DOÑA LONA

DOÑA LONA

A Novel Based on the Life of Doña Tules

Facsimile of Original 1941 Edition

by

Blanche Chloe Grant

New Foreword
by

Marcia Muth

SOUTHWEST HERITAGE SERIES

SUNSTONE PRESS

SANTA FE

Sunstone books may be purchased for educational, business, or sales promotional use. For information please write: Special Markets Department, Sunstone Press, P.O. Box 2321, Santa Fe, New Mexico 87504-2321.

Library of Congress Cataloging-in-Publication Data

Grant, Blanche C. (Blanche Chloe), 1874-1948.
  Doña Lona : a novel based on the life of Doña Tules : facsimile of original 1941 edition / by Blanche Chloe Grant ; new foreword by Marcia Muth.
     p. cm. -- (Southwest heritage series)
  Originally published: New York: Wilfred Funk, 1941.
  ISBN 978-0-86534-604-8 (pbk. : alk. paper)
  1. Barceló, Gertrudis, d. 1852--Fiction. 2. New Mexico--Fiction. I. Title.

PS3513.R2919D66 2007
813'.52--dc22
                                        2007026989

WWW.SUNSTONEPRESS.COM
SUNSTONE PRESS / POST OFFICE BOX 2321 / SANTA FE, NM 87504-2321 /USA
(505) 988-4418 / ORDERS ONLY (800) 243-5644 / FAX (505) 988-1025

The Southwest Heritage Series is dedicated to Jody Ellis and Marcia Muth Miller, the founders of Sunstone Press, whose original purpose and vision continues to inspire and motivate our publications.

CONTENTS

I

THE SOUTHWEST HERITAGE SERIES

The history of the United States is written in hundreds of regional histories and literary works. Those letters, essays, memoirs, biographies and even collections of fiction are often first-hand accounts by people who wanted to memorialize an event, a person or simply record for posterity the concerns and issues of the times. Many of these accounts have been lost, destroyed or overlooked. Some are in private or public collections but deemed to be in too fragile condition to permit handling by contemporary readers and researchers.

However, now with the application of twenty-first century technology, nineteenth and twentieth century material can be reprinted and made accessible to the general public. These early writings are the DNA of our history and culture and are essential to understanding the present in terms of the past.

The Southwest Heritage Series is a form of literary preservation. Heritage by definition implies legacy and these early works are our legacy from those who have gone before us. To properly present and preserve that legacy, no changes in style or contents have been made. The material reprinted stands on its own as it first appeared. The point of view is that of the author and the era in which he or she lived. We would not expect photographs of people from the past to be re-imaged with modern clothes, hair styles and backgrounds. We should not, therefore, expect their ideas and personal philosophies to reflect our modern concepts.

Remember, reading their words and sharing their thoughts is a passport back into understanding how the past was shaped and how it influenced today's world.

Our hope is that new access to these older books will provide readers with a challenging and exciting experience.

II

FOREWORD TO THIS EDITION
by
Marcia Muth

Blanche Chloe Grant was born in 1874 in Leavenworth, Kansas. Like many other women of her time, she was from the first an independent spirit. She was interested in the arts and literature and saw a role for women that did not include the usually prescribed domestic life. A graduate of Vassar College, she also studied at the Boston Museum School of Fine Arts, The Pennsylvania Academy and the Art League in New York City. She soon became known for both her landscape paintings and her career as a magazine illustrator.

In 1918, she was asked to go to France as head of an art project under the auspices of the Y.M.C.A.

A move to Taos, New Mexico in 1920 brought about dramatic changes in Grant's life. She developed an intense interest in the rich and varied history of the area. She took on the job of editor of the *Taos Valley News* and began her years of research into the history of Taos and the Southwest. This led then to a series of books, many of which were about Taos and the people who lived there.

Her art also changed and she painted Native American and Western subjects. Although an active participant in the Taos art scene, she continued to show paintings in New York. Gradually her main interests turned to her writing. Her books included *When Old Trails Were New, Taos Indians* and she edited a biography of Kit Carson based on his notes.

One of her last books was *Doña Lona: A Story of Old Taos and Santa Fe*. It is an exciting and a true story about life, love and politics during the time when "Manifest Destiny" was the slogan of choice in the United States. It was in the first half of the nineteenth century and the land we now call the American Southwest was a place of turbulence, turmoil and trouble. Grant's heroine is based on the real person Doña Tules Barceló (María Gertrudis) but for literary reasons, she calls her Doña Lona Barcelona, although other persons in the book are given their real names. She may have taken as her example Willa Cather who, when she wrote *Death Comes for the Archbishop*, used another name for her main character even though she was writing a true, historical account.

Doña Lona like her counterpart was a woman who went from a poor background to a place of wealth and power. Leaving Taos for Santa Fe, she became the owner of the most famous gambling establishment in the Southwest. It was here that Doña Lona got to meet and know all the men of importance in the area. She was privy to the secret political machinations and later used this to help the American army.

Grant in her own preface to the book says that she felt some of the early writers had maligned Doña Tules and because of her own research, she gives a gentler portrait of her and her life. This does not contradict the facts that are historically correct.

After a long and busy life in art and literature, it was one simple fact that Grant wanted to be remembered for after her death. Her tombstone in the Sierra Vista Cemetery in Taos has this inscription: "Historian of Taos."

III

FACSIMILE OF 1941 EDITION

DOÑA LONA

Books by Blanche C. Grant

WHEN OLD TRAILS WERE NEW

TAOS INDIANS

TAOS TODAY

ONE HUNDRED YEARS AGO IN OLD TAOS

Edited by Blanche C. Grant

KIT CARSON'S OWN STORY OF HIS LIFE

DOÑA LONA

A STORY OF OLD TAOS AND SANTA FÉ

by

Blanche C. Grant

Publishers

WILFRED FUNK, INC.

New York

MANUFACTURED IN THE UNITED STATES
OF AMERICA BY THE VAIL-BALLOU PRESS

To

E. B. T.

and to others,

among whom are many Spanish

Americans, who gladly gave me

valuable information.

THOSE FAMILIAR WITH THE HISTORY OF OUR
Southwest will recognize Lona Barcelona as Madam Barcélo
of Santa Fé, who, more than a century ago, established the
most famous high-class gambling salas in that section of the
country. She was successful in this business that was accepted by Spaniards as definitely respectable.

Since I have not been able to find many facts about her
life, either in books or in tradition, my story can lay slight
claim to the word "biographical." For this reason, I have not
used her name.

The principal characters in the book with the exception of
Rudolfo, Marino, Pedro, Pablita and those obviously minor,
were men and women who actually lived between the years
1826 and 1851, the known date of Madam Barcélo's death.
When I learned as fact that two worn volumes of Shakespeare
were found among Ewing Young's effects after his death in
Oregon, I felt that the man I had imagined was fairly like
his real self. Bill Williams may have been of rougher nature
than I have pictured him but he came of good stock. Both
men undoubtedly knew the vivacious, attractive young woman
gambler.

As for Madam Barcélo herself. I have word from her that

she was from the South. She told one of her adopted daughters that she came from Mexico. Years later, the woman told Juan Garcia, who eventually passed on the information to the late Harry C. Yontz of Santa Fé, and he, in turn, told me. Tradition in Taos runs that, as a child, she came from Spain with her mother who died in "New York Port"; that she was well born and probably of aristocratic parentage. In Taos, Madam Barcélo was called "Doña," a distinctive title not lightly accorded by Spaniards.

Later, Madam Barcélo went to Santa Fé where she was respected and became a power. The elite of the capital flocked to her salas, located, at first, across from *La Fonda* of today and then on the site bordered by San Francisco Street, Burro Alley and Palace Avenue. There she made a fortune.

Madam Barcélo has been given the credit of assisting the American Army to the extent of a thousand dollars. One wonders if she was reimbursed? She is also said to have been brave enough to pass on the word which saved the Americans from conspirators bent on their death in December, 1846.

Careful analysis of what was written of Madam Barcélo by Josiah Gregg, George Brewerton and others has made me veer away from what historians are determined that we should believe of her. Not a man ever said that he really *knew* her. Seemingly these early commentators felt that she must necessarily conform to the type with which they were familiar, the disreputable frontier gambling woman. My own research through many years convinces me that they have maligned her. It has been my intention to draw a fair portrait of Madam Barcélo and her astonishing career in old Taos and Santa Fé.

Blanche C. Grant

Taos, New Mexico

viii

DOÑA LONA

HIGH OVER THE CARAVAN, LONG-LEGGED cranes flapped through the crisp November air. Birds and caravan were headed north toward the dusty green and yellow fields and the white walls of Chihuahua. The wagon drivers sang;

> *"Oh, give me to eat a tuna*
> *Even if it pricks my hand . . ."*

"They are more than four hundred leagues from the land of tunas," said Lona, moving slightly to ease the bumping of the coach.

"So they are, Señorita *mía,*" answered Pablita, her chubby half Indian maid.

"I suppose even now, after all these weeks on the trail, they still ask you who I am. But mind you never tell them. It's nobody's affair. I think I'll take a new name before we reach Santa Fé, not because I'm ashamed of a noble family but because I want to start a new life."

Pablita's small bead-like black eyes rolled quickly to the face of her mistress.

"Sí, Señorita, they do ask about you even now. They think

3

it—very—queer that you have no duenna and travel so bravely with but Pedro and me."

"Yes? But they know Señor Gonzales is my escort." Lona leaned forward, her hand on the window sash warming now in the Mexican sun. She looked out over the desert, forbidding and silent save for the grinding of wagon wheels, the thud of horses' hoofs, and the crack of whips. The cranes were far ahead.

But the desert was gloomy. Lona sank back on the cushions. From habit she rearranged the black mantilla over her parted hair, lifted the long braids on either shoulder and flung the lace to the left. She closed her eyes. The fine straight nose, the poise of her head, the long tapering hands folded in her lap, marked her an aristocrat. In repose her face had a maturity beyond her age.

Behind closed lids Lona thought of her nineteen years. Most of them she had traveled alone, going into strange countries, leaving behind people whom she loved. Even now she grieved for the father who had died in Spain, the soldier whom she barely remembered. Perhaps he had loved indiscreetly for he had fallen under a dagger in Barcelona. Then followed the long voyage to New York Port, the death of her mother and the burial at sea. The gray loneliness of the trip to Vera Cruz with no one but the Archuleta women to care for her, swept over Lona again, loneliness for the beautiful French mother who used to tell her about the apple trees and wisteria blooming along the Loire. Did she grieve for France or was her mother happy after she married a Spanish grandee and went to live in Barcelona? Was that why she called her daughter "Lona"? There was a story. Aunt Rita had hinted more than once of a romance between her mother and the Spanish king.

Lona opened her eyes and pulled from her bodice her mother's gold locket, an oval set with pearls surrounding a royal

4

coat of arms cut deep and topped with a small diamond. As long as she lived it should be her luck piece. She pried the locket open and stared at the miniature within, love and hate struggling for mastery of her face. Again she tried to release the ivory and throw it away but it would not loosen. Did it mean that she could not tear Rudolfo from her heart? At least she need not look at him.

The locket snapped shut but Lona could not blot out the image of Rudolfo flaunting his red cape, stepping lightly out of the path of the charging bull. How dextrously he had twisted his sword with death on its tip. How the crowd had shouted "vivas" for their matador, unlike the others, a grandee of purest Spanish blood. She would not be here in this coach headed North if he had not taken the rose from Dolores, silly, pretty Dolores. Lona would never forgive him. Only the night before the bull fight he had stood below her grilled window, whispering undying love, and had promised to accept no other rose but hers. No, she would not think of him.

Caramba! There were other men. Army officers perhaps. General Santa Anna? She admired him even if they did say he was crude. She had seen him but once, riding in a state coach, so handsome and proud. Well? She would see.

Swiftly, for the hundredth time Lona's mind touched the high lights of the long journey through flowering lowlands, deserts, villages, a splash of green on the trail. It was at Quatitlan that Marino de Alvarado had discovered her. He turned his horse sharply on its haunches when he saw her watching the campfires near the stone meson of the trail.

"*Por Dios!*" he exclaimed. "You, Lona, with the caravan?"

"Yes. Here I am. And you?"

"Oh, I'm a veteran of the trails. But you, Lona de—"

"Hush! Do not use my name, Marino. No one knows who

5

I am. I do not wish to be known as yet. My veteran friend aged twenty-two. Why are you going?"

"Oh, I'm on a search for gold. Uncle found some good veins, you know. But, Lona, you must turn back. The trail's no place for you."

When Marino was convinced that she would not return, he appointed himself the girl's guardian. Lona smiled as she thought of the first time she had watched a game of monte, there at Querétaro. Often since then, Marino had declared, "I could hardly pull you away. Your eyes were glued to the cards." He had been quick with his dagger, that night at Lagos, when the man beside her began to draw her winnings into his pockets during the confusion at the end of the game.

That was so long ago. It seemed to Lona that she had been on the trail for centuries, moving always North toward Chihuahua—and what? Suddenly a party of ragged, friendly Indians trotted by on sturdy ponies. Their quivers were full of arrows, and bows were slung over their shoulders. They were probably on the outlook for Comanches and Apaches but now they were gay, singing like boisterous children;

> "Now, yes, now I have,
> Now, yes, now I have
> Two shirts to change,
> One that they have promised me,
> One that they have promised me,
> And another that they are to give me."

From the coach window Lona watched the Indians out of sight. The caravan neared the city. Weary hoofs pounded on. The sad complaining of the cranes flying again overhead, was punctured by short sharp chirps of gold and black plovers. Quail and pheasants rose from mesquite and yuccas. Through the awkward cactus, antelopes scrambled, frightened by the

6

wagons. The caravan followed a dry river through groups of cottonwoods and willows. Ahead was a long, arched aqueduct, beyond the outlying fields of corn.

The two girls looked out when the wagons rolled between the stout loopholed towers of the gateway. The crooked streets were fronted with one-story, gray-yellow adobe houses warm in the sunshine. Women in bright skirts and rebozos were carrying market baskets or shaking rugs in their doorways. Men in striped serapes thrown over their white suits squinted under sombreros as they lazily drove mules with hampers on either side of their painted saddles. No gardens were in sight but tops of tamarisk or cottonwood trees above adobe walls hinted of patios.

The streets became straighter and led directly into a large plaza. Small shops had pushed their way in front of fine old homes but the parish church with its two solid towers and carved façade, stood its ground.

The glare of sunlight on canvases across the plaza caught Lona's eyes. "Those must be the big wagons from the North, Pablita. We'll ask Señor Gonzales to take us over."

"Oh, I'd like to see them right now," begged Pablita.

"So would I." Lona stepped from the coach. "Let's go. We can not get lost here. We do not need Señor Gonzales."

Shielding their eyes, the girls walked toward the wagons. They were clumsy. Heavy wheels supported wide box-like beds about four feet high. Curving above, over oak poles, were sheets of canvas tied down at the sides and drawn together into an open oval at the rear. One of the wagons was untouched, but the canvas on the two which had been opened, flapped and cracked in the wind. Rough-looking, unshaven Americans in bulging trousers tucked into high boots and dirty cotton shirts with sleeves rolled above the elbow, lifted boxes and carried them into shops or loaded them on small carts. Some

7

of the bundles were untied and the contents were sold there in the street. Men staggered away with bolts of cotton cloth, iron tools, hickory sticks and cartons of trinkets. As yet the men of the North had not had time to purchase their return cargo. Señor Gonzales had told Lona that here they would buy wines, ammunition, metals, cheese, candy and tobacco. They worked with undue haste it seemed to Lona. Unlike Mexicans, not one was singing.

Crude, awkward and stout for the trails, Lona thought as she walked around the wagons. "Where did they come from?" she asked aloud of no one in particular, and was surprised to hear a strange voice answer. She glanced at the owner of the voice, a tall man, dark. His sombrero was pulled down to cold, unpleasant eyes.

"They are all the way from Mis-uri," he said in a thick voice. "Two years back the first of them traveled over a thousand miles through Indian country from the East to Santa Fé. This year these three came with our South-bound train. Next year there'll be more of them on the trails. But the Indians are bad! Downright bad!"

"Thanks, Señor." Without looking at him Lona motioned to Pablita and walked on. She did not see him follow.

The two girls sauntered around the square looking at the tawdry articles which merchants placed on mats before their doors. Farther along they saw a game of monte. Lona slowed her steps to watch the cards fall. Pablita suggested that they go into the cathedral.

Prayers were said hastily in the dark grim church and when the two returned to the plaza, boisterous shouts tore the air as five hunters dashed around the square. By their strange clothes Lona guessed at once that the men were American mountaineers. Four of them had small dead antelopes hanging from their saddles. One man had a bear. They galloped around

8

several times whooping in harsh voices and shooting into the air. Finally one of them pulled up and dismounted near Lona and Pablita.

"Whoa, I tell ye. Blarst yer hide!" Turning toward Lona, he took off his cap with its pointed ear-shields. "Wal, what d'ye think of this hyar baby bar, gals? He was makin' himself scarce ter his ma. Fine un but he needed killin'." The man nodded vigorously and added, "He sure did."

Lona started to move away.

"Oh, ye needn't be skeery of me. I ain't no bat outah Hell ter frighten ye. I reckon I shoulda waited fer an interduction, eh?" Noting that the girl was listening, he continued, "My name's Bill Williams. Jes thought ye might like ter look at a real bar. Beggin' yer pardon, I am, Miss."

Lona never understood why the note of apology and something indefinable about him made her turn and walk out to the horse. She looked at the small grizzly but more at the man. "The mountains hyar are raggeder than the Rockies," he said. "Harder ter climb."

Lona did not reply. She watched the stranger. Raw-boned and awkward he was and taller than any man that she had ever seen. His clothes were different, made of buckskin, and fringed along the sleeves and trousers. His freckled, clean-shaven face was long with a wide square jaw and prominent thin nose. His gray eyes squinted but were kindly and surrounded by tiny wrinkles of laughter. He rolled them quickly, taking in everything at a glance. His hair, red and thick, curled slightly at the ends as it reached his shoulders.

"I'll remember this man if I ever see him again," Lona said to herself. "Tall—red hair—gray roving eyes. And his name is Beel Williams."

"Finest young un I evah see, as shore as me gun has hindsights," Bill said. "Caught him jes a-comin' out of a cave ter

9

look the weather ovah and probably wishin' spring 'ud ante
up. He come right toward me, thinkin' I was a tree, I reckon,
but he didn't think long 'cause one of me branches come down
awful sudden with a gun. Stranger 'round these parts, air ye?"

Lona nodded.

"I say, Miss, beggin' yer pardon but what's yer name?"

"Lona," replied the girl hesitating slightly and then with decision, "Lona Barcelona." She liked the sound of it.

"Wal, Miss Barcelona, I jes want ter tell ye that ye'd better
be a mite keerful 'round this durn town. Ye savvy?"

"Yes," answered Lona slowly, venturing on the fair amount
of English that she knew. "I think you mean take care?"

"Jes so. Did you understand me blarney? I mean what I've
said all the way through."

"Not quite all. Some words are strange. I think I understood
fairly well," said Lona. "But, if you will speak slower . . ."

"Yeah, I know," interrupted Bill at a more deliberate pace
but still in English. "Ye wander 'round like 'n American gal
but it ain't safe hyar, I tell ye. Listen, ef ye evah need a bit o'
help, Miss, I'm the man ye kin call on. Remember! My name's
Williams, jes plain Bill Williams. Goin' North? Tomorrer's
train?"

Lona nodded again.

"I be too," Williams added before he threw his legs across
his saddle and pulled his cap over his hair. Then he lifted a
thin finger and said, "Remember! Bill Williams. They call
me 'Ole Bill' but I ain't a thousand years older'n ye air ef I am
a wid'wer. Ole Bill from North Caroliny, 'riginal."

"I'll not forget," smiled Lona.

"All right," he called out and rode away muttering to himself, "Durn the language anyway. Folks all oughta speak the
same way. She's a likely gal. Looks a leetle bit like Mary, 'cept
fer that long hair. Seems ter be no older woman taggin' arter.

10

Not like most Spanish gals. Wonder why? Got more guts, I reckon. Allus some in every generation." With that Williams dismounted and rolled his way to a *pulquería* where he ordered a drink and stood gulping it down while he watched Lona and her maid across the plaza. He saw them enter a shop and come out again. Then a fellow motioned to the smaller girl. Her mistress evidently bade her go and see what the man wanted.

While Pablita's back was turned, Lona was startled to see beside her the Spaniard who had answered her question earlier in the day. He was smiling with eyes so intent on her that once more she did not look squarely at him. But her second impression of the man was better. He asked her if she would like to see a very old part of town and assured her that she would be quite safe with him. It was not far. She hesitated. Yes, she would like to go.

Lona called to Pablita who was talking to Pedro, but did not realize that the girl had not heard. When Lona followed the man around the corner through a narrow passage into an old patio, forlorn with age, Pablita was not behind.

Two dead trees stood in the place. Building stones lay here and there among rubbish. In spite of faint sounds of the city, a grim silence seemed to brood over the enclosure. The doors and windows of the stone rooms which lined the patio were boarded across. Clinging to one post of the portal was a vine drooping in ragged lines, its lower branches flung across the red flagstones. Lona shuddered at an adobe wall peppered with bullet holes, man-high. In a corner of the wall rose a low tower with loopholes. It had been a place of quick death, this patio.

"Beyond are the dungeons," said her guide. "The rings and chains are still there." He threw open a heavy door with some effort. Lona stepped inside and the man followed. He let the door bang shut. It left them in utter darkness. She heard the man's hard breathing and before she could speak he had clutched her violently. She tried to push him away, but his face, pressed against hers, muffled her screams.

Williams had seen Lona walk away with the man. "That damn rascal Manuel!" He almost leaped across the plaza. When he reached the patio he could hear Lona's smothered cries. With long strides he was at the door, swinging it open. "Come outah thar," he commanded.

The man freed Lona. She ran into the patio. He followed, glowering. "Ye old skunk! I'd like ter shoot the liver outah ye," growled Williams. His fist crashed into the man's face. The fellow slumped to the ground unconscious.

"Beel!" sobbed Lona, clinging to him.

Bill put a protecting arm around the girl and led her across the patio.

"*Santa María! Yo no pensé* . . ." Lona was trembling. No further words came.

"Yes, Miss, I knowed ye didn't think," answered Bill as the two went through the narrow corridor to the street. "That goddam son of a . . ." He caught his words with a snap of his lips and then continued brusquely, "Wal, now looka hyar, Miss. I tole ye! I warned ye! Ye be keerful. Nobody'd knowed whar ye wus. Now where's yer outfit?" He did not wait for an answer. "Out hyar the durn cusses air doin' anything they like, clever with the gals ef they see 'em alone, cheatin' a-dealin' keerds, and hidin' under that pious look o' their'n. Oh, yeah, I know they're not all like that. I've seen Spaniards that's gentlemen all right but, Miss, mark me words, 'Be keerful!' "

Bill said no more when he saw the maid running toward her mistress. Lona quickened her steps.

"I can not tell you how I thank you," she said turning to speak to her new friend. But Williams was gone.

12

Before Lona stepped into her coach, the next morning, she glanced around the plaza and the trail station but she did not see Williams there nor anywhere along the line of wagons. When the caravan was many miles on its trail to El Paso, he galloped by on a dark horse with stirrups drawn much higher than most riders liked them. Her eyes followed the lanky figure with horned cap far forward, the red hair flying and the fringes of his buckskin suit playing antics in the wind. She laughed outright, for Williams on a horse was a sort of animated geometric puzzle. Ridiculous or no, he had saved her yesterday. What if he had not come? How foolish she had been! If she had only studied the man's face she would have known! She wondered how long the fellow had lain in the patio.

Suddenly Williams rode by again. "Soul of fibre, heart of oak." That phrase of Cervantes fitted the man. Then she smiled. How different he was from the polished gentlemen of Mexico! But she admired Williams. Some day she might even like him.

Marino rode by. How utterly unlike Beel! He did not rein in his horse but hailed her as he passed. His red-lined cape floated in the wind. Red! She leaned against her cushions and looked with unseeing eyes over the desert. She was in Mexico again, in the arena, in her own yellow room. She was at the theater. Rudolfo and she were dancing!

The coach rocked. Indians trotted by. Lona was on the trail again. How sharply that easy life in the South stood in contrast to the discomforts of this long trek. Once she would have believed it impossible to endure such a meager existence as this of the caravan. Her hand touched the locket at her throat.

"It did not save you from that bad man," said Pablita. "My Pedro says that he can not understand. He hopes my coin will be kinder to me. But then, he'll always be near me."

13

"Pedro. Bless his heart! He will be near us both in the future. Señor Williams will help us too, at least on the journey. He's going through to Santa Fé." In Lona's voice was a note of confidence and relief.

"I don't think we'll have any more trouble," said Pablita. "Pedro says that it won't be long, not very long before we'll see Santa Fé."

THE COACH WAS NOT MOVING. LONA ROUSED from sleep. Her eyes, still blurred with dreams, saw no cause for delay. The windows framed nothing more hostile than leafless willows flaming red-orange on the banks of a thin stream which zigzagged lazily across the square of light, changing color like a chameleon. Gaunt whitish cottonwoods stood in wrinkled lines. A few twisted leaves, high on their branches, made angular designs against the stubble of maize on a small hill beyond.

Lona stood and leaned out of the window. Close by the trail was an adobe mansion of a hacienda. It is like a fortress, oriental in its seclusion, silent and mysterious, Lona thought while she watched the corner towers and the high loop-holed walls glow yellow. Far down their length the wooden gates opened slowly. Men thronged out, waved a welcome with sombreros, shouted, but gave passage to a man who was evidently the ranch owner. He walked toward the caravan with sombrero held stiffly straight in the air, like a command.

The captain of the caravan rode forward and leaned over to listen. A moment later, he raised a hand. His mounted messengers rode forward at once. A quick command, and the horsemen galloped down the line, motioning the while for drivers to leave their wagons. A word or two was whispered and the men rode on.

Señor Gonzales soon reined in his horse by Lona's coach.

"We are to stop here for the night, Señorita. This hacienda is used sometimes as a station when further travel is unwise." He caught his word for correction. "Impracticable, I mean. Here are many rooms; the corral ample and the patio large enough for coaches like yours and the most valuable carts. It's much better than an ordinary meson, Señorita."

"The other wagons, Señor?"

"Oh, they'll be drawn into the usual circle outside. Guards will be posted. Everything will be all right."

His explanation defeats its purpose, Lona thought. She would not have him guess that she understood. There are hostile Indians about, she guessed, and the men don't want the women to know.

Bill and Marino rode by, halted for a moment but neither spoke of danger. Nor did she. Earlier on the journey she would have been swift to question but not now. She could wait.

A few moments later Lona was inside the huge patio. The *ranchero* was ordering extra fires built on the mud roof and men were packing wood up the ladders. Her eyes caught those of one older woman after another. They were bright with anxiety but each was holding her tongue, lest someone had not understood the preparations for the night.

Later, a few of the women went aloft to sit by the bonfires. Lona went with them. A few feet away from her, Pablita huddled with her blanket drawn about her chubby face. Her eyes gleamed in the firelight. Lona threw her serape back, readjusted her long braids over her shoulders and drew her knees close with her arms. She watched men pile wood on the fires, and light torches. Others stood by the small cannons in the towers.

16

Suddenly Bill Williams stepped to her side.

"*Buenas noches,* Miss Lona," he began in a low voice. "How d'ye like this hyar trip so fur?" He leaned over, picked up a corner of her serape and threw it gently over her. "The night stings a bit."

"Oh, well enough, but I long to reach Santa Fé," answered the girl looking up at him. His head far above her seemed like a mountain crag ruddy in the firelight.

"Wal, we'll git thar some sweet day. I jes come ovah ter tell ye . . ." Williams looked at her quizzically, rubbed his new beard and sat down. "I reckon I wont skeer ye ef I say . . ." Again he hesitated.

"Indians about! I know, Señor Beel."

"Ye know? Why the men warn't ter tell . . ."

"They did not have to. There's hardly a woman who has not guessed."

"Wal, I swan! Now I come ovah ter tell ye ef ye hyear any whoops ternight ye git outah yer rig and make fer the fust room and stay thar. Arrers have a way of curvin' down sometimes. I ain't hankerin' ter frighten ye but I've made tracks around and I'm not likin' the signs I found down ter the pool. They're fresh er I'm a skinned coon. I figgur that Injuns was hyar 'bout 'leven last night. Been waitin' fer more of their band ter ketch up, I reckon. By the great horn spoon, the guards'll keep their peepers open ternight er I'll know the reason why."

"Do you think we are all in danger?" Lona asked quickly.

"Oh, ye'll be safe nuf ef ye do what I tole ye. Ain't any real danger, Miss." Then thinking to change the subject, Williams continued, "This hyar place is a likely fort. Minds me of plans I've heerd the Bent boys talk 'bout up on the Arkinsaw. Ye don't know 'bout the Bents, course. They air two gritty boys from Missouri. Father's a big Mogul in the law somehow down ter Saint Louie. I'll be damned ef they ain't fust-rate trappers and fighters. Ain't been in the kintry long but they're pow-wowin' 'bout buildin' a fort of their own. I wisht I could see 'em and tell 'em 'bout this place. Makin' a few changes like buildin' a tower ovah the gate fer a man with a spy glass and addin' a couple rooms somewhar, they'd have a mighty good fort. This hyar un is shu-ah needed 'bout these parts, I'm opinin'."

Williams sat hunched up like an Indian thoughtfully look-ing into the flames, but after a few moments he unfolded and rose. He threw a stick on the fire and said quietly as he turned to leave, "Good-by, Miss, don't git ter worryin'. 'Tain't nevah done no good. It jes makes yer stomick try ter dance *La Jota* and it cain't make it."

Lona smiled and looked at Pablita who was rubbing her hands together and trembling.

"Oh, Señorita Lona, Señor Beel says not to worry! Is there any danger?" she asked as she clutched her mistress's hand, her eyes big with fright.

"Probably not, Pablita. Anyway, we must be as calm as we can."

"Let's go below, please," begged Pablita. "My coin! It hangs by the window. I must have it! Perhaps it will help us!"

Lona led the way down the ladder and found a couch on which Pablita soon went to sleep. She herself was still fully-dressed. She loosened her bodice and put her slippers near at hand. Then she lay quiet, listening.

Williams wrapped himself in his blanket and stretched out by the fire which the guards kept burning. He ached for a brush with the "critturs." He had heard of the attack on the last caravan some weeks before. Several men had been killed but that was up North on the hundred mile desert, the *Jornada del Muerto*—the Journey of the Dead Man. No water there and fine hiding places for Indians.

Williams roused to look at the stars. There was time for a doze, he knew, and promptly turned over and fell asleep. But in that eerie period before dawn when all living creatures stir in their sleep, he woke at once. He listened but could hear no sound. It was still very dark and would be for two hours or more. Yet it was time. There might be some fools who had not cleaned their guns. He had weighed the quality of the men, even the master of the wagons, during the early evening, and knew that he would have to take charge if there was a fight.

With his silent Indian-like step he walked among the sleeping men, saying quietly, "Yer horse. The corral gate. Quiet er I'll . . ."

"Indios?" questioned one or two.

"Not yit but we must be ready. I know the varmints. They'll attack at dawn, maybe sooner, er I'm plumb loco."

"Ah, I don't believe it," said one sleepy fellow who rolled over but Williams gave him a substantial kick, saying, "Don't be a fool er a coward. Come on. I know what I'm talkin' 'bout."

As silently as possible the horses were saddled and led out to the corral of the wagons beyond the gate. It was so intensely dark that it was not easy to find the way but the long, lean arm of Williams indicated the direction. Not a word was said. Williams dropped the reins of his own horse and walked again among the men to caution them about talking and smoking. They followed his lead without comment.

In time a faint light filtered through the Eastern sky. As yet there was no sign of Indians. The men began to relax because, if the enemy were planning to attack, they should be at it by now. There were none in sight by the bushes, under the trees near the pool, nor on the ridge.

"Guess Ole Bill be wrong in his ca'culations this time," drawled one fellow, "I'm fer goin' back and gettin' a bit more shut-eye."

As he spoke, Indians swarmed from beyond the pool and over the hill with sharp war whoops, their lances high and bows taut. The few guns which they possessed began to crack. Prodding their horses, the Indians galloped around the wagons.

The noise awakened everybody in the hacienda. Lona was quickly out in the patio. She climbed the ladder before any of the women had opened the doors of their rooms.

"Down there is the place for you," cried out one of the guards. "No place for women up here."

"But here I am and I'm going to stay. No other woman will follow, I am sure," said Lona determined to see the fight.

In a corner near one of the towers the girl found a tree-stump seat near a loophole. She peered over the five-foot parapet for a second, before she ducked and sat at the loophole. By this time there were eight guards, two in each tower with torches ablaze near the small cannons. They were too busy to pay any attention to Lona and she was glad of that.

"Father was no coward. I'm not," she whispered to herself as she looked out and saw that the hacienda itself was not as yet a target for attack. Unconsciously her hand felt of her locket under her bodice.

Flintlocks spit fire. With the men of the hacienda Lona noticed that the firing was timed to cause blast to follow blast. One fired while another reloaded and primed his gun. In the gray light Lona could see Williams on his horse, more ridiculous than ever.

Flash! An Indian rolled from his horse. Another fell. The noise grew louder. As far as Lona could see, no one of the

20

hacienda men had been wounded. Yonder was an Indian in the dust creeping toward one of the wagons. A light! He had a torch! He was trying to set fire to one of the wagons. Did the men see him? Lona stood without realizing her own danger. She wanted to shout a warning but she clapped a hand over her mouth. They had seen him! More than one rifle cracked. The Indian fell in a huddle, his torch out in the dust.

One of the men in the wagon corral had been hit? No! He aimed. His bullet reached its target and an Indian, who appeared to be a chief, toppled from his horse.

A wild sad whoop came from the Indians. They wheeled their horses, lay flat over their necks and rushed for the bushes, through the trees and on over the ridge. The men left the wagons, and raced after the Indians.

Lona paced the roof while she waited for their return. More than an hour dragged by before the men came back over the rise. Tired and dirty, they dismounted near the wagons. Lona's eyes ran over the group. Yes, Williams was there. Now it was time to go below. She was spared the sight of Williams scalping the chief nor did she see him hang the bleeding top-knot on a nail on the wall near the gate.

When Lona next caught sight of Williams he was inside the patio and busy cutting notches on his Hall rifle but he looked up when she approached and said, "Jes makin' me record up. Thar!"

"Oh, eet one beeg fight, Señor Beel," exclaimed Lona. "I see eet."

"See it? How in the thunderin' dicks did ye see it?"

"I was on the roof."

"Wal, I'll be hornswoggled. Didn't they tell ye it wus po'ful dangerous to be up thar?"

"Sí, Señor Beel, but I wanted to see the fight."

"Warn't afeard then? Wal, by the jumpin'! Ye're made fer

this kintry all right. Good fer ye, gal. Didn't expect that of ye. Saw the hull durn affair? Huh, I swan," said Bill turning to pick up a child who tugged at the fringe of his trousers.

"Eh, thar, little un. Don't cry. Thar! thar! 'Twas only a brush, not much of a fight, Miss Lona."

"Well, I hope no more brush come. I'm glad that you . . ." Lona's voice was lost in the sound of the breakfast gong.

It took longer that morning for the trail master to get his wagons in line and the people calmed down. Finally on the trail the fever of the night was succeeded by the lethargy which falls upon travelers when they regain a sense of safety. In the late afternoon the riders broke into hilarious shouts. Williams rode to Lona's coach. With cap waving, he shouted, "That cut in the mountains is Paseo del Norte. El Paso is not far now. It'll take us another day and night but the stations air built proper strong."

Lona asked if Williams had seen any more Indian signs.

"No. Injuns got plenty o' fightin' back thar. Besides I know the varmints have ter make medicine up in the mountains."

"Make medicine?"

"Yeah. Bonfires. Dances. They're sort of prayers fer courage and success."

"So! What do you think our chances are in the *Jornada?*"

"We're too many fer 'em. I don't ca'culate they'll trouble us any more. Might be a few strays. Not likely though. The moccasin newspaper will have reached 'em afore we git thar. I'll let ye know ef I see signs. Stay close to yer coach, gal, anyway. 'Tain't no joke fer a woman ter be captured by Injuns. No! I'll swan it ain't." With that Williams jammed his cap on his head and rode forward.

El Paso brought relief to the travelers. The small town was flat and low. It spread out along the West side of the Río Bravo del Norte and was flanked on the East by a pueblo of friendly

Isleta Indians, the descendants of those who had accompanied the Spaniards when they were driven from the country long ago. Lona had never seen so many types of men. There were more Americans than she had seen anywhere along the trek. More Englishmen too and Frenchmen who talked of Louisiana. She found the shops full of strange things for sale but she bought little and soon returned to the wagons, hoping that the necessary repairs would be made in time to go Northward on the morrow. Everyone talked of the *Jornada* or Santa Fé.

The next morning the master of the caravan rode by to warn the travelers that every canteen or skin for water must be full. "We are soon to enter the *Jornada*. It's the loneliest part of the trail," he said. "There is no water for a full hundred miles."

The *Jornada* was a sorry land of burning yellow sand, brown rock, desert plants, and, far ahead, of mocking blue water. Bones of men were strewn along the trail. Skeletons of horses and mules scorched white in the sun. Not a living thing stirred among the mesquite bushes. Lona noticed that their branches slanted North, always North. The yuccas stood in groups, with knife-like leaves and thin stems thrust skyward. The stems held yellow pods from which black seeds fell. Not far beyond, on either side of the trail, patches of hoary grass made patterns on low hills rounded against the blue of jagged mountains.

Hours rolled into days. Lona recoiled from the spirit of this savage land. When the caravan reached the great lava rocks, Williams rode by her coach on one side, Gonzales on the other. Neither man said a word but the girl knew that here Indians often hid. Williams was right in his prediction. There were no Apaches about.

Relief again spread the length of the caravan when the wagons pulled into the narrow fertile valley of the Río Bravo del Norte. To the West the river was flanked by mountains. On the flat stood Socorro, once a pueblo, where, long ago, Don Juan de

23

Oñate had found succor for his hungry men and women. Now it was a straggling adobe town. Indians and Mexicans, sauntered along old irrigation ditches or abandoned the shade of great ancient cottonwoods to see the wagons in the treeless plaza.

Night was coming on but the master ordered the train forward to ford the river two or more miles beyond. He hired three mounted natives to tread out the way through shifting quicksands under the water. When the men had safely climbed the far side, the wagons followed. At camp in the open, that night, Lona heard that, in spite of the care taken by the mozos in the rear, several burros had wandered from the line and were sucked quickly out of sight.

For several days the caravan climbed hills sparsely dotted with piñon trees or cleaned bare by desert winds; some were yellow but others were a glorious rose-red. When possible, the wagons skirted the Río Bravo. Its swift water lapped against boulders and much of the grass on its banks was still green in spite of winter. At last the desert was left behind. Finding the trail station and plaza in use, the travelers camped in winter-rusty fields near a village named for a Spanish duke— Alburquerque.

At night they danced and sang for here was no danger from Indians and their goal was almost at hand. In the morning the caravan followed the river. High mesas stretched away for miles with their flat tops darkened with pines and then gave way to range on range of blue mountains. Toward evening, a great valley of rolling land widened out and the train made its last camp at Bernalillo, a village so old that many of its adobe houses were in ruins.

"Thank God, this is the last stopping place," said Marino as he sat by Lona near a campfire. "And now, you have made plans for the city, Lona?"

"Beel said some time ago that one should stay at Pino's place. It is the best inn."

"Beel!" replied Marino with a hint of a sneer in his voice.

"Yes, Beel," laughed Lona. "He is odd beyond words, I know, but I like him. Don't be an idiot, Marino. I'm Spanish, am I not?"

Marino stared into the fire. It had been all too obvious that Lona liked the crude mountain man—a consummate rascal probably. Damn these Americans anyway. Then to the girl,

"The captain has promised to stop on the very first hilltop from which Santa Fé can be seen."

"Yes. The end of the trail." Lona did not look up but continued to pile a few small twigs to a point from a circular base. Then she glanced out of the corner of her eye at Marino. "Now if I had a bit of soft buffalo skin, I could finish a tepee. Beel says that he has often lived in one." Marino was solemn again and Lona laughed outright.

There was no chance for further conversation for the mozos had set everybody singing lustily:

> *"Tres años hace que estoy amando,*
> *Y un sentimiento ma has dado a mí,*
> *Tu bien lo sabes cuanto he sufride,*
> *Y estoy a sufriendo solo por ti."*

When the old song died away, Williams began whistling "Yankee Doodle." He strode over to Lona and said when the lively air was finished, "Thar's the tune fer me. I'm gittin' up near my kintry. I'm rarin' ter climb the Rockies agin."

From the time her coach was on the move in the early morning, Lona watched the land ahead. When the caravan pulled out of the lowlands, she could see mountains white against the wintry Northern sky. Odd geometric designs in dark and

25

light lay on lower slopes, black pines splotched with snow.

Shortly before noon came the order to halt. Everyone climbed down from the wagons or coaches and looked, shielding his eyes with his hands. In the distance on the valley floor was a low line of adobe walls glowing in the sun. Santa Fé!

III

THE WAGONS WOUND THROUGH FORTIFIED
haciendas, along a little murmuring river bordered by trees.
Dry whispering leaves held tenaciously to their branches and
shivered in the wind. Everywhere were corn fields, the yellow
stalks stacked in pyramids. They filled the air with a sharp tart
odor. Among them Lona saw small box-like adobe houses with
orange pumpkins, melons and red peppers on their roofs.

On the main street of Santa Fé the houses joined each other
and were crowned with parapets which, at the moment, were
rapidly losing the glow of the reddish lowering sun. In the
shadows below on both sides of the roadway, crowds were
gathered under the mud roofs of the portals.

Señor Gonzales had told Lona that it was the custom for all
the villagers to gather in the plaza to hear the words of the first
messenger from the train. "Luckily," he said, "he could shout,
'All's well! We have not lost a single man.' "

Younger men waved sombreros, shouted "vivas," joked with
girls in bright colors, and bowed sedately to black-shawled
duennas. Younger girls looked out of grilled windows under
the portals even as they did in old Mexico. A quick warmth
swept over Lona when she caught their eyes over the heads of
the crowd and waved her kerchief to them. Older men scanned

the newcomers with interest. So did many sad-faced women in
black mantillas, who knew well the dangers of that long trek.
Many had lost loved ones in the terrible *Jornada* or in battles
with Indians. The coming of a caravan choked them with sadness mingled with pride because it had come through.

The wagons were halted. Bells tolled. From a cross street
near the large hay market, a funeral procession on foot followed
a long wooden box on an open cart. The delay gave Williams
the chance to ride forward to Lona's coach. "Wal," he asked
her, "what do ye think of this hyar town?" but, spying an ac-
quaintance, he did not wait for a reply. "Hey," he called out,
"who's gone beaver?"

"*Quién sabe?*" was the answer. Williams laughed.

"Who knows, eh. Wal, now ef they'd jes bury the other fellow '*mañana*' they'd git somewhar in this blasted kintry." He
chuckled to himself.

Lona smiled and said nothing. The wagons had begun to
move and were entering the plaza.

She stepped out on the hard mud pavement under the western portal of the plaza and looked about eagerly. There was
nothing grand. She was disappointed. Before her was a rectangular barren space with a fairly high adobe sundial in the
center. She had heard that it was the only public clock in the
town, built recently by order of Governor Narbona. On all
sides, save where churches stood, portals with thin posts fronted
the one- and two-story flat-roofed houses. The walls were well
plastered but there were few windows facing the plaza.

Señor Gonzales stood by Lona.

"On the South side is the soldiers' church, *La Castrénse*," he
said. "Sometimes it is called the chapel of Our Lady of Light.
Plain enough with its two towers. Within is a beautiful réredos
given long ago by a Spanish Governor. That is the main
church on the East, *La Parróquia*." Señor Gonzales was well

28

launched. "It has better towers, I think. These buildings on the Northwest are the soldier's barracks. There on the North is the old palace."

"The old palace!" exclaimed Lona. "That a palace! Is it fine inside?"

Señor Gonzales shook his head. Her eyes ran the length of the low building with portal and parapet. Here and there adobe plaster had fallen and exposed the huge mud and stone bricks. Old, it certainly was, and how neglected!

"Señor," she said, "I did expect something better. Let us go through the market and see the inside of the palace."

The market was not unlike others that she had seen in Mexico but here were fewer vegetables for sale. Meat swung from strings hung between the posts. Poor farmers from the outer ranches were drawing blankets close over their clothes of skins and stamping their feet in moccasins. Drivers of scrawny burros overloaded with wood, looked half frozen in their rags. On the ground squatted Indians selling pottery, moccasins, bows, arrows, blue corn and pemmican. Lona stepped gingerly among the mats on the pavement. She drew her own cloak more tightly around her even as the Indians had drawn their bright blankets or buffalo skins.

"Few windows, you notice, Señorita," Señor Gonzales spoke in a louder voice to be heard above the welter of sounds in the plaza where trading was brisk. "I have been told that there was a time when none faced the square. The danger of Indians invading the town was always possible, of course, and windows would have been out of the question then. But such hazards are past. American fur traders and men of the new Eastern trail have laughed people out of such fears. They have demanded more light in the rooms where they trade. At any rate, there are more windows every time I return."

Through the main front door of the palace, Señor Gonzales

and Lona entered a fairly large hall which ran through to a patio shabby with dead flower stalks from which dangled withered leaves. Rooms were all about; those to the left, poorly furnished offices; those to the right, the home of the governor which Señor Gonzales said was sumptuously appointed.

Lona smiled at that news. There was, then, something of beauty in the old palace after all but there were no balustrades, no gold decoration and no palms anywhere. She had not known that the city was far too high from sea level for tropical plants. How poverty stricken the whole place was.

Once more on the plaza she watched the people, Spanish, Mexican, Indian and a few "foreigners," Americans, Englishmen, and Germans. They were dressed in everything from tatters to satin. Over the babble of voices came the shrill cries of vendors in the wagons, hoping to sell their merchandise before dark. Even now lighted lanterns were swinging under portals.

As Señor Gonzales went to make arrangements at the inn, Marino de Alvarado joined them. He had little to say for he, too, was drinking in the scene before him. Was he lonely, she wondered. Not a face was familiar until she spied Williams striding toward her.

"Hello thar, Lona. Eh, Marino," called Bill. "Not so bad, this hyar town, is it? Ye haven't been ovah ter the inn yit? Wal, as I said, Pino's place is best. Sometimes they call it *La Fonda* 'cause it is an inn even if it is the home fer the Pino family. Then ye'll have a squint at some rooms ovah thar North o' the church, I reckon." Bill pointed across the square. "Leastwise, I found good uns that maybe ye'll be likin'. I'm cuttin' out. Business. I'm leavin' airly in the mornin'. Come some moons, I'll flash in agin. Good luck and good-by, Señorita Lona. Good-by ter ye both!" Without another word, he lifted his hand in the air and disappeared in the crowd. Biting his lips he

30

muttered to himself, "I'll be durned ef she ain't a leetle bit like Mary!"

Marino watched Bill go. Calls her "Lona," does he? His frown betrayed his thoughts to the girl whose eyes glinted with amusement. She knew that he was hoping Bill was gone forever. How silly of him! Before Marino turned, the girl's face was composed save for a quiver of the lips which she could not control.

Marino and Lona inspected the inn. It was built in the good old-fashioned style except that the entrance was aslant the square. The huge corral at the rear faced the old Río Chiquito trail. Through the double entrance doors they entered a small office adjoining a barroom; both rooms opened on a patio paved with red flagstones, centered about a full-branched tamarisk tree. Bushes had been planted at the corners of the place, their rose hips dark now. Tawny vines with limp leaves clung to some of the posts. From cages hanging here and there, birds roused to chirp feebly and then tucked their heads under their feathers. Two parrots rose on their perches and stretched clipped wings. One threw out his chest and chattered, "Here Pino! . . . Cards for me!" and the other followed with "You win! . . . Don't cry!" and then chuckled, "Luck! Luck! Luck!"

Marino and Lona laughed outright but Señor Gonzales only smiled for he had often heard the birds.

Señor Pino, a short, stocky Spaniard with sharp eyes, bustled into the patio and explained that the birds learned to talk in the gambling rooms where the players had great sport in teaching them. Sometimes they seemed uncannily intelligent. "Why, one night, I was losing," said the inn-keeper, "and one of the rascals came out with, 'Cross your fingers, Pino! Better luck!' and the other kept on with 'Next time! Next time!' I'd never heard them say that before and, by the great Picurís serpent, they were right!

"Do you play, Señorita Barcelona?" he asked.

"I know how to play, Señor," replied Lona glancing at Marino.

"Well, it is quite proper for a young woman like you to play in my rooms. We are not as formal as people in the South. The best folk of the town come here and they also play under the portals around the plaza. Good game—monte. I win and lose a fortune often. I have a young son who is positively crazy about the game. I'm almost afraid that he will bet the inn itself some day and lose."

Madam Pino joined the group, a little woman, stout like her husband, with good-natured, intelligent blue eyes.

During the evening, Madam Pino accompanied Marino and Lona to the gaming rooms. Out of the corner of her eye she studied the girl. Fine type, she thought. Young, but she will learn. Strange, that she has no duenna but she looks capable of taking care of herself. Aristocratic. Yes. Dresses well. Unconscious of Madam Pino's glances, Lona stood by the tables, her eyes glistening, her hand on a locket that flashed on her green silk dress. By her side, Marino watched with growing concern. He did not like this interest in cards. Finally he felt impelled to say, "Won't you leave the cards, Lona? It is midnight."

The next morning, Lona and Pablita went to look at the rooms of which Williams had spoken. They were poorly furnished but Lona knew that she could make them attractive with her own rugs and hangings. Nevertheless, she decided to stay at the inn where Madam Pino had already been very kind. She chose three rooms, one to be a reception sala. Following the prevailing fashion, she ordered Pedro to roll mattresses against the wall to be used as seats during the day, and covered them with her own beautiful blankets. Rugs were laid on the mud floor and soft yellow curtains were hung at the windows.

Madam Pino gleaned sufficient information from Marino and Señor Gonzales to justify her in stoutly defending Lona when some of her older friends made sly innuendoes. The orphaned girl's duenna had been too old to come North. Why should she not travel with a caballero and two servants? "She is very much a lady," she assured everyone. "Yes, she had brought letters of introduction," but Madam Pino never added that she had not seen them.

During the winter, Lona made many friends. Women liked her. At the dances she flirted impartially. But she kept lovers at a distance. In time, she would know her own mind, she thought. And as for marriage, she had tasted a freedom that she did not care to lose.

Almost every day she rode with Pedro far out to the desert. The solitude fed her spirit. She liked to watch the desert quiescent under the sun, sinister and mysterious under the clouds, exuberant in the wind. Often coils of dust spiraled upward. Now and then a column flamed red in the sunset. Flaming dust! Flame for life—dust for death. Lona remembered the inscription on the sundial in the plaza—*"Vita fugit sicut umbra"*—Life flies like a shadow. No! Life must blaze for me, she thought, and then it may fall.

Once as she was returning from the desert through one of the many winter-bound fields, she was met by a rider who wheeled about and asked permission to accompany her. Lona looked to see that Pedro was following and then smiled consent. The short, lean Spaniard asked her name, giving his in return—Facundo Melgares.

"Melgares? Then perhaps you are the former governor?"

"Sí, Señorita Barcelona, and although no longer in office, if I may ever be of any service, pray command me."

He talked pleasantly about the life of Santa Fé, about the

33

great celebration when word of Mexican independence had come, and the good-humored surprise of the people when they had to dance to a different tune. By the way, did she know General Santa Anna? No, she had seen him. She understood that he was a country gentleman at the present. Señor Melgares had been away all winter on a *rancho* playing the country gentleman himself, although he sorely missed his wife who had died not long ago. He glanced at the girl appraisingly. She blushed and turned her eyes toward the road. Señor Melgares continued to tell her amusing stories about city politics until they reached the inn.

Melgares, once a governor, thought Lona. She admired men who accomplished something. The younger men whom she knew . . . Perhaps she would meet Señor Melgares again some day?

When Lona was not riding, she often made the rounds of the plaza, accompanied by Madam Pino, and watched men playing at the gaming tables under the portals. When invited by a man whom she had met, she lingered by his table. Sometimes she joined in the game but she preferred to play at the inn.

Marino was rarely present now when Lona played monte, nor was his presence necessary. He knew that and, now that spring was burgeoning, he was often out of the city. Long ago he had told her of his uncle Bernardo Castro who had searched for the *Cerro del Oro*—the hill of gold, in the early years of the century and of his death before he could find it. Marino had his maps. He had dreamed of being a mine owner ever since he was a child.

For several weeks there had been talk of the first caravan from the South. One morning a messenger rode in to announce that a rich wagon train was approaching and, except for a mozo

34

from Chihuahua who had been shot in a drunken brawl, all travelers were in good health and the cargo safe.

Lona waited impatiently for the caravan. She hoped that someone whom she had known in old Mexico would be with this first train. When the wagons were expected, she told Pablita to wear her best. She, herself, dressed in a bright red gown, long gold earrings studded with pearls, and the chain with her locket. Last of all she swung over her high comb her loveliest white mantilla.

Leaving the house the two walked quickly along. The heels of Lona's black velvet slippers clicked on the flagging and flashed red. Meeting Señor Melgares, she gave him a friendly but reserved greeting. Since he had not come to the inn to see her, she did not linger. She would urge no man.

Turning into the street of the cottonwoods, she could see the wagons lumbering along toward them. She and Pablita waited under the portal where they had first looked at the plaza. Now she was among the welcoming crowd. Perhaps there would be travelers as disappointed as she had been. A coach stopped near her. A young man alighted, tall and strangely familiar. He turned his profile. It could be! Yes, it was Rudolfo!

Lona felt her throat contract and tears start. Had he cared so much? She checked the impulse to fly to him. Instead she grasped Pablita's hand and hastened to the inn.

Rudolfo stood for some time looking at the plaza, barren except for the sundial.

"Rudolfo!" In the bronzed, roughly dressed man who grasped his hand, he hardly recognized his onetime friend, Marino. "I don't wonder that you scarcely know me," said Marino. "I've just come back from the mountains where I believe I have discovered a real vein of ore."

Rudolfo gave Marino news of the South before he asked eagerly about Lona.

"Lona? Yes, she is here, stays at *La Fonda* yonder. We are little more than strangers these days though we meet often enough. Of course, I am away in the mountains much of the time. Her mountain man has gone to the West."

"Mountain man! *Por Dios!* What do you mean?"

Marino told about Bill Williams, the affair in Chihuahua and the subsequent friendship between the two, hinting that the girl had shown unusual warmth of interest in the crude fellow.

"Nonsense! Marino! Such a man is not in her class. Lona's no fool. Why, Lona de Es—"

"Listen, Rudolfo. Her name is now Lona Barcelona."

"Santa María! Is she married?"

"No. On the way North, she took the notion to change her name, said she was coming to a new life and wanted to sail under a name of her own choosing. She would not use the letters of introduction which the Marqués had given her. She would make her own friends and manage her own affairs. Queer whim! I tried to talk her out of it but to no avail. Then finally, I heard this fellow Williams speak of her as Señorita Barcelona and knew that no words of mine would alter her decision. To me she seems much changed since she took to the cards."

"Cards?"

"Yes. She is no longer the girl that you knew. Quite a woman now and already an expert at cards. How she does love to play! She has grown so independent, stands squarely on her own feet, I tell you. Of course, as one might expect, life up here is less conventional except in some old-fashioned homes where they almost bend over backward to be like the Spaniards in the South. The girls in such families chafe at the restrictions, I know, because I have heard them say so. As for Lona's affairs, I know precious little."

"By the saints, Marino! I can't understand it. I'll go over to

36

the inn and get settled. Then I'll find Lona. Meantime, good luck. I'd like to join you some time in the mountains. I do not expect to return until fall."

An hour later, Rudolfo was ushered into Lona's little reception room decorated with rugs and draperies which he remembered. Pablita had greeted him and had gone to call her mistress.

"Rudolfo!"

Lona had never looked lovelier. Her eyes glowed. Her long dark braids hung down over the folds of her yellow silk dress and white mantilla. In her hand a turquoise blue fan swayed when she curtsied. She was like a happy bird free of its cage. Rudolfo threw his head back to contemplate this new picture of the girl he loved, then bent over her hand and kissed it with his grandest air.

They sat facing each other where both could glance into the patio. The scent of early spring floated in through the twilight. Lona plied Rudolfo with questions about Mexico. He studied this new Lona with her quick, eager voice, her greater charm.

"It is a new land, Rudolfo," she replied when he questioned her. "New customs. New faces. New names. I am freer here than I ever could have been in Mexico." Smiling over her fan, she asked, "Will you join Marino in his search for gold?"

"Hardly. You know why I came. You are my gold."

"But, Rudolfo, when I left Mexico, I left all behind—even you—and . . ." She looked away and shrugged her shoulders slightly.

"You mean Dolores! She is nothing to me, Lona, and never was." Rudolfo's hand pushed back his hair. "Will you listen to me, Lona?" In the excitement of the bull ring, the mad shouting, the confusion, the blinding sun and sea of faces he had lost all consciousness of what he was doing. The rose? Yes, he had taken Dolores' rose. That night, when he had wanted to be beneath her window, telling her how it happened, he had been called to his father's bedside. When he had returned to the city a month later, she had left with the caravan. There had been no chance in the world to catch up with the wagons. Now he had come on the very first spring train. Would she understand? There had been no reason for anger.

"Oh, I am not angry any more. But I am a different girl. Life is new here and I like it. Dolores, after all, will make you happier."

Rudolfo winced.

"No, Lona, no! You know I love you. Do you think I would have endured that awful journey for anyone but you?"

"Perhaps not. Well, now that you are here, shall we be friends? They make a fine point of friendship in this country. Love?" She spread her fan in a slight questioning gesture.

When Rudolfo rose to go, he ceremoniously pressed his lips to her hand. This was the first time they had ever talked like this—alone. He bowed again. His blue eyes challenged hers.

"Must the grille always be between us?" Before she could answer, his arms were around her. Lona smiled up into his face. In spite of herself, her lips answered his.

IV

A FAMOUS MATADOR FROM MEXICO COULD NOT
long remain undiscovered in a town like Santa Fé. Rudolfo
was soon feted by the old Spanish families, especially those in
which there were daughters, but Señorita Lona was not among
the guests of these people who "almost bent over backward"
to be like the Spaniards in the South.

Constantly Rudolfo was plied with questions. Is it possible
that the Señorita from Mexico has no duenna? Who was
she, anyway? Some say that she is of noble birth but, if so,
who . . . ? She is too young to be so independent . . . not
becoming! Did she not play monte too often on the plaza? Of
course, others did also. Then aside . . . Señor de Godoy always speaks in the highest terms of her but then he is a gentleman. Have you noticed that he gives little real information
about her?

Soon Rudolfo declined invitations in which Lona was not
included. Daily he pled with her to fix a wedding date. His
name would protect her from innuendoes and spying curiosity.
But Lona laughed. "How do I know that you will always be
faithful?" This was not only a new Lona but a new type. Why
had he never thought of a girl as a comrade? Perhaps he was
changing too. But of one thing he was sure, he loved her more

deeply than ever. To Lona, never was there a gayer, more tender lover. He could not doubt that he was master of her heart but her mind was her own and he could not fathom it.

One morning Lona noticed Pedro and Pablita passing arm in arm through the patio. Pablita's face was aglow. Lona guessed that they were already mated. Some day she must see that banns were read.

The lovers came to the door.

"Doña Lona," asked Pablita as she clung to Pedro's arm. "We are so glad that we are here. Are not you glad too?"

"Yes, Pablita, I am," answered her mistress. "But . . ."

"You? Pedro and I are troubled. You . . . You are not going to old Mexico with El Señor? We should not ask, I know," said Pablita. She withdrew her arm from Pedro's and came to stand near Doña Lona.

"Perhaps Don Rudolfo will decide to stay in Santa Fé, Pablita. Then all four of us will be happy. I do not know. Now go and help Pedro, if he can find something for you to do."

Pablita flashed a smile at her mistress. She took Pedro's arm and danced across the patio. Lona's mind was engrossed with thoughts of Rudolfo.

"Darling, I do love you!" she whispered. "I love everything about you! I could smother you with kisses, this moment. But, oh, this matter of marriage?" She stared into the patio and tried to understand why she saw marriage in such a gloomy light. If other girls thought of the restraint of marriage, they never spoke of it. Perhaps they wanted just that, but she did not. She could not return to Mexico. In some inexplicable way she belonged to this new country. No matter how deeply her emotions responded to Rudolfo, even when the world was blotted out in his arms, something whispered, "Before you tie yourself to him irrevocably, make him love you enough to want to stay in this Northland."

40

The weeks danced by. Lona and Rudolfo were in the saddle, galloping along the trails, sometimes waving greetings to travelers who sang if they came from the South but shouted and roared if they hailed from the East. Sometimes, Lona led the way to the foothills and up the higher slopes carpeted with wild beauty. One day, she wheeled and reined her horse by his.

"I love those twisted old piñons and cedars. And the desert! Under the rain it has a delicious odor, never sullen and bedraggled. Even in winter when coyotes race and wolves prowl among the *chamisa* bushes, it thrills me. Do you love it too, Rudolfo?"

"No, it appalls me, Lona." Rudolfo shook his head. "It makes me creep. It is like death. The mountains are friendly. The desert scoffs."

"But it is so free. See that dust cloud lift. There! The wind catches it. Watch it rise, ambitious to reach the sky. Rudolfo it reminds me of the dream that I have for my own life." They both were silent. When the dust was lost against the ragged horizon, Lona turned her horse. "Now let's take the canyon trail close to the mountains. I love them too."

Rudolfo followed without speaking, depressed because he could not feel Lona's love for this uncouth land. Mexico had its deserts, its mountains, and much more lure. Had she forgotten the palms, the roses, and the fountains with their clouds of bright hovering birds, forgotten the beauty of the land, the ease, the wealth, the charm of an ancient culture?

Not long after this ride which neither forgot, Lona confided in Madam Pino and her friend, Madam Alarid, that she was trying to make Rudolfo content to remain in Santa Fé. Some day she might venture marriage but she never would consent to go South again. They heartily seconded her plan and began to give dinners and dances at which Lona always sparkled, especially when she danced *La Jota*.

With rare broadmindedness, Madam Pino and Madam Alarid never criticized Lona for riding alone with her lover, nor did they interrupt when they saw Rudolfo and Lona sitting under the tamarisk tree in the patio or chatting in the candlelight of the girl's sala.

"Times are different," Madam Pino told her friend. "They will know each other better and, after all, it seems the sensible thing to do. I wish I had been as free as Lona when I was young."

The inauguration of a new governor was the occasion of a grand fiesta. The day broke cool and sharply sunny. Very early the plaza was noisily astir with merchants who were brightening their windows with new goods. Under the portals all about the plaza, gamblers sang as they placed tables and dusted benches. Here and there a tricky professional dealer secretly examined the edges of his cards.

Long before time for the midday ceremony, Lona, Madam Pino, Rudolfo, and Marino, all gay in Spanish dress, pressed through the crowd and found places near the sundial. Around them people talked of the new governor, curious but not enthusiastic. This Don Manuel Armijo was no soldier, was not even to the manner born, but he had been appointed. How matters would go now, no one could foretell. But this was his day.

Tiring of the long delay, Lona suggested that they go to play at the inn. There dignitaries had already gathered. Someone whispered to Lona that Don Manuel Armijo was among them but she did not see him when she went into the sala for special guests.

Madam Pino was proud of the long room which had recently been washed down with light yellow adobe. Against a four-foot dado of orange cloth stood fine old carved chairs

42

stained brown as the woodwork. Over the tables lay fresh green felt which had been brought in lately from the East. From the ceiling of spruce poles supported by heavy beams of fir, swung strong chains holding candelabras and in the corners of the walls were shiny tin lanterns. The room had none too many windows and, at times, candles were lighted even in the daytime. On this day, however, the glow of the outer sunshine gave plenty of light.

Among the players already seated, Lona noticed friars in brown-cowled robes; army officers in blue, red and buff uniforms; merchants in brown or green, some with the new-fashioned long trousers, all with chokingly high white stocks. There were also a few ranchmen in rough clothes and one or two mountain men in new buckskin suits with fringe and bead embroidery.

The party found their table, called their favorite dealer and were soon absorbed in a game of monte. Rudolfo watched Lona. What would her cousin Andreas think if he could see her now in a public inn, playing with the air of a professional? Her hands reached out with avidity toward her winnings. They curved. The long nails shone. Not quite like human hands, thought Rudolfo, more like beautiful panther claws. He shook his head in disgust at such an idea.

As the game went on, he noticed a tall, angular fellow in buckskin, with red hair down to his shoulders. He was leaning against a wall and looking intently at Lona. In his hand was a black felt hat decorated with a red plume. He rolled his eyes around the sala and looked directly at Rudolfo for a second. Instinctively Rudolfo's glance crossed swords with him. Whoever he was, Rudolfo disliked him.

When the game was ended, Lona straightened, smiled at her lover and pointed proudly to her winnings. As she rose, her eyes discovered the man in buckskin.

43

"Why, Beel! Oh, I am so glad to see you," she exclaimed, running to greet him. "My dear Beel friend!"

That was all Rudolfo heard. He stood transfixed, staring at the two who started to walk through the crowd. So Lona had forgotten him for the moment, even as he had forgotten in that affair of the rose? But she turned soon and beckoned to him. Reluctantly he stepped forward to be introduced.

The three walked into the patio and found a bench near the parrots swinging on their high perches.

"Where did you come from, Sir?" Rudolfo asked. The "Sir" almost choked his throat.

"Wal, from every darn place but hyar and I'll be from hyar afore long," answered Bill.

Rudolfo sharpened his sword. He need not be funny with me, he thought. I'll put Lona right about this crude fellow. What if he did rescue her down in Chihuahua. Any man worth his salt would have done it if he had had the chance.

Meanwhile Bill eyed the young Spaniard, sizing him up as he had sized up small craft floating by on the old Missouri when he was a lanky boy swinging his feet from a rock on the bank. Rolling his eyes away, he thought, "Know his kind. His keel ain't scarfed to suit me."

"Staying long in these parts?" Bill asked curtly without looking at Rudolfo.

"That remains to be seen. Lona will answer that question," replied the Spaniard in a possessive tone implying that he, and he only, claimed her. Then he rose and excused himself.

Williams watched the young man saunter away. " 'Tain't none of me business, Miss, but I reckon ye won't be marryin' yit nor goin' back ter Mexico neither, ef I've larned ye proper."

"I hardly think so, Beel," she replied. "But what about your trip? Have you been trapping? You have been gone so long."

"Wal, in the winter, yes, but summer's no time fer beaver.

44

Their fur's too thin. I wus jes out o' the world for a spell. Didn't ca'culate ter be gone so long but days flew some'ers. Then I got wind o' the big doin's hyar terday. Been dressin' up fer the occasion, ye see," said Bill who looked down and fingered the red plume on his hat.

Lona smiled. "That's gay but I like your two-eared cap better, Beel. You once said you always had one of them on hand. Are you really going away soon?"

"Me? Ain't I nevah tole you that settlements don't shine with me fer long? Jes thought I'd look ye up fer a minute. I'm leavin' ternight after the fandango ef I don't git sich a load on as'll keep me from gittin' me legs ovah me ole nag."

They walked out to the front door of the inn. Bill put out his hand. "I'll git goin' now. Will be seein' ye agin some fine day. Luck ter ye. Good-by er how is it the Frenchmen put it? O riv-or! Why they air allus talkin' 'bout the Missouri, I dunno." His eyes twinkled while he swung his absurd plumed hat to his breast with all the suavity of a courtier. Then he turned and vanished down the street.

Lona returned to the gaming sala.

"Ready?" said the dealer as she took her place. "There's an hour yet."

"I'll join the game, if I may," said a man, a stranger to Lona but all the others knew him. Conscious that the man was looking at her, she did not glance at him but blushed uncomfortably.

"Pardon, Señor Armijo, but it is your turn," said the dealer.

Armijo, the new governor! Lona glanced at the man. Showily dressed in blue and gold; hard smooth-shaven face; large nose bending over the upper lip; lower lip protruding; cold steel-blue eyes. Where have I seen such eyes before? Lona dropped hers for he was looking at her again and smiling. She did not return the smile. Watching the cards, she kept on wondering

45

where she had seen the man before. Somewhere! On the plaza? On the trail? She could not remember. Perhaps she was mistaken. She dismissed the matter.

Huzzas in the street drew all the players to the windows. The dealer put down his deck hastily. The lower card flipped and showed a king. Armijo rose tardily, lingered by the table and when he thought all eyes were watching the parade he dextrously changed one of his cards. No one saw him except Lona who, at the moment, had given a sidelong glance at the table. She turned quickly toward the window and heard Señor Armijo clap his hands as he edged into the crowd.

"Narbona! Chief Narbona! Don Antonio! Bravo!" shouted the people as a straight military figure rode by.

Good heavens . . . ! thought Lona. Is he to be succeeded by a fellow who cheats at cards . . . ?

When Colonel Narbona had passed, the game began again. Armijo claimed the stake. The dealer eyed him questioningly. Lona did not look up for fear her eyes might betray what she knew. After another bet she rose.

"Not going?" inquired Don Manuel Armijo. "There are twenty minutes yet."

Lona pretended that she did not hear.

"Hum! She does not speak to me? Good Lord! What a girl!" Señor Armijo muttered. "I wonder . . . ?"

Promptly at twelve, bells rang. Flags whipped upward in the wind. Music of guitars, banjos and drums filtered through huzzas. Soldiers marched to their places. Officers curbed excited horses. Gamblers reluctantly left their tables and mingled with the crowd which was forced back as friars passed to a dais in front of the main door of the palace. On this platform were several chairs. One with a higher back was covered with a square of purple velvet edged with gold. An American who

46

stood in the crowd nudged a companion. "See the chair? The New Mexicans may believe in a republic but they never forget the purple!"

Drums rattled and people cheered wildly when Colonel Narbona rose, impressive in his full military uniform glittering with gold braid on red and blue. He raised his hand for silence and spoke in short terse sentences. He made no references to his own work, but built a picture of the future and urged that all stand behind their new leader and wish him well. Then introducing Don Manuel Armijo, he motioned for him to take the chair with the purple cover.

When the applause died away, Governor Armijo began to speak. He stammered, chose his words badly, grew more and more bombastic. The cheers which followed were perfunctory. In an effort to hide his chagrin, Armijo waved the attention of the people to his predecessor. When the applause thundered, he smiled and bowed as if the huzzas were for him. As the crowd drifted away from the dais, the new governor stood erect. He was taller than most men. His face was set in cruel lines, his eyes squinted and his lips curled in an ugly sneer. He would teach the people to shout huzzas a-plenty.

"Think of appointing such a man to take the place of a gentleman like Colonel Narbona, Rudolfo!" whispered Lona, as she leaned on his arm while they walked back to the inn. "It is incredible!"

"From what I can learn he is at the head of a powerful clique. They forced his appointment. He is a crude fellow. I have heard much disparaging talk about him during the past few days but always in whispers. They all fear him even the men who cringe about him. There may be trouble ahead. I believe, if the rank and file dared, they would revolt right now.

Don't you see, Lona, that Mexico is the sane place for you?
Santa Fé is fine for a visit but it's a poor village compared
to Mexico. I cannot understand why you want to stay."

"Yes, that is probably true. But in spite of everything, I like
Santa Fé. I mean to stay." Lona looked up eagerly into Rudolfo's face, hoping that he might decide at that moment to do
what her heart desired. But his eyes avoided hers.

"Lona, darling, when will you marry me and go back home?"
The girl shook her head.

Silence fell between them as they walked through the lazily
moving crowd. At *La Fonda* Rudolfo bade her good day. Lona
went directly to her room and flung herself on a couch, crying
as if her heart would break. She had made her final answer
but she loved him! She could not believe that he would go
back to Mexico.

V

FOR TWO BREATHLESS AUGUST DAYS LONA DID not see Rudolfo. On the third evening he escorted her and Madam Pino to a dance at the home of Señor Gómez y Alarid. Duty held Señor Pino at the inn. They walked the short distance under the light of the plaza lanterns, stepping aside, at times, to avoid pools of wine spilled by drunken fellows gambling at the tables. They dodged ragged Indians and singers with wide sombreros tilted back, serapes and guitar straps thrown over their shoulders. Out in the roadway, soldiers staggered by in ragged uniforms. Rudolfo took Lona's arm. A tremor ran through her body, a sharp stab of anxiety. But she tried to keep her voice light.

"Soldiers haven't had much to do lately, have they? I should think they would try to better their condition."

"It's the old story. The merchants as well as the soldiers in this town are indolent. Remember? 'Many in the stirrup are still afoot.'" Rudolfo's words were edged with bitterness. "There is too much indifference, too much ease. Lazylegs never climb. True, we have them in Mexico but—well, it is different."

"I simply can not understand how anyone can be without ambition."

49

"And your ambition is . . . ?"

"I don't quite know yet, Rudolfo, but I have it deep inside."

Rudolfo's mouth twitched. So, she was ambitious. What on earth could she want to do? Women belong in the home. His mother was right. No woman should do anything out in the world.

They had arrived at the great door of the Alarid house. The host ushered his guests into the sala with the customary greeting, "May God grant good to you."

On a small platform at the far end of the room, musicians with fiddles and guitars swayed and tapped the time of the *valse redondo*. When the music ceased, the dancers sat on mattresses rolled against the walls and covered with blankets. Madam Alarid claimed Madam Pino and Lona.

"Have you heard that balls of fire bounded down the mountainside last night? They say that they are really witches in disguise, Lona. The other night a man declared he chased one. It became a rat and scurried under the *chamisa* bushes. When he followed, it turned into a huge dog. Yes, that's what he said. It jumped over his head and disappeared under the willows by the river. Those fire-balls usually come before some disaster." Madam Alarid sighed. "I am anxious about my son, Carlos. He is with Don Marino in the mountains. I know that *el señor* is careful but . . ."

"Yes, he is," replied Lona. "You need have no anxiety for Carlos. Don Marino will surely find gold. When he was in the city he showed me samples of ore, stray bits of stone—I think he called them 'floats.' He will find the mother lode. He thinks that the Ortíz mountains to the South may be very rich. He and Carlos will be very rich some day."

"Sí, that may be. But I wish I had not heard of the fire-balls. Perhaps the music will drive my fear away."

Madam Alarid forced a smile and glancing at the musicians

50

said, "I see the *bastonero* points his bow at Don Rudolfo. That means *La Jota* and you for his partner, Señorita."

When the floor was cleared of all other dancers, the lively music began. Rudolfo in black satin with embroidered bolero and green sash, Lona in white silk and brilliant red, yellow, and black shawl; a handsome couple, the crowd thought. The two bowed to each other and posed with one hand upward in salute. Then came the sprightly dance—the bowing, the swinging away, the quick return, the circling of each other, the stamp of feet, castanets rattling furiously like a clash of swords. It was a dance of old Aragón, sensuous languid measures followed by quick flight and pursuit, ending with hands flung high in the spirit of conquest deferred.

Rudolfo led Lona to her seat. He bowed quickly and walked away.

When the bells struck for midnight, the two were in the dark patio at the inn. Madam Pino had left them. Rudolfo touched Lona's arm. He was staking all on a last plea.

"Lona," he whispered in a husky voice, "I am leaving on the caravan at noon tomorrow."

"No! No! I won't believe it. Rudolfo, you know you are my very life. Can't you be content with me here?"

"Content! Content as matters stand now? How could I be? You will never marry me and I am not satisfied to be always your suitor. If you really loved me you would come with me. It is best that I go. I bid you farewell now." He pressed his lips to her hand, then crushed her to him. "My love! Lona, *querida mía.*"

"*Querido!*" she whispered.

At last Lona broke away. "I can not go! I can not. I do not know why but it is so." Sobbing she ran into her room. The door was open but she knew that tonight he would not come.

Rudolfo's ruse had failed. Now his decision had become iron hard. He wandered about the twisted streets until the sun came up.

Across the patio, Lona tossed for hours. Why was her heart so stubborn? It lay like a stone between them. She did care. But she could not go back to that life in Mexico. It would choke her. Why should love demand such a terrible sacrifice? Rudolfo! She had been cruel to him. If he loved her enough, how could he leave her.

When morning came Lona dressed in green, coiled her braids crown-wise and threw a gold-embroidered darker green rebozo over her head. Her lips glowed but her eyes were dull. She walked through the patio where a foolish parrot screamed, "Luck . . . luck . . . luck!" Beyond in the office she met Madam Pino. The older woman put her arms about Lona and whispered, "He loves you, do not let him go!" But Lona did not answer.

At the corner stood Pedro with her horse. In the confusion on the plaza Lona barely heard the curses, the songs, the guitars. Her ears strained to hear the call, *"Listo! Adelante!"* How grim and savage it sounded when it came. The wagons began to move. Men galloped by but she did not see Rudolfo. He would not leave without a word of farewell?

"I have looked everywhere for you," Rudolfo drew rein beside her.

"Yes, we have missed each other."

"Lona, dearest! You would have ridden to bid me Godspeed? I shall not forget that!" He leaned toward her. "If ever you want me, Lona, send for me. I will come. I beg you, do not remain too long in this Godforsaken land. The wagons have gone. May God be good to you!"

Rudolfo caught Lona's hands and held them to his cheek. Tears glistened in his eyes as he said his last, *"Querida mía!"*

52

Suddenly he straightened in his saddle, took up the reins, put on his sombrero and pulled it down. Then waving his hand he rode swiftly around the corner and out of sight.

"Despedida!" called Lona after him. Tears blinded her. She sat for a moment until she could brush them away, then drew the reins and followed.

Far down the road she went. On a desert hill she pulled in her horse to watch the line of wagons wind in and out among haciendas below, top a rise and dip again. Now dust was all she could see. She started to gallop after the caravan but her mind said, "Too late!" A light wind blew the dust aside and she caught one last glimpse of the tiny moving line. When it disappeared, she turned her horse back to the city, gave him the reins, seeing nothing. She set her teeth hard. Her rebozo fell from her head and wisps of her hair whipped in the wind.

Rudolfo rode with bowed head. His thoughts were at war again. Did he hear his name? He looked back. On a hill was the silhouette of a woman on a horse. She had followed! Rudolfo turned in his saddle and watched until the dust shut her out. He settled himself more easily in his saddle. Had he been too proud, too jealous? Had he lost the race in the last heat? But he must go on. For several hours Rudolfo's memories lashed his weary spirit. The jogging had already become tedious. It was unendurable! He did not want to go South. He would not!

"Turn back!" he shouted to his muleteers, "back to Santa Fé."

Grumbling in astonishment, they obeyed. Horses, burros and carts were pulled out of the line. Sullenly they took the trail Northeast.

It was dark when Rudolfo reached the inn. Neither Madam Pino nor Lona was about so he waited at the bar. Toward mid-

53

night he sauntered along the plaza portal where he found Facundo Melgares and others playing.

"Come on. Try the game, Don Rudolfo," invited Señor Melgares.

"No, I'll wait until tomorrow." He was not drunk but whisky had made his tongue thick.

"Afraid to try your luck?" sneered the dealer.

"Afraid! What do you mean? I am never afraid."

"No?" answered the challenger, raising his eyebrows. Rudolfo leaned over the table.

"I'll bet on the knave." He threw a handful of coins on the board.

"Eh, there you are. You win, by Heaven!" shouted the dealer who thought drink had befuddled the handsome Mexican's brain. But Rudolfo understood and watched closely. The fellow was a stranger to him and apparently to the others.

Pesos piled up for Rudolfo. He called larger bets and began to lose steadily. He kept his eyes on the dealer's hands and, lightning quick though they were, caught him in a crooked deal. He pushed back his stool.

"Thief!" he cried. "Contemptible cheat!" His hand felt for his dagger. The dealer was quicker. He plunged his own into Rudolfo's side, withdrew it, brandished it menacingly and disappeared in the crowd.

Rudolfo fell backward, his face white, blood oozing from his wound. Señor Melgares made a pillow of his cloak. He tried with kerchief after kerchief to stem the blood. He felt for the pulse, tried again. Someone had run for a doctor.

The crowd grew larger. Parties were breaking up at the sound of the midnight bell. Among them were Madam Pino and Lona who had been playing long whist at a friend's house. Lona had lost heavily. Madam Pino understood. She did not wonder that the girl's bids went wild.

54

"I played badly," Lona said. "I kept seeing the dust from the wagon train lifting on the desert and horsemen galloping away. The dust actually seemed to pass in front of my cards!"

"Yes, I know. What does it matter? Look! There is a crowd under the lantern. What has happened?"

"Someone is hurt. There is the doctor." As the crowd parted Lona caught sight of the man on the ground.

"Rudolfo!" she cried, forcing her way after the doctor.

Kneeling, Lona took Rudolfo's head in her arms. "Speak to me. I thought you were gone. Speak to me, Rudolfo!"

The eyes slowly opened. The lips tried to smile. "Lona, darling! You do . . ." His head fell back.

"I do! I do love you. Speak to me. You must live. You must not die. I did not know I loved you so. You must live!" she pleaded, caressing the white face. Then she fainted.

Señor Melgares lifted the girl and carried her to her door. Pablita opened it, eyes wide with fright.

"What . . . what . . . has happened?" she stammered.

"Señorita Lona is ill. She . . . Señor Rudolfo has been killed!" Señor Melgares answered. His own voice was none too steady.

He laid Lona on the couch. The doctor bent over her. He called for water, both hot and cold. Pablita rubbed her wrists, crying silently. But it was a long time before they could arouse her from the stupor.

During the succeeding days both the doctor and Señor Melgares called often. Lona stirred only occasionally. Later, she stared with wide open unseeing eyes, uncannily large in her thinning face. Rudolfo gone! The fire-balls! Madam Alarid . . . cards through dust . . . always dust . . . wagons disappearing . . . dust . . . wagons . . . the crowd . . . Rudolfo's face . . . She could never be happy again. She . . . she was to blame!

VI

WORK FORCES MEMORY TO BEHAVE, THOUGHT
Madam Pino. She invited Lona to go with her to the room reserved for spinning and weaving. At several high-built looms
women were making fashionable black and white checked carpet. Lona watched the pattern grow as hands swung swiftly
and feet made pedals creak and thump. One loom stood idle.
She looked down at her own thin hands that so far had done
so little.

"In this country we all learn to weave, Señorita," said
Madam Pino. "I know that in the South such work is left to
servants but here we make most of our own cloth. Of course,
some comes on the wagons from Chihuahua and from the East
now, but there is rarely enough. I use this loom. It is good fun
to create new designs."

New designs, thought Lona. Yes, she must make new designs for her life. For the present she might as well learn to
weave. She asked if she might try her hand and, after a few
lessons, spent much time at the loom. The very monotony, the
motion of her hands, across and across, up and down, soothed
her mind.

One Saturday afternoon, Pedro met her. His big hands fum-

56

bled with his hat. He hung his head and stammered, "Señorita Lona, I've wanted . . . to ask you something . . . for a long time. It's about Pablita . . . I want . . ." Pedro hesitated and then blurted out, "We want to marry. Will you see the priest, *Patrona mía?*" Pedro straightened his shoulders. "I love her, you know."

"Yes, Pedro, I know. I'll have the banns read tomorrow. Indeed, I will. I'll arrange everything. Bless your heart!" replied Lona and hurried on lest the servant see the tears in her eyes.

Pablita had watched from the door of Lona's sala. She stepped back to let her mistress enter. "Oh, Señorita Lona. We can be married?"

"Of course, you dear little Pablita. Did you think for a moment that you could not?"

"Oh, no, not really," chuckled the maid. "Did you know, Señorita Lona, that Felix Areta is in town again and he has promised to stand up with us? He and his sister. They came on the last caravan."

"So you have your plans, Pablita. Tell me about them." Lona sat down to listen. Pablita prattled on, ending shyly with, "Could I have a pair of high-heeled slippers like yours, Señorita *mía?* You see I'm working for the finest lady in all Santa Fé and I want to look grand!"

"Of course, you may. We'll begin at once."

Three weeks later, the five o'clock morning mass in a small side chapel at *La Parróquia* was finished. At Señorita Barcelona's request more candles were lighted. A priest stood waiting.

The small group of people gave passage to the bride and groom. Over her full-skirted black cotton dress Pablita wore a long white muslin veil with a crown of cotton flowers. Pedro was proud in his new black suit and shiny high boots, the gifts of his mistress. He put Pablita's arm in his and stepped for-

57

ward. Pablita swayed a little in the strange new slippers and tripped slightly as a heel caught her veil. Señorita Lona could not refrain from a smile as she noted that Pablita's crown had slipped awry, but her face was solemn when Pedro and Pablita held their single lighted candles.

Felix Areta opened the small carved chest which Pedro had made for his bride. In it was the *arras,* a few bead necklaces, silver rings and the customary thirteen coins. He lifted out the wedding ring. Then he handed the chest to Pablita. The priest flung a wide white satin ribbon about the shoulders of the two, tied it and continued with the ceremony. Pablita and Pedro were duly married and blessed.

They came to receive Lona's blessing. Pablita's beaming face beneath the crown, now quite on one side, forced her to smile. Pablita was so radiantly happy. Lona patted the little girl's shoulder. It was her day.

After the wedding Lona tried to weave but the shuttle fell from her hand. She stared at the design on the loom. Through its black and white she saw the yellow sanded arena, Rudolfo waving his red-lined cape. Rudolfo singing. And now—she stood in the patio and it was dark. Lona left the shuttle on the floor and walked out into the sun.

"Lona, dear," called Madam Pino, looking up over her rectangular gold-rimmed glasses, "you are tired of weaving." She had waited under the tamarisk tree, apparently engrossed in her sewing. "I need assistance in the office. Would you like to learn how I keep my accounts?" Lona nodded but did not speak.

For many weeks, Lona was daily with Madam Pino. She enjoyed the business of the inn more than she had expected and became expert in handling money. Meanwhile, Marino, who now lived in a shack at the entrance to his mine, came into the city occasionally and always called at the tavern to chat with her. Señor Melgares came almost daily. She liked him. Not once did she consider either man as a suitor.

Throughout the long winter, Señor Melgares talked of local affairs and then of mountain trails, fine distant views, unexplored arroyos and ruins of pueblos. He fired Lona's imagination. When spring came, she rode with him when small parties of people left for the hills. Sometimes she rode with him alone, again defying custom.

"Señor Melgares and Señorita Barcelona ride well together," said neighbors. Men gossiping in the sun, pulled at their pipes, pointed with their thumbs and commented, "One may count on Señor Melgares to choose a beauty. She smiles more now. Too bad that young man had to go."

Dismounting one early October afternoon, Lona spied Bill Williams at the door of the inn. He turned when he heard the horses stop. The girl welcomed him so cheerfully that Señor Melgares bade her a crusty good day.

"Ah, my big Beel friend," exclaimed Lona as she looked up into his friendly gray eyes and offered her hand.

"Eh, Lona. It's right glad I am ter see ye agin. Wus gone longer'n I expected ter be . . . as usual." Bill walked quiet-footed beside her through the inn and on to the patio. They sat down under the dusty-green tamarisk. Both were at a loss for words.

A slight acrid scent from frost-bitten plants filled the air. Bill rolled his eyes about. He missed the small birds. Sensible leetle uns ter fly South! But the parrots were there with wings clipped. Each opened an eye and promptly closed it again. From the windows of the gaming salas came no sound and the looms in the distant room were still.

59

Finally Bill broke the silence. "Had some trouble since I wus hyar, I'm tole. Sorry, mighty sorry. Mind tellin' me 'bout it?"

"Not now, Beel. Later. Tell me first about your trip, will you?"

"Not much ter tell. I've jes been workin' by main strength and awkwardness. Been out West in Apacheria. Had a bunch o' pelts hid down thar at an ole copper mine, in whar it wus cool. Found 'em as I left 'em. Wus short on hosses. So I went inter Californy and tuk all I needed."

Lona smiled at Bill who grinned sheepishly and then laughed outright.

"Sh, Mother Confessor, hoss-stealin' ain't no great sin out thar as I figgur. It makes the fellers mad though and some of 'em tuk arter me right smart but I got away. Then Injun varmints tried ter steal from me, did get some and made it purty hot fer me but I cleared out, one night, by runnin' me stock up a river fer a spell. Wal, they won't miss them animuls fer long arter they git ovah bein' mad. Plenty more down thar."

"Had any luck since you came in, Beel?"

"Yeah, sold some furs. I ca'culated there might be some airly buyin' in Santy Fee. Wus right. I've made a coin er two. Pockets in me jeans wus a-yearnin' fer 'em."

Bill thought best to say nothing of the arrow which had struck his leg, another which had killed his mount under him, and his final escape from the Indians by catching a fresh horse and losing himself in the great red rocks of the Western desert. He puffed vigorously as if his life depended on such breath and finally blurted out, "How 'bout ye, Lona?"

Noticing Pablita open the door to her sala, Lona motioned to Bill and led the way within.

"People will come soon into the patio. The parrots will cackle their nonsense but they'll not disturb us in here." In a low con-

60

trolled voice she told Bill about Rudolfo beginning with the day of the red rose.

"Gol darn! Now that's too bad, Señorita. Ef I could be shu-ah of the feller who done the stabbin' thar'd be some singin' 'round hyar that he wouldn't hyar. Ain't nevah killed a man yit." Bill caught the high arching of Lona's eyes and added quickly, "Oh, Injuns? Yeah, but they don't count only as notches on me Fetcham. All-fired sorry, I am. Reckon ye couldn't go ter the funer'l?"

Slowly Lona shook her head and whispered, "I have never asked about it, Beel."

"From all I evah heerd, that young chap made a good many friends 'round these parts. I reckon Madam Pino had plenty of fine food handy and turned the mirrors ter the walls likely. Seems folks down hyar think ef a body sees himsel' in a mirror at sich times, why he'll be the next one to be carted out. Wal, I had a 'sperience mesel', Lona. I kin understand how ye feel. Mine want eggsackly like your'n, 'course. I ain't nevah tole anybody 'bout it since I come ter the mountains." He hesitated. Perhaps he could distract her from her grief.

"Tell me about it, Beel. I've always wanted to know where you came from and about your family."

"Wal, me folks wus Welsh and good stuff, Ma and th'ol'man, too. From all I kin larn I wus born near the Skyuka Mountain back in North Caroliny, forty years ago. Afore I knowed what they wus up ter they'd named me William Sherley Williams. I can count more years than ye can, gal. I know now, but I tuk ye fer bein' older'n ye air on that thar trip from Chihuahua."

Lona nodded and waved him on as she lighted a cigarette.

" 'Course, I don't recolleck much about them airly days but I do remember that mountain. 'Spect I'd call it a mole hill now but I swan ef it wusn't some mountain then, 'bout three times the size of any of the Rockies I've evah seen. Ye see th'ol'man wus a soldier in the Revolutionary War when everybody most wus hell-bent on bein' independent from England. He fit in more'n one battle. I allus believed he wus in the big un on top o' King's Mountain. Anyhow a bunch o' me uncles wus thar.

"Wal, arter the war he got a tarnel hankerin' fer wanderin'. He tuk a new farm in the Southwestern part of North Caroliny and stayed a spell and then he wanted ter git goin' agin so he piled us all inter wagons and 'long with some other folks we went travelin'. We brung up at Whiteside Station on the Mississippi, and arter argu'in' with some officials across the river we got ovah inter Spanish kintry."

Bill puffed at his pipe. "Is that 'bout all ye kin stand, Lona?"

"You know better," replied the girl. "Do you remember much about that long trip?"

"No, I don't recolleck much 'bout that trip 'cept it tuk a hull piece of forever. St. Louie. We lived thar fer a spell with as jolly a bunch o' French people as evah wus. Come darn neah gittin' a chance ter fly with the angels onct in the ole swimmin' hole. Head got ketched 'tween some logs way down but a feller rescued me and then sat laughin' his fool head off at me a-shiverin' and scatterin' water ovah everything like a yeller dog. I sang a bit louder'n usual next time Ma had meetin' and she smiled at me, not knowin' I needed a switchin' 'cause she'd tole me ter keep out of that thar hole."

Bill began industriously to clean his pipe. "Then Pa got the movin' fever agin and dickered with the Spanish moguls fer sev'ral hundred arpens up on the Missouri near the ole Boone Trace."

"Did you have any schooling, Beel?"

"Yeah, soon's Ma could, she set us boys ter figgurin', writin' and doin' sums. I learnt right smart 'bout subtractin' later. I'll say I did when Injuns got ter stealin' pelts. Later my folks sent

62

us ter a genu-ine school. We had some teachers that didn't know a hull sight more'n we did."

Bill laughed, lit his pipe again and shifted his long legs.

"Let's see. I wus a boy. Yeah, I used to sit swingin' me feet and watchin' the keel boats and barges makin' yeller foam on the Missouri. The singin' Frenchmen wus arter beaver a heap sight airlier'n Americans. I ust ter wish I could go 'long but th'ol'man wouldn't hyar ter it yit.

"Time I wus seventeen, I had reeligion plenty and started ter preach. Should say I helped me older brother, Lewis. I allus called mesel' a parson though. I tuk ter circuit ridin'—with brother 'course. That's ridin' 'round and tellin' folks 'bout ree-ligion. When I got the chanct, I shu-ah tole 'em 'bout hell-fire and brimstone a-plenty. Guess I skeered some inter behavin' theirsel's fer a while anyway. Arter we'd had a good feed, Lewis would preach 'em damnation and hell-fire and then ride on fer ten miles, and, maybe I'd spell him and go at it agin. We had 'em on the road ter Heaven er I'm a bawlin' calf, all 'cept Hank and Sam."

Bill laughed outright and rumpled up his hair again.

"Yeah, all 'cept Hank and Sam. Want no kind o' boostin' could evah have got them fellers through the gate. Saint Peter would shu-ah have give 'em a kick back ter ole Booneville. Then the devil, he'd a tuk them no-counts in and afore long he'd a-kicked 'em outah Hell fer playin' in the ashes."

Bill shook his head and glanced at Lona, saying, "Right I am. They wusn't wuth kickin', I tell ye."

Lona laughed, and sent circles of smoke into the air.

"Time come when a deacon and me had a hoss trade. I knowed me ole nag wusn't up ter snuff but I lost me head, hell-bent on a trade. I let the deacon think the hoss wus all ter the good. He tuk mine and I tuk his'n. Wow! The deacon couldn't

63

manage ole Maria and she up and heaved him off. He went sprawlin' in the dust. I knowed he wusn't hurt and rid away but I heerd the darndest cussin'. He wus sayin' things that ain't ca'culated ter git nobody inter Heaven—not on the fust knock anyway. I wus mad, rid back, got down and hit him on the jaw. Didn't do much good 'cause he worked that jaw ovah time a-tellin' everybody in sight and out 'bout how the parson had cheated him."

"An old rascal you were even then. Didn't you have any sweethearts, Beel?"

"Yeah. I had a gal, Mary, in them days. She wus purty as a pictur'. Smart too. I wanted ter marry her. I rid up ter see her a few days arter that and she turned me down flat, 'count o' that fuss with the deacon. Made me feel like a durn dog with me tail 'tween me legs. I wus young nuf ter feel some hurt.

"I went home and sat down by the river and done a tall 'mount o' thinkin'. I figgur'd 'twant no use stayin' 'round ef Mary wus agin me. I knowed it want no ust ter argufy with her neither. So I saddled up, yelled ter Ma and tuk out up the river. Didn't git fur. Stopped with the Osages. Know'd a lot o' them Injuns. I stayed on thar but I didn't git nowheres with preachin' fer they kept right on worshipin' the sun, moon, stars and some animuls. The ole chiefs wouldn't listen ter a young un like me. Guess it's all right. I learned a lot from 'em and jined White Hair's tribe. Folks said I'd jes made mesel' inter an Injun."

Bill rubbed the stubble on his chin and looked at the heavy beams of the ceiling. Then he ducked his head and glanced out of the corner of his eye at Lona. "Couldn't forgit Mary. Nevah have. She moved away som'ers. Married I reckon. Hope 'twant Hank got her. He wus the ornerist ... Ye make me think o' Mary, Lona, jes a leetle bit. She wus dark-haired and had big shiny eyes, like your'n.

64

"Wal, I stayed on with them Osages on the Swamp of the Swans as the Frenchmen call it. They had a purty village. The houses wus square er oblong. Ridge poles 'bout twenty feet high and roofs slantin' down ter walls, 'bout four er five feet up. Logs, brush and mud they wus. I trapped with them Injuns, camped with 'em and fit fer 'em. They called me 'Red-headed Shooter.' 'Tain't quite clear how they got that, is it?" Bill grinned and scratched his mop of red hair.

"Arter a while, I got ter hankerin' fer me own hut so I married the purtiest gal in the tribe. I tole ye onct thet I'm a wid'wer, ef ye remember? We lived mighty happy tergither fer ovah ten years. She wus a fine squaw, I tell ye. We had two leetle gals. One of 'em, the fust one, had me red hair and I called her 'Mary.' Folks thought I named her fer me sister. Let 'em think so. Guess the Osages air bringin' 'em up right. 'Er mother's got 'em."

Bill fell silent. He brushed aimlessly at his trousers or untangled buckskin fringe.

"And what of the wife?" asked Lona finally.

"My leetle wife died. I didn't want no other Osage gal and wus fer cuttin' out when 'long come Major George Sibley and said he wanted 'n interpreter. I jined up with him and come down hyar. Arter all, I'm white and might as wal be with me own kind, leastwise fer a spell. When we got ter Santy Fee and he'd paid me off, I jes disappeared. Ain't nevah tole anybody whar I wus. That wus when I went down ter Chihuahua. 'Course, they know I've been out West but that's all. I'm goin' back afore long."

Bill paused and looked embarrassed. He had not talked at such length for many a year. With little ado he bade Lona good night and slipped out into the dark.

Several days passed and Lona did not see Bill. One morning

she was walking along the plaza when a man strode by. He resembled Rudolfo so strikingly that Lona caught her breath and gazed at him with widening eyes. Unconsciously she started to run after him but checked herself. She sank down on a bench, buried her head in her arms and wept bitterly for the first time in many months.

"Eh, thar, Lona, gal," came in a familiar voice. "Ye mus'n't be sittin' hyar. What on airth is the matter?"

"Oh, Beel," she sobbed. "It can not be! But I saw a man so like Rudolfo."

"Come, gal, hants don't walk o' days. Ye're tired, I reckon, and need ter git ter yer rooms. I'll walk 'long with ye."

When they reached her door, Bill broke out with, "Darn this hyar town, Lona, why don' ye go up ter San Fernández de Taos? Jes Taos is what we men call it. It's a fine leetle town up in the North kintry, not so very fur away. Jolly nuf when the mountain men come in. Maybe ye'd be happier up thar. Wont be anybody ter remind ye of Rudolfo. Good folks up thar. Fine young American doc'. David Waldo's his name. Indians air friendly, as fur as I know. Ef ye want the keerds, wal, they've got 'em and the coins too."

"Taos? San Fernández de Taos? Yes, I have heard about it. I don't know. Well . . . maybe . . . for a while. I'll think about it." San Fernández de Taos? She played with the idea. Señor Alarid was going up there soon.

VII

"HOW MANY DAYS WILL WE BE ON THE JOURNEY, Señor Alarid?" The merchant carefully folded some papers and put them in his cloth bag, then he straightened up and answered Lona.

"Let's see, we leave at seven. Perhaps four or five days. It may be more because it takes extra time when I trade on the way. Indians must sit around and smoke before they barter. As I go, the trail is long. I must spend a night at Santa Cruz. Then we'll go over the sand hills and through the draw to Embudo Plaza. We'll probably make camp there. Next we'll climb into the Picurís country and beyond to El Llano Largo. That will be rough going for the whole land is little but rock. People say it should be called 'Peñasco.' The mountain road on to Taos valley is none too good but it has been passable for centuries and we'll get through."

Lona bowed. Then she lifted a blanket curtain and went to bid good-by to Madam Alarid whose wren-like face lighted with pleasure. Sticking her needle in her embroidery, she said cheerily, "The stars are right—very propitious in fact. Furthermore Maria was cleaning the house this morning and had all the doors and windows open. No bird flew in—Death is not stalking any of us."

Madam Alarid left the room and returned with a small jewel chest from which she drew a string of corals. She hung them around the girl's neck. "There! Danger lurks on any trip. Coral is a sure charm against the evil eye. You are going among strangers and through Indian country. One can not be too careful." She smiled as she stepped away, lifting a hand in blessing.

Madam Pino's face grew solemn and told Lona better than words how much she would miss her at the inn.

"You'll not wish to remain long in the North, I think. You'll be returning some day."

"Undoubtedly I shall. Santa Fé beckoned to me once. Probably it will again. I shall miss you, my friend."

Lona rode beside her *carreta*. This hundred miles or more to Taos did not mean much. She could easily return. But today is today. She touched her treasure bags behind her saddle. Other bags were safe in the wagon.

Three long tedious days later, Lona felt that she was being lifted into the air. The trail was winding higher and higher, disclosing mountains to her left. There was no sign of life in that blue distance nor any about her except that of the caravan. The travelers seemed to be the only people on the globe.

The next day, the road curved suddenly and the wagon train dipped below to the Picurís pueblo of flat-roofed gray adobe buildings huddled together in a valley. Finishing his trading quickly, Señor Alarid brought an old chief over to Lona's wagon, where she sat perched on the high seat out of the sun. It had been a hot day, so the aged Indian wore a wreath of fresh leaves around his forehead. His small lack-luster eyes were dull with fatigue in his heavily wrinkled face. Down either shoulder over his gray shirt hung his hair in a plait wrapped with green tape. Around his waist was a thin red blanket, beneath which were

68

deerskin leggings swinging low over beaded moccasins. He limped along, aided by a dried cactus cane.

Urged on by the merchant's questions, he told Lona that he had seen many friars come and go at the old towered church. Often his people had taken refuge within its thick walls. With his stick he pointed to the site of a ruin which had been erected long before the Picurís had come into the valley. Again he pointed, this time with pride, to the house for scalps. The front wall of an upper room was gone so all could see the gruesome trophies. Then suddenly without another word, the old chief waved his hand and hobbled away.

Surprised, Señor Alarid watched the Indian go.

"Perhaps I did not give him enough *tequila*. Sometimes he tells about a great serpent which, the Picurís believe, lives in caves hereabouts and sometimes writhes its way to deserted kivas where it feasts on newly-born deformed children, deserted by their parents."

Lona shuddered. She would be glad to leave this pueblo. The pall of bloody days, not so far gone, hung over the place.

In the early afternoon of the following day, the caravan was wearily crawling up and down an old trail which showed occasional glimpses of a range of high mountains stretching Northward and rising apparently out of opalescent mist. As she rounded the last hill, Lona saw the wide valley of Taos. Its undulating multicolored floor quivered in the sunlight, gray green of sagebrush, yellow of corn stubble, dull ochre of desert, gold of cottonwoods, rust and green of bushes along irrigation ditches that were streaks of silver.

Several hours later, the caravan approached Taos. The orange glow from the low sun transformed the town into a great crown of gold. The two towers of the mission church shone like oriental topaz ornaments.

Nearer, loopholes could be seen as the only openings in the connecting home walls. Several houses were detached from the main compact mass. Were these the homes of men less fearful of Indian attacks, she wondered?

"No," Señor Alarid told her, "those are the houses built on land granted by the king of Spain to poor people about thirty years ago. I have been told the alcalde led out no less than sixty families at that time. When they had chosen their land, they took possession in the old-fashioned way by plucking up grass, casting stones and shouting huzzas to the king. Some of the men have managed since to bring in many good crops of beans and corn and are no longer poor. Taos is quite a place, you must know, almost as old as Santa Fé."

The light had begun to fade but one mountain, a distant, tooth-like pile of rock, shone like a solid yellow metal. Small wonder, thought Lona, that the old Spaniards had talked so wildly of a peak of gold in the North. Men still believed that tale. She wondered if Marino had found his wealth. Beel had talked of gold also. Beel? He must be on his way to Apacheria since he had not been about when the caravan left Santa Fé. Yes, he had talked of gold but he was not interested in mines.

Once he had said, "Plews in me paw are gold enough fer me. You folks have it right. 'A bird in the hand is wuth a hundred flyin'!' Yeah. Them mountains have their secrets but I ain't one fer pryin'. They tell me that ole carpenter, Jim Purcell, who ust ter be in Santy Fee had some mighty fine lookin' rock but he wusn't fer tellin' nobody whar he fetched it from. Wal, he had 'em goggle-eyed, I'm tole. 'One fool makes a hundred,' ye know. Now when it comes ter huntin' through that hull range fer gold—wagh! I cain't keep one eye glued ter the ground and t'other watchin' fer Injun varmints. Mine don't work that way."

The caravan stopped at the Western gate of Taos to let

70

herders drive their sheep into the plaza for safety during the night. Some of the muleteers began singing; others gave war whoops and cracked their whips as the wagons pulled into the center of the village. Only a few huzzas greeted the newcomers. There was no special interest in any small group of wagons coming from the South.

Not unlike Santa Fé, thought Lona as she looked about, save for the sheep. The houses are similar, but here is no palace to lend dignity. Under the portals, windows of mica twinkled with candlelight. The air was flooded with the scent of newly-made tortillas, frying fish or venison and sweet pastry, until suddenly burning beans conquered all smells.

At the common well in the center of the plaza, Lona could see men watering their sheep. Now and then blanketed Indians on pinto ponies galloped through the other gateway on the East toward their pueblo home two leagues away.

Señor Alarid knew the town well. He walked with Lona to a group of rooms just off the West side of the plaza. She found them to her liking and engaged them at once. Three were for herself and one adjoining was for Pedro and Pablita.

During the first winter, Lona made friends even though she had no duenna. Social recognition or the lack of it did not bother her. She found that, here also, a few families held themselves aloof like Southern aristocrats, but, in the main, life was more easy and unconventional than in Santa Fé. The men declared for her. She was the handsomest woman who had ever come to town, they said, and a good sport when she gambled. Clever she was at cards. In fact, she was such an unusually swift dealer that she could keep a game of monte lively from beginning to end. What if she did play under the portals? Others did, just as they did in Santa Fé. Perhaps she did flirt with that red fan of hers but how about girls who had duennas? No social decrees could govern eyes. Señorita Lona danced divinely and favored no special admirer. Oh, little Pablo Garcia thought she did but then he was a fool. The newcomer was a real lady, an aristocrat. Did not people call her *Doña* Lona?

One day late in the spring, an expedition from El Paso rolled in. The men had brought wines and brandy, as well as silks, satins and varied-colored cottons. Lona bought generously as soon as the curtains of the wagons had been untied, then asked for an introduction to the lanky American leader, William Wolfskill. She was eager for news from Mexico.

"Of course, I heard about affairs in Mexico when I was in El Paso, Miss Barcelona. Several wagon masters had just arrived from the South," replied Wolfskill to Lona's questions. She motioned to a bench under the portal. Flinging off his wide sombrero, Wolfskill uncovered a white forehead but the rest of his face was as dark as that of a Spaniard.

"You see they had a fake presidential election down there," Wolfskill continued, "General Santa Anna got mixed up in it and there were hints of plans to hang him."

"What did General Santa Anna do?" asked Lona. "He may be a rascal but he has power and does things for the people."

"I should say he does! They may knock him over but he bounces up every time. Why, last September, one faction actually deposed Santa Anna as Governor of Vera Cruz. In six days' time, he got some soldiers, cavalry and field pieces together and made the fortress at Perote surrender before they could say 'Damn!' Deserters from the government troops joined him and, by Wilkins! there was a real live revolution on again.

"The government declared him an outlaw mighty soon. That was quick action for Mexicans. But that is what they told me. The upshot was that a general was sent out after Santa Anna. But get him? Not him! Before we left down there, Santa Anna was the real power."

"I should say he is!" broke in Lona. "His enemies are jealous

72

of his ability, I think. They say he's unscrupulous but he does get somewhere."

"Unscrupulous? Well, I guess that's true enough, Miss Barcelona," Wolfskill laughed outright.

"Come on over here," he said motioning to a group nearby who obviously wished to hear the conversation. "I'll tell you a funny story that I heard down in El Paso. Santa Anna needed money for his revolution. General Calderón was after him and did get him on the run but finally, by thunder, they actually made a truce. Nevertheless, Santa Anna went on and took Oaxaca anyway.

"Then he decided he'd capture Calderón. His spies found out that the general went to mass at a certain convent not far away. One morning there were many priests present at mass. Nobody thought anything of that. Suddenly the priests got up in meeting and threw off their robes. Soldiers, they were! Yes siree! They told everybody that they were prisoners. The general was not there so they did not get him. Finally the soldiers agreed, apparently reluctantly, to allow the prisoners to buy their freedom and they surely did. They paid a-plenty! Then the soldiers bundled up the money and picked up the alms box as well and skedaddled back to Santa Anna. He beats all for winning!"

His last words were lost in the laughter of the crowd.

Lona thanked Señor Wolfskill for his news and was out of earshot when a mountaineer motioned Wolfskill aside and drawled, "Way folks air talkin' down in Texas, some of 'em Mexicans too, I reckon there'll be a revolution down thar some day afore long. An' I've heerd men 'round these parts say, kinder secret-like, that they don't keer a tinker's damn 'bout Mexico and would like ter see the United States come in and rescue 'em 'cause, with all the fightin' down thar, Mexico don't give a damn continental ter help the people in this part o' their kintry."

"Is that true? Well, perhaps that will happen. Who knows?" replied Wolfskill in non-committal tone. He did not care to admit that he himself had talked often about such possibilities to the miller Rowland and the storekeeper Workman here in Taos and Ewing Young, his one-time partner.

"By the way, have you seen Young?" he asked. "He should be in from that trapping expedition down on the Gila."

"Young ain't come in yit. I heerd someone say only this mornin' that some fellers wus on the trail and might come in right smartly."

Early the next afternoon, when Lona was walking around the plaza, she heard wild shouts and the crack of rifles. Several mountain men rode in followed by burros loaded with pelts. The girl scanned each face. Could Beel be among them? No. They were all strangers.

Since Lona was taller than most Mexican women, she chose to stand on the outskirts of the gathering crowd and watch the men dismount. Suddenly the largest of the trappers caught and held her eyes with a look that changed from admiration to wonder. It was such a look as human beings exchange in moments of immediate understanding.

Lona guessed that this tall, compelling man was Ewing Young. All winter she had heard of him.

He continued to look at the girl after she had blushed and turned away. A stranger in Taos, he knew, and a girl with something fine and hardy deep beneath that surface beauty. He would make inquiries when the crowd scattered.

"Gambler, is she? From old Mexico. French-Spanish, eh?" the mountain man exclaimed later. "Here, with servants but no duenna. The devil take duennas anyway. I like her mettle. I'll dance the high fling with her. See if I don't! 'Honest' you say? 'Square'? No lover? Oh, that small, insignificant Pablo Garcia thinks he's on the way, does he? That little fellow? Well!"

"On your guard, Young. Garcia is a spit-fire and all too ready with his gun."

"Yes, but remember, I've a quick finger myself. I've been about."

Young sauntered away. He was broad-shouldered, with a graceful swing and a square, blond, well-shaven face. His stride had the assurance of a leader of men.

The arrival of the mountain men always meant a fandango. Preparations had already begun. That night the mud floor of the sala was carefully swept, the benches dusted and placed along the wall. Cheap candelabra blazed over the dancers who already swayed and stamped to the music of violins and guitars. The musicians sat on a small platform in the corner of the hall. They were singing a short ditty in derision of some dandy who was forcing his way out into the night air to cool his anger. There he would find company for singers often evened an old score during a dance.

Young had been watching the door. When Lona entered he sought her at once. "Señorita Lona Barcelona, I am told. I'm Ewing Young from ole Tennessee. Will you dance?"

It was surely the custom with these mountaineers to care nothing for convention, Lona thought, as she looked up at the tall man. What difference did an introduction make, after all? Away they went, trying to keep time to the music and out of the way of the Americans, some of whom had already taken generous drinks of "Taos lightning." Something was about to happen and Young knew it. The Americans were whooping like Indians and singing "Hi-ya-hi-ya!" Yelling "Thump it!

Thump it!" they stamped their feet and, when their partners had slipped away from them, began an Indian dance in the center of the room.

"I do wish the fellows would wait a while for their rough penny gaff stuff," said Young swinging Lona to a far corner of the hall. "You dance like a real Spanish girl. I hear that you came from Mexico? They call you *'Doña.'* Been married?"

"No. People here have always called me *'Doña.'* It is proper for older women like me whether married or not, you know."

Young smiled down from his six feet two at his partner, as dainty and pretty as any American could wish. And she was certainly not old. Hearing an extra high whoop from the other end of the room he said, "When they get too rough, you clear out, will you? I'll be seeing you tomorrow, Doña Lona, if I may?"

They were dancing again, when she caught sight of Pablo Garcia leaning against a wall, watching her bend and sway to Young's improvised steps. She smiled into Young's eyes, glanced again at Garcia whose brown face was turning a dangerous red. He was pushing his way now through the dancers to claim her from Young. Lona whispered, "Look out, Señor Young. Pablo Garcia is coming. He has no claim on me. He is danger itself when he is angry."

"No, you don't," blurted Young when Garcia came up. "You cain't shine hyar. You make tracks."

"Like Hell, I will," snarled Garcia and, little fellow though he was, gave the American a heavy blow.

Young swung Lona to one side and struck out furiously. Garcia staggered, fell to the mud floor, but soon regained his feet and drew his dagger. He could not reach Young for, in that moment, the Americans had gathered together and stood back to back in the center of the room. They punched heads with their fists, for knives could be drawn later, if necessary. Those

76

who did not yet know what had happened began to hit their neighbors out of sheer exuberance.

Lona stood on a bench near the entrance door with a few other women who had also refused to leave. She could see that blow after blow from the Americans sent many Mexicans sprawling on the floor. Someone lifted a chair. Young grabbed it and held it high and was hurling it downward when Lona saw Garcia make a lunge with his dagger. The American fought on unmindful of blood running down his arm and side.

It was not long before the room was free of all fighters. Several Mexicans lay unconscious on the floor. Laughing in the dim light of the few candles left burning, the Americans stood apart. Young did not move.

"Guess I won't go beaver, boys, but one of them *palous* sure gave me a nasty 'Green River.' "

He tried to stand but his legs crumpled. There was a deep wound in his side.

"Let me by," said Lona as she rushed forward, her face ablaze with anger.

"Better take him to my room," said Wolfskill whipping out a kerchief, trying to stanch the blood. Little Kit Carson, Young's cook, begged that his master be taken to his own room. "I kin take keer of him, Sir," he urged.

"No! Carry him to my home," Lona ordered in a voice of command.

"Best thing to do. Let the woman have her way. It's the nearest place," said Dr. David Waldo who was leaning over Young. "Here men!" With that, the men lifted the wounded man and carefully carried him to Lona's rooms. They undressed Young and covered him with blankets. Then they stood by while Lona and the doctor worked to bring Young back to consciousness. The men withdrew when they heard Young sigh and mutter, "That damn *palou!*"

VIII

IT WAS NOT QUITE DAWN WHEN LONA CREPT into the room where Young slept. She leaned over and whispered to young Kit Carson who had insisted on rolling himself in his blanket and sleeping near the man he idolized. The sick man stirred, opened his eyes. "Kit, where am I? Doña Lona? Oh, I remember. Got scratched last night."

"It wus more'n a scratch, Mr. Young. Doctor Waldo tole the men ter bring ye hyar 'cause it wus handy. I begged 'em ter take ye home. I could take keer of ye."

"Yes, I know you could. Doña Lona, when Kit was only sixteen years old, a man in his caravan was shot in the arm. Mighty bad. What did Kit do but saw it off, burn the wound with an old king bolt and plaster it up with tar! Saved his life." Young's voice was weak.

"Hush," said Lona, laying her cool hand on his forehead. "Don't talk."

"Anyway, glad you brought me hyar," he murmured. Closing his eyes, he was soon asleep.

Wolfskill, the miller Rowland and others came to sit up at night or stopped by during the day to inquire about Young's wound. Busy young Antonio Martínez, the priest, came often and always, as he left, said, "One fine man, Señor Young. One fine man."

78

On the third day, Young developed a high fever. Kit ran for Doctor Waldo as fast as his short bow legs would let him.

When the doctor arrived Young was delirious. "I hoped that this would not happen." His voice was anxious. "The Friars' Balsam did the trick here on his side. That's all right. But the arm? I'm afraid some kind of poison got in here. The dagger probably nicked the artery. He lost much blood. Get a fat meat poultice."

"The fever, Doctor?" ventured Kit. "Geronimo's squaw makes good medicine out of herbs."

"That's right. Get some of that as soon as you can. It beats all, Doña Lona, but the Indians seem to be a jump ahead of us white men when they are willing to discard what the medicine man tells them." The doctor lifted a package from his case, measured out a tiny quantity of powder. "That much every hour. Cinchona is good for fever. Quinine, I should say. That's the new name." He picked up his bag, and when he stood at the door, the doctor put his hand on Lona's shoulder and said quietly, "I'm glad he is here. Don't worry about the gossips. They get busy right away in this town, I know. I'll take care of the cusses—I appreciate your doing this. Young is a splendid fellow and we must pull him through."

Day after day, Doctor Waldo came and sat by his patient. He would draw up a chair, brush back his shock of dark hair and tell Young all the news of the town. Behind his octagonal spectacles, he studied the man. He had let blood, given quinine, done everything that he could think to do. At night he pored over his pitifully few books on medicine but could find no further help. Why did that other patient of his with a similar wound get well so rapidly? He was sickly and weak naturally but this husky fellow was burning with fever and not yet able to leave his bed.

Gradually Young's rugged constitution brought him back to

health. He rarely talked but his eyes followed Lona as she went about the room. To his ears the rustle of her skirts was music. The touch of her hand was better than brew or powders. "What can you think of a big fellow like me not being able to stand a bit of stabbing?" he queried.

"But, Señor," she answered, "the doctor says that you will be well soon."

"Señor again, eh? Won't you call me Ewing, please? The doctor? If I get well, you shall have the credit—Waldo, you and Kit. Good boy!" He caught Lona's hand as she bent over to give him a dose of quinine and kissed the finger tips.

Gently she drew away and stepped into the patio to keep him from seeing her eyes. The patio was barren of flowers but at the far end a small ditch was lined by several old cottonwood trees. Beyond was Taos Peak, near enough to be friendly. Should she let herself love this man? Foolish! She already loved him. Rudolfo! She had loved him but he was gone! She could never love another in quite the same way, yet she could love. She looked again at the mountain and her heart began to sing.

One morning Young asked Carson to bring over his books. "Only have two, you know. They're on the high shelf.

"Damn!" he exclaimed. "If I'm not the jumpin' son of the carcague to be lyin' hyar so long. Plumb froze to get goin'. Damn!"

Catching sight of Lona in the doorway, he choked back his words. "Oh, excuse me. My tongue gets mixed with mountaineer jargon sometimes. I've been out hyar so long. I ken good English. Back in Tennessee my grandfather was a scholar, and father after a fashion. Ma was eternally reading. I'm not one for boasting, Lona, but I had good training for frontier country."

"I had training too in old Mexico," said Lona. "What was that animal you mentioned?"

"What? Oh, the carcague?" Young smiled. "Mountain men believe that there is a beast, half wolf, half bear—an awful creature. They declare it's so quick that it can bound into camp, grab meat set out for cooking or even already on the fire, and make way with it before any of the men can see it clearly. Of course, I don't believe there is any such animal. Anyway, I've never met a man who could swear that he'd seen a carcague— that is, none I'd believe."

Presently young Kit returned with the books. "Here is my trail library, Lona." He fingered the two worn calf volumes lovingly. "My father gave them to me when I left home. Shakespeare. I have read them from cover to cover. Loaned them once to Williams and he nearly choked over the *Comedy of Errors!*"

"Shakespeare? I've read many of the plays but that was when I was in Mexico. I have not seen such books since I came North. Do read me something you like, Ewing."

"I'm in the mood for *Romeo and Juliet.* Let's see how it goes." Young leaned back against the pillows, pulled up his knees to support the book, and read aloud. Now and then he glanced at Lona and asked, "That's true, isn't it?" or "How much he knew, eh?" He read on. "That's enough for today. I think a lot of these books. They've kept me from growing too lonesome on the heights. I shall keep them as long as I live."

Impulsively Lona took the volume from Young and ran through the pages. She picked up a pencil from her desk and on the inside cover wrote her name. Around the four letters she drew a circle. "There, that's for remembrance. That's for a thought of a girl you knew in Taos sometime when you are specially lonesome on your long treks." Young answered her smile and noticed that she too was stirred.

Soon Young was able to walk, haltingly at first, to his disgust. One morning he sent Kit "to dig out his cave." When Lona brought his accustomed glass of wine, he quietly closed the door behind her. Setting the glass carefully on the table by the couch, he turned to face her, holding his arms wide.

"Lona, darling." Lona flushed. For a moment she stood silent and looked at him. Then she tossed her head and walked straight into his arms.

That afternoon they sat in the patio beside the cottonwoods.

"I've done a deal of thinking while I've been hyar," Ewing said. "I know I'm no marrying man. But fair or not, I could not keep from loving you. I've tried to believe that I might settle down. I undertook to do that, last year, when I bought out Wolfskill's caravan stuff but I could not stay. I had not met you then. I know even now that I must carry out my plan for one more trip West. Then perhaps my wandering spirit will be tamed. But I do love you. You know that."

"Sadness and joy run side by side, Ewing. I also know what it is to be free. I shall wait for you."

Again and again Young postponed his trip. In the morning the mountains and desert called him to be gone. He would go to win a fortune for Lona. This he told himself but he knew well that the real reason was the chafing of his restless spirit. Yet his heart bade him stay.

In the evening he and Lona were quietly happy exploring each other's childhood, wondering that fortune should have drawn them together, one from Mexico and the other from far Tennessee. Lona would not think of Ewing's departure or let it sadden their days together. Once he asked her, "Shall we have the padre?" But she answered, "No, not until you return. We belong to each other. What does it matter about the banns."

Late in August, plodding into town on a tired horse with pack mule following, came Bill Williams. Within an hour he knocked at Lona's door.

"Gosh A'mighty, I'm glad ter see ye," he exclaimed as he looked down into Lona's face. "Months ago, a feller in South Apache land tole me ye'd come ter Taos." He sat down, stretched his long legs and reached for his pipe in a coat pocket.

"It got so tarnel hot down thar I thought I'd come up hyar fer a bit of air. Got a fine place. I jes heerd how Ewing Young has been makin' up ter ye. Wal, I reckon I cain't be blamin' him. He allus knows a real gal when he spots one. They tell me Garcia had some sort of a cat fit ovah Young. What's been happenin' anyway?"

"I like it here," answered Lona. "You thought I would. Have you any news from Mexico?"

"Happens a feller from down thar did come inter my camp when I wus in the Mogollons. He said that General Santa Anna . . . I've heerd ye talk 'bout him . . . wus cleared of bein' an outlaw, last spring sometime, and wus tole ter make Vera Cruz and git goin' as gov'ner agin. He made a side trip ter Jalapa though . . . jes a-visitin' . . . with only a thousand soldiers 'long."

Bill's eyes snapped with amusement. "Yeah, only a thousand guests 'long with him. He tole the folks that he'd come as a friend—but they'd have ter ante up with some seven thousand pesos! Seems he didn't git what he wanted. Said he wusn't fer usin' force. They might jes give him the list of them as had paid and them as had not." Bill knocked the ashes from his pipe and pointed it at Lona. "Ye see his ole neighbors knowed him. They didn't dare do nothin' but jam down in their jeans and haul up. I'll bet he done a heap o' laughin' ter himsel'. Seems the hull kintry down South is full of spies fer the Spaniards. People air afeard the Spaniards'll take ovah the gov'ment. Reckon as long as Santa Anna kin kick, the kintry'll be safe nuf—fer him anyway."

83

Lona asked what in the world he had been doing in the Mogollon country so far down in New Mexico.

Bill looked a bit foolish.

"Guess I wus sight-seein'. Oh, blast it! Ye'n Marino got me kinda het up onct ovah mines and when a feller ast me to go inter the Mogollons, I hit the trail with him, cussin' mesel' all the while. Shu-ah nuf, he had a hole. Hyar's a piece of silver ore I brung 'long. I wouldn't eggsakly recommend yer takin' a trip down thar ter see more. No."

"Oh, Beel." Lona studied the piece of rock. "I wish Marino could see it."

A knock at the door interrupted them. Lona answered it.

"How are you, Señor Garcia?"

Seeing old Bill stretch his neck to catch sight of the caller, Garcia made short his errand. He assured Lona that she could have her Young for all he cared because he was affianced to Rafaelita.

"I'm delighted," Lona answered in her most honeyed tones, "that she should love you."

The last words only caught the ears of Young who was a few paces behind.

"Love you!" gasped Young. "My God! That little greaser."

Through a window Williams saw Young's stricken face and guessed at once what he had overheard. He saw Young shut his lips hard, whirl and walk away. Williams smiled for although he admired Young, he mildly resented his attentions to Lona. "Good Lawd," he said to himself, "ain't he grow'd up nuf ter know that words kin be like straws pintin' the wrong way on a trail. Feller has ter see some real sign afore he plunges down a ravine."

The next morning Lona learned that Young's party had pulled out at dawn. He had left no word of good-by. She was

84

puzzled and furious. This was not like Ewing. Perhaps Beel would know. She sent Pedro to find him.

"Yeah, I know." Bill told her what he had seen and what he suspected.

"But Beel, why didn't you tell me?"

Lona's eyes gleamed with anger. She said sharply that he would, have to straighten the matter out. She would write a letter and he would have to explain. When she disappeared into the sala, Bill called after her, "Reckon ye're right. I'll come 'round later. This ole hoss has got ter git his fodder and some new traps afore pullin' out."

It was late in the afternoon when Bill came again. Lona chided him for not starting earlier. Without answering, he took her letter, bade her a short good-by and warned her, as he had often done, that "wurryin' is like a balky mule, it don't git no-whar." He promised Lona that he would see to it that Young sent back an express or he'd come himself but as he was heading for the "Col-o-row" and up North, he'd make the fool behave himself.

Long before morning, Williams drew in the cinch of his saddle. His two pack animals were tandem-hitched to the tail of his own horse. Quietly he rode out of town. With a flash from his flint he found signs and picked up Young's trail.

Once he lost it but turned back and two hours later, picked it up again. Young had turned Southwest.

"Southwest, eh? Ain't got no licenses and foolin' officers. Southwest suits me," he growled and tore a fid from his hunk of tobacco. Jabbing huge rowels into the horse's side, Williams thrust his head forward and drew up his knees. He talked on to himself as lone men do. "Ain't afeard of officers but I'll be damned ef I stay in this scalp-takin' kintry. Too flat."

Prodding his nag along, Bill kept his eyes alert. In the early evening he saw smoke signals on top of high lone Ute Mountain. He snapped his reins close and read slowly, "One . . . white . . . three . . . West. Yeah, one white man with three horses headed West. West? Wal, I'm headin' Southwest. I'll beat 'em ter the mountains. Time this chile wus cachin'." Not until Williams was well within the canyon ahead did he cease prodding his horse. Then he made a trail of his own behind huge boulders on the side of the mountain and soon saw Young's party making camp below.

"Hey, old hoss. Decided to join us?" said Young when Williams came in.

"How! Yeah, fer a spell. Ain't much on jinin' a hull party but hyar I be," said Williams as he dismounted and jerking his thumb over his shoulder he warned, "Injuns. Smoke signals on Ute. Tellin' only 'bout one though. Reckon the varmints ain't seen ye yit. Need plenty o' guards. I'm cachin' up in the rocks. That thar fire needs waterin'."

Young gave quick orders. The camp was made as safe as possible; horses staked; saddles piled in a circle and guards doubled.

Later, Williams found Young ready to wrap himself in a blanket for an hour or two of sleep. He stumbled up to him and blurted out, "What's up, Young? Leavin' Doña Lona without a word?"

"That's my business," snapped Young.

"Maybe so. But I tole the gal, some years back, that I'd stand by when she needed me and I'm gwine ter do it. Hyar's a letter she rit."

Young took the letter and shrugged his shoulders. Looking narrowly at Bill he said, "She told me about you. Only a good friend, eh?"

86

"On me honor," answered Williams opening his eyes wide and raising his right arm. "Me? Good Lawd!"

"I might as well tell you. I heard her talking to that damn Garcia. I got hot clear through. I'm leaving her flat if that's her make."

"'Spected as much," drawled Williams pulling on his pipe. "Listen ter me, ye young fool. Ain't ye evah heerd 'bout there bein' two sides ter everythin'? I wus inside that house and heerd every word. She wus jes repeatin' what Garcia had been sayin' 'bout his new gal. I seen ye turn and git. Lawd, man, Garcia er nobody else has had a chance ter shine since ye come. Green ain't becomin' ter yer style o' beauty, Young."

"By all the gods, is that true?"

Pocketing the letter, Young strolled back to the dying bonfire and stirred the coals. He squatted and began to read the quaint mixture of Spanish and English.

Young sat for a long time flicking the paper against his hand and gazing into the ashes of the fire. He did not hear its occasional snap nor the stamping of animals tethered near, nor the low voices of men half asleep. He reproached himself, called himself no end of a fool.

Finally he fumbled in his saddle bags for a candle and climbed up the side of the canyon to a group of rocks behind which he flinted his candle, drew some paper from his pocket and wrote his answer. For a long time he struggled to put into words his love and remorse for his mistake. Now he could not return but some day he would. Snuffing out the candle he folded the note carefully while his mind weighed the Indians in his party. Eagle Feather was his choice. Williams, he hoped, would stay on for he needed another American.

Just before midnight, when Young was to stand guard, he sought out Eagle Feather and roused him from sleep. He whispered to him. The Indian said nothing but rose at once and nodded. He found his horse and tied a small package of food to his saddle. The leather pouch containing Young's letter and his quiver of arrows he secured to his belt. "I go, white friend," he said. "I find you again, maybe."

IX

MONTHS WORE ON. LONA HAD NO WORD FROM Young or Williams. She could not understand. She knew well that there was danger on every trail but messengers usually came through. Both men had failed her. In spite of herself bitterness grew in her heart. But she was gay and tossed her head. During the autumn and winter she played monte, danced, and flirted. But she gave no man her favor.

Meantime, out on a Northern waste, near a canyon pass through the mountains, a paper fluttered in the sagebrush, farther and farther from the body of an Indian lying face downward with scalplock gone and two arrows in the back. Blanket, quiver and bow were gone also, but near him lay a leather pouch torn open.

Life in the village stirred into activity when spring brought the wagon trains. Caravan men always brought news. A man from Chihuahua told how the Spaniards tried to reconquer lower Mexico.

"I met a sailor who had come from Cuba on the flagship," said the stranger. "Rear Admiral Laborde and Brigadier Barradas quarreled over plans for the expedition. Why, one time, they threw dishes at each other! Must have been a fine sight to

89

see! Officers fighting with plates and cups! Yes, the Spaniards landed, left the ships some fifty or sixty miles below Tampico. They marched overland in the terrible heat and just walked into town."

"Where in God's world was Santa Anna, Sir?"

"Well," said the newcomer, "on the very night after the Spaniards landed, the word reached Vera Cruz. It was past ten o'clock but General Santa Anna ordered the bells rung and when the people were rounded up in the plaza, he commanded them to begin at once to celebrate victory. *He* was to march. But first he must have twenty thousand pesos! There was nothing for the citizens to do but dig up pots in their gardens. Santa Anna got the money all right, then he commandeered the ships in the harbor for his infantry and sent his cavalry across country. By the middle of last September, the Spaniards surrendered. Everywhere in Mexico the people went wild shouting of General Santa Anna as 'the hero of Tampico.'"

"Santa Anna" was constantly on the air until a caravan from the East arrived. Then two names mingled—Santa Anna and Sam Houston. They were drifting slowly toward each other, the one from Mexico and the other from Tennessee.

"What manner of man is this Sam Houston?" Lona asked Señor Wolfskill.

"Well, he was governor of Tennessee. Early last year, he married a girl of good family and three months later he left her. Nobody could drag a reason out of him. What did he do but resign and leave the country. Mind you, he was not only governor but was talked of as the next President of the United States! The whole affair had everybody gabbling a fellow deaf. They say Sam was in love with her all right. But he took out overland for the Cherokee tribe where he had been when he was a youngster. They call him 'The Raven.' Maybe he's crazy.

90

I don't know. Anyway that's where he is—with the Cherokees not far from Texas."

Could Ewing Young go Indian? Lona hardly thought so.

She held her head high as she turned away from the square. She did not hear the soft tread of moccasins behind her until someone spoke her name. There stood Bill Williams.

"Of all things!" she exclaimed. "Well, what will happen next? Here's all this caravan news and then you walk in! Where have you been, Beel, these many months—over a year now." Her voice was hard until she looked at him again. "Why, Beel? Small-pox?"

Bill fell into step beside her. "Yeah. I wusn't much of a beauty afore but I'm one unholy sight now. Had a run of pox up in the Injun kintry but I come out of it 'tween the Injuns and a mountain man er two at Bent's Fort. Wal, now I'll be tellin' ye 'bout me travels and me sins, little mother confessor. Gosh! Take too long ter mention me sins though."

"I'm sorry, Beel, that you've been sick, but you have your fine gray eyes still and they are what count."

"Yeah, got me winkers. I'm jes in from Bent's Fort where I sold a batch of pelts. Made some eleven hundred dollars. 'Course I ain't got that much now fer I busted in a barrel er two of whisky back thar and went dead drunk as usual. Then I lit out fer hyar. Lona, I tuk yer letter ter Young and he answered it 'O.K.'"

Lona's eyes widened. "Yes. 'O.K.'" she tossed back. "He did nothing of the kind. I have never heard from him."

"What? Ye nevah heerd from him? Reckon Eagle Feather nevah got through then."

"Eagle Feather? Why, Hawk-in-the-Sky told me, long ago, that he was found dead on a desert up North."

"Dead, eh? Wal, he's the Injun sent back with Young's answer. That I'll swar. I seed him swing off down the canyon and Young a-standin' starin' after him. I didn't know but I'd have ter grab the hind-end of his shirt ter keep him from ketchin' holt of that pinto's tail. He ca'culated he'd been too hasty and he looked glum enough ter fly with the owls."

"When is Señor Young coming back?"

"Ain't any way of knowin'. He tole me he wus fer trappin' all the rivers and streams clear ter Californy. The ole thunder box! Makes a lot o' noise 'bout his plans and then does as he damn pleases. He said he wus comin' ter Taos agin, but, by the jumpin' hind legs, I swan I cain't make a guess fer ye."

Lona looked away to the mountain. Her eyes gleamed and for the first time in months her smile was real.

"Been thinkin' of a leetle plan o' mine that I want ter talk ter ye 'bout, ef you care ter listen."

"Let's hear it, Beel."

"Thinkin' of settin' up a store." Williams noticed Lona's mouth quiver in amusement but he puffed a bit harder on his pipe and continued. "Yeah, right hyar in Taos and see ef I kin stay put fer a spell. The last caravan brought a good bunch of stuff. I've still got money. Went up inter the Coeur d'Alène kintry way up North. Worked fer the Hudson Bay Company. Good Lawd! It wus cold. I got a bunch of pelts of me own that the factor didn't know 'bout. I turned in plenty ter him though. Now hyar I be with this tarnel idee buzzin' in me noodle."

"That might be a good plan, Beel. Why don't you try it anyway. It would be something new. We have no real stores."

"Ye see, a feller has ter git set som'ers sometime. 'N anchor is what every man needs. Reckon life nevah mounts ter much without it. Leastwise, that's my way o' thinkin'."

Bill found a small room on the North side of the plaza and bought a stock of cotton cloth and "other trinkets." When all

92

was ready he put a chair in front of his door in which he tilted back and swung his long legs waiting for customers.

People came to look out of curiosity but usually went away without purchasing for they preferred to buy direct from the wagons. Bill would bow, bend his head down and look over his new spectacles and say only, "Ugh!" Then he would pull out his pipe and sit again under the portal.

Often Lona asked about business. "Comin' but I ain't seen it yit," he answered. "Fact is, it kinda rushes by in the mornin' and kinda falls off in the afternoon."

One day, Lona found Bill showing some bright red calico to a Mexican woman and she waited by the rough counter, listening.

"Purty, I think," he was saying. "Make a good dress er shirt. The price is half a peso more but what's that? Cain't have all the prices alike, ye know. Ye ain't buyin'? Wal now, folks has ter have clothes. Wont do fer ye ter be walkin' 'round without 'em, I reckon. Might come some day that folks'll think the sunshine is nuf fer clothes. Like as not, we'd all be better off ef we weren't all tied up. I'd be glad ter see the day," he ended laughing outright.

Lona laughed too and then bought something that she did not need. Bundle in hand, she asked, "How's the anchor holding, Beel?"

"It's a-creakin', I'm thinkin'. Ef these women don't stop hagglin' ovah prices and a-wastin' me time with their tarnel lookin' and lookin' that thar anchor may bust. But I'm hangin' on fer a spell anyhow."

It was just a month to a day until Bill's anchor "busted." Thoroughly disgusted at himself for dallying in a settlement anyway, and at the whole town for not buying his stock, he suddenly began throwing out his goods by the bolt, good cotton cloth worth a dollar a yard. He yelled like an Indian and told

93

the women that if they would not buy, he'd give 'em the stuff. They could get their scissors and "git ter cuttin'."

When the shelves were clear, Bill took his gun. He passed by Lona's window and called, "Bye. The anchor's gone and I'm driftin' ter the mountains."

It was a long summer. Lona rode her horse as far to the West as she dared, toward the purple distant Jemez mountains. But no messenger came. Perhaps her lover lay face down on some desert?

In early autumn, Wolfskill and a party of Americans and Mexicans were leaving to make a new trail west to California. When she had an opportunity to speak to him she asked, "Send me a message somehow if you ever hear anything about Ewing Young, will you?" Wolfskill promised, reminding her that it could easily take more than a year to do what Young had planned.

In September the whole town joined the annual fiesta of the Taos Indians. Lona and her friends galloped toward the pueblo of the tribe. The block-like, terraced buildings reminded Lona of the rough pyramids she had seen in Mexico. Dignified and stolid, they were against the mountains. Along the walls, unbroken by doors or windows, Indians, Spaniards and "foreigners" displayed their wares. Stout ladders led to entrances in the roofs. Against the dull yellow adobe walls Lona found the stalls where men played monte. This was more interesting than the black pottery, silver bars, and gold and copper jewelry.

Rhythmic booming came from underground clan chambers. Finally a group of old men with blankets drawn over their heads came up into the sunshine. Beating their drums, they marched to the square in front of the old mission church. Behind the drummers came young braves clad in breechclouts of buckskin, their faces and bodies streaked with earth colors

94

and their black hair decked with feathers. In their hands were small branches of yellow and green leaves. Facing each other they began the slow steps of the sun-down dance, in thanks for their abundant harvest.

In the crowd, Lona caught sight of a tall man swaggering about with a gold-trimmed, blue cape and high plumed hat. Manuel Armijo, the governor of Santa Fé. He caught sight of her and walked jauntily to her side.

"So you live in this North country now. You are lovely as always, Señorita Lona."

"Do you come often to Taos?" she said, without meeting Señor Armijo's glance. "I find it a delightful place to live although I sometimes long for the greater excitement of the capital."

"So excitement is what you crave?"

"Excitement is part of an active life, Señor!"

While he walked by Lona's side, Don Manuel was not insensible to envious glances nor was she unmindful of the fact that people noticed the flattering attention of this important *político*. When he left her, he bowed with a swirl of his hat and said, "May I come to your sala this evening at nine? You may wish to hear of happenings in Santa Fé."

That evening when Pablita opened the door Lona could see only Armijo's face like that of a giant with no body leering down at her. Had she made a mistake to let him come? He waited until the maid had disappeared. Then he threw off his great cape and hat and at once took Lona's hands in a hard grasp.

"I missed you. What possessed you to come to Taos?"

"I just took it into my head to come," replied Lona. "But tell me of Santa Fé."

For half an hour they chatted about Madam Pino and the others. Suddenly Armijo flung himself down beside Lona on

the couch. She pushed him back. "No! No! You mistake me."
She rose. He rose too, and caught her in a vise-like grip. She
leaned back, her eyes as fierce as his. "Surely you would not
force me?"

"Why not?" For a second his arms relaxed. She pulled away.

"Pedro," she called.

Armijo whirled, his face distorted with anger, his tongue
powerless.

Instantly the door opened and the servant appeared.

"Never mind, Pedro. Señor Armijo is just leaving."

Pedro closed the door but Armijo knew that he stood behind it.

"Yes," he growled, "I'm leaving but you have not seen the
last of me."

For some time Lona had entertained the thought of a gambling establishment of her own. Spaniards everywhere considered it highly respectable for a woman. She had money; she
would make more. She would forget Ewing Young and make
a life for herself here in Fernández de Taos.

Lona and Pablita searched the plaza and could find no suitable house. Then they investigated a suburb, called "La Loma"
—a low hill, lying to the West only a short distance from the
center of the town. On the winding roadway leading back to
the town she found a series of rooms. The doors were unlocked
for misusing property of others was not one of the sins of the
villagers.

"Pablita," observed Lona, "see the fine view of the town and
the mountains. What a fine sala for monte. That room will be
for faro and dice; the third for long whist; the fourth for
canute."

"*Canute?* As long as I have been here I never have seen it
played."

Pablita ran into the fourth room. "Yes," said Lona, following her, "there is plenty of space for the sand piles at either end. The treasure pot of beans could be put on that shelf over the fireplace. Along the walls, the men with drums can sit and sing as the game goes on. The Indians will come. They love to play *canute*."

Opening the door, the two strolled out into the patio. It was barren save for a well in the center and a cactus or two near the ditch at the Western end. On either side were rooms for their own use.

"Mine will be a place for gambling only," said Lona as she and Pablita went down the hill. "I know some men who will be angry and will attack my reputation but I'll prove them babbling gossips. I'll have plenty of good wine and some of that new whisky they call, 'Taos lightning.' Players will pay well for drinks but woe to the man who gets drunk."

Within a fortnight the place was ready. Walls had been replastered with light adobe; roofs rid of weeds and tramped down; mud floors retamped. One day, when a man was at work on a floor, he looked up at Doña Lona who was inspecting the room and remarked, "Americans say that we should put down board floors. What nonsense! Nobody has them. I think what was good enough fer our forefathers should be good enough fer us. Doesn't this floor look smooth?"

On the evening of Lona's opening there was free wine for all her guests. The townfolk crowded in to look at the place with its new benches and tables. The walls were relieved of stark whiteness by a drapery here and there. Bowls of black pottery brilliant with autumn flowers stood on the window sills. The hostess was dressed in her favorite blue-green, a white mantilla about her shoulders.

Such a reception had its reward because, although the people of Fernández were not given to making quick changes in their customs, it was not long before many deserted the old cantinas and salas on the plaza in favor of Lona's rooms on the hill. No one could remember finer gambling rooms, nor such a hostess.

Lona was happy. Money and more money fell into her chests. Late at night she sat at a small desk in her own pleasant room, and counted her winnings. She kept accounts as Madam Pino had taught her at the inn in Santa Fé. Usually she stacked her coins and then tipping them over, thrust her hands through them. The feel of pesos was delightful, soothing and reassuring. Was she learning to love money? It was better than dreaming of Ewing Young. Love needs a brisk breeze of devotion to keep it burning, she thought, and hers—alas, hers was all but dying in a flagging wind.

During the long winter, messengers from other expeditions arrived, but for her there was no news from the West. Already a new year was well under way, and yet, in spite of herself, she kept alive a faint hope that her lover would return.

Early in April, the people of Cordoba, a small village a few miles West of Fernández, announced a fiesta. When Lona heard of it, she decided at once to have a gambling stall.

When the morning came, she and Pedro galloped along the road, their saddle bags clinking with silver coins. Fording the blue Río Lucero, they struck up the trail to Cordoba. Standing like a solid mass of yellow adobe, its flat skyline was broken by a chapel belfry and a slightly higher sentinel tower. As Lona approached the desert village she remembered that an aged man had told her, "Cordoba is like Fernando de Taos thirty years ago." Lona remembered he had used the older name.

Delighted that Doña Lona had come to their feast day, the townfolk brought piles of blankets and helped build her gambling booth. Everything was soon in readiness. By the time the Mexicans in their red sashes were strolling about, plucking their guitars, monte was in full swing. Winners greedily claimed their stakes but silver fell constantly into Lona's money bags. Suddenly a cry from the sentinel tower galvanized the crowd.

"*Indios!* Apaches coming! Three miles. *Indios!*"

Terror seized the people. They heard the Western gate clang shut. Families climbed into wagons and were gone through the gate to the East, lashing their horses. Children were snatched up and hurried indoors where barricades were thrown up. Wooden shutters banged. Grabbing their guns, men climbed ladders and pulled them up over the parapeted walls of the roofs where boxes of ammunition and bows and arrows were kept. One old man helped draw a cinch. When his son put a foot into a stirrup, he cried, "Tell the men in Fernández to hurry. There is little time."

Lona's horses pawed the ground nervously as her money bags were piled on. She handed Pedro a dagger, felt for the one hidden in her own bosom and her small gun at her belt. Leaning forward both struck spurs and dashed through the Eastern entrance. Men crashed the great gates together behind them. The guard in the tower shouted, "One mile!"

"I'm not afraid," cried Lona. "We have time."

"Aye, but you do not know Apaches," called Pedro, the wind catching his words.

The two riders galloped through sagebrush toward Fernández. Dust soon screened them somewhat. Lona halted for a moment to look back. Pedro turned also. They could distinguish Indians with red bandeaux fluttering and lances shaking. The war whoops were lost on the wind. They were circling Cordoba. To Lona's horror, she saw a small band of the savages detach themselves and swoop down the Taos trail.

"They are coming for us," screamed Pedro. "Hurry, Doña Lona. Apache ponies are like eagles. They fly!"

Rounding a ridge, Lona caught sight of a dark line of horsemen. "Taos men!" she shouted and spurred her mount again. They reached the dark rocks. Her horse stumbled and she was thrown to the ground. Feeling no injury she leaped to her feet and caught her horse's bridle, but he had strained a fetlock. She looked about hurriedly. Pedro had galloped on and then, missing her, wheeled and came back.

"Hide, Pedro," commanded Lona. "They'll find me more easily than you. I'll demand a parley."

"They won't listen to you. I'll stand by."

"No! Go, I tell you," ordered Lona.

Reluctantly Pedro led his horse behind the farther rocks.

Lona trembled while she waited, ready to give the signal. Apaches would care little for a sign from any woman but she would try. Peering close to the ground, she could see the Indians charge over a hill and hurtle forward, an avalanche of fury.

The Apaches gave a hideous yell when they sighted Lona. They turned quickly and halted near her, amazed that a woman dared give them the sign which asked for a parley. Courage in an enemy always made them pause. And here was a comely Spanish woman standing bravely before them.

"No arrow!" commanded the chief who dismounted and walked toward Lona. A grin spread over the red-painted face under his fine feathered bonnet. He had been in Fernández and knew who she was. Her saddle bags would be full of money. He motioned for a scout to find her animal and strode farther toward the woman.

Lona's hand was still high. "Chief! Braves! We give the race to you. All the money I have is yours if you will let us go. We have done nothing to harm you or yours." She drew herself up and held her head proudly to keep from trembling.

"Ugh! Woman brave," the chief muttered. "She'll be mine!"

Over the bend of a hill, rode the men from Taos. Their rifles spit fire. Indian after Indian fell. The chief threw himself on his pony and dashed from the rocks. Galloping for their lives, others followed with the Taos fighters at their heels. More Indians rolled from their mounts. Only one remained. "Let him go. He'll tell the tale," shouted the leader.

Rounding up the ponies of their enemies, the Taos men checked their horses and slowly took the trail back to the rocks, where Lona and Pedro had stood motionless watching the fight. As the riders drew near Lona started. Her hand flew to her throat. Ewing! She swayed forward but stopped. Let him come to her. She had waited long. Ewing Young dismounted and, unmindful of his neighbors, took Lona in his arms.

"WHAT ABOUT ALL THIS GAMBLING BUSINESS,
Lona?"

"Oh, it has been such fun." Lona lifted her rose silk skirt
in a curtsy. "Your Honor is most welcome." Her delight in her
establishment forced Young to smile. She crossed to the window and rearranged a branch of pussy willows in a black vase.
In the farther sala, Pablita was lighting candles.

They walked slowly through her rooms where piñon wood
burned in the fireplaces, filling the air with a faint bitter-
sweet odor. All was in readiness for the night. Leaving Pablita
and Pedro in charge, Lona threw a cape about her and led
Young along the portal to her own sala facing the patio in
which the rain was beating a furious tattoo.

Sitting on the mattress bench against the wall, close to each
other, they had no need for words. Young looked at the flames
in the fireplace, the warm color of the room, so snug against
the rain. Candlelight fell on Lona's desk and glowed on a
handsome leather-bound chest. Why could he not accept this
venture of hers? Why did his American blood flare at the
very thought of it?

"Darling, why did you do it?" Lona felt the troubled note in
her lover's voice.

102

"I wanted to do something. My treasure bags were growing flabby. I believed that I could make money right here in Taos. See the chest?" Lona crossed the room and threw back the lid. She lifted coins by the handful. Young shook his head as he watched her hands let the pesos fall. Obviously she was delighted at their clinking. "Many people come to play. Such a place as mine is perfectly respectable, you know."

"But you? You, my Lona? I can not bear it. Girls in the East never do this sort of thing." Young's face went very sober. Irritation gave way to a sadness which Lona could not understand.

"But I am from the South," answered Lona cheerily when she sat by him again. "It is all right here, Ewing. You will see. Tell me about the expedition."

Young rose and walked back and forth. He picked up a quill from the desk, flicked it across his hand and played with the fringe on his buckskin shirt.

"About the message first, Lona. When Williams made our camp and gave me your letter, I wanted to return at once, but I couldn't. We were well on our way. I had to send Eagle Feather with my answer. I hope it brought you some relief? I know I was something of a skunk."

"But, Ewing? Don't you know that he was killed? Your letter never reached me."

"What? He never got through? He was a good scout. . . . Poor fellow! Of course, I supposed you had received my message. It was well nigh impossible to send another. That was a bit hard on you." With that he dismissed the matter, for the man who wanders far never realizes the burden his silence imposes on those who remain behind.

Young sat on an Indian rug in front of the fire while Lona gaily told him about Williams and his store. Young shouted in glee, "Just like the old codger! I wonder if he really made money? Coins run through his fingers like quicksilver. You should see him slapping down his horsehide cards on a blanket in the light of a campfire, playing 'old sledge' and betting like a millionaire. He's odd as a porcupine, pricking with words sometimes but keen and not illiterate either even if he does use the jumbled talk of the high camps. Bless his lonely hide!

"I had news of Bill in San Gabriel Mission and in the Sacramento Valley. There we ran into Pete Ogden with his company of Hudson Bay Trappers. We summered around those parts but we didn't have much luck. Had a little diversion at the Mission. Injuns stole about sixty head of our horses."

Lona sighed. "Danger everywhere and not much luck."

"I reckon danger is the very heart of any adventure, Lona. But we had some luck after we left the Pueblo de Los Angeles. We trapped the Col-o-row way down to tide water and then struck East. We had some two thousand pounds of pelts when we all reached Santa Fé. We sold but the money had to be divided." Young filled his pipe, puffed hard and looked into the fire like a man who had much more to say and did not want to say it.

"Yes, and in California," queried Lona, "did you see Señor Wolfskill? He left for the far West last year."

Young nodded and pushed down his tobacco. "Yeah, I wanted him to join my next party."

Lona lifted a hand across her mouth to hide its quivering. "What about your promise to me?"

"I know, sweetheart. Would you marry me and go West?"

Lona did not answer.

"What's the use of marrying and leaving you in Taos when I may have to stay in Californy. I didn't make the money on this trip that I wanted for you, darling. This is no sort of life for my wife. Would you . . . would you give up this infernal business?" Young caught his knee in his hands and rocked

104

back and forth. "I don't see anything for me to do but leave in a few months. I'd hire a rig of some kind and try to take you with me on the safest route I know if you would go."

"I don't know, Ewing," said Lona slowly. "I have dreamed of a home here and happiness for you and me. You once said that a mountain man never gets into town that he doesn't begin to plan for the day when he will leave again. You have the wandering spirit and you'll never lose it." Tears gathered in her eyes. "You know I love you!"

"Come now, girl, we must not have any tears." Young put his arm around her. "We'll work this out somehow. We'll have a royal time for five or six months and see. You're mine now!"

Two months slipped by happily, on the surface. Each hoped that there would be no fork in their road, yet feared to look ahead. They overlooked no opportunity for pleasure, attended all the fiestas, the cockfights and bullbaitings. The latter Lona thought no sport at all. She remembered Mexico with its great arena and brilliant crowds. But never did she wish for a second to return to the South. Nor did she want to go West.

Sometimes on horseback they followed trails into the foothills where men gathered wood, cautious always with horses headed toward the town. They galloped over the low hills beyond Del Rancho until they stood on the high canyon wall of the Rio Grande. When Lona chose the course, they rode to the North along the "Old Taos Trail" on which occasionally they met a wagon train or a group of mountain men whooping and shooting into the air.

"This glorious desert!" cried Lona one day. "Let's go right into it toward the Abiquiu mountain."

Snatching off her black velvet cap, she threw back her braids and loosened her red cape to catch the wind. Her eyes filled with pleasure as she dashed ahead in and out of the sagebrush, now and then crushing a branch that filled the air with sweet medicinal odor. Young followed, his hand on the trigger of the rifle across his saddle, on guard against rattlesnakes that coiled in the sun near the thick purple stems of sage. Finally Lona pulled up her horse, the wind stinging her cheeks.

"Ah, this is *my* country."

Young nodded but said no word. Lona had changed subtly. She was a much stronger character than she had been when she came to Taos—impelling—but she must not prove stronger than he. She wanted him to stay in Taos but he could not. It was his will pitted against hers. His silence made Lona realize that the conflict was astir between them. She plied her quirt, wheeled about and galloped toward Taos.

That evening, Ewing Young gambled at monte and later spent some time with Lona in her own sala but he left early. He must think this thing to a finish. It was weeks now since he had spoken of Lona's business. He knew that he resented such independence of thought in any woman. His own mother . . . ? Well, she was different. Lona was stubborn and unreasonable. In advance of her times? Maybe. But this business? It was absurd! He would not argue with her again until he was about to leave. And leave he must.

Several afternoons later, Ewing was sitting in the plaza nodding in the early autumn sun. A young soldier stopped before him.

"Mister Ewing Young, unless I am much mistaken."

Young nodded. "Why, Ed Stanley! Where did you fall from?"

"A wagon. Just today, Sir."

"You've grown some since we boys yanked you out of that swimmin' hole back in Knox County. Soldier, eh? Sit down, Ed, and tell a fellah 'bout Tennessee."

106

"Well, I enlisted and was sent down to Cantonment Gibson in the Injun country." Stanley leaned forward as Young had done and twirled his cap. "I resigned. Had a talk with Sam Houston . . ."

"Houston? Crash on. You know Sam Houston!"

"A lot of folk still growl at him in Tennessee." Stanley laughed. "When he was back in Washington, last year, they say he had a different blanket for every occasion and plenty of beaded buckskin. Even went all dressed up like that to see President Jackson."

Young laughed outright. "No tellin' what a man like Sam Houston will do. And now?"

"He's married to a half-breed, Tiana Rogers. Injun fashion, I reckon. She's right smart on looks. Houston seems to think a good deal of her but he lets himself drink an awful lot. Somebody told me he was planning a Rocky Mountain expedition. I don't know. But some of the soldiers are betting that he will not go to the mountains but to Texas."

"Texas, eh? From what I've heard 'round hyar, Ed, things are none too steady down there. So Houston's got the whole country jumpin' sidewise wonderin' what he'll do next, eh? There's so much power in the man. It's bound to break out somewhere."

"And what about you, Sir?"

Ewing and the young soldier slipped into tales of old-times. Tiring of the bench, they wandered along the portals, drinking at one cantina after another.

At the far end of the plaza they came upon a man whistling "Turkey in the Straw" while he whittled dowels. He stopped in the middle of his tune and called out, "Ewing Young! Wal, I declare! Why ain't you pulled out fer the trails? Sold all the nails I brung 'long so these hyar dowels have got ter steady her. Been sleepin' in a bed, by gumpity, and the damn thing's

107

wobbly. Dreamed I was slidin' down a precipice all last night, hangin' on ter a whisky bottle so *it* wouldn't git smashed." He looked up at Young. "Several years since last I seed ye. Like trappin' better'n followin' the trail, eh? 'Course ye heerd 'bout Charles Bent bringin' in wagons with oxen fer the fust time? They do git along. Makes you feel like a prince, ridin' in state." Young nodded and the man whistling, sharpened his knife, and began to whittle again.

Young and Stanley strolled on to the ramshackle inn and sat down at a table in the small eating-room, dark in spite of candles, and reeking with the scent of ancient cooking, old wine and worse air. A forlorn little woman in black brought beans, tortillas, beef and liquor. With a satisfied smile, she put down a plate piled high with savory *empanadas*.

A whiff of air broke into the place when a man stomped in with boots already heavily spurred. He spied Stanley and called that a bunch of fellows were riding out for Santa Fé the next morning at five. If he still wanted to go, he'd better see to his nag and meet them at the big spring at the foot of the slope.

Such news meant that Stanley must bestir himself. Young bade him good-by, downed his whisky and started to the gambling establishment on the hill. He found Lona busy in her cheerful sala.

"This afternoon," she told him, "I heard that Señor Josiah Gregg has come in with the biggest caravan yet. One hundred wagons, two cannons and goods worth $200,000! What do you think of that? This is bound to be a great country for making a fortune."

"I told you that more Americans would be driftin' in. Hooray!" shouted Young, slapping his hand hard on his knee. "It's a comin'—big American trade. Maybe you are right." He smiled for he knew what was in Lona's mind.

108

Young watched Lona arranging flowers in a row of black jars. "I've been thinkin' matters over, Lona. What you say of traders makin' money hyar, in Santa Fé and far below may come true before long, but, after all, I'm a trapper. I like the business. Every mountain man I meet tells me that the streams 'round hyar and up San Luis way are worked out. I must go back to Californy and just possibly up into the North. I don't know. You've got your business hyar, whether I like it or not. Right now I can not give you the home that I want for you. God! I wish I could. I see nothing for it but to saddle up again. Honest. You'll nevah know how I hate to leave you but, if I make good I'll be back. It may take some time but I'll come not later than September of '33. I'm comin' back sure as . . . as God makes little coons!" Young kissed Lona before she could reply.

Lona drew back her head and tried to smile. "Something told me all along that I was losing. Gambler's luck, I guess. Win only for a time and then lose. I did so want you to stay." Her voice quivered but she braced herself. "I'll have to content myself until Fortune catches up with you, Ewing. The saddle bags do not have to be over-full, my dear. My heart urges me to go with you but a woman on the trail would be no help, not on a mountain trail for beaver."

"Honey, that's one of the reasons men love women as they do," said Young tenderly. "One reason. But, my dear, you beat us men to a finish on endurance. As a general rule, you women dream beyond us too. When a fine woman loves, she's incomparable. And you are fine. I'll return, if I can. Be sure of that."

Young glanced sidewise at Lona. "Sounds as if I were preachin' but I mean every word I've said. Let's be happy until next Tuesday. After that we'll hope. So thar!"

On the morning of his departure, Young stopped at Lona's door to say good-by. On the table he laid a spy-glass.

"I've two of these. Keep this to remember me by, Lona, girl."

Lona took the glass and ran her hands down its length. "I'll remember without it," she said, her voice trembling. "I'll treasure this because it was yours, my dear."

XI

IN HER IMAGINATION LONA FOLLOWED THE trappers along the route Young had described. She fancied that she could see Young camping on his way to Santa Fé, to Alburquerque and beyond, riding up and down barren hills. Then came his first letter written at Santa Fé. All was well but there was little news. She kissed the crackly paper and hid it in her desk.

Three weeks later, another letter came. Young had scribbled it in the old inn at Socorro where the great cottonwoods shielded the walls against the sun. Lona remembered it well. "From here," Young wrote, "we strike out on a trail away from the wagon routes. This may be the last place I can leave a letter for you, my darling. Some day, you will hear from me again."

Letterless weeks bogged down the days. Lona saw Young's party with their heavily loaded pack mules plodding heavily over deserts. How dark their slow-moving line must be against the bases of the red castle rocks of Apacheria. Perhaps they had reached the Gila. Ewing had told her of its rim of dun-colored flat land. Now, surely they were in the mountains, crunching over hard snow, clicking traps into place or drying and packing beaver skins. Or fighting Indians! God forbid!

Now, he was lost to her. The party was full three months

gone. Were they high in the mountains or were they pulling over the last pass and entering California, the promised land, where flowers bloom in winter? No doubt Ewing was comfortably warm this pleasant December day. It was graying in Taos and the air had the feel of snow.

Happily for Lona, she could not see her lover hunched up under his heaviest blanket in front of a campfire chary of its heat. The bitter cold froze his breath to his new beard. He was thinking of Lona in her warm salas, smiling at other men. He could almost hear the swish of her silk skirt through the clinking of the coins.

The hoot of an owl cut across his thought. Its tone was slightly false. Young lifted his head and listened. It came again. "Sentinel to the East," he said, dragging himself up from the fire.

Plowing through two feet of snow, Young found the man who pointed his clumsily gloved hand and whispered, "Yonder, Sir. Do ye see anythin'?" Young drew from its case his long spy-glass and looked steadily for a moment or two, then he answered, "It's a slow-moving line. Too thick for Injuns. Single file's their custom. Too thick. Now I see. It's a bunch of deer wandering in that streak of moonlight. Adjust your own glass better. See?" The man, a greenhorn on his first trip West, agreed that Young was undoubtedly right. Then the captain continued, "Ye may not believe me but Injuns are smarter'n we are in lots o' ways. They are wily, cautious and know enough not to strike toward the high peaks gone white. Any Injuns who've spotted us have probably grunted out that our parcel o' fools can freeze to death for all they care. However, keep yer eyes peeled anyway."

"Thank God! We are in Los Angeles at last," wrote Young several weeks later. "We pulled in with a fair amount of pelts and have a few pesos jammed into our pockets. But—not enough for me to turn back to Taos for you, my dear. The authorities here are more friendly to us than on our last trip. They invited us to an inn. How the men did eat! They are gambling now with a bunch of soldiers from the garrison and listening to jokes not meant for such as you. They are drinking. You should see the huge hookers that we have out here! I drink too, but not much, as you know. I don't care to wake up sprawled in the street and wonder what world I'm in nor have to turn my pockets inside out to search for a possible coin left behind by the fellow who stole my wallet. No, not me!

"Somebody's calling me. I'll write later. A ship's captain is outside. More, later. . . ."

"Damn!" he said. "I wanted to finish that letter so's it can go on the first caravan East." He slipped the paper between the two books of Shakespeare which he always packed in one of his bags and went to meet the captain, a big hearty fellow from the East coast.

"All right, sir," answered Young after he had listened to the man. "We've many pelts yet unsold. I'll be down at the Mission by tomorrow night. You'll be aboard by then?" The man of the ship nodded, said he would send a messenger ashore and bade Young good day.

Young strolled down the street and entered a cantina where he knew some of his men loafed, whether they had the cash for drinks or not.

"Ship off shore," he called.

"Ship off shore? Hooray! Whar? When air we pullin' out?"

"This afternoon," answered Young. "She's ridin' Sou'west of the point, down coast near San Capistrano. Men of New England. Boston, likely."

Late the next afternoon, when he and his men rode through the gate of the Mission of San Juan Capistrano Young was thinking how much Lona would enjoy the place. The cacti before the heavy arched portal were damp with the salt mist from the Pacific three miles away. Near them walked several friars with brown robes flapping.

In the early twilight, Young sat with his old friend Padre Miguel under the cloister portal facing a rectangular frost-touched garden. The smoke of their cigars floated away into the light mist. Behind them the bells were ringing in the four stone arches connecting the mission with the earthquake-ruined church. Young did not hear the moccasined feet of an Indian who touched the sleeve of the padre's robe. "Padre Miguel, a sailor stands without, asking to speak to Señor Young." The padre glanced at his trader friend and replied, "Bring him in, Juan." The padre rose to leave but Young urged him to wait and hear what the sailor might have to say.

The seaman, cap in hand, rolled sidewise along the portal. His black hair was brushed back from an expanse of forehead and his eyes were intensely blue. As he came forward, he spoke and his brogue was so unmistakable that Young greeted him with, "Man of Ireland, eh?"

"Sure'n don't I look it, Sor," he answered with a grin. "Got the vury map o' good old Ir'land on me face. I'm after tellin' ye that me captain held he'd be runnin' dories to San Juan Point in th' marnin' ef ye be of a mind te trade, Sor?"

"Good," he answered when Young replied that he would be ready by dawn. "Now, I'll be after reportin'. It's biddin' ye good day, I am, Sor."

The sailor started to leave but Young motioned him to a seat. This was too fine an opportunity for news to let the man go unquestioned. "How did ye happen to take ship fer Californy? How d'ye fare?"

"I shippit on the *Pilgrim*, Sor, to try me luck standin' on me head. It's a good sturdy ship. I was after lookin' her over afoor

114

we h'isted sail. Had scurvy, o' course, but we ran harrd for Aires. Anchor'd in th' outer roads. Then we pullit for shore after food'n a good toime. At Valpariso too. Vile smellin' port, that. Some of it's still crawlin' outah the mess the airthquake left for 'em back in '22."

"What about the Horn, young man?" broke in Young eagerly.

"Aye, it's the Horn ye'll be wantin' te hear of. It was battlin' we did, standin' on our heads with the good ship hangin' te our feet. Had sich seas as only the deevil himsel' coulda kickit oop. Sich a blow! Lost the tops'l and come nigh losin' one o' th' masts. But the ship's a winner and our captain a mahnn—a mahnn, Sor. When I spied the cliffs through the mists, I said me prayer that Manannan would whistle daown th' wind. He's our Irish God o' th' Headlan's, Sor, an' a friend to us men o' th' sea."

The sailor rose again to go. "This is the best part o' th' 'Mericas, I'm thinkin', for the mahnn as can bide it ashore. I'd be barrin' Oregon if what I've hurrd is true. There's a land for sich as ye, I'm thinkin', husky and big as ye air."

"Oregon?" echoed Young, interested.

"Oregon. Aye, it's a land good for fields 'n for fur with a great river runnin' wide to th' sea. And winter a-plenty to keep a mahnn fit."

"I've heard as much from the traveling brothers," commented the padre. " 'Tis true they do not wander that far but they've heard tales of the North at Yerba Buena. 'T would seem a fair venture for men of the mountains."

Young stood as the sailor bade the two men good day. "I'll be thinkin' of Oregon," he said.

In his cell-like room, Young threw a blanket about his shoulders and lighted several candles. He sat down at the crude wooden table and whittled a fresh point on his quill. Then he

115

wrote of his trip to the Mission, of his visit with the padre, of the Irish sailor, and Manannan, his God of the sea.

The following night he added: "We loaded our pack mules and made for San Juan Point, this morning. When we reached the cliffs, we could see the *Pilgrim* riding at anchor a mile or so out and small dories coming in to shore.

"I went below with a few men. The trail was plenty narrow among the rocks. When the sailors pushed their boats on the sand, they balanced boxes on their heads and waded ashore. I motioned for my other men to drop over the bundles of pelts. Had to do some sharp trading but we got tools, iron, cooking dishes. Clothing too. Wish I could send you some of the satin. We got all sorts of stuff. The men insisted on selling at once and we did for good money here at the Mission. Word got around that we'd be thar, this afternoon.

"Two of my men will travel on the first caravan bound East. One will take this letter. The other will bring a short note. I reckon one of them will get through to you.

"I know that you could not send me a letter as yet but, my dear, I beg of you to send one down to Santa Fé in time for the first trade caravan. My heart gallops back to you more often than you know."

The next morning, Young gave his letters to the two men who were going East. He watched the fellows mount their mules and stood by an outer wall of the Mission until they dipped out of sight.

Suddenly he threw his head back and realized that he was looking North. "Oregon?" he muttered. "It may be a good country but so is Californy. I've a mind to loaf in this balmier land. But Oregon?"

XII

IT WAS MID-APRIL OF 1832 WHEN LONA RECEIVED
the letter and the note. She spread them out on her desk and
tried to read between the lines. He had written nothing of his
plans. Was he still at the Mission? "He writes better than he
talks," she thought to herself, "but I'm glad he slipped in a
'thar.'"

A month later another letter came. Ewing was in San Diego.
He had made a friend of a fidgety old cabinet maker. "I still
love the smell and feel of freshly-cut lumber," he wrote. "Yes,
and of yellow wax. I like the sound of hammer and saw. That's
queer when, you know, I hated that kind of work when I was
a towhead. This fellow is from Germany too like old Jacob in
Tennessee, but he is not old enough to talk of pirates on the
Mississippi. How my eyes used to bulge at tales of Mike Fink,
the bully, on the Ohio and of the great black strumpet, Annie
Christmas, who queened it over the water front in Orleans.

"Life out here is like milk and honey, Lona. I find myself
doing too much loafing, but, by fall, I know I'll be up in the
mountains again. I'm telling you this now so you'll understand if you get no letters for a while."

One early June evening when Lona returned from a party,
she found Bill Williams seated on the floor in the monte room,

with his long legs drawn up under him. He was slapping down cards. His red hair and beard were smoothed down, a sign that he was winning. When Lona entered, he rose quickly and strode forward to greet her. "Wal now, howdy, Doña Lona. Been gamblin' awaitin' fer ye ter come in. It's good fer the wits ef a body has any. And how be ye?"

"In the glow, thanks." Lona dropped her black mantilla across her low-cut crimson dress and gave him her hand. "Coming suddenly is your long suit, Beel. When you close up your game, will you meet me in my sala?"

Bill smiled at her approvingly and returned to his cards.

Slightly lifting her wide skirts, Lona rustled through her rooms, bowing and smiling to her patrons. All was in order, dice rattled, gamesters watched each other over the faro layout. In the whist room men played in intense silence. She did not enter the canute room but through the closed door she heard the accustomed rumble of drums and low singing.

When Lona returned to the monte room Williams swept his coins into his pockets and rose. "I'll be followin' yer trail now."

In Lona's sala, Williams pyramided a few sticks of piñon in the fireplace. A snap of his flint and a blaze flared quickly. "Cain't be so high from the sea without a bit o' fire even in June," he said more to himself than to Lona. "Well, gal, what luck?"

"Luck? It is a relative thing, Beel," she answered, looking down at her long, well-kept hands. "I've made money if that's what you mean. But I lost . . ."

"Yeah, I know. Young's been hyar and whooped out agin. He's allus on the go, same as me. May come a time when he'll be ready ter settle down, but ye kin tell him fer me sometime that I ain't recommendin' storekeepin'."

118

"Beel, you were a whole circus, tiger, monkey and clown, all in one."

"Mostly monkey, I guess."

Lona told Bill news of Young's trip while he nodded in understanding. "Ewing's going to try and make a fortune this time," said Lona. "He's been gone since last September. One has to wait so long for a letter. I wonder . . . now you must not laugh! . . . I wonder if the time will ever come when there'll be a post road from here to California, like those you've told about back East?"

"Ye jes don't reckon how fur it is, woman," replied Williams. "Why, the Injuns'd have ter be quieted down and I cain't figgur out jes how that could be done unless they wus all kilt dead. Even then there'd be damn scoundrels who drift away from the settlements and the law and I'll swan ef they wouldn't rob and murder. No stage coach er express rider would be safe."

"I suppose that's true. But Young said that in England, not so many years ago, they built a railway of planks with iron over them and a horse could pull carts with coal easier and quicker than any other way. Then he talked about an engine of some sort called the 'Puffing Billy.' It pulled wagons, too, and even carried passengers. Silly, I suppose, but I've often wondered if your men in the East wouldn't do something like that."

"Wal, now! I recolleck that a feller talked to me 'bout that 'Puffin' Billy,' a long time ago. Another man said that in Pennsylvany—in '29, I think he said—some men run a steam enjin. Fifteen miles an hour! That's goin' some. A feller could git som'ers. But sich a train could run only a few miles. Why, Lona, in this kintry there's miles and miles, thousands of 'em. Rivers and mountains ter cross. No, there'll nevah be any sich enjin runnin' 'round these parts. Why, men'd have ter stop at the

Mississippi. If they built on this side, then they'd have the passes in the mountains ter make and that'd be jes impossible. Might be that men'll manage some kind of a way ter git 'cross ter Californy, four hundred yeahs from now. I reckon you 'n me'll have ter keep on makin' our journeys by hoss, mule er oxen."

"I suppose so, Beel, but I like to stretch my imagination. What's been happening to you?"

"Been roamin' 'round South'ard. Then I heerd 'bout this feller John Harris a-makin' up a party hyar fer the Comanchy kintry out east so I skedaddled up hyar ter jin up. He's a good feller but part of his brain needs workin' ovah by 'sperience. Reckon I'll have ter be boss afore we're many miles out."

Bill tossed his black felt hat into a corner, filled his pipe and struck his flint. "Thought I'd nevah see ye agin a while back. I wus ridin' me hoss near an edge and me darn animul stumbled and fell rollin' ovah and ovah down hill. Me feet didn't mind me, got tangled in the stirrups. Me traps wus bouncin' all ovah me. Guess I wus most ready fer wings when I come ter a stop. The feller with me scrambled down and picked me up. I wus some dizzy and fer the fust time since I wus a young un I had ter let a body help me mount. Got a breeze in me face and come to and, by the jumpin' hind legs! ef I didn't beat him ter the best place fer settin' traps. Wus he mad! Takes more'n a tumble ter kill me."

A knock at the door. Pedro came in quickly. He had been running.

"Doña Lona, a man in yonder has drawn his dagger. I made him put it back. He tried to strike me with his fist. He's good and mad."

Lona sprang up and started across the patio. Williams followed. He had never seen Lona in action. He watched her walk to the card room, unhurriedly, her head high. Across the table now littered with cards, chips, coins and wooden markers two men glared at each other. One was a Mexican obviously of the better class. The other, a rough-looking, slit-eyed American, held his deck in a small box. Neither man was conscious of Lona.

"Put that snake to bed, you damned gopher," yelled the Mexican. "Put it to bed, I tell you. That isn't the first time you've played me short. I'm on to you."

"So ye cain't take a fall for a loss, eh?" snarled the American.

The Mexican lifted his dagger, "Let me have a look at that box."

"Oh, no, ye don't," growled the American, putting his box with its hidden copper wire far down in his trousers' pocket.

"Let me see . . . ," the Mexican suddenly realized that Señorita Barcelona stood by, "I'm begging your pardon, but that simpleton thought he could . . ."

"Men are expected to be gentlemen in my place. Put your dagger away, Señor. And you, you march and use the quick step too," Lona commanded the American. "You think this is a gambling den? Any man can tell you better. Such as you can stay out."

Again the Mexican apologized and bowed while Lona's glance swept his swarthy genial face and heavy figure in embroidered velvet waistcoat and correct black broadcloth. "And you, Señor?" she asked.

"I am Luís Cortazar of Durango. I came yesterday on the caravan. I understood that your place was high class. That's the reason for my surprise and anger. I am sorry. A thousand regrets, Señorita."

"I understand. Your apology is accepted. Sit down. Pedro, clear the table. Come, Beel," she said introducing Williams.

Since no one else was in the room, Lona asked the stranger to tell her of affairs in Mexico. She assured him that she was still deeply interested although she had been now almost six years in the North.

"At your service, Señorita, I'll gladly tell what I know. Well, General Santa Anna woke up last summer some time."

Lona leaned forward.

"Thought so," Bill broke in. "Last fall, I heerd that Santa Anna sent word to the Texians saying he wus their friend and that he'd see to it the folks thar got some special gov'ment, somethin' suited ter 'em. Did the gen'ral git an army together?"

"Yes, of a sort," answered Cortazar. "He appropriated over 200,000 pesos of federal funds and assumed control of the customs receipts of the port. Always a high hand. Now he is besieged in Vera Cruz."

From that night on, Luís Cortazar was often seen with Doña Lona. During the weeks that followed, he paid her ardent attentions. On the plaza men told him of Ewing Young. He winced but then such a charming woman would have many suitors. Lona found him attractive and basked in the warmth of his admiration. One evening he spoke of Williams with ill-concealed jealousy. Lona frowned.

"Pray do not be silly, Don Luís. Beel and I have been friends for years. I know his story; he knows mine. Love between us? It's impossible. *Santa María!* I'll allow no man to demand that I thrust Williams out of my life. He has an understanding of friendship, rare enough in men. Then too, he once did me more than a good turn down in Chihuahua." Lona shuddered. She had not thought of Chihuahua for many a day.

Before the caravan departed for the South, Luís Cortazar begged Lona to return to old Mexico with him. She gently shook her head. "I like you, Luís, but I do not love you. Mexico? No. My life is linked with this North country."

When the wagon train went South with it went Luís Cortazar. Lona did not watch it go. "Señor Cortazar," she said to herself, "is just another man who is going out of my life, probably forever. Men ride in and men ride out. Cortazar is gone and so is Beel."

Two months later, Williams galloped into the plaza with a group of mountain men. "The Red River kintry was *no bueno,*" he said briefly as he made for the nearest cantina. When he had cleaned up and bought him a new outfit of buckskin he zigzagged up the hill to see Lona.

"Wal, hyar I be agin," he began after greeting Lona in the patio. "That thar man Harris didn't know A B C 'bout leadin' a party. I had ter take holt. But Albert Pike! Git the name—Albert, by gumpity!—I jes couldn't stand fer him. He was allus writin' in that book of his."

"You old rascal, Beel. Tell me more about Señor Pike. I didn't even see him when he was here," said Lona.

"Pike wus mighty partic'lar 'bout food. We wus most starvin' onct and kilt an old mare. Pike and his mess wouldn't eat any of the meat. No siree! No hoss meat fer them. I come near dyin' holdin' in from laughin' but I jes had ter git some o' that meat under me belt so I 'tended ter business. Ye see, it wus up ter me ter do the huntin' fer the hull party and onct I couldn't see nothin' ter shoot but a crane. When I brought that in, Pike's eyes bulged out but he didn't git more'n his share and that wusn't more'n a bite fer anybody.

"Did some record shootin' while I wus out, Lona. Some of us got ketch'd in an ole adobe. Injuns stole a march on us. A big bunch of 'em. We did some shootin' but kinda held back fearin' a rush on us when the damn varmints wouldn't parley. Then one of the Injuns climbed on a rock. In sign language, he told how he despised all whites and wished 'em ter Hell. Wal, I jes riz up, took keerful aim and fired. The Injun toppled ovah.

It wus the longest rifle shot I evah made er heerd of." Williams
stalked around the room, swaggering a bit. "When it went
home like that—jes one shot—the Injuns gave a yell and tuk ter
their heels so fast we couldn't see 'em fer the dust."

Lona smiled. "You old rascal, Beel."

"Wal, 'twant no use wearin' a feller's life clean ter the bone
in that blarsted Red River kintry."

Bill refilled his pipe. "Afore I left, I polished up me language,
best I could, and had a pow-wow with that feller Pike. I told
him somethin' 'bout the Rockies and Californy and 'bout some
books I know and Injun legends. Ye shoulda seen him look at
me. I mighta been some new kind of animul. But I didn't crack
a grin. Reckon he thought I know'd a thing er seven afore I left.
That night I ketched sight of him a-writin' like the deevil wus
aftah him. Wonder what he rit 'bout me?" Williams stuck
both thumbs in his belt and lifted his shoulders.

"Did you hear any news about your country in the East?"
asked Lona when she thought Bill had strutted long enough.

"Yeah. 'Course. Seems they had a rip-roarin' campaign afore
they reelected 'Old Hickory' but he come through on top. I
heerd South Caroliny has been buckin' like a steer. Jes cain't
be any cuttin' out o' the Union er nullifyin' federal laws neither.
That's what they're talkin' 'bout down thar. Jackson's plumb
center on that. Ef they git inter a war, I'm goin'. Now I ain't
President but ef I wus . . ." Williams paused. He ruffled up his
long red hair, stroked his beard and glanced sidewise at Lona.
"Wal, guess I've bit off more'n I kin chaw. Tomorrow I'm
goin' North."

Williams took Lona's hand. "Good-by, I'll be seein' ye agin."

"September '33, at the latest." How positive Ewing had
been. No letters had come for several months. He was well
when Antoine Leroux, the Taos scout, had seen him in the

124

spring, and he talked of returning to Taos then. "Mountain men rarely write. They just come back." That is what Ewing had said once when he begged Lona not to worry. "Anyway," she told herself, "this is his month. Today is the first of September. He is coming!"

Day by day, the month wore slowly away. Doubts besieged her. In spite of herself, her smiles faded quickly after greeting her guests. Problems of the gaming rooms irked her. Rarely did she deal monte throughout an evening. Often when she left the monte room she noticed concern in Pablita's black eyes but she hurried on with a sharp rustle of her full silk skirt. Both Pedro and Pablita had seen more than one lucky player look about in vain for Doña Lona and leave without her customary gay good night. They realized what this might mean. One or the other must warn her.

At twilight on the last day of the month, Lona entered the monte room and walked to a front window, her new black silk dress swishing. Her dark hair was parted and drawn closely over her fine forehead. At her neck shone a rosette of ribbon, fresh and red. She touched it. Young always liked red in her hair, she was thinking as she turned toward the players.

A newcomer from Louisiana was trying to arrange a game of poker. He was the handsome Creole from New Orleans who had lingered one evening not long ago and tried to make love to her. Had her sharp words taught him a lesson? The young man rose to his feet and bowed with elaborate ceremony. What a patrician, thought Lona, slender, black eyes, curly black hair. Spanish and French, too. She could have liked him well, had he not been such a fool at love-making.

"Poker? Is it new?" questioned Lona, trying to keep her tone impersonal.

"Fairly new, Señorita. In our country anyway. I've been told it's a grandson of the old *primero* of Spain. It has been played

125

for some years in Louisiana and on the Mississippi river steamers, I'm told. I learned the game in New Orleans."

Lona asked to watch the play. Refusing to be seated, she stood for several moments until she caught the main run of the game. Then she went on. In the monte room she took the cards to relieve the dealer. Her face brightened for, as usual, she felt the lure of the cards. Suddenly came the dull roll of the midnight bell on the Loma. She finished the game indifferently, bade her guests short good nights and hurried to her own sala.

By the candle-lighted desk, Lona reread Young's letters, the pitifully thin packet of them. September was gone. Ewing had not come. Would he return? Was another in his thoughts now? Men were fickle—far more so than women. She had met several men who attracted her. The Creole was one. She would never see him again for he was leaving in the morning. She might have forgiven the young monsieur—perhaps. Not one had touched her inner heart. That belonged to Ewing Young.

When dawn came, Lona was standing by her window. Daylight brought her face to face with her problem—life without Ewing and with a money chest in which her pesos were steadily diminishing. Pedro had chided her for not paying more attention to her business. It was only when the caravans came in that she made real money. She must make a plan for the future. Outside, the wind was playing with fallen yellow leaves from a cottonwood tree. Their edges were blackened. The wind quickened. Winter was at hand. Must she start on another trail!

For a year Lona drifted, postponing a decision. A few short letters had come from Young, one in which he deplored his inability to be in Taos during that September of '33. His messages of love were heart-warming but she noted that he never answered her question about his return. During that year her gambling salas lost their popularity. True, players still came, especially the Indians, but it became more and more evident to her that many men preferred to play at the new cantina on the village square or to loaf about the big stove, cold or hot, in the thriving Bent and St. Vrain store on the plaza. She saw more caravans now with bigger wagons and richer goods but the wagonmasters rarely left the center of town.

In October Antoine Leroux knocked at her door. "I come, Señorita Barcelona, from the West. Many months ago I saw Señor Young. He was in the best of health. Oh, yes. He'd come in from a trapping trip some time before but he told me he had had little luck. He's jolly whether he wins or loses, is Señor Young." He pulled a letter from his pouch. "I got sidetracked on my way back so this is late in reaching you. I'm sorry."

Lona extended her hand for the letter. It was worn and soiled. "Many thanks, Señor."

Breaking the seal as she walked along the portal, Lona tore open the letter and read eagerly.

Monterey, June 2, 1834

My darling Lona,

Your last letter of many months ago reached me here. I have read it until it is almost in tatters. Yes, my dear—September '33? I did not forget but I could not return.

I have tried to strike it rich out here but I seem to be just a jockey for the horses of the wind. Right now I'm joining a group of men with Hall Kelley as leader. We leave tomorrow for Oregon which Kelley thinks is a sort of Heaven. I sincerely hope I'll not find myself there "wedded to calamity."

Lona, I have reread "Romeo and Juliet." Do you remember the summer evenings when we read it together?

127

I still love you, Lona—my Juliet. But it is only fair that I release you from your promise to me. It may be that I'll never return to Taos. Certainly not without a fortune. Out here I've done everything from otter hunting to climbing for fur. But money? I've never had enough. Here's to good luck for you! I'll always remember my Taos sweetheart but I may be lost to her in those North woods.

I must look to my horses now. It is almost morning. We start early.

Love and farewell,
Ewing.

P.S. I've just looked over the play again, tonight.

> *"Night's candles are burnt out, and jocund day*
> *Stands tiptoe on the misty mountain tops.*
> *I must be gone and live, or stay and die."*

It fits my case, Lona. E.

For several moments, Lona sat stunned, dry eyed. But she was calm. She could not tell why. Perhaps it was because lately she had been waiting for release from this hideous uncertainty. Now she would forget love and try her fortune in Santa Fé. Business was poor. Everything was awry. Young would never come, she knew. "Troubles come in battalions," Ewing used to say. He was right. But through them there is always a path leading beyond. With youth and skill she would follow that trail and win. Lona drew a long breath and raised her head. She would not be hurt again. Walking rapidly across the patio, she entered the monte room where Pedro and Pablita were dusting.

"We must pack. We are going to Santa Fé."

XIII

A SHARP NOVEMBER WIND FRETTED THE CAN-
vases of the two *carretas* and stung the faces of the three riders
ahead. Against the yellow-pink of the foothills, Lona could
see the two square towers of the mission and the plain adobe
mass of the pueblo of Santa Clara. As they approached through
fields of sullen corn stalks breaking through drifting lines of
snow, Lona heard the sound of drums muffled by underground kiva walls.

"Pedro," she called, "I had forgotten that this is a gala day
for the Santa Clara Indians. We'll try our luck. Arrange my
booth just opposite the church."

As she rode through the main gateway to the plaza of the
pueblo, Lona knew that she was recognized. "Barcelona! Barcelona has come to our fiesta," the villagers shouted, "Doña Barcelona of Taos!"

With blankets flying, Indian men came on the run. Their
Mexican guests followed, lifting their sombreros. Squaws waddled forward in their clumsy buckskin boots, leaving their
tortillas to burn, eager to see this Señorita Barcelona so famous
in the North. A chief's wife invited her to the midday meal.
Others, seeing Pedro drag poles, brought out their finest rugs
and helped to arrange the booth.

Throughout the day Lona and Pedro kept monte cards flashing and coins clinking into the saddle bags. Now and then, a Mexican or an Indian would clear the boards. The sight of pesos cupped in his son's hands, drew an aged Indian to the booth. Lona noted his ragged suit of buckskin and his small pouch of money. He played with shaking hands, his eyes gleaming with youthful eagerness. Little by little, the man emptied his pouch, but he held his head high when he stumbled away. "His pride is like mine," thought Lona. Motioning to Pedro to take over the game, she strolled along in front of the other booths. Her eyes followed the old man. When he entered a door she was behind him.

"You lost your all, Señor?" Lona asked. "It is perhaps not always well to throw the last peso. Will you do me a favor? Lend me your bag a moment."

The old fellow's black eyes widened with amazement as he held out to Doña Lona his worn leather pouch. Silently he watched her refill it from the beautiful beaded bag which fell from her own belt. With a finger at her lips she warned, "Say no word," and went as quickly as she had come.

Next morning Lona neared Santa Fé, richer by several hundred pesos. In buoyant spirits, she galloped along through bad lands with their reddish sandstone columns. At a cross-road, she spied a horseman jogging along from the Tesuque pueblo down near the river. He was too tall for an Indian but he rode like one and seemed to be making haste to join her party. When he turned into the main trail, Lona saw the two ears of the man's cap and knew at once that the rider was Williams. She waved a hand in greeting.

"Hi! Ho! Beel friend! Here, after all these many months. Are you just bouncing in and out as usual? Where are you going?"

130

"Wal, I'm a blasted son of a coon ef it isn't Doña Lona!" exclaimed Bill. "Whar am I goin'? *Adelante, yo no soy cangrejo*— Forward, I'm no crab! Whar on airth air ye goin'?"

Lona's horse shied. She pulled in the reins and patted his neck. "I'm going to the moon. Want to go along? Can't you guess where this horse is headed? For Santa Fé. You once told me to go there if things went stale in Taos. Well, they did. A new cantina on the plaza and Bent's store were too much for me. Anyway I've been there long enough."

"Wal, I reckon that's not a bad idee. Gone beaver in luck thar, don't mean same'll happen in the next place."

"I hope not! Where have you been all this time?"

"Been in Californy. Got tired of the settlements finally and struck out for the Rockies and down hyar. Thought I'd take a look at Santy Fee and then make for Taos. Has Young got back?"

"No," said Lona.

"Reckon he won't, neither. Last I heerd, out West thar, wus that he wuz headin' fer Oregon. Nevah mind, gal, thar's bigger fish in the pond ef ye kin find a pond in this hyar dry kintry."

Lona looked away, "Eh, Beel, where did you get your fine horse? Steal it?"

"Naw, I nevah stole a hoss in all me life. You see I jes saw a rope layin' easy on the ground. I picked it up and the durn animul wus at t'other end of it."

"No! You old rascal!" laughed the girl as she watched Williams' solemn face, until his white teeth gleamed in a smile through his red beard.

"Wal, it's jes as I tole ye onct. Cain't seem ter keep from helpin' mesel' when I need a hoss. I left me ole nag back yonder. They kin fatten him up. I had ter be movin'."

When darkness set in, Williams suggested camping but Lona

131

shook her head. With Beel along, she wanted to push ahead and reach Santa Fé. The stars came out and made the trail visible. In the plaza lanterns swayed above men still at play under the portals. Riders and *carretas* dipped down the hill past the old *garita* where only the jailer's lamp made a dim light.

"Good place fer ye down thar beyond the old palace," said Williams reining in beside Lona. "I know the folks thar."

At a door in a long unbroken line of adobe homes, Williams dismounted and knocked. Soon the mistress of the place came to peer out, holding a candle high.

"It's jes Ole Bill. Ye know me," said Williams. "Got some friends hyar who need beds. I reckon ye kin take 'em in, even ef it is late."

"Sí, Señor," was all the woman said. Lona, Pablita and Pedro followed her candle. The drivers of the *carretas* knew the town and disappeared. Williams wandered back to the plaza to watch the gamblers. When their last game was ended he found a bench. Wrapping himself in a heavy blanket, he stretched his long legs. Like many who live much alone, he began talking to himself. "I'll be damned ef I kin see how she's goin' ter make out down hyar. Thar's so many gamblin' places now. But she's as purty as a pictur' still. It's too durn bad Rudolfo had ter git himsel' kilt. And Young? He'd nevah stayed put anyway. I reckon she'll ketch another soon. 'Pears like I cain't see nobody but Mary in her, 'cept fer her gamblin'. Wal, maybe her luck will behave." With that conclusion he fell asleep.

In the morning, Lona dressed hurriedly. She looked about at the house, the usual type, rooms and portal about an open space in which stood a well surrounded with cracked dry flower stalks. Only the south side was different. There rose

132

larger and higher walls with a few windows. She was looking at them when Pedro joined her.

"Those rooms are a store and warehouse. Beyond, to the West, is the pit for cock fights."

"Yes," she replied absently. "I wonder if this place is for sale? I wish I could own it. There are possibilities here, Pedro." She raised her voice slightly, for over the flat roofs came the sound of rattling carts and shrill cries of men driving burros in the narrow lane to the West. "I must hunt for rooms at once," she added and went indoors.

Later, throwing a heavy cape around her shoulders, Lona went to the plaza. Not much had changed here. The old palace, patched with new plaster, looked forlorn. So did the military chapel. More windows broke the walls of stores and homes facing the great rectangle. On the far corner, she saw the inn. It shone with clean white earth well applied. From the number of men talking near the wide front door, Lona saw that the place still had many customers.

"Wal, now, ye're up airly, ain't ye?" called Old Bill waving to Lona from the Southern portals.

"Yes, for I've a great deal to do today."

"Now, ye jes listen, gal," said Williams, holding up a long finger, "keep a wary eye out in this hyar place. The gamblers air on ter more tricks than up ter Taos. Ef you do, ye'll likely be makin' good afore long."

"A wary eye? Yes, I will. Don't worry. Are you staying long enough to see how my plans work out?"

"Me? An ole grizzly like me needs ter be nosin' out a camp fer the winter in the mountains. It's me fer makin' tracks. Must be gettin' plews a-plenty afore spring. Ef I stayed 'round hyar, I'd be growlin' afore long. I'm leavin' come mornin' agin. Now let me warn ye once more, Lona. You know the

133

old Spanish sayin'?" Bill struck his right forefinger on three fingers of his left hand, one at a time, narrowed his eyes and spoke slowly, " 'One hundred tailors, one hundred millers and one hundred weavers are three hundred thieves.' Now ye look out!" He took off his blanket cap, flapped it over his heart and bowed so low that his long red hair swung out toward Lona. "I'll be seein' ye agin some fine day."

Lona watched him out of sight then went on to *La Fonda*.

When she reached the office of the inn, she found little changed except for a new deer head or two against the wall, one directly over the high counter. Madam Pino came bustling in.

"Why, Lona! Lona Barcelona!" she exclaimed. "Bless you, child! You have come to Santa Fé? To stay?" Lona nodded. "What a woman you have grown to be! You are more than welcome, my dear. Do sit down. I have heard of your success in Taos, Lona." She folded her hands primly in her short lap and leaned forward eagerly waiting for the younger woman to speak.

"Yes, I had a degree of success there. It thrills me to be in Santa Fé again. There are more people now."

Madam Pino bobbed her head vigorously and Lona saw how gray she had become.

"Do you know of any rooms where I can begin?" Lona continued. "I mean to have the best gambling salas in all the capital, barring yours of course."

"Rooms? Let's see. Why, yes, there is a group just across the street. I imagine that you can rent them immediately, if you like. It is a good location. I'll be glad to have you there. We have more players than we can accommodate here. Our house has become literally the end of the trails, you know."

"Thanks. I'll see them. I'm glad you want me so near. Tell me of Madam Alarid?"

134

"She's well and just as bird-like as ever. 'A wee bird busy about much' you used to say. Señor Alarid has made good money trading. They live in fine style. Perhaps you knew that Marino lived with them for some time? He left for the South, last spring."

"I heard that he had gone. Why did he leave?"

"Truth to tell, Don Marino was thoroughly discouraged. He did find some ore but never enough to make a fortune. How he did search for his uncle Castro's mine! He studied those maps until I thought he must go crazy. But he finally gave up. When he left he said that he might stay in El Paso for a while and then go to Texas. Some big land grants have been made over there this past year but whether Marino received one, I do not know."

Lona rose to go. "I must call on Madam Alarid and look at the rooms across the street."

The place was suitable although not large enough, she thought. A few days of cleaning would suffice to make it ready. There could be no room for *canute* but this game never was as popular in Santa Fé, she remembered.

When Lona established herself across from *La Fonda*, curious men and women wandered in. For a time, the players were few and Lona began to wonder if she had made a grave mistake.

One morning when a belated caravan from the East arrived she walked to the wagons to see what had been brought. In one of them she found two tall mirrors. These she purchased at once. When the merchant delivered them and placed them with their marble topped walnut bases against her walls, she flushed with pleasure. The man eyed her with open admiration. "I'll be over after nightfall and try my luck. Am half froze for a good game of monte on something better than a buffalo robe."

With a full house that night, Lona felt that fortune smiled again for she knew that almost all the Americans would have to spend the winter in Santa Fé. She had guessed right. Luck was with her. For the first time she heard herself called "Madam Barcelona." Before another autumn she decided to buy the place on the corner of "Burro Alley," the house where she had stayed on the night of her return to the capital. To enlarge it she bought the adjoining high-walled store and warehouse with an entrance on San Francisco Street. She gloried in these big plans and hired a score of workmen to begin renovations at once.

The largest room on the South facing San Francisco Street soon had more windows and the smoothest mud floor in town. Huge candelabra were hung from the heavy beams of the ceiling and smaller ones installed between the pier glasses. Curtains of deep red hung at the front windows. Madam Barcelona herself placed between them three flags, Spanish, French and Mexican, which fell from their poles in stately folds.

A hallway divided the ball-room from the smaller rooms and led to the patio. Here Lona ordered rugs spread on the earthen floor. Her especial pride were the cozy salas for private parties and one for conferences. Lona made few changes in the living quarters on either side of the patio and in the North rooms which faced the soldiers' barracks. In these rooms, she set up all sorts of gambling devices.

Finally everything was ready for Lona's first great *baile*.

Madam Barcelona invited guests personally and sent cards to all the leading families of Santa Fé, even to those who still "bent backward." Perhaps they would come now that she was successful. Throwing her best black mantilla over her high comb and across her dark red silk dress, she went to the old palace to invite the new governor, Colonel Albino Pérez, and his retinue. When they promised to come she smiled triumphantly. She was riding the crest of fortune and it did not matter now whether Ewing Young knew or not. She could live without his love.

For her gown Lona chose heavy white satin. On the night of her opening ball, she felt well satisfied with the fall of the wide flounced skirt and the snugness of the bodice, trimmed with Brussels lace. On her feet were white satin slippers with red heels. She had always liked red heels. In the braids coiled about her head, were two strands of her mother's pearls. On her hands glittered diamonds, also her mother's. Like a scepter she carried a scarlet fan.

Among the early guests was the distinguished Señor Antonio Barreiro, who recently had been elected to the Mexican Congress.

"I am highly honored, Señor," said Madam Barcelona.

"Not so much as I," responded Señor Barreiro bowing over her hand. "May I wander about your delightful salas?"

"Indeed you may, but I'll gladly act as guide. This, you see, is my ball-room." She paused at the door of the great room where dancers were swinging and bowing to the music of guitars and violins.

"Well done, Madam Barcelona. There'll be many a *baile* here."

"Now this way along the hall. This room is for poker players, and this, for long whist. Now it's but a step to my conference room, Señor."

Lona led the way to the elaborately furnished small sala where already a group of leading statesmen of the capital were gathered. They bowed as Madam Barcelona and her guest entered. She walked directly to the center table covered with a rich tapestry. On it lay Señor Barreiro's own book, *Ojeada*

137

sobre Nuevo Mejico as well as copies of the political paper which he had been publishing during the summer. Señor Barreiro was flattered. "So you too are interested?"

"Yes," replied Lona. "And here you may talk politics to your heart's content. The door closes well."

With a low curtsy, Lona withdrew, "I'll send my man with wine and *cigarros,* Señores."

When Pedro had brought a decanter of fine sherry, Don Ramón Abreü carefully closed the door.

"We are all good friends and can speak without restraint here," he said at once and lifted the little volume from the table.

"Señor Barreiro, I have enjoyed your book and share your opinions. I glory in your daring to publish them."

"Thank you, Señor Abreü. If I may say so among friends," answered Barreiro, looking keenly about the room, "I fear the return of Manuel Armijo. He is a man to be reckoned with. Colonel Pérez does not know this country and may not last long as governor."

"Right again," said Abreü. "I see that Armijo is here to-night, dressed like a king—the dog! He's as ill-bred as a sheep-herder—he was one, you know—and has less conscience than a burro. He seems to have made something of an impression on Madam Barcelona."

"Doubtless," replied Barreiro. "While I am gone to Mexico, it will be well to watch her. She does not know his kind. Any-one can see that she is well-born. I hear she is the daughter of a Spanish grandee. I believe she is not as sophisticated as she would have us think."

"We'll remember," said Don Ramón, "but it is not I who would like to warn her."

The men talked on for half an hour, mainly about maneuvers to keep Armijo from winning the governorship again. Sud-

138

denly one of them said, *"Por Dios,* Señores, if we linger here much longer, someone will believe that we plan a conspiracy."

They dispersed as they left the room. The men who went directly to the ballroom, noticed at once that Manuel Armijo was whirling Madam Barcelona in the dance. She smiled as if she were happy and, to a degree, she was for she was proud of having, as a partner, a former governor. He was still powerful. She had not forgotten the Armijo she had known but tonight he seemed to be a different man. She needed his patronage.

Thoughts of another character were racing through Armijo's mind. Here was a charming young woman whom he would cultivate and use to his advantage. In such a place and business as this she would be in a position to learn much. He would teach her to listen. She should be his aide. Was she not a beauty? He needed her.

Armijo lingered after the guests had departed and asked Madam Barcelona for an interview. She preceded him into the conference room, leaving the door open and ordering Pedro to bring wine. Then she sat down to listen to the man. She would like to know him better, she thought.

"I shall do all in my power to see that you are not taxed as highly as the others, Madam Barcelona," began Armijo abruptly. "I am chief disbursing officer now, as you may know. My word also carries weight in regard to taxes. You have a splendid establishment and should succeed. I'll do all that I can to help you."

"Thank you, Governor," said Lona, noticing that the man squared his shoulders slightly when she mentioned his former honor.

"You can keep your tongue?"

"Of course. In my business, I must."

"Mark my word. I am coming to Santa Fé as governor

139

again. Colonel Pérez is no man for the place. I am making plans. I need your help. I wish very much that you would listen to the men who have been here tonight. They will come to play. It is a simple matter to learn their plans if they have a little more whisky. If they talk in their cups, why, I might as well know what they say. There'll be no harm in that." Armijo eyed the young woman for a moment, then went on, "If you will assist in learning about what is going on, I'll make you a power."

Madam Barcelona narrowed her eyes and looked sidewise at him. She lifted her cigarette. "You would have me be a spy?"

Arching his eyebrows, Armijo answered quickly, "Spy is a harsh word. Just tell me what you happen to hear. That is all." He raised his shoulders and put out his hands as much as to say, "You see that is not exactly spying."

When he stood up to go, Armijo asked as casually as his voice would allow, "Have you no room for a belated guest like me? My wife is not here. You know that I live in Alburquerque now."

"No, Señor, this is my home. The salas are for gambling only."

Armijo walked straight to the great front door. He must use diplomacy with this woman. She was no longer a girl. Then he turned, expecting to bow over her hand. Instead she was curtsying at a little distance from him.

"Ah, you play the grand lady with me? So? I will bring you fortune. You will help me, won't you?"

"Perhaps," replied Lona taking a step backward and making a curtsy again.

"I bid you good night," Armijo opened the door and swirled his great cape over his shoulder.

Lona did not sleep for hours that night. She lay thinking

about this man who had crossed her path again. She knew definitely that she could never like him. That he was a brute, she knew, stubborn and insufferably domineering, but he had power. Where did he get his power? Was his personality so compelling that men followed him willingly or did he hold their loyalty through fear? He had said that he would make her powerful. She would like that. She wished to be something far more in the community than the mistress of the finest gambling place in the whole Southwest. She could do much for herself but she might need help.

Love had failed Lona. She would forget Rudolfo, forget Young, forget love itself. Power was the thing! She would not be a spy but she would play Armijo's game. Her wits were as sharp as his.

XIV

FOR A FORTNIGHT, MANUEL ARMIJO CAME OF-
ten to Madam Barcelona's. He brought men who were politically
important but usually not of the better class, she noted. In turn,
they brought others. Lona understood. Señor Armijo was trying to convince her that he would make good his promise.
Money, plenty of it, made for power. He always managed to
have a quiet word with her, asking if she had heard anything
from the players. "The Abreüs, for instance?" Invariably she
answered that she had heard nothing of importance as yet.
"But you will in time," he would reply. "I'm counting on you."

Armijo was growing impatient at lack of information and
furiously eager to carry out his personal enterprise. He came
unaccompanied, late one evening, and whispered that he would
wait, he must see her alone. Lona watched him as he walked
on to the conference room. She saw his hand swing out in an
angry gesture as he passed Pedro who was already cleaning the
hall.

When she swished into the room, he grumbled, "Can I
never see you without that *peón's* being about? Tell him to
leave."

The tone of command grated on Lona's ears. She was tempted
to refuse but perhaps it was better to let the man have his way

in such a small matter. She knew that Pedro would remain within call. She stepped to the door, gave Pedro his orders and turned to face Armijo.

For a full moment there was a battle of eyes.

"We'll be alone tonight or I'll break his head," Armijo muttered. He closed the door noisily and felt for the key. It was not there. Armijo frowned and shoved a chair in front of the door. Then, blunt as usual, he walked directly to Lona and catching her hands, blurted out, "What have you heard? Nothing?" She shook her head. "Nothing! *Por Dios!* Again!" He frowned down at her and searched her eyes which gave back steel for steel. Then he laughed and touched her cheek.

"We need to work more closely. We should mean more to each other," he seized her so quickly that Lona was off guard. She could not free herself but she bent her head away.

"What? You do not want me?" Armijo's tone was meant to convey surprise and hurt. "Lona, you have called me for years. We can be happy together and accomplish much. I love you, girl." He bent his head against her neck. "I want you. But I want you willingly." Straightening up he smiled down on her. "You are a woman who can make her own choice."

Armijo's voice broke with a semblance of emotion, "Come!" he said and stepped away. This time he stretched out his arms toward her.

Free, Lona moved back. Her eyes held his steadily. "I understand," she answered slowly. "But I have no wish for a lover. We live in easy times, I know, but I resent your request." Walking to the far side of the table, she sat down and exclaimed, "Oh, let us talk."

"Talk!" Armijo sat down opposite her. He reached for her hand and kissed it violently. "No one with your lovely eyes can be cold," he thought, "but I can wait."

Armijo dropped her hand and bent forward. These were his

143

plans. He was slowly creating allegiance to himself in Alburquerque. When the time was ripe, he would have a small army
at his command. "I've told no one except you. You will not
speak of this?"

Lona shook her head, looked Armijo in the eyes and said
nothing.

"You would lose much if you did."

Again he denounced Governor Pérez. It was necessary that
he learn more of what men said about the governor, especially
what were their plans. He urged Lona to try this tack and
that to make men talk while they gambled.

"But men do not talk while they play. Not as a rule, you
know," said Lona. "I appreciate what you have done for my
place, Governor." On the strength of his rising pride, she continued, "I hope that we may continue to be friends." She almost
smiled at the idea of Armijo's being a real friend to anyone, especially to a woman.

"Oh, yes. Friends!" Armijo all but snarled and rose to go.
He would be lenient with the girl this time. She might give
him valuable information some day. Reminding her again
that he must know how men stood, Armijo bade her good
night.

Lona sighed. If she could always manage so well! Armijo
loved her. Bah! She was through with love. But *if* she ever
did love again the man would not be Manuel Armijo. That was
sure.

Lona herself was thoroughly interested in the news of the
capital. Men often told her of such matters as she might hear
from others but they did not speak freely about their own
opinions. She had been seen too often with Manuel Armijo. But
one afternoon a man who had been drinking too freely, burst
out with, "I hear that your friend Armijo is to lose his job,
Madam Barcelona."

"Is that true?" answered Lona, "and why . . ." Her question was cut short because a companion drew the man away on the pretext that he was late for a meeting at the palace.

So Armijo is to lose his position? That was the kind of news she could relay to him because he would soon learn of this himself. It would seem like real information. How furious he will be!

"Pedro!" called Lona. "Go search for Señor Armijo. He may be on the plaza. Tell him that I wish to see him at once. See to it that you speak privately with him."

Pedro had no difficulty in finding Armijo, who was standing under the portals of the square looking with closely drawn eyes at the palace across the way.

"Yes, I shall come immediately," he answered. "Now go on around *La Fonda* and return by another road, *hombre.*"

Armijo stood for several moments as if unconcerned. Others might have seen Pedro. Then he took a short route and before Pedro could possibly return was being received by Lona at her great door. He came in blustering, swinging his cane, looked cautiously around and went directly to the conference room. There Lona joined him.

"Señor, you asked me to listen. At last, I have something to tell you."

Armijo closed the door quickly.

"What news?" he whispered, his ears pricking up like a wolf's.

"Not long ago, a man told me that Governor Pérez is to relieve you of your office. Your predecessor is to be reappointed."

"Oh, he did?" snapped Armijo. "Did he say anything more? Who was the man?"

"No more. It was just one of the many who drift in here, Señor. His *compadre* took him away at once."

"But who? I like to know who gets such news before I do."

Lona shook her head although she remembered well enough. She would tell him only as much as she wished.

"You remember. Who was it? I want names. I have told you that often enough." Armijo caught Lona by her shoulders and looked into her eyes. "It may be that Pérez is going to replace me. At present, I'll be unable to do anything about it but, by God, I'll not forget such an insult. The day is coming when I, not that fool Pérez, will be in the saddle. You do not tell me the man's name. I'll guess that it was Don Ramón Abreü?"

Lona drew in her lips but she could not control the tell-tale flush which spread over her face.

"In my business, I must not tell names, Señor. You surely must realize that."

"I realize nothing when you are listening for me," Armijo replied gruffly. "I see that I guessed right. Don't play with me, my girl." He stepped away from Lona keeping his blue eyes steadily on hers. With a curt bow, he strode out of the room.

During the next few days, Governor Pérez did remove Manuel Armijo and he left the capital in high dudgeon. But he kept his tongue carefully under control.

Lona sighed a great sigh of relief. Armijo had left Santa Fé without a word to her and was safely some sixty miles away in Alburquerque. Pedro told her that men said he was undoubtedly "pouting and plotting." She knew this was true and she could guess the sort of plotting he was doing but she said nothing.

Within ten days, Armijo was at Madam Barcelona's door and again late at night.

"This time, may we go to your own room?" asked Armijo.

"No, the conference room serves well," answered Lona positively.

146

Once more there was a battle of eyes. Armijo glared but Lona smiled. She would be mistress in her own home.

"See here, Lona. What's the use of being so stubborn?" Armijo said as soon as the two were alone. "I've been good to you. I've been building up your business and you know it. I love you, girl. Let's go to your own sala." His voice ran the gamut from anger to persuasion. He had put his arms about Lona but hesitated at a kiss.

Lona stepped away. All the pride of her ancestors seemed to rise in her and the man, unaccustomed to dignity of spirit, was momentarily confused.

"It is news that you want?"

"Yes. News? What is it?" He seated himself by the table. Once more she had sifted what she had heard and would tell him what he could learn within the hour if he wandered about the plaza.

"You know, of course, of the Governor's plans?" Lona began.

"I have heard something."

"He means to tax all the people. There is much grumbling at this high-handed attitude."

"Has the news become so generally known as all that? I thought Pérez would either act at once or alter his plans before the people are aroused against him. But then what do the people amount to anyway? A governor should act independently. But this Pérez? He should not dare. The people should rise," said Armijo, contradicting himself.

"Has it become known? Why, there's not a girl of fifteen in town who has not talked about this, not to mention her father. As a matter of fact, I myself think that Governor Pérez's plan for schools is excellent. Taxes should be levied for that."

"Taxes for schools. *Dios!* Why bother? The rich can see to

147

it that their boys have enough schooling. The girls do not need much. They should learn from their mothers how to run a house and obey their husbands. As for the poor? What difference does it matter whether they ever see the inside of a school."

Lona's eyes flamed.

"The poor need schools as much as the rich. Girls need education as much as boys, if not more so. Padre Martínez was awake to that in Taos. He teaches them both. The day is coming when women will no longer be slaves to men. They need to have their own money too."

"Don't be silly, Lona. I always give my wife money when she asks for it. As for Padre Martínez? He's crazy."

" 'Money when she asks for it!' " Lona repeated. "What humiliation when she's earning it keeping your home." Glancing out the door which had swung open, she shook her head. How glad she was that she did not have to ask for money.

"You've been listening to some of these fool Americans. I know about American women. But, even if their men do let them have ideas of their own, such conduct here would be absurd."

Again Lona's eyes flashed but she held her peace.

"Let's talk of something else," she said finally.

"Have you heard what men have told Pedro on the plaza? He tells me that he is to be taxed for living with his little wife, Pablita."

"Ho, ho! That *is* news. I think that I have heard everything but this. That is news. My men are clever," he went on without explaining. He pounded a clenched fist in the palm of his other hand. His mind did not readily work out new plans but built rapidly when given a hint.

"What are you going to do?" queried Lona, sensing intuitively that she may have done mischief. Yet, she thought, I need not blame myself, for Armijo will hear of this also and right soon.

Armijo rose. "Never you mind," he whispered. "You keep your ears to the very dust, Lona. What I do is my own affair."

When he turned to bid Lona good-night, he opened his arms and said, "One kiss?"

"No."

"No. Oh, well. You are a woman like all the others."

Lona's throat tightened. She shook her head.

"So?" His heavy chin moved forward. "Well, there are others. You shall pay for such obstinacy." Catching up his cape and cane, he hurried down the hallway and slammed the door.

Lona lingered in the semi-darkness. "A man like that will make me pay. He will come late. Men will lift their eyebrows and wag gossipy tongues. Mexicans and Americans too. They will call me Armijo's mistress. The lie will get afoot and, Heaven knows how long it will follow me. But, so help me, God, it will always be a lie. I despise the man."

Manuel Armijo walked about the plaza. A gambler under the first swinging lantern called out, "Eh, Señor Armijo. Have you heard the latest?"

Leaning against a post, Armijo listened, his wide black hat far over his eyes. The man embellished the rumor. When he had finished, Armijo said simply, "Is that so?" and went on. He had an errand. Four errands in fact. He turned the corner and a moment later raised his cane.

One knock. Two short knocks. He waited. The door was opened by a cautious hand. Striding quickly to a rear room, Armijo found three of his henchmen eating a midnight meal. He ordered the serving women to be gone.

"Listen to me, and tell Lorenzo Baca what I have to say. You," he commanded, "go West. You, East. You, South.

Lorenzo Baca, North to Taos. Drink with men at cantinas and tell them that Governor Pérez intends to tax every woman for the chickens she has, no matter how few. Tell the men they are to be taxed for living with their wives. You get that? Here is money. Get your horses and be off before morning."

Armijo never tarried with his men. On a side street he found his team and harnessed them to a light wagon. When he had cleared the outskirts, he swung Southwest. Such false tales—for he knew well that no governor could be such a consummate fool as to mean what the rumor had said—such false tales—would start a veritable conflagration, "Pérez, ha!" he said aloud for the desert has no ears, "Pérez will do well if he keeps his head on his shoulders."

For many months, Lona saw Manuel Armijo rarely. To annoy her, he continued his practice of coming late and remaining until after the players had gone home. Both knew his conduct would add weight to the rumor that she had become his mistress. She avoided meeting him when she could, but when she could not, the news she gave him remained of the same type, only such as he would hear shortly himself. He did not speak of love again.

Lona rebelled when she heard her name linked with such an ill-bred man as Armijo but she could think of no way to check the falsehood. Madam Pino and Madam Alarid urged her to hold her tongue. "Vigorous denial revives belief," they said.

Some days later, in the early afternoon, Lona saw Pedro open the front door with a wide swing. He made an especially gracious bow as he did always when someone of importance arrived. In came Doctor David Waldo. Almost running to the hallway, Lona greeted him. Taos men did not come to Santa Fé often and here was the doctor of whom she was genuinely fond. She plied him with questions.

"Well, the little town seems to be waking up a bit," he told her. "More traders are coming in. Business is good. Mountain men do not come quite as often. They say that beaver is done for. Silk hats are in style. Most of the trappers go much farther North now."

"Have you seen Williams?"

"Yes, the old rascal was in for a night some time ago. He didn't start a store." The doctor laughed with Lona. "He grows more peculiar all the time. He has a notion in his head at present, that if he ever has a dream that a bear has struck him with his paw, he'll be dead *pronto*. I do my best to shake him out of such ideas but one might as well try to move the Rockies."

"Yes, he does grow more and more queer, every year. Did he drink a good deal and start a fight or two?"

"I suppose he did. But we all like him just as you do. There's something compelling about him."

"Are there any newcomers?"

"There are always a few. Lately a man by the name of Lorenzo Baca has been wandering around stirring up trouble. I've seen him in the cantinas and under the portals and heard of him in the small villages. He says he lives here. Who is he, I wonder?" Lona shook her head. "He's talking a lot of nonsense about the Governor's plan to tax women for the fowls they may have and men for living with their wives. A number of people have come to me to ask whether such things could be. I thought I'd come down and see whether there's any truth at all in these rumors."

"Colonel Pérez rarely comes here. I've heard men say that Señor Pérez is no fool. I feel sure he intends to do no such rank injustice, Doctor. He must levy taxes if his plans for the betterment of New Mexico are to work. That's certain. People are not used to taxes, especially the poor."

"Yes, I know. I asked this fellow Baca who sent him to Taos

but he declared that he had come because he thought the North country should know what's going on. Since I have been here, I have met a man from out Pecos-way and one from the South. They tell me strangers have been in their towns, telling the same sort of tale. There's some one person back of all this. I can not imagine who it could be."

Lona flushed, for she could guess.

"I wish I could get at the bottom of this matter," continued the doctor. "But I must be going. I'll drop in for a game or two about eight. Now I must buy a supply of medicines and search for any new books that may have come to town."

For the evening Lona chose a yellow silk gown. She lifted a package from the lower drawer of her dressing table. Slowly she unwrapped an old fan, as fresh as it was when she had put it away so long ago. It was of turquoise blue. Rudolfo always liked it. Why keep it unused? She would carry it sometimes. Perhaps the doctor would like it.

Promptly at eight, Doctor Waldo walked in. He smiled at Lona with her blue satin fan.

"Doña Lona does not lose her beauty. We all enjoy it, girl," he said. "I thought I'd have a game of poker and then slip away and get a round night's sleep."

Lona led the doctor to the poker room and presented him to the players. She noticed a small box on the table beside a man of whom she had been suspicious for some time. He was a rough-looking dark American with a heavy scowl. She saw the pile of pesos growing beside the man. The doctor should not lose any large amount of money in her place. Motioning to Pedro, she stood near the door. Suddenly her quick eye caught the American drawing a card from his sleeve. In a flash Lona reached the table. Her hand clutched his box. The man looked up in astonishment.

152

"I saw this man draw from his sleeve, gentlemen. An old trick, not deftly done. I will not have that sort of thing here. Leave your pesos. Don't you dare touch one."

The man was too startled to speak. He rose quickly and gave back Lona's stare.

"Pedro," she called. "Get this man out of here at once."

"I thought a few too many pesos were going his way," grumbled one player. Another said, "I sensed something wrong but I could not catch the fellow in trickery."

"I'll go without any servant showing me out," muttered the American. "I know the way."

"Now the game can go on, Doctor. These others are gentlemen, I know," said Lona and smiled as she left.

When Doctor Waldo rose to go Lona joined him. They walked to the great entrance facing San Francisco Street. Lona partially closed the door behind her.

In a low voice, Doctor Waldo said, "I've been scouting for opinions since I saw you this afternoon. There are a good many guesses going the rounds. Not a few men think a friend of yours is behind this Baca business. Be wary of Manuel Armijo, Doña Lona."

"He may be, Doctor. I do not know for certain. But pray, do not think he is really a friend of mine. I must be gracious to all who come here. But he? He has been most troublesome since he became angry with me one night. When he comes here, he insists on arriving late and staying on. I say nothing but to you, my good friend. Armijo means worse than nothing to me. He is no lover of mine, nor has he ever been."

XV

"PEDRO, DON'T SWEEP THAT DUST TOWARD ME. That's bad luck!" said Pablita waving it away with her hand. She looked across the small garden waking to spring growth. "Doña Lona's door is open too. Don't you see?"

He stopped sweeping and leaned on his broom. "Didn't see you, little one." He pulled out horn-like bunches of his black hair, and head foremost dashed at Pablita. "Bad luck? Yes, and the Texians'll get you if you don't watch out!"

Pablita caught his hair and raised his face for a resounding kiss. "Now what about the Texians?"

"Some horsemen got in today. The Texians are claiming land clear to the Río. If that's true they'll come and take us somehow."

Lona came out of her sala and asked almost breathlessly, "What did you hear, Pedro?"

"Seems General Santa Anna took the Álamo, whatever that is. Down in San Antonio."

"I know. An old stone mission. It was turned into a fort, no doubt. What else?"

"Fellow said General Santa Anna's letting his men kill all the defenders. Said the Texians had declared for independence

154

from Mexico. I'm not afraid of Texians. They're a long way off, Doña Lona. Guess I'll have time to get the garden swept up before they come."

"Yes, and probably a moment or two to spare," said Lona smiling. She returned to her account book and flicked the quill against her hand. Pedro was right. There was plenty of time. Armijo would do something to save Santa Fé from the Texians. There was nothing to fear. How the interwoven pattern of events did build itself, she thought, events from the Mississippi River to the Pacific, from the northern Rockies to the plains of Mexico! One could see it plainly in her rooms. She was proud that in no other place in Santa Fé were affairs of this part of the world more thoroughly discussed. She did not hear all the news. Often small groups of men gathered around a fireplace and did not invite her to join them. Long since, she had discovered that they kept from her gruesome details of horrors on the trails. But she was abreast of her time. Many a man of the trail, as he sat by the campfire, thought how he would embellish his news for Madam Barcelona of Santa Fé.

On an evening in May of 1836, a tall, angular fellow walked into Madam Barcelona's establishment. He introduced himself as George Brown of Texas.

"Of Texas?" exclaimed Madam Barcelona.

"Yes, and I wouldn't be in Santa Fé if urgent business had not brought me here."

"You have real news? First-hand knowledge?"

"Reckon I have. I've been down there close to Sam Houston all the time."

"News of Texas means much to all of us." Madam Barcelona lifted a hand to halt the games. "Here's a man who was there! In Texas. Let's hear him."

The men and women left their tables and crowded about George Brown.

"From Texas, eh? Do the Texians claim all the land to the Río Grande?" queried one man.

"I don't know about that but I'm from Texas. Was in the thick of the fightin'. Close to Sam Houston all the time. Have you all heard of the battle of San Jacinto?"

"No, not San Jacinto. Shoot the news," shouted an American against the wall.

George Brown sat on a tabletop and lighted a cigarette.

"I'll tell you as far as I myself know. I happened to be in Washington-on-the-Brazos when the convention was meeting in March. There was a norther on and the men had no place to go except to a chilly shed. There are not many people in Washington, you know, and when they heard that the men had declared the independence of Texas, they had a bad case of 'Let's get out' fever, I'm tellin' you. They knew guns were thunderin' at the Álamo. They were plumb skeered. Even the men down at the shed were for leavin' but Sam Houston was there and he told the convention to keep on workin'. He'd go to the relief of the Álamo, he said. I wanted to go too. I borrowed a suit of clothes. The General had no uniform. All he had were his buckskin, a Cherokee coat and a big hat with a feather, and Mexican spurs on his boots. I was one of three volunteers to ride out with him and his aide, George Hockley. Five of us against Santa Anna's army. But we knew that there were some soldiers down at Gonzales more'n a hundred miles away.

"When we got out on the prairie Houston halted us and rode on alone. He got off his horse and put his ear to the ground, just like an Injun. When he came back, he was shakin' his head. He said that he feared the worst at the Álamo. The firin' had ceased. 'Course, we heard what had happened soon after we reached Gonzales."

"Were all the men killed?" interrupted a man with a Southern drawl.

"Yes, Sir. All of them. Way over a hundred and fifty."

"There, at Gonzales, the General just kept on drillin' the men he had. We had two cannon and another bein' fixed at a blacksmith shop. But we didn't have horses."

"*Dios!* no *caballos!*" exclaimed a Spaniard unheeded.

"Late one pitchy night he sank the cannon in the river, piled all the ammunition on one wagon with four oxen hitched to it. Then he gave the command to retreat. We all had to hoof it. Women and children were bringin' up the rear in baggage wagons. Houston wouldn't leave 'em behind. We grumbled and kept on retreatin' when we wanted to fight! It began to rain and how we did wallow along! God, how it did rain!

"How in that God-forsaken, rain-soaked country Houston himself ever kept goin', I can't make out. He didn't sleep nights. I know 'cause I was near him all the time. Come mornin' he'd kick off his boots and snooze for a spell. We slopped along, most of us cussin'. In spite of the Devil, Houston is the kind of a man who keeps men followin'."

"Where was Santa Anna, Señor Brown?" asked Madam Barcelona.

"Comin' after us. Santa Anna was makin' for Lynch's Ferry. So were we, only we didn't know it then. About that time, the 'Twin Sisters' joined us."

"Eh, twin sisters? We don't want to hear about womenfolks. When did Santa Anna ketch up?"

"Hold on, Sir. The 'Twin Sisters' were iron six-pounders, man."

"Whar did they come from? Grow out of the ground?"

"From some friends back in Cincinnati, so Houston told me. Heaven knows we needed 'em. The blacksmith cut up rusty horseshoes for ammunition."

"Hay, laddie, be after the foightin'," called a Scotchman, grabbing his pipe from his mouth and pounding the ashes out with

157

a bang.

"Yes, the 'foightin',' " smiled Brown. "Well, we got in sight of Lynch's Ferry. Santa Anna couldn't make it. We were just a few miles nearer. But he kept a-comin'. Houston marched us up under some big oaks with lots of moss hangin' down. In front of us was the prairie. Santa Anna just had to come that way. And that's the way the 'Sisters' were pointin'. We'd been beat out of breakfast to get to Lynch's Ferry but this time we had steaks sizzling when in rode some scouts with word that Santa Anna was just beyond the rise. Houston ordered us to the edge of the wood. We ached to go forward, but the General rode back and forth on a white stallion and held our line. Then . Santa Anna's one gun was rolled into a position not more'n three hundred yards beyond us in a clump of trees.

"One of our 'Sisters' banged. The shot struck the gun carriage. A captain fell. Another ker-ash!" Brown's hand came down with a bang on the table. "The Mexican gun answered but its shot tore overhead. Skirmishers opened up. We had to hold our fire though. The 'Sisters' blasted away. Then the Mexicans backed down the slope and quit. Houston let Sidney Sherman and some men try to capture that gun but they didn't get it. Nevertheless, Sherman was our hero for the moment for he and the spy, Deaf Smith, managed to capture a ferry-boat with some Mexican flour. We had fine baked dough on sticks that night."

Brown paused and lighted another cigarette. His listeners were bent forward. One called, "Get along, man, or we'll attack."

"All of a sudden, in the middle of the next afternoon, Houston gave the order to form. At four, he raised his sword. A fife and drum struck up 'Come to the Bower.' Well, we were comin'. 'Hold your fire!' was our command. We crept through the tall grass toward a Mexican barricade of pack-saddles and

158

the like. The enemy began firin'. But not until we were within about twenty yards of them, did Houston raise his hat. Over we went with the 'Sisters' crackin' their best. Our guns poppin'. Our knives ready. Then came the cry, 'Remember the Álamo!' Good Lord! I can hear that yet. And the screams from the Mexicans, *'Me no Álamo! Me no Álamo!'*

"That," said Brown, "was the battle of San Jacinto."

No one spoke for a full minute.

"How many men did Houston have?" came from somewhere in the room.

" 'Round eight hundred, I reckon, Sir. The Mexicans had several thousand, I think. You see, we surprized them. Some were cookin'; some bringin' in wood; some asleep. Arms were stacked. The retreat was a rout proper.

"At the end of the battle—it didn't last but about twenty minutes—Houston was ridin' on his third horse. We didn't know for some time that he'd been struck and his right leg shattered."

"So Santa Anna escaped, did he?" questioned Madam Barcelona.

"Wait now. Say, I wish you all could know Joel Robison. He's a big-eyed chap a little younger'n me. He and four others scouted for prisoners. Toward evening, Joel came in with a Mexican mounted behind him. He was a little fellow. He had on a blue smock and red felt slippers. Some uniform! How we laughed. Joel was just about to turn him in when, by Heaven, the caps of our prisoners came off and the cry went up, *'El Presidente!'*

"And there he was—Santa Anna himself, the President of Mexico! I'll never forget Joel. He looked like a frightened owl. Everybody laughed except Santa Anna. He straightened up with as much dignity as he could have in a blue smock and red slippers. It was some dignity at that. That's what we all thought when he asked to be conducted to General Houston. He walked away as if he had on his dress uniform. When that smock flapped in the wind we had to laugh but we didn't laugh as loud.

"There they were. Sam Houston in his Injun trappin's propped up against a tree. Santa Anna standin' in that ridiculous garb. If it hadn't been so damn serious, we'd have laughed out loud. Well, it didn't take long for Santa Anna to write out orders for all Mexicans to skedaddle out of Texas. Deaf Smith took the papers out. Now, the Mexican army is all gone. If something else doesn't bob up, Texas is free."

"Will the Texians get the land clear to the Río Grande?" again someone asked.

"I don't know about that, Sir. All I know is that Texas is free!"

Brown stood up and waved his hat.

"That's quite a story, Señor Brown," said Madam Barcelona. Santa Anna and Sam Houston! She paused and stared blankly over the crowd. Her onetime hero and Young's had met. And Santa Anna was down! She was silent for a few seconds, then lifted her hand. "Do you wish to start the games once more?"

But games were no longer interesting. Players crowded about the young man and plied him with questions. Some of them followed when Madam Barcelona led him away to talk in the gaming rooms on the North side of her patio where, throughout the evening, men came from the street, from the barracks or from their homes. Word that the young fellow who was there had flown over Santa Fé.

Such important news brought more men to Madam Barcelona's salas. One night, not long after, a player told her, "It's true. All this land East of the Río Grande actually lies within the boundaries of Texas! I wonder when they'll be coming to annex Santa Fé."

XVI

FOR MANY MONTHS RUMORS AND COUNTER-
rumors shook the capital. Lona's patrons grew reckless, played
for higher stakes. At *La Fonda,* Lona found Madam Pino always on an even keel, but little fluttery Madam Alarid was different. She assured Lona that there was surely trouble of some
kind ahead.

"I know you don't believe in most signs, Lona dear," she said
shyly, "but, the other day, I saw a black cat run right in front of
Governor Pérez. He paid no attention and went on. I wonder if
he knows that some of the men who play at being friends of his,
actually sneer at him behind his back. I'm sure there is danger
of the evil eye now-a-days. I do wish you'd wear your coral
necklace. I wear mine."

"Well, we'll hope for the best," Lona patted her friend's hand.
Once more in her room, she took from her jewel chest, the
string of coral Madam Alarid had given her years before and
clasped it about her neck. "I don't believe it will help but it
won't hurt to wear it," she thought and smiled at her own re-
flection in a mirror. "Anyway it doesn't show."

Rumors of revolution were so thick in July of '37, that they
almost achieved the status of fact in Lona's mind. She was

thinking of them one midnight when she stepped down into her patio after her patrons had gone.

"Howdy, Lona!"

The light of a lantern above the door fell on Bill Williams. He was examining something which sparkled, polishing its surface. "Beel! Beel friend, where did you come from?"

"Oh, this time, I slid down the rainbow. See hyar?" Bill said, coming to her door. "Old Fetcham's got a new pup. Glue yer eyes on this. A revolvin' cylinder. See? It's a six-shootin' pistol. The likes ain't been out long. Traded plenty of plews fer it up North. The feller said they're usin' 'em in the army down in Florida. Look. Load. Shoot six times without reloadin! I cain't git ovah it."

Lona took the six-shooter and looked at it carefully. "How Ewing would have liked it, Beel," she said. "I'd like to have one, some day. Before long at that. Affairs are in a bad shape here. I'm glad you've come, Beel. Where have you been lately?"

"So I've heerd. Oh, I've been livin' with the Utes. Got a squaw up thar. They made me a member of the tribe. Hell-bent on fightin', they air, more'n the Osages. Purty good folks at that. Left 'em ter trap fer a spell out in the Apache kintry and when I knowed the floods wus comin', I tuk ter the mountains agin. Met a trapper up thar. He tole me things wus hummin' right smart down hyar and there might be trouble. So I ca'culated it wus time I dragged me ole carcass down to Santy Fee. Fur's no good this time o' year. Then I allus tole ye I'd stand by ef thar wus any trouble and I could git hyar. Kinda think I'll hang 'round. Don't like what I've heerd 'round these parts."

Lona began to tell Bill what she knew and what she feared. She mentioned Manuel Armijo.

"Armijo? Yeah. He's mixed up in this trouble, I gather. He's a hissin' snake. Worse'n Injuns. More undah-handed. I heerd

162

he wus a friend o' your'n—lover, maybe?" Bill glanced side-wise at her and lifted his eyebrows.

"Men would say that. He's no lover of mine. Honest, Beel. The fact is I've met no man who touches me, since I came to Santa Fé. I'm through with love."

Bill smiled slightly. "Um, through with love, eh? You! Reckon nobody evah says a word 'bout lovin' ye. No!"

"That's different, Beel. Of course, men flirt with me. Some-times they think they're in love. But I give them back the spar-kle and laugh them down. Love? *Santa María!* Above them all, not Armijo. Of course, I have to treat him decently in my salas. Just between us, Beel, he wanted me to be a spy for him."

"Spy, eh? Bet you didn't do it."

"No, Beel, nothing but what he'd soon learn himself ever passed my lips."

"Ye nevah spoke with a forked tongue that I knowed of, Lona. I've been achin' ter know the truth."

Bill drew out his six-shooter and looked it over again.

"Kinda wish I could draw a bead on that damn rascal. I've knowed what he wus fer yeahs on end. I say, gal, kinda think it's time I wus askin' ye somethin' else."

"Fire away, Beel."

The mountain man patted his beard. His questioning gray eyes caught hers, then he looked away.

" 'T ain't nevah been any o' my business ter meddle with ye and yer choice of friends, has it, gal?"

"Never."

"Nevah have, but I reckon it's up ter me now ter give ye a pointer." He met her eyes squarely. "Have ye evah really studied Armijo's face?"

"Yes, I have. His eyes always have puzzled me for some rea-son. I never knew why."

163

"Didn't ye evah see 'em afore ye got to Santy Fee, the fust time?"

"I never even thought of that. I wonder?"

"Nevah saw 'em afore? Remember Chihuahua?"

"Beel! Was that man Manuel Armijo? Saints above! Beel, you don't mean that?"

"Yeah, I do. He wus the feller."

"But, Beel, that man had a beard; was dark."

"I know. He wusn't white-livered as he is now. But beard er no, the man was Armijo. I kinda thought ye didn't know the man. Didn't tell ye 'bout him 'cause I didn't want ter meddle. But now ye must be keerful. Shy off him ef ye kin. Kinda build a wall 'round yesel', even ef ye do have ter meet him in those salas of your'n. And mind ye, don't let a hole git in the wall neithah. Remember that ole sayin' from Spain?

'When a draught gets at ye through a hole,
   Go make yer will and pray fer yer soul.' "

Lona trembled. "He's capable of anything. Beel," she continued slowly. "Somehow, I feel that I'll have revenge on him, some day."

"Wouldn't be surprised. But I'd advise ye ter hold yer tongue until ye're sure he's leavin' fer somewhar and ain't comin' back, maybe. Men like him that think they're so damn smart git into a jam sometimes and walk right into a trap. I perdick he will."

" 'When he's goin' somewhar and ain't comin' back,' " quoted Lona staring into space. "I'll remember, Beel."

"O.K. Ye got me straight. I'll shuffle me shanks along. Be droppin' in now and agin. I'm fer visitin' gamblin' dens in this hyar town sich as ye've nevah seen. It's thar a feller gits the feel of a place. Unless I'm dogged mistaken, a fever's risin' in this kintry and, this time, gold ain't got nothin' ter do with it. Night."

164

Bill swayed along the portal and through the North rooms. On the street, he muttered to himself, "Bill, ye ole coon. Ye nevah said a word 'bout the gal's success and her fine place. Ye ain't got no perliteness left in ye."

Two nights later, Lona again found Williams under the lantern. He was striding back and forth. The fringe of his trousers and sleeves flapped raggedly. His six-shooter was at his belt. His rifle and wide black hat lay on the bench.

This time his greeting was brief.

"Messenger got through tonight, his hoss all a-lather, Lona." Williams spoke more rapidly than was his wont. "Trouble's more'n jes brewin'. It's b'ilin'. Seems Don Ramón arrested an alcalde up ter La Can-ya-da. Don't know what fer, 'cept it wus 'bout money somehow. The folks demanded his release. They're rarin' ter fight. Men and Injuns air on the way from all ovah the North. They're yellin', 'Down with Pérez! Down with taxes!' Hit a man's pocket book and ye got somethin' doin' right now. Seems Santa Cruz de la Cañada's the place the men air headin' fer."

"Will there be a real revolution? Will the mob swoop down on Santa Fé?"

"Shu-ah as shootin'. Ain't nothin' ter hold 'em back. Jes wanted ye ter know. Now I've got ter keep me ears donkey-wise. I'll trot along. I'm sleepin' hyar somewhar from now on. Don't git ter worryin'. Listen ter Ole Bill." Williams shook a long finger at Lona and looked intently into her eyes. "No gittin' up on the roof this time ter see the fight ef thar is one in the plaza. Now remember. Them's orders from the big boss, General Bill Williams."

The trapper-general was gone when Lona stepped into her patio the next morning. The babel of rumbling carts and cracking rifles came to her over the roofs. Men were testing guns in

165

Burro Alley. A faint smell of burnt powder filled the air. A spent bullet spattered dust near her feet. She gripped the locket under her red dress and stood wondering. Strangely enough she was not afraid.

Pedro called to her and she went rapidly to the North rooms.

A man had hurried in to tell Madam Barcelona what Williams had already told her. "The Governor's calling men to join the soldiers. They aren't coming in as fast as they should. I wouldn't be in his boots for a million pesos." He was interrupted by an excited Frenchman who asked from the door if Madam Barcelona had a gun? Ammunition? "Yes, but not many cartouches," replied Lona. A few minutes later he returned. "Too beeg," he said when Lona produced her small Spanish gun. Again he rushed out and in again. "Here's the right size, I think. Let's see." He tested the bullets for the muzzle. "Keep indoors, Madam Barcelona," he urged when he handed back her gun. "You have many friends, Madam, and they do not want you to get hurt. The rebels are coming. We haven't enough men to hold the city." Everybody in the room stood spell-bound. Finally Lona spoke, "If you please, gentlemen, find your own homes."

At sundown, Lona sat on the portal. In her hands was her locket, her luck-piece. She listened. Not a sound. Her silk dress rustled. She jumped nervously and then laughed at herself, startled by her own skirt.

A footstep on the flagstones. Lona turned astonished to see Williams leading his horse into the patio.

" 'Scuse this hoss, Lona, but I had ter bring him in through the room. Too many men a-lookin' fer a hoss. Jes came to tell ye I'm jinin' the Governor." Bill yanked his pipe from his mouth and sat down.

"Evah have a talk with somebody who ain't thar?"

Lona smiled. "Yes, I have. I didn't know anybody else ever did."

166

"Wal, I've been talkin' ter Andy Jackson, that ole hero o' mine, and he seemed to say, 'Ole Bill, stick by the gov'ment. Stand by the Gov'nor.' So says I, 'Ye're right.' Now I'm leavin'. I ca'culate thar won't be any danger fer a spell. Ef thar is, I'll come a-whoopin'. Pedro's promised me he'll stay right hyar. Got plenty of grub handy? Yer gun?"

"I'm ready," answered Lona.

"I'll bet me six-shooter Armijo's the big un behind all this. And I don't bet me gun easy-like. Now ef it comes ter a battle, the damn rebels'll nevah make this ole hide ef mine go undah. Don't ye worry. Good-by Lona."

"Good-by and good luck. Do be careful, Beel." Lona walked with him and his horse through a North room to the street.

During the next two days while the Governor and his men were gone, many a manservant knocked at Lona's door. From Madam Pino, from Madam Alarid, from various patrons all over the city came the same urgent request that she join them in their homes for greater safety. But to all, she sent her thanks and word that she was safe. Meanwhile the silence over the city was almost unbearable. Lona would have welcomed a scream or a sharp snap of rifles but none came.

Night once more. And Williams was leading his horse into the patio. He barely nodded to Lona but called Pedro.

"Come with me," he said curtly. "We must git some hay and oats in hyar. Back soon, Lona."

In a few minutes both men returned under heavy loads. They were out twice more before Williams declared there was enough for his horse.

"Now fer the news, Lona, gal," he said as he walked to the bench near her door. Pedro and Pablita, who were carrying tapers to light the lanterns, listened.

"We marched out to Pojoaque and inter the Cañada kintry.

Did a bit of shootin'. But, by the great carcague, ef most of the Gov'nor's men didn't desert to the rebels by mornin'. Nevah saw the likes. Couldn't believe me eyes. Want more'n about twenty-five men who galloped like the Devil himself wus aftah 'em toward Santy Fee, hopin' ter keep their scalps on."

"Deserted the Governor?"

"Yes, siree! Deserted him right out thar. But not this chile. I started with 'em flyin' back but then I decided they'd all make it. The rebels hadn't got started yit. So I turned off to stop at the Hernández ranch. Hoss needed water and I wus some thirsty mesel'. Up come Señor Hernández and helped me git water and feed. I ast him ef he'd been ter the battle. He said that when the men wus comin' down they halted at his upper ranch and tole him that they needed his head. 'Wal, I tole 'em ef they needed me head,' says Hernández, 'I'd bettah take it ovah mesel'. So I ketched up me rifle, threw me serape 'round me and tied onto the saddle a lunch me wife had fixed fer me.' Ye shoulda seen him talkin' and wavin' his hands, Lona. Wal, when he'd mounted his burro he wus 'off ter war.' When the fightin' wus ovah he reckoned he'd bettah git back home. So he looked fer his burro. Want no whar 'round. Then he hoofed it ter his house. Thar he found his animul. 'When I got home,' he says ter me, 'I tole me wife that the burro had more sense than I did. He knew nuf ter come right back home.' Hernández laughed, a-holdin' in his belly. Then he said that the other men could go on with their foolishness ef they wanted to but, as fer him, he wus stayin' on the ranch and mindin' his own business. Smart man, I say. Maybe he's right.

"We'll shutter the windows and barricade the doors right now. I'm stayin' hyar. It's every man fer himsel'. I tole the men I'd be hyar guardin' the place and, ef worse comes ter worse, a bunch of 'em's comin' ovah and give the pass word, 'Jackson' and I'll let 'em in. The rebels air a-comin', I'm shu-ah. Ain't a

168

mite skeered of 'em. We'll jes cache hyar and me 'Barker' will dust 'em off ef they git funny and try to break in."

For Lona the sequence of events was tangled during the days which followed. First it was Williams with news; then Pedro. The arrival of the *insurrectos* on the plaza needed no messenger for she could hear the war whoops of the Indians and the yells of the Mexicans from the North. Suddenly the noise and confusion, the spurts of rifle fire were followed by an ominous silence. Pedro mounted a ladder to the roof and creeping on hands and knees reached the low parapet of a neighboring house where loopholes faced the plaza. He returned to report that it was deserted. Apparently there had been no battle.

"Um, deserted," said Williams, frowning. "Somethin' back o' that. I'll see." He strode out but in a few moments he returned to the patio, saying that the rebels had left for a camp a mile away. There had been no looting or killing in the city. The Governor and many of his officials had fled South and "God only knows what is happenin' to 'em!"

A few hours later, Pedro stumbled in with the news that Governor Pérez had been killed. He gave no details. So again Williams left. Going from place to place under cover of night, he learned the full truth. Pérez had fled on his horse. Then he had let his animal loose and on foot reached a rancho. But the Indians had tracked him. They had killed Don Ramón and Don Santiago Abreü as well. Williams, like Pedro, said nothing further. Why tell Lona and Pablita that the Indians had cut off the Governor's head and were using it as a football? Why tell them that Santiago Abreü had been killed by inches? Hands and feet had been cut off one at a time. Eyes and tongue had been gouged out while the Indians taunted him!

Lona did not need to use her gun but kept it ready during

169

the interminably long days of that month when the whole town expected disaster. Her courage lifted when she heard that an assembly was meeting, but fell again when it was announced that the new governor was none other than a Taos Indian, José Gonzales!

"All the men can say for him, Doña Lona," reported Pedro, "is that he's a good buffalo hunter! I might as well be governor for all he knows about carrying on affairs."

"An Indian! And Armijo in the assembly!"

"Talkin' 'bout the new Gov'nor?" asked Bill as he stalked into the patio. "Armijo? Yeah, but give him time. That's what he's stallin' fer. Gonzales, a gov'nor! Might as well elect me burro. He's claimin' all of the Pérez property. Others takin' their share. It's a purty mess. Jes heerd that Gonzales has declared against Mexico and talks of sendin' fer help from Texas. Wow! Now what with Texas a-wantin' this hull kintry and the people hyar agin jinin'!—Wal, there'll be another mess!"

Once more quiet was restored to the surface of life. Men came to Lona's salas. They declared that they might as well be gambling. Every evening her rooms were full of armed men until the September night when a messenger burst in with the news that Armijo was on the way to Santa Fé *with an army!* "He's announced a counter-revolution. He'll demand that we all stand with him. Woe to the man who will not, I'm thinking."

Gathering up their money and cards the men rushed from the doors and disappeared.

"If you or Pablita do go on the roof, keep well behind the parapet. I'm going to Madam Alarid's. Close and bar the place, Pedro," ordered Lona early the next day. "I'll carry a key to the monte room."

Walking along the deserted street, Lona peered around the corner before she went on. A few players were at tables under the portals. Suddenly they gathered up their coins, decks and guns and scattered like a flock of birds.

"What in the world is happening now?" asked Lona as little Madam Alarid drew her within doors.

"A messenger runs along the portal. He is probably telling the men that Armijo's army is not far away now."

"I want to wait here and see what happens."

"It will be something awful, I am sure. My maid broke a mirror this morning. It fell in splinters, not just cracked," whispered Madam Alarid with her chubby hands half covering her face. Her small dark eyes glistened with tears which she could not control.

The two women were never far from the window which commanded the plaza. Soldiers passed in uniform. Citizens marched after them because they dared not do otherwise. All carried guns, rifles or small arms and not a few had bows and arrows.

It was midafternoon before huzzas echoed in the plaza. Lona and Madam Alarid stood back from the window and watched General Armijo ride by, sitting his horse in haughty dignity. The plume of his high hat waved as he turned his head and noted the people who gave him welcome. His dark blue cape lifted slightly and displayed his red and blue uniform bright with yellow braid. One shoulder showed an epaulet with heavy gold fringe. They watched him dismount at the palace.

"He's . . . he's the cruel sort. What . . . will he do?" stuttered Señora Alarid.

An hour later, Señor Alarid puffed into the room. "Armijo has proclaimed himself governor and *comandante-general*. He has sent a message to Mexico requesting troops."

Madam Barcelona reopened her establishment. The endless nightmare weeks passed until January. Governor Armijo did

171

not appear to play. Men guessed that he was afraid to be seen abroad. Lona suspected as much and, for her own sake, she was glad.

Then came the day when she stood on the roof nearest the plaza with a group of neighbors and watched the soldiers from Mexico march in, four hundred strong. A few hours later, from her North window she saw all the soldiers gallop away with General Armijo. She knew they were to meet the insurrectionists, perhaps two thousand of them, in the Cañada country.

"Are you going?" asked Lona when Williams sauntered in as soon as the army was lost in the dust.

"No. I am not travelin' aftah any leader like that rascal Armijo. He don't mean honest gov'ment. Reckon Jackson wouldn't go."

When the enemy were routed, it was the men from Mexico who drifted into Madam Barcelona's salas and dared to denounce Armijo. "Why," said one fellow, "Armijo is a downright coward. He shook like a leaf when we were all set to make for the rebels. He actually wanted to retreat. If it had not been for Captain Muños of our Vera Cruz Dragoons, we would have had the enemy at our heels. He begged permission to rout the whole lot of 'em with his own company. He did it too. Now Armijo talks of a great victory! He says little, I'll bet, of shooting down José Gonzales without a trial and others too."

A day or two later, the same soldier spoke openly again in the North room. "Armijo's giving orders right and left for the execution of many of his former *compadres*. The folks say that they are good citizens, fine men. Somebody should plant a dagger between his ribs. I'm glad we are leaving. I'd get into trouble if I had to bend a knee to that fellow."

"I heard the rifle shots this morning. Who was killed?" inquired Madam Barcelona.

"The Montoyas for one group."

172

"The Montoyas! How dare Armijo do that. They have helped him. They were not criminals. Can nobody intercede?"

"Might as well try to intercede with the Devil. General Armijo won't listen to anybody. He's a contemptible cur."

Lona did not reply. She trembled with relief that he had never sought her out in these past months. No one could say that she had influenced him.

XVII

WHEN THE FIRING HAD CEASED BEHIND THE *garita* walls on the hill, Williams began to hanker for his own campfire. "Come airly mornin', Lona," he said, "I'll yank mesel' out North."

At dawn he was collecting his belongings and fuming aloud because he could not find a buckle which had fallen from his saddle. Across the patio, Lona was already dressed to bid Beel good-by. She heard him talking to himself as she approached the open door.

"To whom are you talking?" she asked, stopping on the doorstep.

"Ter a gentleman, by God. I'm talkin' ter mesel'," growled Bill, continuing his search. Suddenly he yelled, "Got 'er. Mornin', Lona. Now when I fix the saddle, I'm trottin' out. Had me breakfast. Pablita's a good little soul." Williams patted down his long hair, stroked his beard and pulled down his buckskin coat. "Now I'm ready and it's high time," he said. "Imagine Bill Williams sleepin' in a room all this time. Heerd a new un t'other day. Ye Spaniards are the beatenest fer old sayin's. *'Cada chango á su petate y cada perico á su estaca.'* 'Every monkey to his palm mat and every parrot to his perch.'

174

Reckon I'm not colored up nuf fer a parrot but I'm the monkey all right, and me mat'll be in the Rockies. Had nuf of a city ter last me the rest of me life."

Williams led his horse through that North room for the last time, listening to Lona's words of gratitude and admonition that he take care of himself. When he had mounted, Lona put her hand on the saddle and looked up. "Beel, if you ever hear anything about Ewing, either send me word or put it securely in your memory for me."

"That I will. But aftah all, 'twould be bettah ter forget him, gal. Bettah spend ye time bein' on ye guard." Williams jerked his head and turning in the saddle looked at the old palace. "When things git cooled off a bit, Armijo'll try ter git in ye good graces agin. Look out. He may pretend to take it easy in his berth thar. Beware! Ye know, 'Not all who snore, sleep.' "

"Yes, that's true, Beel. There'll come a day when I'll even scores. Meantime, I'll remember, 'If I can't bite, I won't show my teeth.' "

"Right! Good-by. Good luck ter ye," said Bill, lifting his wide black hat.

For fourteen dreary months Santa Fé did not arouse itself from the gloom which had settled upon it during the revolution. Fear of the man in the old palace ruled the city. Lona's salas were almost empty. No one wished to dine or play away from his own home. Lona herself found relief only when she mounted her horse and rode out on the trails.

On a brilliant April day, Lona rode with Pedro, as usual, a short distance behind her. Dipping through the Mascara Arroyo to the North, she struck Eastward on the trail to the Chaves ranch. Snow lay white under the piñons and pines but the *chamisa* was already green along the road. Lona reined in her horse and listened to the desert. She lifted her head. Now and then she could see Santa Fé sprawling below with its box-like

175

houses dun-yellow in the red plowed fields. Refreshed, she turned her horse toward the city.

As Lona neared the arroyo, an officer in the blue uniform of the Vera Cruz Dragoons hailed her. She pulled in her horse for she recognized him as one of the few who had remained in the North after the revolution. He had often been in her salas. He asked if he might accompany her to the city.

"Certainly, Lieutenant Miera. Do you too like to ride alone?"

"Yes," said the young officer, "it is so peaceful out here on the desert."

"I wish it were in the city," replied Lona. "Such a pall of gloom hangs over Santa Fé. Would it be possible to have a ball, I wonder?"

"That would be a fine gesture, Madam Barcelona. May I bring a friend from Mexico? He came on yesterday's caravan."

"Surely you may. We must try to be gay."

Upon the night of the ball, Lona's large sala was cleared of gaming tables. More than a hundred candles were reflected in the mirrors. Young guests in bright costumes danced light-heartedly in gay contrast to the solemn duennas who sat like a frieze of draped black figures about the room.

The Governor arrived late, announced by a deep-voiced guard. When he entered, the dancers paused where they were and curtsied. Armijo in his general's uniform was a resplendent figure. Bowing to the assembly he waved them on with the dance and seated himself in a high-backed chair between the great front windows.

When Madam Barcelona came to greet him, he immediately claimed the dance.

As far as they dared, the guests watched the two dancers. Armijo was bursting with pride. Lona laughed and chatted, apparently in the best of spirits. When she swung away with her next partner, Lieutenant Miera, she caught his frown.

"Armijo is trying to play the fine gentleman tonight," said the officer.

"He, a fine gentleman? The brave soldier of La Cañada! *Caramba!*" she whispered.

"Have a care, Madam. We must talk of other things. Pretty ears may belong to spies. Ah, here is my friend."

Madam Barcelona curtsied. She studied the stranger's face. Where had she seen this Señor Lucero? Was he not the man whom she had passed so long ago on the plaza—the man who—? He did even now resemble Rudolfo. Older. But Rudolfo would have been older now. His mouth, tilting at the corners was not like the firm straight lips of Rudolfo but the general contour of the face was his.

"Since you came from Mexico I'll wager you know the old dances. You have castanets?" suggested Señor Lucero, "Let's show them how they dance in the South."

Lona's eyes sparkled. Señor Lucero clapped his hands. "And now Señoras, Señoritas and Señores, if you will allow us, Madam Barcelona and I will dance for you as they do in old Mexico. Please stand against the walls." In a lower voice, he added, "I promise not to shoot you."

Lona's eyes flashed quickly toward Governor Armijo but he appeared to be engrossed in conversation.

Lieutenant Miera pushed his way to Señor Lucero and whispered, *"Por Dios!* José, hold your tongue. Armijo has many spies."

In the center of the room, Lona bowed to her partner, her black braids gleamed under a white mantilla and her white silk dress, embroidered in red and black, circled wide. Hand held high in salute the two began the swirling *El Járabe* with its sudden stamp, quick swing and sharp retreat. Señor Lucero threw his sombrero to the floor. Lona danced on the brim and

177

clicked her castanets. With a flourish, the dance ended. She and Lucero bowed to a round of wild applause.

Governor Armijo stirred uneasily in his chair and frowned. He joined feebly in the hand clapping.

Madam Barcelona stole a look at him. Let the man in the chair frown if he would, she thought. Here is a man I honestly wish to know. Throughout the evening she and Señor Lucero danced often, laughing and covertly studying each other. Toward the end of the evening, while they circled in a waltz, Lucero whispered, "Governor Armijo has been watching us."

"I know. I have pretended not to notice. No one can trust him. I shall do as I choose, but he is dangerous," warned Lona.

Governor Armijo rose to leave earlier than was his wont. Lona excused herself to Señor Lucero and went to the door to bid Armijo good night.

"So, you have found a new friend," he burst out.

"Apparently, Governor."

"Let him take care. No stranger shall edge between us."

Lona curtsied and left him to finish her dance with Lucero. In amazement Armijo watched, his eyes narrow and green. Haughtily he stalked through the door held back by Pedro.

Last of the guests to leave was Señor Lucero who turned back for a final word. "Madam, if you will honor me, I know where we can find a quiet midnight supper not far away. Will you go?"

"I do not often but I will tonight."

The two stepped into the starlit street. Lona glanced about. She could see no one lurking near. "We must be cautious," she said. "Attacks are not uncommon, Señor."

"Yes, I have heard. This way." Taking her arm, he did not speak again while they walked by the great hay-market, down a narrow lane to the home of the widow Montoya who now eked out a meager living catering to fine appetites. At the door Lucero glanced quickly over his shoulder.

"It is as I felt. We were watched. I saw a big fellow and a smaller one whispering at the corner." Lona raised a warning finger. For two hours they talked of Mexico, Santa Anna, the affair in Texas, avoiding any mention of Santa Fé. When Lucero cautiously opened the door, the street was empty. Both thought they had outstayed the men who might have planned to waylay them.

"There seems to be no one abroad," Lona said as Lucero swung her in a wide circle at the corner.

"Apparently not," he answered, "but run if I am attacked."

At that moment a small fellow muffled to the eyes, sprang from the shadow of a doorway and lunged at Lucero. The Mexican swirled and parried with his own blade. Lona found her voice. *"Guardias,"* she cried, *"guardias!"*

At the sound of her voice, a larger man, also muffled, ran by, striking at her with his dagger. *"Vagamunda,"* he growled.

"Guardias! Guardias!" A few soldiers came running, pulling on their coats.

"Por Dios! Madam Barcelona!" The first one cried. "Are you hurt?"

"No. Not I nor Señor Lucero, luckily. But the dagger thrust at me by the larger fellow cut my cape here."

"Who were the men? Have you any idea?"

"Both were muffled. One short. One tall."

"Aye, muffled. Short. Tall. It is not hard to guess who they were but unless we know for certain no guard dare speak. Nor you, Madam, if you have your suspicions."

"I understand. A thousand thanks, gentlemen. Now, Señor Lucero, let us go. We will not be attacked again with the guards awake."

Walking on with her arm in his, Lucero whispered, "You are a brave woman as well as a beautiful dancer. Why didn't you run?"

"I? Run? Not I, Don José. It was all too sudden anyway."

The two said no more. When they reached Lona's great door, Lucero asked, "You guess?"

"Yes. The tall man was none other than Armijo. But I'll hold my tongue."

"As I thought. Good night, Doña Lona. You are one in thousands."

Absurdly confident that his flimsy disguise had been successful in the dark street, Governor Armijo came to Lona's sala ten days later, with a party of friends. He bowed with elaborate courtesy. At the door of the small private gaming room he turned and looked squarely at Lona with hungry inquisitiveness, but Lona's eyes were blank.

In the outer hall, Pedro met his mistress with the message that the men in the North room had asked her to deal monte for them. She walked with him. In the patio she whispered, "Go, tell Señor Lucero that I request him not to come this evening and will explain later."

When Madam Barcelona entered the monte room, she saluted all with a lift of her hand. The game took on new life. Coins fell. Bets ran higher. When midnight neared, she gave an assistant her place. Telling Pedro to excuse her to the governor when he left, she went to her room.

Following his usual custom, Armijo inquired for Madam Barcelona soon after the church clock had struck twelve. Pedro gave him the message.

"Aha! Retired, has she? Well, that's new. Retired?" Turning to his friends he bade them go. He would speak to Madam Barcelona.

Armijo stepped into the patio. He knew which was Lona's room. A light burned behind the closed curtains. He stepped along the path between bushes in spring flowering and tapped on her door with his cane.

"Lona, I wish to speak to you." Lona had heard his heavy tread. She hesitated. When he spoke again, she opened the door wide. Candlelight threw an aura about her fine defiant head.

Armijo did not step forward. Lona's eyes deterred him. He had no wit to understand why he found himself helpless against her power. "You send me away without a word, this evening?"

"Yes, Governor," Lona's voice was cold, as slivered ice.

"I want to have a friendly chat with you," pleaded Armijo, his voice gaining fire as he took a step forward.

Lona drew back and slammed the door. She had bolted it before Armijo pushed his stout shoulder against it. With a snarl he threw his full weight against the door.

"No, you shall not!"

"How dare you? You . . . *vagamunda!*"

Again he hurled himself against the door.

"You can not frighten me," Lona called. "You can not strike me now."

"Strike me?" Armijo caught the implication of her words. She had recognized him that night in the lane.

He recoiled from the door. Without a word he gathered his cape and hurried across the patio.

Pedro posted at the front exit infuriated him. He lifted his cane. No! Not that.

"*Peón,* tell me where Señor Lucero lives," he growled.

"Your Excellency, since he was not here tonight, Señor Lucero must have left the city," replied Pedro, trembling.

"If I find that he is still in Santa Fé, it will go hard with you. I do not tolerate lies," snapped the Governor.

Armijo's cane swept down. Pedro dodged. The blow fell on the great door and shocked the Governor's wrist. Pain always made him cry out. Dazed, he stepped into the street.

"Guard?" he called. With cane in the left hand, he lashed the fellow across the shoulder. "You lazy brute. Walk along there."

Wincing under the blow, the soldier set out at a brisk shamble ahead of the Governor.

When Lona heard Pedro's shoes clatter upon the flagstones of the path, she unbolted the door and called. Pedro ground his teeth. "I'll kill that old wolf yet. He is looking for Señor Lucero."

"Lucero! Go, Pedro, bring Don José here at once. Fly. Take your gun."

Lona paced the portal, her green skirts rustling slightly as she moved. In Burro Alley someone was singing to a guitar. She listened until the song faded away. The church bell tolled one. Finally the door of the North room creaked open.

"Don José," Lona ran to meet him and caught his hand. "The Governor . . ."

"Yes, I know. Pedro told me. May we talk somewhere else? Even roofs have ears."

"My room," she said, leading him across the patio.

She locked the door. Her other hand closed tightly over his.

"Señor Armijo is very angry. He'll kill you if he finds you in the city. You must go. The caravan for Chihuahua is not far on the trail."

"Do you want me to leave?" asked Lucero, facing her in the candlelight.

"No."

"No?" repeated Lucero. "Do you mean that, Lona?"

"Yes." Lona lifted her head. Their eyes met. "You know I want you to stay. But you must go."

"Ah, Lona *mía,* you love me. I will remain. What is danger!" He lifted her braids and wound them around his neck. "See, I am bound." Gently she drew back.

"I suppose I should parry a while with love. But I am no

182

young girl. I can not. My heart cries, 'Stay, my darling,' but I beg you to go."

"You feel sure I must go?"

"It is wise, José. We must wait."

"Wait! I loathe the word. We Spanish are too prone to send the heart far ahead. Mine leaped to you that first night when we danced together. I've learned to wait until my mind should catch up. It did. Now I know for certain that I shall love you always."

The bell in the church struck. A dog growled over a wall. Another answered.

"You have but four hours to catch the caravan, José. Go, lest I hold you."

"I shall return on the next caravan but one. Affairs in Mexico must be arranged. When I come I shall stay. You will marry me then?"

"Yes. I'll waken Pedro and he'll help with your horse while you gather your belongings." She walked with Lucero to the door.

"Kiss me quickly and go, lest I play coward. God be with you, my darling."

Lona snuffed out her candles, all but one on the desk. It would be four, no probably six months before José came again. Her mind galloped over the trail. Up and down to Alburquerque. On to Socorro. The grim Jornada! El Paso, busy little El Paso. The dreary plains of Chihuahua. The awful desert.

But it was better not to think. She sat down by the desk and unclasped her locket to put it in the drawer. Opening it, she looked steadily at the miniature, thinking not of Rudolfo but of the resemblance to José. In the open drawer lay a thin bundle of letters. She did not take them from their hiding place. Ewing! Word had not come from him for five years. Yet she could not believe that he was dead. At any rate, he was out of her life. She had not told José about either man. Her past life was her own, just as his belonged to him. She would be true as steel, as she hoped José would be, but tell him of love which belonged to others, that she would never do.

XVIII

THE ANTIDOTE FOR LONELINESS, MADAM BAR-
celona knew, was work. But neither balls nor the duties of her
salas could relieve the cheerless night hours when she bent over
her desk adding accounts, thinking, longing and planning for
José.

During business hours, Lona spent more time in her salas.
She dealt monte more frequently. Whipping her face into
smiles and her eyes into flashes of interest, she discussed politics
with an eager flippancy. Men noticed that Madam Barcelona
listened with scornful lips to any news of the Governor and
his parasites in the old palace. An occasional word of fierce
contempt told them that she hated him now. Although they
did not know her reason, they trusted her and dared to talk
before her.

Again and again, men said that the rich were growing richer,
the poor, far poorer. She had seen new wealth ostentatiously
flaunted on the plaza, shiny new carriages, better horses, glittering diamonds on rough hands. She had also noted that many
more barefooted ragged *peóns* and country folk loafed and
begged as they squatted in the shade of the portals. Men said
cautiously that the Governor was to blame. He overtaxed wher-

185

ever he could, diverted public money into his pockets and those of his followers.

Occasionally, when Lona, accompanied by Pablita, went to the market at the Northwest corner of the palace or when she walked on to chat with Madam Alarid or with Madam Pino at *La Fonda,* she caught sight of Manuel Armijo strutting about with a guard always at his heels. She was glad that he came infrequently to her rooms. Probably, she thought, Armijo, harried by fear, not only felt but actually was safer in his own little office. There had been threats against him. He must know that daggers had been sharpened and rifles loaded by enemies. But recently, a fellow had drawn an arrow on him. Lately she had heard that Indian scalps and ears strung on leather thongs hung in his office. Lona shuddered. But there would come a time! The brute would overstep himself.

In midafternoon, whenever he was not on duty at the barracks, Lieutenant Miera came to see Madam Barcelona. Lona called him "Don Orlando" now and urged him to talk of José and his mine. He told her that José had aroused him to tell of his great luck on that night when he had left so hurriedly for the South. Orlando liked to tell her of his own Lucia whom he hoped some day to bring North as his bride. It banished their loneliness to make plans and talk of love.

Sometimes they sat in the patio when children of the neighborhood gathered after school. Don Orlando let them play with his sword and told them tall stories of Indian wars. Lona always had a cake or a candied fruit for Anita and Luísa, the daughters of Madam Labarta, a soldier's widow who lived in a small adobe on Burro Alley.

One May afternoon, Lona sent the children home when she heard shouts from the plaza greeting the caravan from Chihuahua. With Don Orlando she hurried to the small post-office and waited impatiently while mail bags were emptied. Letters

186

there were, two for Madam Barcelona and three for Lieutenant Miera. José had written at Alburquerque, and again at Socorro, and binding them together, had left them to be picked up by someone on any North-bound caravan. To Lona he wrote of happenings along the way, news of Santa Anna's escapades that he heard from travelers from the South, and of his longing to return.

The summer sped by without a shadow. Lona was so confident that she threw off all fear of ill befalling her lover. Now it was July. He would return in August. In her patio, Lona watched humming birds whir above overblown flowers. Suddenly one of them flew over her head, into her room and out.

Her hand flew to her mouth to smother a cry, "An ill-omen!" Madam Alarid! How she prates of omens. But there was no truth in them. Ewing! How he had tried to cure her of believing in them. He had said that it was foolish, childish. He had well-nigh convinced her in those days. "If ill-luck is due, it will come willy-nilly," he insisted. "Shadow lurks wherever sunshine lies." And now the bird? Lona shook her head as if trying to shake the omen from her mind.

On the next day but one, Pablita came across the patio, her eyes swollen and red with weeping. Pedro followed, fumbling at his sombrero.

"Ah, Doña Lona," sobbed Pablita. "Mother Labarta caught the awful fever and died last night."

"Fever! That terrible typhoid, probably. Mother Labarta dead! I know. The bird!"

Pablita looked at her questioningly, gulping her sobs, but, since Doña Lona said nothing further, she continued, "Luísa and Anita are quite alone. They have no relatives except an aunt who lives far down in Mexico. At first, they cried but now they sit stunned, like very old people."

187

"Are you sure they have no relatives?"

"None, I'm sure. They call for you, Doña Lona."

Madam Barcelona walked with Pablita to the small adobe home on Burro Alley. Men who turned into the far end of the lane strumming their guitars quickly hushed the sound with their hands and, with sombreros off, passed silently through the people at the door. In the back yard, a bright colored washing swung mockingly in the sun. Madam Labarta had worked to the last. Although burning with fever she had hung it out before she staggered indoors to fall on her corn-husk mattress. Out in the sun, men hammered and sawed, making ready a box coffin. The neighbors would not hear to wrapping Madam Labarta's body in only a blanket for burial. She deserved the best they could provide.

Within the house, where women moaned and swayed back and forth, candles were lighted at the head and feet of the dead woman. As Lona entered she noticed that the one cracked mirror in the room had been turned to the wall.

The two girls threw their arms about Lona. Both of them began to sob. Finally, Luísa, the older, said, "Doña Lona, they tell us mother will never waken again. What shall we do?"

"I'll see to that, my dear," answered Lona hugging the girls close to her.

When the twilight procession to the chapel and to the hallowed burial ground was over, Madam Barcelona sent for the children. Their eyes were wistful and questioning. "Would you both like to be my little girls now?" she asked.

Dark-eyed Luísa, older than her twelve years, nodded. The younger one looked up and said timidly, "Doña Lona, we love you. We'd be glad to be your girls now. We'll try to be good."

During the next few days Lona made plans for their care, not at her own home, but with a Madam Suazo who lived

188

farther up the West street facing the barracks. She made it clear that she wished the girls to be brought up very strictly as ladies. To the surprise of Madam Suazo, she engaged as tutor one of the young army officers at the post who instructed boys.

"They are to be taught to read and write. Teach them just as you teach boys. Later they shall go to the priest," she told the officer. "I want my girls to have as good a chance in life as boys have. Padre Martínez in Taos believes in that and so do I. Some day they may help me with my accounts. I do not want them to know life as I see it in my salas. Some time, before long, I want you to teach them to ride. Take them out to the hills where they can see the desert and the mountains. But be careful of their mounts, Señor."

That evening, Lona went to the inn. Madam Pino bustled toward her and took both hands in hers, exclaiming, "My dear, what is this I hear? Children? Well, bless you, my dear. You have undertaken more than you know."

"Perhaps, but I hardly think so," replied Doña Lona. "After all, I'm a woman and it is natural that I should love children. I may never have any of my own."

"Of course, that's true. The girls will have more advantages than most children in Santa Fé, I know that. But somehow it seems inconsistent for you to—"

"Surely not," interrupted Lona. "That's just a notion that people have. Why follow what others decree? When I was in school I learned this from Cervantes, 'I would have nobody to control me; I would be absolute; and who but I?' How my aunt would have smiled if she had known I was wondering about that when she scolded me." Lona laughed.

"What of Señor Lucero?" Madam Pino asked.

"I believe he'll love me whatever I do. I'll know soon. Meantime, I'll wait before adopting the girls legally. Don José gets in on this next caravan."

189

The forerunner galloped into the plaza. The Chihuahua caravan would arrive late that afternoon.

In her full-ruffled green dress and her finest black mantilla,
Madam Barcelona stood under the portal when the tired, dusty
travelers rolled in. Unmindful of the shouts, the grating of
wooden wheels, the cracking whips and thin string music, she
scanned every man's face when the wagons and horses went
by. Narrowing her eyes, she walked around the plaza until she
found the master of the train.

"Did not a Señor Lucero from Zacatecas join your caravan?
He must have come."

"Madam, we had no Señor Lucero with us. Perhaps he was
detained."

"Thank you, Señor," said Lona, and no more. Swinging
about she hurried home, her heart pounding.

"Pablita! Pedro!" she called. "Don José did not come. I can
not understand."

"But Doña Lona," argued Pablita, putting an arm around
her mistress. "If he could not come at the last moment, you
will have some message. That's certain. Señor Lucero is a fine
gentleman. We both think so, don't we, Pedro?"

"Never seen a better," answered Pedro, running his hand
through his heavy black hair.

"Of course, Pablita! A message. I did not think to ask. Go
and see if a letter came."

Pablita listened at the post-office. She did not hear her mistress's name. When all the others had gone out, she asked the
man in charge if he would kindly search the mail that was left.
There must be a letter? He obligingly shuffled through the letters and packages again, and turned to say, "I'm sorry. There's
nothing here for Madam Barcelona. Sorry."

How shall I ever have the courage to tell her, thought Pablita,
but she did not have to speak. The news was in her face. Mak-

ing no remark, Doña Lona went directly to her room, threw herself on her couch and buried her face in a pillow.

For a quarter-hour, Pablita sat by, wondering what she could say or do. She leaned over, gently touched her shoulder. "Ah, Doña Lona, do not grieve so. *'No hay camino tan llano que no tenga algún tropezón*—There is no road, however smooth, without some obstacle.' There is then some great reason for this."

Doña Lona did not stir. Save for her breathing she might be dead, Pablita thought, and closed the door against harsh voices of teamsters already drunk and carousing in the alley. Then again she sat by.

A door latch clicked across the patio. Quick footsteps tapped on flagstones. Pedro was at the door knocking softly and saying, "Pablita, a messenger is here."

"Messenger?" exclaimed Pablita, echoing the hopeful tone in her husband's voice.

Lona heard the words and roused herself. She was composed when the young man reached the door.

"Madam Barcelona?" He doffed his sombrero. "I bring you a letter from Señor Lucero. He requested me to deliver it to you personally. I came as soon as the wagon master would let me go."

"Do you know why Don José did not come?" Lona asked breathlessly.

"Yes, he is ill."

"Seriously ill?"

"A rock fell . . ."

"At his mine? He was hurt?"

"Yes, Madam, I am distressed to report. He lies in a long chair with a leg badly broken. It will be some time before he can travel. He told me to beg you not to worry about him. He will come North as soon as he can. I wish . . ." The young fel-

191

low paused. "I wish I could have brought better news. But I might have brought worse. Had the rock fallen a foot farther over he would have been crushed. He bears up well under his misfortune. I saw him a few hours before we started. He told me that he would watch the wagons when they rolled up out of the ravine. He is game, Don José. He even jokes while he lies there as disappointed as you are, Madam."

"Does he suffer much?"

"Yes. But he does not suffer as he did at first. He will get well, I am sure. Now I have another letter to deliver to Lieutenant Miera. I must find him."

"Yes. At the officer's quarters across the way."

When the young man was gone, Lona broke the seal of her letter.

Zacatecas,
June 28, 1839.

Lona, *querida mía,*

The caravan leaves tomorrow and I must remain here. Your disappointment at such news will not overtower my own. How I have counted on coming to you! I've been prancing to be off for weeks. And now, I can not go!

The nurse has propped me up in my long chair so I can handle a quill. I told him that I *had* to write. But I must be brief.

Now the question is: Why was I not created a jack rabbit instead of a jackass? I've cudgeled my brains sore trying to find out why I stood there fascinated when the great boulder slowly loosened itself to fall. I jumped. Yes, but too late. The rock caught both of my legs, broke them below the knee. By a strange quirk of fate, it was worn into a hollow just below the top so that my feet were bruised but not crushed. So matters might be worse.

Why was I such a clodpate? I have known for years that

192

such a thing might happen but it had been so long since any rock had fallen that I stupidly believed none would. Now I pay the piper but I'm not dancing. I will, a few months from now. You are not going to lose your partner for 'La Jota'—not if I can help it. We'll swing more gaily than ever, some day.

I've begged the doctors to tell me when I may be well enough to travel but they only shake their heads. Something on my right leg seems to trouble them. Some bruise or other. But I'm coming to you in time if I have to hobble on crutches. Do you hear?

Meanwhile, believe me when I say that I love you more than ever. My life is *dedicated* to you.

As for letters. I'll send one on every caravan but remember, that sometimes I may not know the hour for *'Adelante!'* Neither of us must be too downcast if no message arrives. So do not worry.

Courage, girl! Never forget that I shall be growing stronger every day because of you.

They will not let me write longer now. So with my deepest heart's love, I am

Your own
José.

"I must go to him," she said aloud and gripped the letter. "How terrible for him, lying there day after day. I could leave on the return caravan." But would José want her to close her business? He would think that unwise. Then there were the girls. She must remember them now. He did not know about them. Perhaps it would be better if he did not until his return.

At her desk, Lona began to write rapidly. She would write every day until the caravan must leave. That was all she could do. But she wanted to go to José! When she threw sand across her paper, she looked up suddenly. Surely she felt a hand on her shoulder. How foolish. Of course, no hand had touched her, yet somehow, she sensed José's presence very strongly. His spirit had come to her across those weary miles?

Lona visited her girls at vespers when they stood for a moment's prayer. She would adopt them. There was no reason to wait.

The following morning Madam Barcelona found the office of the proper official in the old palace. He fumbled through a pile of documents; chose one to his purpose and began copying the correct preliminary form. "This is not quickly done, you know," he said as he asked for her signature and pointed at the line.

"Nothing ever is with us, Señor," commented Madam Barcelona leaning over to sign her name. She hesitated a moment, then wrote firmly Lona Barcelona. Perhaps some day she would tell her real name to José.

XIX

"NO! NO! SEÑOR. MY HEART'S IN MEXICO," MADAM Barcelona stepped back. The candles burned low in the deserted sala. Her eyes flashed with friendly interest, not with anger. "No," she repeated when the tall buckskin-clad American trader took a step toward her, thrusting forward his eager squarish face.

Burton Hart had remained after all the other gamblers had left. Ever since he had come in with the fall caravan, he had lingered to chat and laugh with Madam Barcelona, flirting with blue eyes that still squinted from the habit of the trails. His heavy light hair and full voice reminded Lona of Ewing Young. How slight a resemblance stirs my memory, she thought.

When Hart gambled, his glance always lingered on her face, watching her as long as she was in the room. Nodding brightly and swinging her fan, she would pass on, with a smile that seemed meant for him alone. Now he was surprised.

Again Madam Barcelona declared, "No, Señor. My heart belongs elsewhere and when I love, I am true."

"But I thought . . ." Hart checked himself.

"I know. Men misinterpret my cordiality too often. A greeting, a laugh, a snap of my eyes do not mean that I am falling in love. No grown woman tumbles as fast as she did at nine-teen."

"True. But I care and I hoped you did. I've been too hasty, too presumptuous. I'm sorry." Hart's voice grew thick. His hands went into his pockets. "So your heart is in Mexico—a long way from Santa Fé?"

"Yes. My lover would be with me now, if he had not been seriously hurt at his mine. He writes that he'll not be able to travel North for a long time. Alas!"

"He has a keen eye, Madam Barcelona. I've had sweethearts a-plenty back in Missouri but never have I met a woman like you. I'll confess that I rather lost my head. My congratulations to the lucky man." Hart used a longer time than necessary to light a new cigar.

"Like other men, you thought that marriage is the all-in-all to a woman. I wonder why men never suspect that we may have other desires? I appreciate the honor you have done me, however." Madam Barcelona curtsied and, motioning to a table, said abruptly, "Let's talk of other things now. You know the trail trade. They tell me it is growing better every year."

"Yes. There's good money in it but not as much as there should be after such a long tedious journey. Governor Armijo is most unjust to charge so much for wagon entry. But even so, we make a fair profit, usually," replied Hart looking at his hands to keep his eyes from meeting hers.

"Doctor Gregg is a good trader? I've been told so for years."

"He is that, Madam. He's clever in his choice of merchandise. He directs most of the buying but he brings so many wagons that, sometimes, others select goods for him. I came with him, you know, as far as Santa Fé. I hear that he made good money in Chihuahua during his last trip. He leaves soon for the East and I shall go with him. I shall not return to Santa Fé."

"Rarely does Doctor Gregg come to my rooms. Apparently

196

he cares little for games. I would like to talk to him. I wonder if you would be willing to tell him so. I want to confer with him about some business that I have in mind. Thursday afternoon late would be a good time. Tomorrow I am due at the fiesta down on the Galisteo ranch."

"Josiah Gregg has an ear for business, I'll certainly be glad to tell him."

The church bell thundered out one o'clock.

"It's time that I was leaving." The trader, rising, bade her a courteous good night, and turned sharply on his heel.

Thursday afternoon found Doctor Gregg in the conference room; Lona greeted him in a voice of admiration. She noted his shock of brown hair which reminded her of Doctor Waldo. Something about his habit of tilting down his head and the meagerness of his spare figure hinted of ill-health.

"Thank you, Madam Barcelona. Did you have a good day at Galisteo? I understood that you were at the fiesta and, as usual, had the most popular booth."

"I did have a fine day except for the incident with the rascal who grabbed a pile of coins and ran. Of course, Pedro caught him," she said. "It's a fine ranch with large acreage," Lona continued. "All sorts of people were there making holiday. There was music and to spare. Food. *Santa María!* How they all did eat! I wondered how they could."

"I've wondered too. Your fiestas in this country are doing a lot of good. At such gatherings people talk and learn more about governmental affairs. That's a fine thing. They are beginning to understand us Americans better too."

"Yes. I know that is true. Just between us, I've heard many a man say that, in his opinion, we would all fare well, were we under the stars and stripes."

"Thanks to the early mountain men," said Doctor Gregg.

197

"And the traders, Doctor," added Madam Barcelona quickly. "In Taos, caravans brought news. In Santa Fé, they have brought more. The traders have driven home the ideals of freedom, of the rights of all the people, but our leaders here, especially Armijo, have crushed us until no one dares raise his voice. We are underlings. We know it and speak about it among our friends but let no word slip on the plaza."

"That is wise. From what I have learned on this one trip, not to mention the many others down here, I am convinced matters are in a sorry plight. But such a condition can not last forever."

"What we need, I believe, is more Americans who will live here. Of course, there are many who are against Americans. Jealous, I think. For years I have liked Americans, Doctor. I'll confess that I have been hurt when I learned that they judge me by the standards of gambling women of their frontier towns. Surely that is obviously unfair. My business is perfectly legitimate and respectable."

"And you make good money too, no doubt, Madam."

"Yes, and now I think of investing in the trail trade. That is the subject about which I wished to talk to you. You are the topmost man in the business, Doctor Gregg. I wonder . . . I wonder if you would buy for me?"

"You do me honor," said the trader, leaning forward with interest. "But this is my last trip."

"Your last! I am sorry to hear that. But . . ." Madam Barcelona paused to reorganize her plan. "But . . . you could do the buying in the Eastern markets, take your fair commission and ship with some trader in whom you have confidence?"

"Yes, that could be done," said Doctor Gregg. "But, I hardly think the time ripe for your venture. Not this year and maybe not the next. Governor Armijo is a problem."

"Even so," answered Madam Barcelona unconsciously putting a hand to her bodice under which she could feel her locket. "Even so, I would like to have you take a chest of silver with you, if you will. I'll entrust ten thousand dollars to you, Sir."

"Very well. When we are ready to leave, I'll drive my own wagon to your North door at dawn, load the consignment, and give you the receipt. By taking time I will be able to select the choice merchandise you will want. Now, just what do you want?"

"Silks and satins of the loveliest colors, ribbons to match, fine laces, slippers. Do not forget that I like slippers with red heels. I wore them as a girl and I still do. Oh, there are many things. I'll make a list and then you may choose other articles which women especially like and men love to see. No hickory, iron or tools in my wagons, Doctor. I'll surely make a good profit. You have, on this late trip to Chihuahua as well as here, have you not?"

Doctor Gregg nodded.

"Tell me about your journey South. I came by that trail, you know, 'way back in 1826. Has it changed much?"

"Not much except that there are undoubtedly many more wrecks of wagons along the route and far more crosses at graves. The roadbed is beaten to greater firmness. The trail is much more traveled now, of course, than fourteen years ago."

"Did you have any unusual experiences?" Madam Barcelona was thinking of herself, sitting by a loophole watching a battle with Indians, and later watching Bill Williams kicking a man he called Manuel.

"Unusual? I guess that's the word. I reached Chihuahua a few days after the *grande fête d'hilarité* given every year in memory of the onetime Emperor Iturbide. They call him now the 'Father of the Republic,' you know, of course. Well, there were many merchants in town so we set up store at once. Many of

199

the wealthy class came to our room, especially in the evenings. They bought, too."

"No doubt," interrupted Madam Barcelona. "There is more money in Chihuahua than there is here."

"Yes. Chihuahua is the finest of the Northern Mexican cities. It is laid out better than Santa Fé and has much finer buildings. There is money there, all right. Everything was going well when, one day, who should walk in but the alcalde and several friars. They demanded that I give them part of my merchandise. You probably know that the feeling runs high against Masons and most of us traders are Masons. What these men wanted was a few dozen handkerchiefs."

"*Por Dios!* Why?" exclaimed Madam Barcelona.

"Well, to my surprise, they unfolded one of the kerchiefs and showed me that it was stamped with a print of the 'masonic carpet.' I did not know that they were so marked. I never do all the buying in Missouri. I have too many wagons to fill. So there they were. Those men gathered up all the handkerchiefs and condemned them to be burned publicly, making out of the affair an *auto-da-fé.*"

"Poor little 'kerchiefs. They were terrible enemies to the church!"

The trader smiled faintly. He never laughed aloud.

"What happened next?"

"Oh, I soon sold out and started North."

"Did you have any trouble?"

"I should say I did," continued Gregg. "Since the man who was to deliver sheep to us never turned up, we were soon out of meat. There was plenty of wild beef about so I sent out three of my men to get some, intending to pay for it when I should come on a *mayordomo* or some of his *vaqueros*—cowboys, we call 'em—and goldarn, if the youngster of the three wasn't captured and taken to Torreón some miles to the West. I went

200

over and tried to reason with the magistrate but, no sir, he was determined to take the boy down to Chihuahua and have him tried for robbery. My patience whisked away. I told the boy to mount his horse and make for the wagons."

"Of course, you were warned of dire consequences?"

"Yes, but I went on, madder than a cornered coyote. Then two American gentlemen caught up with us and told me that I was accused 'of rescuing a culprit from the hands of justice by force of arms!' Soldiers arrived two days later. I was to return to Chihuahua with my three men. We were then about one hundred and thirty miles from Chihuahua. I could have ridden on North but I finally made up my mind to return. By this time, I was ready to snarl, I tell you."

"How did you fare?" asked Madam Barcelona.

"The upshot of the matter was that, after several days, I signed a memorial to the Governor and was allowed to leave with my men."

"Such foolishness! The delay must have irked you. Were you put in jail?"

"No. One of the finest men that I have known, Don José Artelejo, was allowed to entertain me in his home. But the injustice of the whole matter! Even the fellow who started the trouble said he was sorry that it had gone so far. I'll not forget and I'm never going back there again, good trade or no."

Josiah Gregg struck his right fist into his other hand, shut his mouth hard and narrowed his eyes defiantly. "Never," he said once more. "For me, the Santa Fé trade is not enough to warrant my taking such a long journey."

"And now, you are soon to leave . . ."

"Doña Lona! Doña Lona!" screamed a woman from the patio. The high voice shook with terror.

Quickly the doctor and Madam Barcelona looked out of the window facing the patio. A heavy snow was falling.

"It's . . . Soledad Abreü. Poor child!"

"Don Santiago's daughter?" asked Gregg. As he followed Doña Lona to the door he caught her troubled, "Yes."

"The soldiers! They were coming straight for me. Oh, Doña Lona, hide me. It's Governor Armijo."

A sob choked the young Soledad. "I will not . . . I will not go with them. He is horrible!"

"Let's take off this snow-covered cloak, first," said Lona. "There. Sit down and tell us what is the matter and how you happened to be out in this storm?"

Soledad sat shaking with fright, jumping at the slightest noise. She stared as if she were unconscious of her surroundings, of Doña Lona, of Doctor Gregg, now the sympathetic physician. He stroked her hands and assured her that she was safe. Finally his voice soothed the girl but she said nothing.

Doña Lona rang a bell and when Pablita came with her black rebozo flecked with snow, she ordered tea and supper ready as soon as possible. "You will stay with us, Doctor Gregg?" The man nodded. "Remember, Pablita, Lieutenant Miera promised to dine with me this evening." Turning to Doctor Gregg, she added, "He'll know what has happened. We'll not bother little Soledad now."

"Let's take her to your room, Doña Lona," urged the doctor.

When the three had reached the room and shaken off the snow, Soledad was gently urged to drink a cup of hot tea and lie down.

"I must go home. . . . Aunt will tell my family where I am. Your door was open, Doña Lona. I ran in. I feared the soldiers would march me to the palace. Poor Uncle Ramón! Poor . . ." The girl fell back on the cushions and, thoroughly exhausted, fell asleep.

Hardly had Lieutenant Miera seated himself at the dining

table with its fine linen and silver glinting under the candle-light, when he burst forth, "We've come mighty near a revolution today. If the soldiers had kept faith with Ramón Baca and marched to the palace, I'll wager my last doubloon, Armijo would have fled the town. That's all it would take. A hundred guns leveled at him and he would have run out a back door, jumped on the horse he always has ready for him, and plunged away to the South. He has not enough friends in this whole country to help him return. I did what I could to make the men see their big chance but they are blind or utterly fear-ridden."

"A revolution!" exclaimed Lona. "Well, that's what we need. Do tell Doctor Gregg what's been happening, Lieutenant." Bending her head toward her other guest, she asked, "You know about trade but perhaps not about some of the under-currents of trouble here?"

"I suspect that's right, Madam. I've heard many unsavory rumors. What about the soldiers today, young man? Then tell us of Madam Soledad Caballero."

"For one thing, Doctor, just lately Armijo tried to force about twenty soldiers to accept corn from his granary in lieu of wages. Four dollars a *fanega* was his price."

"Four dollars! Why traders on the plaza get only something over a dollar," ejaculated Doctor Gregg.

"Yes, I know. When the men had the nerve to refuse the corn, Armijo had them thrown into prison and loaded down with plenty of iron. Naturally that frightened the whole army. I can not quite blame them for what they did today. Yet . . . Well, I'll tell that later.

"Now here's where pretty little Soledad comes in. Why, Doctor, that libertine has tormented her for several years. He could not win so he managed a marriage with Esquipulas

203

Caballero, an ensign of his. Probably Armijo thought he'd have clear sailing after that, but he floundered." Miera leaned over, picked up a glass of wine and drank.

"When a man like Armijo is aroused to anger, he'll know no bounds," interposed Gregg.

"Right. When he found he could not win the girl he went after her husband and her favorite uncle, Ramón Baca. He played from under the table. There were two fine young officers of whom I suspect Armijo was afraid. Anyway, he ordered a grand review and proceeded to promote inferior officers and even a private from the ranks above these two men. Imagine their mortifying disgrace! Later they petitioned the Governor to reinstate them. He threatened them with death if they, ever raised a voice again. Then pretending that Soledad's husband had been favoring these officers, Armijo had all three thrown into prison and decreed that by today Soledad's uncle, Ramón Baca, should leave the country, an exile."

"So that is what Soledad meant by 'Poor Uncle Ramón!'" interrupted Lona. "Today? Why, I saw Don Ramón this very morning with his sword at his side walking along the palace portal. He stopped and talked with the soldiers."

"Yes, he was there. I met him and he declared to me that he would not go into exile. At that time, he thought that he had the soldiers on his side, that they were ready to revolt. But when the moment came to act, they hesitated. They did not dare. This afternoon! You should have seen Don Ramón, mounted, and in full uniform—a fine manly soldier. Over at the barracks, he made a farewell speech, moderate not fiery, to the very men who would not follow him. Then he proudly rode out of town."

"Ramón Baca, an exile! I can hardly believe that."

"Neither can I," said Trader Gregg, agreeing with Madam Barcelona. "I'll wager if timidity had not made cowards of the

204

soldiers we'd have had the quickest downfall of a tyrant ever known in the history of the world. But his day will come!"

Doña Lona nodded her head.

Lieutenant Miera glanced inquiringly at the physician who caught his unspoken request.

"Never fear, young man, no word of this account which you have given us will escape my lips."

"It would mean irons for me if the Governor ever suspected me, you know. I can not have respect for the cur," answered the officer. "That does not make me a traitor to the department, however. I'd fight for New Mexico as quickly as the next man. If I may say so frankly, I believe that I have earned promotion but I did not get it. I've wondered why?"

"Undoubtedly Governor Armijo knows that you are my friend. I've braved the rascal more than once," broke in Doña Lona.

"Possibly, but if that's the case, I prefer your friendship to a higher office in Armijo's army."

"You do me great honor, Don Orlando."

"It's well merited, I assure you. Now, if you'll excuse me I'll accompany Madam Caballero to her home."

"There'll be no danger?" asked Doña Lona as she walked with the men over the crunching snow to her room. It was colder now. The snow had ceased to fall and the stars pierced the dark blue overhead. They found Soledad waiting, her cloak about her.

"No danger of an attack on a night like this," said the officer. "The soldiers have hardly enough clothing to keep them warm on an ordinary day, not to mention a snowy night. I'm lucky to have an old greatcoat for an evening like this."

When they were gone, Madam Barcelona and Doctor Gregg sat by a lively fire in the conference room again.

"A sorry plight for the whole country. Americans would

not stand for it, Madam. The common people—and we are all common people in the eyes of the law—would revolt before morning. No tyrant could keep them down."

"I do wish something could have been done today but if a man like Don Ramón Baca can not lead on, there's little hope for the present. But, as you say, a day will come." Lona stared into the fire with speculative eyes.

"Now about your venture? Do you think the Governor will make trouble for you when your goods arrive?" asked Gregg, once more the trader.

"Oh, probably. But I'm not afraid of him. He would not dare to throw me in prison. I know too much about the man and I have many friends."

"Well, then we will go on with our plans. I am more than ever convinced, however, that your merchandise should not come to you for a long time. I'll keep an ear to the ground for conditions out here and I'll learn, for the men do much talking when they return to Missouri."

"When do you plan to leave?"

"By the twenty-fifth, if possible. Some of my men came down with the small-pox a few days ago. More may come down with it. I was glad to note that those who have been vaccinated have shown no sign of the disease."

"There's a real epidemic, Doctor. After all the typhoid we've had for the past two years, it does seem as if the pox might have passed us by."

"It's no respecter of persons or localities. I wish we physicians knew how it spreads. Through the air doesn't sound like a sane theory. Anyway, nobody in my company is seriously ill. It's time I was looking in on the men."

The twenty-fifth of February 1840 broke dark and cloudy. Just at dawn, a covered wagon rolled up to the North door of Madam Barcelona's monte room. Across the way a lone sentinel paced his beat on the portal in front of the officers' quarters. No one else was stirring. Even the soldier had disappeared into the patio of the barracks when two heavy chests were hoisted into the wagon and pushed under the driver's seat.

Doctor Gregg greeted Madam Barcelona as he hurried into the room and to the table where candles stood lighted. He drew out his agreement which she read over rapidly.

"We have counted the money very carefully, Doctor. I'll guarantee that it is all there."

"I'm sure of that. Now sign here, please."

Doña Lona scratched with the quill.

"Now here's the copy. Compare it and then sign it also."

"They are correct," said Doña Lona rising. "I am so sorry that you will not return, Doctor."

"That's right. Most likely we shall never meet again. This is positively my last trip out here."

"I've not seen you since the night poor Soledad was here, but you know what happened?"

"If the plaza gossip runs fair this time, the story is: Don Ramón captured and thrown into the same cell with Don Esquipulas, Soledad's husband. That's where he found his land of exile."

"Also correct," answered Lona. "Armijo could not stand against the general protest which rang all over the city. But he would not release the men. Today he ordered them to go South. Heaven knows what will happen to them but I dare predict that they'll be liberated when the caravan reaches Chihuahua. The people there have no liking for Manuel Armijo, I've been told."

"It's all too outrageous. For your sake, as well as for everybody in Santa Fé, I shall keep on hoping for the 'day.' I must

207

bid you farewell. My men are waiting. I'm glad to have had a glimpse of the real Madam Barcelona," he added and, taking her hand, bowed over it in courtly fashion.

"Good-by, Doctor Gregg. Say good-by for me to Señor Hart for he, too, is never coming back." Doña Lona waved her hand as the wagon pulled away.

When the sun cut through the clouds, Lona stepped out into the street, in her hand a spy-glass, the one Ewing had given her. She raised it to her eye. On a distant hill the long line of Doctor Gregg's caravan was creeping slowly but steadily up, up, over and out of sight.

XX

A LONE INDIAN SKULKED SLOWLY AROUND A camp of Blackfeet in Middle Park of the Northern Rockies. No detail of the scene below him escaped his shifting eyes.

Circling a blazing fire, Blackfeet braves were dancing, whooping and howling. Backs bent and knees lifted high, their bodies swayed to the rhythm of the quivering drum hides. Lances flourished. Horrid painted faces grinned at the sky. War feathers fluttered. Scalp locks flapped on gee strings.

The Indian grunted and stalked ahead.

On went the dance, interminably. On the fire meat boiled in a kettle stolen long since from the whites. With stout branches two old squaws poked the stew. Others threw pine knots on the fire. The Blackfeet were drunk with victory over a group of white men. It was their right, thought the Indian in the brush. He knew; he had been there.

He had seen them rush a small camp of American trappers As they charged, howling, swirling a red blanket, all loose animals and those on weak tether stampeded to join the horses of the Indians. A rear guard struck flints to drying grass which blazed and leaped toward the fleeing white men. Now the Blackfeet were safe, far from their enemies. Young scouts, however, stood guard on the mountain sides above the camp.

No one noticed the tall Indian in the buffalo robe. Many braves who were not engaged in the dance, squatted on the ground examining bows, or testing arrow points while the women mended moccasins or strung sinews into thongs. One pretty squaw was finishing beadwork on a new buckskin coat. She flashed a smile at the Indian behind the bushes. He immediately stalked on. When he reached a tepee near the river where some pack animals were staked, he halted, then walked directly toward the crowd to watch the dancers.

When a new group of braves took up the dance, the Indian sauntered over to the animals, picking up a blanket from the ground as he went. Cutting the ropes near the stakes, he leisurely led the horse and mule to the stream but he did not let them drink. He knew that they already had had their fill, so he walked them upstream.

In the dense shadow of trees ahead, the Indian threw a rope, tied bridle-fashion, over the horse's head, and tossed the blanket as a saddle. Catching up the rifle that he had left there against a pine, and the lead rope for the mule, he swung on the horse and rode away at an easy pace. A few moments later, the Indian turned, looked back at the glow of light over the treetops and muttered, "The ornary critturs! Damn their hides! Did they think Ole Bill was goin' ter let 'em keep his pack animuls? Damn 'em! I jes loaned 'em fer a run. They needed exercise. Yeah. Consarn 'em. Nevah have scalped nuf of 'em ter suit me. Git goin'! Com' on Flopear, ye ole mule. Git goin', Stumbleheels. Git, fer ye life! Ain't any cussed varmints goin' ter rub us out. Git."

Leaving a cloud of dust behind him, Williams galloped on, halting occasionally to dismount and put his ear to the ground. "They ain't followin', Stumbleheels. Now git! Ole Santyfee's waiting yonder. Wondah whar that bunch o' greenhorns air by now? Want no chanct fer any of us unless we scattered."

210

Faithful Santyfee was tethered just where Williams had left him, thoroughly hidden by bushes in full leaf. He gave a gentle neigh of welcome.

"Consarn ye! Ain't I larned ye not ter whinny?" said Bill patting his favorite's neck. "Only fool hosses do that, Santyfee. Mind that thar voice o' your'n." He tied the mule securely to the tail of his pack horse. Tossing the lariat around the saddle horn, Williams mounted Santyfee and pushed ahead as fast as possible. On through the night he jogged, drawing rein at times to rest his horses and the mule Flopear.

Early morning found him far away on the shore of a small lake.

When he had watered them, Williams led his animals to grass out of sight from the shore. While they munched, he drew from his jacket a piece of jerked beef and chewed hard. He was cold but he dared not build a fire, nor did he have anything to cook. The mountain slopes about might hide enemies. He could take no chances.

During the long day, Bill busied himself making pack-saddles. Again and again he rolled his eyes over the lake and over the mountains, his ears attuned to any sound. In the late afternoon, he gathered rose buds, berries and edible roots and stuffed them into his pockets. At twilight he grunted with satisfaction when he threw the blanket across Santyfee. Up over a mountain pass, down and up again he went throughout the night. He cached during the day and not until the next evening did he let his "Fetcham" bark. A young deer fell. Quickly cutting off the back strap, he ate part of it ravenously and tied the rest on the packsaddles. Then he hurried on. He must put distance between himself and the smoke of his rifle. Every hour of this night must count. Before dawn he knew he was on the trail leading to his party's camp where Carson, New, Mitchell and the Frenchman Frederick should be.

Suddenly Williams spied a dull fire. He stopped and raising his hands to his mouth gave two owl hoots. He waited for a full moment and gave two more. He saw the fire flare and he imagined New saying, "That's Old Bill. He cain't fool me but he's good at it." Carson would warn 'em, "Keep yer rifles handy. If he hoots a third time, we'll know." That was surely what they were saying, Bill thought, and then gave the two last hoots.

Half an hour later, Williams rode into camp.

"Hi, thar, boys. Food? Half froze fer a bite and sleepy as a possum," said Bill as he sprawled down on the ground. Bill was tired. He was getting old. He growled his thanks when Mitchell attended to his animals. All the men kept silence until Williams had eaten.

When Carson had given him some tobacco for his pipe and Williams had it burning well, he began, "Wagh! Had a time. Met a bunch o' greenhorns, up North in a ravine. One er two talked of bein' ole timers. Jes puttin' on airs. They wus strangers ter me. Had no idee of stayin' long with 'em. Ain't no use havin' a bunch o' greenies a-yappin' at me heels. I know'd Blackfeet might be 'bout and I tole 'em square nuf to scoot ef I give the sign. 'Vamose fer yersel's,' I said. 'Twant long afore I had ter yell. Whar they went, I dunno."

"Blackfeet eh! The devils!" growled New as he bundled himself in a striped blanket.

"Yeah. They played the ole red rag trick to skeer the animuls. Wanted our hosses more'n our scalps, I reckon, but I didn't wait ter ask 'em. I made the dust reach ter Heaven until Santyfee and me could cache. Then I rescued me animuls." Bill went on to tell of his visit to the camp of the Blackfeet and chuckled, "Bet they wus mad as hornets, come mornin'. No use leavin' Flopear and Stumbleheels ter the marcy of Injuns. I don't wave ta-ta ter me animuls unless me own red hair's in danger. Ain't no habit o' mine."

212

"No, nor mine either," said Carson.

"They might be trailin' ye," said Carson. "I'm doggoned ef I ain't got a hunch that we'd better be beatin' it down to Roubidoux's. Ain't afeard of Injuns as ye all know, but beaver's skeerce 'round hyar and they ain't bringin' much a plew. Ye all know that better'n yer names. What say? Shall we move on, come mornin'?"

"Lost the few I had," said Williams as they all agreed to Carson's suggestion.

Long before sun-up, the party was on its way down to the Ute land along the Uinta River. By late evening, several days afterward, they were at Roubidoux's Fort. They knew there was comfort and security in this outpost with its command of a wide stretch of country. The fort was a good place to summer and the men immediately made themselves at home.

The summer wore away, its monotony broken, at times, by the arrival of trappers. Late in August, an Eastward-bound party rode into the fort. They stood by for a rest of a few days for an exchange of news. Williams liked one unusually quiet fellow called "Matt." One morning, Bill knocked the ashes from his pipe and sat down beside Matt.

"Ain't heerd much outah ye since ye pulled in. Whar be ye from?"

"Well, I thought the other men might as well do the talking. I'm from Oregon. Been out in the Chehalem valley. Great country. I'm on my way back to get my folks in Illinois to trek out there," answered Matthew Ormond.

"Chehalem valley? Yeah, I've heerd of it but I nevah wus thar. Reckon ye know'd the Hudson Bay factor, McLoughlin and his folks?"

"Yes, I knew them well. But I spent most of my time down in that valley. Nice folk are settling there especially since a man, named Young, started his sawmill."

"Young? Ewing Young?" asked Bill.

"Yes. Ewing Young. I knew him better than most folk, I guess."

"Now ye don't say?" drawled Bill lighting his pipe. "Mind tellin' me 'bout him? I know'd him long time gone when he wus in Taos and in the mountains North of thar."

"So! He came up from California with Hall Kelley, you know?" Bill nodded but said nothing. "He's talked with me often of that lower country to the East. Seemed to have a secret longing to return to Taos. Had a sweetheart down there."

"Yeah, I know the gal," said Williams. "Ain't been ter Taos er Santy Fee for some years now. Tell me all ye can recolleck 'bout Young."

"As I said, he came with Kelley. They had a bunch of horses. Word came up by boat that Young was a member of a horse-thieving band. It wasn't true but Doctor McLoughlin wouldn't listen to Young. He had more use for Kelley. The result was that Young was ostracized for several years. He got rather bitter about the matter. Then a few years ago, he went with some neighbors to California, got clear of the charge and drove back a fine herd of cattle for the settlers."

"Young nevah wus a hoss thief," Bill almost yelled. "I'd take a hoss ef I needed him but Young wus fool nuf ter hunt up the owner and fork out good money. 'Course, when we wus out and Young jes had ter have a nag, he'd help himsel' 'long with the rest of us. Ain't any man tellin' me Young wus a hoss thief, proper."

"You're right, Williams. I've known Young since . . . let's see? It's '41 now. It was four years ago that I began working for him, when he was building the mill. He was doing all he could to help the people thereabouts. They liked him but he kept to his side of the river and lived alone. Kindly man, older than his years. He wasn't much over forty, I believe."

214

"We're all gittin' older," interrupted Bill rubbing his knees. "Yit, somehow, I cain't think of Young as evah growin' old. Go on."

"He wasn't old, but graying a little. He kept himself up pretty well. He was always buying blue cotton striped shirts, corded trousers or fine sea boots. I used to spend my evenings with him. I can see him now sitting by the oil lamp, drinking his Twankey tea and giving me orders to get some twist tobacco, a cross-cut saw, some strychnine or a waterproof hat. He'd often add some items such as a pair of women's shoes, or combs for some widow over on the other side. He was good to his French neighbors."

"Bet he bought at beaver price, didn't he?" asked Bill.

"Yes, he did. Smart at trading, he was, but he never made much money. He talked a lot about the future of the valley and laid great store on helping build up the settlement. But he never ended an evening's pow-wow without talking about the past. He seemed to live over and over his days in Taos, going on about his 'Lona' as he called her. He said he never had enough money to go back and marry her. Anyway he thought the North was no place for her."

"So he never married?"

"No. Preferred to live alone, he used to say."

After Ormond had gone on East, Bill wished he had asked more questions. It was not likely that he would ever meet Ormond or anyone else who had known Ewing Young well. But he had learned enough, he thought, as he dragged his hand down over his beard. Wasn't it about time to run down to Santy Fee?

One day Kit Carson said to him, "Bill, I've a hankerin' ter go back ter the settlements and see some of my kin. What do ye say ter clearin' out?"

"Wal now, I had some sich idee mesel' while back. Ain't been in Missouri fer a good many years. Not a bad idee."

"Let's git goin' afore long," said Carson eagerly.

"Not yit. I've got one more lone-lornty trip ter make but I'll meet ye somewhar t'other side of the Rockies er at Bent's Fort, 'long about th' fust of October. Keep yer eyes skinned fur this ole coon. I'll ketch up and we'll go 'long together."

The next morning the men missed Old Bill. He was gone, saddlebags, animals and all. No one had seen him go and no one knew where he was heading.

When Williams reached Taos, he heard the church bell toll nine. Wandering about the dimly-lighted plaza, he met a few old friends, drank but did not get drunk. Before daylight he was on his way again. He wanted to pull into Santa Fé as soon as possible, for he could not make a long stay. He must see Lona.

Just outside of the capital, Williams camped. He stripped naked and wallowed about in a shallow stream and dried himself in the sun. When morning came, he made for the Santa Fé plaza, scouted around until he could buy a new buckskin suit. Then, all dressed up, he hurried to Madam Barcelona's home. He found her in her patio busy over her flowers.

"Hi, thar, Lona," he shouted as he strode across the patio, his old black, square-topped hat in his hand. New suit or no, he would not part with his old hat.

"Beel!" shouted Lona dropping her trowel. "I always have a premonition when you are on the way."

The two raced to tell each other the events of the past three years. Santa Fé, Lona told him, was feverishly excited over the news that Texians were now on the way to New Mexico.

"Of course, people say ridiculous things. As if the Americans will plunder and kill! It's so absurd. They're coming to trade, of course. Anyway Armijo . . ."

"Armijo!" ejaculated Williams. "I caught sight of him to-day. What a face! He looks like Hell sued fer murder."

"I know. He's so unspeakably cruel. Anyway, he sent out some soldiers and they have arrested three men who had come on ahead. One of them is Don Samuel Howland. He has lived in Santa Fé. I know him. Did you ever meet him?"

"Yeah, I recall Howland. Nice feller. Straight shooter. So he's a prisoner?" Bill scratched his head. "Unless I'm pow'ful mistaken he won't stay in jail long. That feller has wits, Lona."

"Well, anyhow, he's in jail now. I wish we could get him out but Governor Armijo is stricter than he used to be. Do you know anything about these Texians?"

"No. 'Cept up in Taos they're bettin' six to one that they want to git the kintry hyar under the Texas government."

"I wonder?" she said and then talked on about her business, her adopted daughters and José.

"Shu-ah, he ain't foolin' ye, stayin' away fer so long?" asked Bill.

"No, Beel," Lona smiled. "He's not that kind. Besides I hear about him through a girl down there. They both say the same sort of thing, only Lucia tells me more. José was terribly hurt, more than he realized at first. He has not been well enough to travel. It's way over two years ago since the accident happened, yet the doctors say that it may be another year before he can come North. It's been a long weary waiting for me, Beel, but we are very much in love."

"Good. Wal, now Lona, I want to talk with ye 'bout a matter."

"Come into my sala, Beel."

Bill sat down on the couch and stretched his long legs out and glanced about. It was the same fine room, he thought. Then he straightened up, took out his pipe, filled it deliberately, lighted the tobacco and sat puffing for a while.

"Ye tole me ter keep me ear waggin' fer news of Young, Lona," he began.

"Young? Have you news of Ewing?" she queried and picked up a quill from the desk, idly examining it.

"Yeah. Met a feller come from Oregon. As luck would have it, he knew Young well. Ewing got to be a big man out thar. He set up a sawmill to help the folks—and himsel' too. But he nevah made much money. This feller Ormond said he ust ter talk 'bout ye ter him. Ye see, he nevah marr'id. Lived alone. All last year he wus ailin' but he kept at his job of gittin' his new grist mill goin'. Had it well up and damn me . . . 'scuse me, Lona . . . ef a tarnal flood didn't come 'long and take his sawmill with it. I reckon it most broke his heart. Anyway, 'long in January er so, he . . . he died . . . all alone, Lona."

"Died alone!" Lona sat very still, her unseeing eyes bent to the floor. "Dead! Ewing! It can't be true," she said. "He still remembered me. Well, I've never forgotten him even if my heart finally did go out to José. Once we love, we never completely forget."

"He nevah forgot ye. That's sartain. Ormond said that Young ust ter read ter him out of a book and he tole him that he'd read ter his 'Lona' too."

"A book. Yes, I remember. It was Shakespeare. He had two volumes. You remember too?"

"Yeah, he let me borrow 'em, long time ago. Wal, Ormond said that he nevah had any more'n those two books of Shakespeare on his shelves. Reckon Young carried 'em everywhar he went. Ormond said that he wus lookin' at the cover of one of 'em onct and he seen a faint circle and inside the circle was a word he made out ter be 'Lona.' "

Lona's head went down on her arms. She sat for so long without moving that Bill finally rose and put his hand on her

218

shoulder. He said nothing for several moments and then he blurted out, " 'Tain't no use grievin', gal. Jes be glad he nevah forgot ye."

Williams waited patiently for a moment or two more. Suddenly he leaned over and whispered, "Thar gal! Now, listen. I've a secret. I need yer help."

Lona raised her head at once, blinking tears away. "Help you?" she whispered in return. "Of course, I will, Beel. What do you want?"

"Three old hats," he whispered again.

"Three hats?"

"Yeah, like mine, trail kind."

"Pedro has one, Beel. He can keep a secret. So can Pablita. They will find others. I get it! I get it!" Lona said excitedly. "Do you think you can do it?"

"Dunno. I got a plan. 'Tain't very original but I'll bet ten pesos it'll work. Ole Bill ain't a plumb fool. Not yit. Yer house like all the old uns? Got a cache?"

Lona nodded understandingly.

"Yeah. Now, it'll be tonight er tomorrow night at the latest. 'Tween seven and eight. Saddleroom door. Mean ter make it tonight, if possible. Get me?"

"I surely do," she replied and bobbed her head once more when Williams put a finger to his mouth and left the room.

Williams strolled over to the plaza. He sat down with some old cronies of his, chatted, gambled but drank sparingly until twilight was closing in. Then he wandered off and by a round about way stopped for a moment at Lona's home and then at that part of the old palace which was used as a jail. The soldiers were all at mess in the barracks across the way. The street was almost deserted as it usually was at supper time. Sitting in an open door loafed the jailor.

Williams addressed the man in Spanish, asking if he were the keeper, if he had an easy job and if he made plenty of pesos.

"Yes, Señor. No much *dinero*. Armijo pay few pesos," answered the jailor in English. He squared his shoulders as much as to say, "See, I can speak your language."

"Mind if I sit down with you?" said Williams in English. "Waitin' for the night guard?"

"Sí, Señor. Guard. Eight o'clock. Yes, I like whisky," he answered when Williams offered him a bottle.

The two men talked on. Williams pretended to drink deeply and kept passing the bottle. Finally when he saw that the jailor's mind was getting muddled, he opened fire.

"Got many prisoners?" Williams asked in easy manner.

"Three Texians. You Texian?"

"No, I'm from Missouri. Sherley's me name. Got anybody by that name hyar?"

"No . . . Señor . . . One Howland . . . Forget names," replied the man too drunk now to realize that he was giving information. Then suddenly he broke out with, "Tins. Tins, Señor. Want come, old pal?"

"Don't mind," said Williams following the man shuffling along unsteadily.

The jailor's hands shook when he fumbled with the key. "Tins," he said as he swung open the door.

The three men handed out their tin plates and looked inquiringly at Williams who winked at Howland.

"Somebody's callin' ye, Señor," said Williams to the little man with the tin plates who stumbled away forgetting the open door.

With a jerk, Williams pulled out the three old hats from his buckskin jacket and whispered, "Madam's— Five minutes— Alley door." Then with a bang he closed the door and made as much noise as possible with the key. He was not surprised that the lock was old and wobbly. Yes, Armijo wanted his prisoners safe but he would spend no money for good locks. The burden of the job should fall on his servants.

"Nobody," said the jailor looking up with bleary eyes. "Key?"

"Yeah, hyar's yer key. I locked the door. You don't want those fellers ter git away, Señor."

The man grinned sheepishly, and drunkenly wove his way to the door. He tested it. It was locked. Now he had done his duty and was about to sit down on the doorstep when, raising his voice, Williams urged him to come and get a swig of much better whisky over on the plaza. Oh, he'd see that he got back to his post. Yes.

The fellow shook his head doubtfully. "Must . . . be . . . here. Armijo get me? Bad!"

"Aw, come on. I'll get you back on time. It's powerful good whisky you'll git ovah thar," Williams assured him and gently dragged the fellow away.

A minute later, the three men had the lock broken and the door open. This they closed carefully. Then jamming their hats down on their heads, they shouldered out of the door to the street. Without undue haste they reached the Burro Alley door.

Meantime Williams kept his promise and landed the jailor on his doorstep. Thank God, the night guard had not come! Hardly had the thought crossed his mind before Williams knew his man was sound asleep against the door jamb. Then with long strides he walked to the alley door and stepped quickly inside. He found only two men.

"Whar's the other feller, Howland?" Williams asked abruptly without greeting the man.

"Rosenburg has already gone. Over there," Howland pointed to Lona's room. "Baker goes now around the garden. I'll follow in a few moments."

"Good," said Williams. "You must be hidden mighty soon. There's likely to be a great hullabaloo. Yeah, pronto! Night guard hadn't come. Me plan worked like it wus greased. Ole trick. Beats all what whisky kin do in this hyar world. Now, Howland. The rest is this. Midnight er a bit aftah, ye make fer the Mascara Arroyo. I'll have three hosses fer ye and me own animuls. I'll ride with ye fer a spell. Must git goin'. Don't know as anybody saw me in action but I ain't walkin' 'round the plaza makin' questions 'bout it. I'm gittin' out."

"Thanks more than I can tell, Williams. Now it's my turn to walk through the garden," said Howland.

"Good," Williams nodded. "Remember! The Mascara Arroyo. I'll ride out with ye."

Weaving as usual, Williams went slowly around the portal. He looked into the monte room where men were already playing. Pablita was lighting more candles for them. The other rooms were, as yet, empty. Satisfied, Williams closed the door and walked on to Lona's room.

Pedro was on the floor. Two wide boards had been removed from under Lona's couch. Rosenburg was already below in the small cell-like room. Lona had given him candles, a basket with meat cakes and a pail of water.

Baker was carefully sliding down from one steep step to another. Howland stood ready to follow.

"Here are some more old saddle blankets. It's cold down there," said Lona. "See? This plank has a handle on the underside. Keep it open for better air. But be on guard and if you hear anyone coming, close it quickly. Undoubtedly Governor Armijo will order his soldiers to search my place. He has accused me of favoring Americans." Turning to Pedro she told him to replace the couch. "There, Beel, the men are safe. How did you manage it?"

" 'Twant hard. Played the old trick. Got the jailor drunk.

Now Lona, I'll hunt up another hoss. Happens, I already got two extry hidden in the arroyo. As soon as the lights are out in the monte room, give the men the direction. See that two go fust, then one foller at a distance. We'll make it outah hyar. Short visit, this time, but my ole hide knows it'll be safer outah Santy Fee fer a spell. I tole ye I've promised ter meet Carson and go back ter see the home folks."

"Maybe you'll see Mary, Beel?" said Lona tipping her head a bit coquettishly.

"Naw. Not likely. Reckon I'll keep outah her way but . . . but I'll manage ter git me eyes on her ef she's 'round. Now good-by, gal. Hope things go O.K. fer the Texians. I dunno. Got me duts with that skunk Armijo hyar. Anyway, come any fuss, ef I hyar of it, ye kin bet on me gittin' back. I don't ca'culate I'll be rubbed out, not right away. Good-by."

An hour later, soldiers did come, as Lona had expected. She greeted them heartily.

"Three men have escaped from jail. Three Texians. Have you seen them? Can we search the place?"

"Of course, you may search all the rooms. Texians would hardly dare to come here. It is too public a place." With a wide wave of her hand, she continued, "Search all you want, Señores. You won't find any strangers here." Lona turned away, believing that she would hear as she soon did, "But, Madam, we want you to come with us."

Madam Barcelona conducted them through her house, opening all doors. When she approached her own room, she spoke slightly louder, "Of course, I would not have the men in here. But there is my dress closet." She pulled aside the curtain and moved the gowns herself. "You can see that no one is hiding under the bed."

"Well, those fellows aren't here, that's sure," said the lieutenant in charge. "Thanks, Madam. Sorry to have disturbed you but Governor Armijo insisted that we search your rooms."

The soldiers bowed, marched with clinking spurs across the patio and out through the monte room.

Madam Barcelona followed shortly. She picked up a deck of cards and dealt for the remainder of the evening, laughing and bantering as if in high spirits.

When the candles were all snuffed, Lona called Pedro in a low voice and he had the planks out quickly. The men were at the North door in a few seconds, eager to be gone.

"Yonder is the way." Lona pointed. "The best of luck to you all. Señor Howland, you must not fall into Armijo's clutches. He is more of a brute than he ever was. *Vaya con Dios!*"

"God be with you," Howland whispered.

XXI

NEWS OF THE CAPTURE OF MANY TEXIANS
reached Madam Barcelona but no mention of Don Samuel
Howland. There were tales of inhuman cruelty to Texian
prisoners at San Miguel, cruelty which most citizens of the
capital deplored. That Governor Armijo courted a terrible
revenge was the general belief.

Pablita heard much at the market where women from San
Miguel brought their wares.

"All women at San Miguel sorry for Texians, Doña Lona.
They give bread. Cakes. Do all they can. The soldiers! Ah,
Santa María! They bad. Wicked!"

One day Pablita waddled back to her mistress as fast as her
short legs could carry her. "Oh, Doña Lona *mía!*" she called.
"Señor Howland! Caught on mountain. No, not Señor Williams. Two shot!"

"But Don Samuel? He lives?" asked Doña Lona sharply.

"Awful! Cheek hacked off. Now, he shot too. In the back.
Armijo no listen."

Doña Lona gasped. "I hope there's a special torture chamber in Hell for Manuel Armijo."

Pablita's beady black eyes snapped with anger. Her fat hand
shot out and lifted as if holding a dagger. "I!"

"No, no, Pablita. That's not for you or me. There'll be some other way. Now, you and Sarah clean the large sala. Sarah is already there," she said remembering that she had set the mulatto girl to work some time before.

Lona returned to her own room and sat down to think. Her mind was troubled with thoughts centuries-old. Why does God allow such men as Armijo to live? Why? Is He all-powerful? All about, death is taking good people. Why not the evil Armijo? Has God forgotten this part of the world? "All-knowing?" Then why? WHY?

The silence of the autumn day was broken by Pablita and Sarah clattering across flagstones. Lona rose with a sigh and a fling of her helpless hands. "I can do nothing . . . nothing. Patience! Yes. 'Patience and shuffle the cards!' "

When Madam Barcelona was informed that all loyal citizens must meet on the plaza and give Governor Armijo a rousing reception on his return, she nodded, but when the mid-October day came she sent Pedro and Pablita. She would not go and knuckle to him. And she was glad that she had not when she learned that Armijo had ordered the Texians to be marched South under the command of Dimasio Salazar, known to be the most cruel of all the Governor's captains. She shuddered at the thought of what might happen.

The first spring caravan of 1842 from Chihuahua brought merchants with news. One of them, a Frenchman from Texas, who now operated out of St. Louis, came to Madam Barcelona's salas as was his custom when in town and, finding her alone, burst out with, "Well, I've seen the elephant! I tell you I've seen the elephant!"

"The elephant? Oh, yes. I'm heartsick and disgusted also, Monsieur Burdette. I don't wonder that you're through. I have had a glimpse of the animal myself. But I *must* stay here," replied Madam Barcelona. "What has happened?"

226

"Some things are too horrible to put into words, Madam. But if ever men deserved to be shot down, those men are Salazar and Armijo. Monsters! Don't think for a moment that Texians won't seek revenge when the truth comes out."

"Tell me anyway, Monsieur. Nothing you can say will surprise me. Salazar is a brute. He has always been quarrelsome here in my rooms. As for Armijo? He is the most hated man in all Santa Fé."

Pierre Burdette shook his head, ran his fingers nervously through his hair. "I know General Elias in El Paso. He told me that Salazar walked into his office to give his report and threw down on the desk, six human ears strung on buckskin. Ears of three men, too weak to march on, whom he had murdered on the way to get rid of them. *Sacre Dieu!* Salazar is a prisoner himself now. Flaying alive would be too good for him!" Monsieur Burdette checked his lips until he was more sure of himself. "Madam Barcelona, good-by. I'm leaving as soon as I can. I'll never come again. That's sure. I've had enough of New Mexico, enough of Armijo, enough of everything. I've seen the elephant, flapping ears to tail, I tell you."

For months after Monsieur Burdette's departure, Madam Barcelona continued to hear about the Texians. Salazar had been relieved of his command but his only punishment was that he return to Santa Fé! The Texians were marched on but were being well treated. Now they were in jail. Yes, Americans were trying to secure their release. Sam Houston was endeavoring to have them set free. So went the news.

Arguments pro and con ran high in Madam Barcelona's salas, often entirely disrupting games. "Don't forget Governor Lamar's proclamation. He urged the people to revolt and come under the lone star flag. That's what it amounted to. No wonder Señor Armijo burned a pile of proclamations at Vegas. . . ."

"But, Sir, don't you want to be free from such a governor as

227

Armijo . . . ?" "No. He's a great general, Señor. . . ." "Your
soldiers say nothing of bravery. . . ." "Perhaps not. In face of
facts, they must be silent. . . ." "Silent? Good Lord! What
about Armijo's own words, *'Vale más estar tomado por valiente
que serlo'*—It is better to be thought brave than really to be
so! . . ." "I know. I've heard him say that myself. . . ." "As a
Governor, he is rotten, Sir. . . ." "One may think so but not
speak, Señor. . . ." "How about saluting that gross wife of his
as *'La gobernadora!'* or *'La comandante generala!'* Ye gods!
She, governor! She, the commanding general! Better scorn her
as procurer—procurer for her own husband at that!" . . . "On
the other hand, Señor, she may act so because of fear." . . .
"But why need anyone live in fear? Texas offers freedom."
. . . "Some day, we Mexicans may be free also." So ran two
streams of thought toward each other, clashing into foam at
Madam Barcelona's until summer brought word that General
Santa Anna had freed at least some of the Texians.

"Santa Anna! So he acted humanely," commented Lona
to herself when she stood under her portal, reading a letter
from José. Her mind lingered on such news for a moment
only, for in the next paragraph, José wrote, "At last, I am well.
I must make one or two trips into the mountains to examine
some new prospects and run down to Mexico as well. Then!
Nothing under Heaven will keep me from traveling North on
the last caravan. I'll arrive in late October."

When Lona put her letter from José in her desk, she noticed that it fell against another, one that she had received recently from Doctor Gregg. He had written that her merchandise should arrive on the late September caravan. The
day would come soon.

Lona's natural gaiety returned. She was happy again in the
thought of José's coming and the imminent arrival of her goods.

228

It was high time, she thought, that final arrangements for her store on the plaza were made, so she hurried to Madam Alarid. The little lady's face was aflush with excitement when she greeted Lona and seized her hands.

"Lona, my dear," Madam Alarid cried. "You are bound to succeed. I know it. Señor Alarid and I both heard a cricket on the hearth of the very room that you have chosen for your store. My husband agreed with me that's a sure sign of good luck. That sala is just the place for you. I've had the rear chamber cleared also for a storeroom. Oh, I'm so glad that times are ripe for your success."

With the aid of servants and Madam Alarid, Doña Lona soon made the rooms ready. They had but recently been washed down with *tierra blanca* and were filled with the smell of fresh clean adobe. In the patio beyond, two carpenters hammered and sawed, making shelves. The sound caused a smile for there flashed across her mind a picture of Williams as he worked long ago getting his Taos store in shape and piling bright cottons on rough boards, grimly biting his pipe the while. She hoped that, for her, business would not "rush by in the mornings and fall off in the afternoons." Dear funny old Beel!

Everything was in readiness when the caravan rumbled in. Heavy chests, trail trunks and boxes were quickly opened in the patio. The storeroom was a jumble of busy women unwrapping bundles and calling out in delight at the rich red, yellow, purple and green satins, soft silks, and shapely slippers. One box brought loud exclamations of surprise. It contained two hats with plumes and veils, marked "Paris." The women examined the queer, utterly new millinery with curious interest. Each one tried on the hats and shouted in glee as she looked in a mirror.

When Doña Lona was alone with Madam Alarid, a few

229

hours later, she took the hats again from their box and looked them over once more. "I'm afraid that they'll never sell. Women will not desert the mantilla and rebozo for such creations," she said. "What do you think?"

"I hardly believe they'll sell, Lona," said Madam Alarid, "but they are the only things that Doctor Gregg sent which may be left over. What a lot of lovely things you have! Between us and our maids, we will sell and sell. You will make a handsome profit. Now don't be foolish and give away much, either in goods or money, my dear."

When a modest sign had been tacked to the front door and the two small windows displayed a few articles, women flocked to Madam Barcelona's shop. It was a novelty to see a store run entirely by a woman. No woman had ever attempted it before.

"We want some of this satin to make a *túnica* like yours," said the señoras, because the style of gown Madam Barcelona had fashioned for herself had now become the vogue. They bought well and smiled at every new dainty thing. How lovely were the sashes, the fine laces, the buckles and the embroidery! How charming were the various trinkets for children. The necklaces were fine but not so beautiful as those their grand-mothers had brought from old Spain years ago, but they were worth buying. But the hats! Small. Funny. Odd. Did women really wear such things anywhere? Did they put them on tilted over their foreheads like this, they asked. Should the veils fall forward or back over the shoulders? Every señora tried on the hats, laughed at herself and then every señora put them carefully back in the box.

A week after Madam Barcelona's store had opened, Governor Armijo stepped in and looked about. Crude though he was, he realized at once that there never had been finer stuffs for sale since the covered wagons had first rolled into Santa Fé, now almost twenty years ago.

230

"So this is what you are doing?" The Governor's lips curled and the color of his voice was green.

"Yes, for a few months," replied Lona ignoring the man's all-too-evident jealousy. "Would you like to take this to your wife? One rarely sees such a beauty of a shawl for sale here."

"No. She has enough," he snapped. "Don't believe in women having too much finery. You will make a pretty piece of money with all this. You're shrewd. That's to your credit."

"Thank you, Governor."

"You should not have to work so hard. Where is your fine Lucero? Left you flat, eh?"

"As you wish to put it, Señor," replied Lona heartily glad that her lover was not in town.

"Why did you not tell me that you were planning to do this?" Armijo blurted out at last.

"Tell you? Why should I? It was *my* business, Señor," said Lona throwing her head high and eying the man narrowly.

Armijo winced under Lona's gaze. "Your business indeed! Women should not be in business," snarled the Governor thinking to prick her. But when Lona shrugged her shoulders, he flung out of the door. She knew he would do what he could to hurt her trade. She was certain that Manuel Armijo was angry solely because she was making money. She was. None knew better than Pedro who groaned under heavy bags of silver which he carried away every night and deposited safely in the underground cache beneath Madam's room.

Meantime Governor Armijo strode along behind his guard, deep in thought. No woman should be allowed to make so much money. The impudence of Lona planning for such a venture without consulting him! Had he not helped to start her place years ago? She should have talked to him. Now she scorned him. He ached to confiscate her goods and tax her heavily. But the taxes had been paid. He must think of some plan to divert some of the profit of her store to his own pockets, if not this time, then the next, for surely she would reinvest.

When Armijo reached the seclusion of his small office, he sat down at his desk and picking up a new quill jabbed it viciously into the wood. His slow mind could think of no plan. He jerked out another quill and some official paper. What should he do? The paper was so blank before him. Finally he crushed it and broke the quill. He would not take action against the woman now. In the spring he would have his plan carefully worked out. No one would guess then the reason for his procedure whatever it might be. He would wait.

It was a glorious October day when the messenger rode in to announce the arrival of the caravan from Chihuahua.

An hour later, Madam Barcelona stood on the corner of the plaza in her finest dark green gown and black mantilla. She watched carefully as the wagons rolled in. Señor Lucero was not among the advance horsemen nor in the wagons, but directly behind them. He rode a fine bay. He waved a greeting with his sombrero, and dismounting at once, walked directly to her. Unmindful of people about, he took Lona in his arms and kissed her with fervor.

Farther down under the portal stood a man who saw that kiss of welcome.

"You are lovelier than ever, Lona *querida,*" said José while he drew her arm in his. His blue eyes sparkled in his thin face bronzed from the journey. Lona, turning, caught Armijo's glance. She tossed her head defiantly.

José turned to look. "Still playing for sympathy with the limp, eh? That's not necessary. The limp, I mean. I know, for I fought for months against a tendency to do just that. I would not have it. He continues to be your enemy, Lona?"

232

"Yes. Our armies are forever drawn up in battle line. Now and then the generals clash."

"Well, I'm one of your soldiers now," said José.

"I may need you or you, me. It's amazing the power Armijo has. Some call him a great general. Bah! Not the men in the barracks. You can wager on that. Great general! That grew out of his trickery with the Texians."

"Heard something of all that. The Texians were marched through Zacatecas. I talked with some of them. *Por Dios!* How they did suffer under Captain Salazar!"

Sitting on a bench in her patio, José and Lona talked on. Their eyes often followed the autumn leaves lifting and floating in the late sun.

"I want to tell you of my two little girls," said Lona.

"Two little girls?" questioned Lucero.

After Lona had explained about the adoption of Anita and Luísa and the reason for not writing of it, José nodded with understanding. "That's just like you. Bless your heart! They shall be *ours* when you consent to have the banns read. When, *querida mía?*"

"I have always wanted to be married in June."

"Sweet, June is eight months away. Must I wait so long?"

Lona brushed his cheek with her lips. "My darling, I love you. True, we have waited all these years. But I have always felt strongly about wedding in June."

"Then June it is," consented Don José, burying his face in her perfumed hair.

"Tell me about your trip South to Mexico."

"You would find the city changed. It has grown much larger. Of course, you know that General Santa Anna rides high as dictator. I inquired about your cousin Andreas. His house is closed but the caretaker was there. He's bent and old but his

233

face beamed when I told him of you. He said that Andreas and his family had gone to Spain to live. Your old duenna is dead. Later I looked up Padre Benvenuto. By that time I had your real name, Lona."

"Yes, I knew you would learn it. Some time I'll tell you why I changed it. Is Marino de Alvarado in Mexico?"

"Oh, no. I thought you knew that he lives in Texas and is reported wealthy."

During the winter, Madam Barcelona was radiantly happy. Business prospered. José was gallantly attentive and spent much time with her but his restless nature demanded a definite interest in business. He bought certain mining claims down at Tuerto and, in consequence, was often absent from Santa Fé for a week or so. He was, however, never absent when a ball was in full swing at Madam Barcelona's sala.

By April, rumor on rumor was rife in the capital. The Texians were keen for revenge. Governor Armijo's anger sizzled. He laid plans to meet the "invaders" and let people know about them in no doubtful terms.

One afternoon as Armijo stood at his office window, he saw Madam Barcelona and Señor Lucero ride by on handsome horses.

"I'll break her yet," he muttered, "and as for the cocky Lucero, I'll break him, too. A merchant with gold bars, was he?" Suddenly Armijo stared wide. He ordered candles and wrote rapidly at his desk. Throwing sand over the paper, Armijo folded it and stamped the wax seal. Then he called for a mounted messenger and commanded, "Ride South within fifteen minutes. Catch the last caravan if you can. If you can not, ride on alone but ride. Find General Santa Anna, give him this letter, wait for his reply and return here by early July. Remember I say, 'early July'!"

Governor Armijo watched the soldier remount and gallop off. Growling to himself he said half aloud, "Now we'll see who has the real power, who can make big money." Armijo's fists came down on his desk with a bang. "I'll catch Lucero and Lona both. And for once Santa Anna will say that I've used foresight."

During this spring of 1843, news surged in wilder currents around Madam Barcelona. In fact, all Santa Fé was agog with interest mixed with foreboding. The air throbbed with anxiety. Trouble was ahead. Governor Armijo would listen to no word of caution. One American after another had fallen under the suspicion of being a spy and had been annoyed by the close surveillance under which he was forced to live.

From conversations in her conference room, Madam Barcelona knew that most men deplored such action on the part of Armijo but when word came that wealthy Don Antonio José Chaves had been murdered by a band of Texians on American soil near the end of his journey, feeling ran high and bitter against all Americans. This touched fever heat when the report came that a Colonel Warfield had raided the small town of Mora Northeast of Santa Fé, but it went down again when men learned that the Mexicans had followed Warfield, recovered their own horses and captured all belonging to the Texians. Laughter at the picture of the Texians afoot, retreating probably to Bent's Fort, undermined the tension which pervaded the city.

The feeling of relief lasted only until the next caravan pulled in.

"Lona, my girl," exclaimed José, "I've just heard that a Texian by the name of Jacob Snively, a Colonel, I believe, is bound for Santa Fé with a large army. Armijo's calling for soldiers."

235

"So? Then we all must suffer for Armijo's dastardly work." Lona pressed her hand hard against the locket under her blue morning dress.

"I'll go to the plaza again and return in an hour. There may be more news."

It was less than half an hour before José hurried into the patio in great haste.

"Lona, where are you?" he called and when she appeared at her door, he went on breathlessly, "I've just heard that I've been declared a citizen of Santa Fé. That means Armijo will force me to serve in the army. He'll probably strike like lightning and allow me no opportunity to say 'despedida' to you, sweetheart. One thing is sure. I'm not running away from him. Send Pedro to my room for my chest. I'll pack a few belongings in the bag that I can carry over my shoulder. Thank God, I have a good rifle and ammunition of my own. I'll take my dagger of course. I'll not be caught unawares anyhow." He caught Lona in his arms and kissed her passionately. *"Querida!* This, and our wedding day so near! It's too infernally bad. But some day we'll marry. Perhaps all this that I imagine may not happen but I have a strong feeling about it."

Lona could not speak. She tried to smile and put her kerchief into her lover's hand. "Take the kerchief for good luck and wear it over your heart. I wish I had a vest of armor for you."

Less than an hour afterward, a small group of soldiers knocked at Lucero's door. He was informed that he must mount at once and proceed with them. To the surprise of the soldiers, Lucero was ready. He snatched up his rifle and mounted the horse which had been provided. By nightfall, he was far to the Northeast bound for Taos.

XXII

FOLLOWING AN OLD INDIAN TRAIL WHICH skirted the Río Grande, the small band of soldiers galloped on as fast as possible, silent for a while, wondering why the greenhorn civilian had been ordered to go with them. Anyway he made the seventh man and seven was a lucky number.

José Lucero gave no hint of the reason for his presence but he knew well enough. Soon, lest the men suspect that he might be in General Armijo's employ, Lucero told them frankly that he was no spy. "In fact, gentlemen," Lucero declared, "I ride with you only because Armijo hopes that I'll lose my life out on the plains."

The country was new to Lucero and he felt lost in a world of gray boulders, yellow desert and purple mountains. His eyes were alert for signs of roving Indians but the men encountered no one until they halted for a few moments at the Tesuque pueblo. There they bought tortillas and boiled deer meat, food for their saddle bags.

The second night of the trek was well advanced and the moon waning, before Juan Duran, the lieutenant in charge, ordered a halt. Nearby was good grass for the animals. The men were hungry and, since no Indian had been seen, they risked a fire in a pocket of rocks. One man stood guard but all

237

were within earshot when Lieutenant Duran said, "Governor Armijo gave me orders to explain our mission when we were well on our way. We are to raise a company of one hundred men in and around Taos. Ventura Lobato of Ranchos de Taos is to be captain. Señor Lucero and I are to go with these 'soldiers.'" Duran snapped his lips hard and gritted his teeth. "'Seasoned men are not necessary,' General Armijo said. Lobato's command is to proceed until it engages Colonel Snively's army in battle. Governor Armijo promised to bring up the rear ready to support us. He leaves soon by the Southern route."

"What about the rest of us, Lieutenant?" asked the sergeant.

"Oh, yes. You five men are to remain in Taos and be prepared for any emergency which may arise there." Duran paused again. "I was just wondering how Lucero and I will fare out on the plains, hotter than Hell, with a lot of ranchmen and Indians, fighters though they all are after a fashion."

"Are Taos Indians to go? I'll wager that they'll refuse. They'll say it's no quarrel of theirs. Right they'd be at that."

"Sergeant Zapata, we must make them go. Armijo ordered that anyone who refused to join Lobato's men must be tied to his horse until the company is far out on the plains."

"I can see Indians consenting to be tied!"

"I doubt if it will be necessary but we will see. We must enlist one hundred men."

In Taos, all seven men were taxed to the utmost to convince the peace-loving citizens and the Indians that orders were orders and one hundred men must march to the plains. It was several days before the required number were ready with saddle bags bulging, rifles and ammunition in condition as well as horses. Both Mexicans and Indians had demurred at the order to leave their fields and become soldiers for Governor Armijo.

238

No one went willingly on that morning when they mounted and galloped away toward the East.

Through mountain forests, across hidden valleys and on to the plains went Captain Lobato and his men. By the middle of June they plodded along over flat country blistering hot in the sun, always searching for the "army" of Jacob Snively.

At the end of each day private Lucero scratched a mark on the under side of his left stirrup. Finally he knew that it was the eighteenth of June—the day Lona had set for their wedding, and here he was, hundreds of miles from her. His eyes saw little but Lona's face, throughout that weary day of pushing ahead although periodically he jerked his mind to the task of watching for the Texians as well as Armijo's army.

"This sort of thing isn't any joke, is it, Lucero?" asked Lieutenant Duran when he rode alongside. "Haven't heard a word from you all day. Dreaming, eh?"

"Where are we?" asked Lucero.

"Well, we're on the plains. Haven't you found that out yet? To the North is the Arkansas river and far to the West is Bent's Fort. One branch of the Santa Fé trail is not many miles to the East there," replied Duran. "Heaven alone knows how much farther we have to go."

"This eternal jogging on puts me on edge, Lieutenant Duran. I'd rather fight and be done."

"So would I. There's Lobato motioning for me," said Duran and rode forward.

That night, scouts were sent ahead as usual and dashed back before midnight with word that the Texians were not far away. Had they seen anything of Armijo's army? No! Scouts at dawn returned in only a few minutes. The Texians were just ahead below the rise of sand yonder. "There is no great army," reported the leader. "Eight hundred? Fie! But there are more

239

men than we have, perhaps a hundred and seventy-five all told. Of course, there might be a reserve company not far in the rear."

Captain Lobato made a brief speech in Spanish and in Indian to his men urging them to be brave but cautious. He ordered them to proceed through a dry river bed. He himself took the lead.

At the bend in what was little more than an arroyo, Captain Lobato heard a rifle shot and a command to halt, spoken in English.

"Who are you?" came from a Texian well-entrenched in sand and out of sight.

"*Mejicanos!*" replied Captain Lobato.

"We are Texians and ready to fight. We give you thirty minutes. Surrender or fight. Raise your sword if you decide to give battle," came back in Spanish.

Captain Lobato wheeled and galloped to his company. He declared a council of war. What did the men think wise? The enemy were well hidden. They themselves were not. They had half an hour in which to decide. Lucero and Duran were silent but most of the Mexicans were stoutly in favor of surrender. The Indians, after mumbling among themselves for several minutes, declared that to a man they were for fighting. They had not come this far to turn and run like women. No. They would fight. They would give battle whether the Mexicans did or not. Finally part of the Mexicans agreed with the Indians and the Captain's sword flashed in the air.

Lucero could see that every man sought what shelter he could and fired, but with wild aim. He kept his own rifle blazing as fast as possible. It was useless! The Texians were too well hidden. Their guns spit fire from many vantage points and within five minutes a score or more of Mexicans and Indians had fallen. Then the remaining men threw down their guns

240

and, begging for mercy, held their hands aloft in token of surrender.

Firing ceased.

In the confusion of that moment of surrender, Lucero
mounted his horse, turned and trotted down the river bed.
Sliding Indian fashion to the far side of the saddle, he urged
his animal up the bank and on until he dipped into a small
ravine. Taking advantage of every sand hill he sped Northward
toward the Arkansas. If he could make the trail, he might sight
a caravan. He must return to Santa Fé and Lona.

When darkness closed in, Lucero scanned the stars. He was
not far off his course. He tethered his horse near a clump of
scrubby trees and searched for water but could find none. A
few feet from his horse, he wrapped himself in his blanket and
lay down to sleep, his mind set for an hour. Awaking he wondered where he was. He listened. There was no sound but the
gentle rustling of birds disturbed in their night slumber. He
scouted about. No one was near so he lay down again.

Shortly after midnight, Lucero was again on his way. He
would put many miles between himself and the Texians with
their prisoners. Was he the only one to escape? How were the
men faring? Was Duran to be shot at sunrise with all the rest?
There was no use pondering on their fate, he had his own to
attend to and pressed forward. During the day which followed,
he hid in a dip in the plain, using every unevenness of the slight
slope to protect himself and his horse from the scorching sun.
Although he watched all day long, he saw no caravan.

When night came he rode at an easy pace to save his horse.
Topping a small hillock, long after midnight, he sighted a distant fire. He gently urged his animal on. The fire was several
miles away. Perhaps it was a camp of the Texians? He must be
wary, but he chose a direct line. His horse seemed to understand and jogged persistently on, gasping through his dry

throat. Lucero's head dropped forward occasionally in sleep but not for long because his tongue was swelling. Neither rider nor beast had tasted water for many hours.

When light broke over the far edge of the prairie, José saw the dark dragon of the desert begin to move. Thank God! It was headed Southward. There were many horsemen? Could it be possible that the Texians had taken a shorter route and joined the caravan bound for Santa Fé? José changed his course at an angle to reach the trail before the travelers could arrive.

Keeping the wagon train in sight, as far as possible, Lucero prodded his horse along. Finally he halted on the trail for a short rest. Then he rode toward the foremost wagon, holding his sombrero high in the air. Faintly at first, his ears caught shouts of welcome. The flat prairie gave evidence that he rode alone.

"Water! Water!" was Lucero's first thick cry.

When the lone stranger had drunk as well as his horse, the wagon master wanted to know how it came that he was alone this far out on the trail. Lucero gave his version of what he had seen and asked if he might accompany the caravan. Consent was readily granted by the leader who swore the air red giving his opinion of "them thar Texians who were out fer no good under Heaven. Ef the Texians air mad, why don't they march outah Austin and go straight fer Santy Fee and git the lickin' done and go home. This business o' prowlin' 'long the trail, I ain't got no dad-blasted use fer."

When the big, husky fellow turned to his own wagon, he asked, "An' whot mout be yer name?"

"José Medina," Lucero answered. He had anticipated the question and decided to use his mother's name. This train was bound for Santa Fé—and Armijo. Perhaps the captain of the caravan might be questioned as to members of his party.

"Live in Santy Fee?"

242

"For the present, yes," replied Lucero.

"Wal, now tell me somethin'. Why don't that goldarn son of Satan, Armijo, help those poor critters 'round the plaza thar? He's makin' plenty o' money. We wouldn't stand fer that sorta thing in the States, I'm tellin' yer."

"You see, Armijo has a lot of clothes."

"Clothes? Now what air yer meanin'?"

"Armijo wants to line all his own pockets, Captain Warner. Then he claims a lot of friends." Lucero's eyes twinkled as he watched the man shake with laughter. Then he added, "You know 'the wheel that squeaks the loudest, gets the grease.'"

"Now yer talkin' sense," haw-hawed Captain Warner pushing back his great straw hat over a forehead that declared him more of a square-faced blond than did his dusty, tobacco-stained beard. "Had ter git that weighty puzzle off me mind."

"We Spaniards have a saying that there are but two families in the world, the 'Have Much' and the 'Have Little.'"

"Yeah. That comes damn near right, Medina. Ain't been down ter Santy Fee but onct an' I wus too goldarn busy gittin' ready ter pull out agin fer ter larn much 'bout affairs. Got a family?"

Lucero shook his head and turned his eyes away but the captain caught his look and added, "Sweetheart, eh? Good fer everybody, I'd say ef you was to fall outah a wagon 'n asked me. Now it's time we wus movin' on." With that, Captain Warner climbed to his wagon seat and started the caravan on its way with a crack of his whip and a lusty, "Git 'long Mirandy!"

XXIII

AHEAD WAS SAN MIGUEL, THE LAST STOP BE-
fore Santa Fé. The wagons dipped down, splashed through a
small stream, creaked up a short steep bank and then pulled
into the great plaza. A fiesta was in progress. The bright crowd
waved kerchiefs or sombreros and hailed the newcomers with
"Los Americanos!" Men with guitars sang louder and plunked
in quicker time. Dancers paused to bow with a swirl of wide
skirts or a deep flourish of flat-topped black hats. Again and
again came the welcome, *"Los Americanos!"*

"Por Dios!" exclaimed Lucero under his breath. "A fiesta!
Lona may be here and I look like the Devil's best friend. This
suit is past redemption."

Turning his horse sharply to the right, Lucero rode around
the old adobe church and sought out a room in which to make
himself as presentable as possible. When his beard was shaved
off, he laughed outright. The lower part of his face was light,
the center very dark brown and the upper round of his forehead almost white. "I might pass for a clown or one of the chif-
fonetti," he said to himself thinking of painted fun-makers
among Indians. "Lona will not know me."

When Lucero stepped into the patio, the woman of the house

244

asked him into her kitchen for lunch. He learned that the great Madam Barcelona had come to their fiesta. "Yes, indeed! Her booth? Over on the other side of the plaza. Fine blankets hang all around. After siesta, you should hunt up her place. All the señores flock there. Yes. She must be getting on in years now but she's as pretty as ever, they say. Can't understand her running a business so well and a store too. Pity, she never married. Husband says she's in love now. Yes. With a man named Lucero, he said. Ever hear of him? Comes from down in Mexico." The woman rattled on without giving Lucero a chance to utter more than a monosyllable.

After the midday siesta José strolled to the plaza in search of Madam Barcelona's booth. He smiled. "So she's in love with a man named Lucero. I'll bet my last peso that she won't know him when she sees him."

Lucero found Madam Barcelona's stall easily enough. It was already filled with gamblers. She herself was seated on a throne-like chair at the end of the monte table, dealing with swift, graceful hands. She looked up and smiled impersonally when Lucero stood at the side of the wide entrance. Then she shuffled the cards.

Madam Barcelona glanced casually over the crowd again. She noted that the stranger had not entered. Once more she smiled. This time the man's gaze held her attention. Strange. He put a warning finger over his mouth. Suddenly she nodded, then looked intently at the layout before her.

Lucero left the booth at once. She had recognized him. That was sufficient for the present.

Not far away Señor Lucero spied Pedro and Pablita, arm in arm, examining a pile of serapes. He walked up behind them and said in a low voice, "Don't be too surprised, Pedro. Here I am again." But this admonition did not have time to sink into Pedro's mind so he turned impulsively with warm greeting.

Pablita exclaimed, "Oh, Don José, we've been so worried. We are delighted to see you here and well. How Doña . . ."

"Hush, Pablita. I am supposed to be either a corpse buried in sand or a prisoner of the Texians. I escaped and luckily met a caravan. The travelers know my version of what happened. You'll hear it soon enough. To them I'm Señor Medina. Is General Armijo here, Pedro?"

"No, but some of his spies are," said Pedro in a whisper.

"Then I'll stroll on. Pay no more attention to me. Where is your wagon, Pedro?"

"Beyond the church in the lane leading West."

With a quick "adiós," Lucero walked leisurely on and soon returned for the afternoon to the safety of the room he had rented for the day.

At the roll of the midnight bell, the fiesta was over. Songs ceased or died away down this road or that or in a distant hallway. Guitars and banjos were silenced reluctantly. The packing was done. One after another, loaded wagons creaked out of the plaza. Everybody wanted the fiesta to go on throughout the night but the priest had decreed that his parishioners start homeward at midnight.

Madam Barcelona was more deliberate than usual. Several men assisted her and Pedro. She glanced at the sky. If she could dally a few moments the moon would be under a cloud and her wagon the last to leave the plaza. She made Pedro refold some of her blankets. She wanted them laid out long. They would not wrinkle that way, she said. Finally the moon slid out of sight and she climbed up to the wagon seat with Pablita and Pedro.

Not until her covered wagon had started to move across the plaza did Doña Lona lean over and say, "Pedro, have you seen Don José?"

"Yes, Doña Lona. I saw him at the serape booth. He did not

246

wish me to speak with him again but I told him where our wagon would be. He should return with us, I think. I have heard that it would not be safe for him to be seen in Santa Fé. How strange he looked. I don't believe anyone recognized him today."

Doña Lona did not answer but bent forward to watch eagerly as the horses plodded around the church. They entered the lane and were stopped at a dark doorway. José Lucero was waiting.

Quickly Lona found a foothold on the wagon step and was on the ground before Lucero could reach her side. He came forward with arms outstretched but Lona raised a warning hand. She heard footsteps.

"José!" she said softly. "My darling! . . ."

Neither spoke as a family passed by and entered a door some distance farther on.

"I understand, Lona *querida*," José whispered. "I can wait."

"Ride to the end of the lane where the trees are. We will meet you there."

A few moments later, Lona's wagon arrived in the deep dark of the trees.

Lona alighted once more. She found José waiting, but he would wait no longer and took her in his arms. She was almost breathless when he yielded to the pressure of her hand.

"Listen, my dear," Lona said. "Armijo's spies are everywhere. If you were recognized today, they hunt for you even now. We must away at once." Still holding his hand, she turned to tell Pedro to tie José's horse to the back of the wagon. "You must be hidden, José. Get into the wagon bed. There is a long pile of blankets. The one on top is for cover. Make yourself as comfortable as possible. There. Now, Pedro, straddle the monte table over Don José."

When all was done and Lona had climbed to her seat, she leaned back and bade José sleep if he could but, she warned, if

247

the wagon was stopped with a jerk, he must cover his face quickly.

"Sleep? I'll sleep soon. I'm infernally tired," answered José stretching out his legs and sighing with weariness. "We started at three this morning in order to arrive at San Miguel in good season. It's no easy life with a caravan at any time but when it heads in—saints above!"

"Sweet dreams, José. We must not talk any longer," said Lona, settling herself more easily on the hard wagon seat. By her side, Pablita soon snored with her head resting on Pedro's shoulder. But Lona was wide-eyed throughout the night. How could she outwit Armijo? If he had word that José was alive, he would have his spies search her wagon before she could reach her home. She drew her small gun from its holster and hid it in her lap. Her dagger was already hidden in her belt. She tried to think of every contingency which might arise. She turned and looked over the back of the seat. Yes, Lucero slept. Bless him! She must keep watch. At four, the heaviest hour of all, Lona saw Pedro nod. Carefully, so as not to waken him, she took the reins and drove on. How she wished to hurry but she knew the value of the steady pace. No one was on the road but there was yet an hour.

Broad daylight made Madam Barcelona's North room a focal point for danger. People sauntered along to the plaza. A sentinel paced the portal of the officers' quarters across the way. Without a suggestion from his mistress, Pedro drove around the corner to the saddle-room. Pablita unlocked the door. Then Lona and Lucero alighted. A blanket drawn about in Indian fashion gave Don José reasonable security from prying eyes.

Once more José and Lona were safe within her own sala.

"Did you hear any news at San Miguel?" asked Lona.

"A little. The señora at the house there did a lot of talking. How she did jabber! She was not unlike some of the men I

have known on the plaza here. Talk! Talk! Well, she told me
that not long ago Armijo's army rushed through San Miguel as
if the Devil himself were after them. That confirms my belief.
Armijo just fled in terror. Now, if he learns that I escaped—
Heaven protect me!"

"The saints help you," said Lona. "I believe it is wise for you
to go South again. I say it against my wish, my dear."

"Probably, but not yet," Lucero answered.

For the next two weeks, Lucero lay low at Madam Barcelona's
and used her rooms by day, the saddle-room by night.

Rumors filled the plaza and swirled about Doña Lona's
salas. Often she sent Pedro out to learn what he could. Several
caravans had moved in lately. Men said that travel on the trails
was heavy, this year; that Texians planned to molest Mexican
wagon trains; that Colonel Snively had cut the throats of all
his prisoners (this was also stoutly denied); that Snively and his
men would be caught and disarmed by U.S. soldiers; that many
Mexicans and Indians had been killed in the battle up near the
Arkansas river; that only one of Lobato's men had escaped.

"Only one?" asked Lucero of Pedro.

"That's what I heard, Señor."

"If so, then I was the man. Was any name mentioned?"

"Today, that Captain . . . What was his name?"

"Warner?"

"Yes, Captain Warner was drunk and talked a lot on the
plaza, Don José. I could not hear what he said but a muleteer
who stood near by told me that he boasted of being the rescuer
of the one man who had escaped. He said that the man's name
was Medina and that he had lost him down at San Miguel."

"That fits me, Pedro."

"I know. If you'll allow me, Señor, I'd like to say that I think
you should not stay in Santa Fé. There'll be a caravan going

249

South very soon. They are not waiting for cooler weather, this year. Your horse is in prime condition, Don José."

At midnight, Lucero and Pedro rode out of town. No one challenged them but on the Agua Fria road they passed a horseman who struck a match to light his cigar just as the two galloped by.

"The light flashed on your face, Don José," exclaimed the frightened Pedro.

"I know, but it was just a lucifer. Even so he may have recognized me. I do not want to worry Doña Lona but you should tell her of our meeting this man."

The two galloped on for a mile farther in silence. Then Lucero insisted that Pedro leave him, cut across cornfields and enter Santa Fé by another road. He himself would go on until he reached Socorro. There, Lucero said, he had a good friend with whom he could stay until the caravan arrived. "A thousand thanks, Pedro. Adiós."

Pedro veered to the left and did as he had been ordered. Once he turned and looked back but darkness had already engulfed Señor Lucero.

The horseman had recognized Señor Lucero. He was not a spy for Governor Armijo but he must pass on any bit of news so he told his friend.

By noon the next day, this friend went to the Governor's office and told Armijo of José Lucero's night ride Southward.

"So Lucero survived and has been in Santa Fé? Why did you not tell me this long ago?" snapped the Governor and struck the man with his cane.

"Your Excellency, I did not know you wanted him," said the fellow wincing under the heavy blow.

"You should know enough to tell me of such men, whether I

instruct you or not, you fool," growled Manuel Armijo. *"El diablo!* None of my spies are worth the beans they eat. So Lucero has escaped me! He isn't worth the effort to arrest him anyway. Now you get out."

Governor Armijo sat down at his desk, alone again. He pecked with a quill, as usual, until he had spoiled the point and tossed it on the floor. His frown deepened. He would get that fellow Lucero yet. Where on earth was that messenger that he had sent to Mexico? He was to return by early July. He was probably just another damnable fool. Late, of course. Why could he not find reliable men to serve him?

Day by day went by. Armijo was more and more irritable. He struck often with his cane until, one day, he realized his cane was doing him no good. Then he decided to gamble for a time and went to Madam Barcelona's large sala.

"How is Governor Armijo, tonight?" said Madam Barcelona gracefully lifting her many ruffled white dress in a curtsy.

"Not as well as I should like but I am about," answered the Governor.

"You wish to play?"

"Certainly. What else would I come here for?"

Madam Barcelona preceded the Governor to a table where men waited for a fourth. The game started but broke up shortly because the others would not stand for Armijo's bursts of temper. Well, if he could not gamble, he would go into the patio. There he found Doña Lona who had gone to her room for extra candles, and was now hurrying back to the large sala.

"Come, tell me about your lovely self," coaxed Armijo. "Your business is going well, is it not?"

So he wants to know about my affairs, does he? "Yes, things go well but I could make more money, of course."

"You made plenty on that trail deal. Of course, you invested again. You expect more goods soon, no doubt?"

"When does the next caravan come in? Have you heard?"

"Within the week, probably. Nothing seems to deter Americans."

A shot rang out in the North room.

"Excuse me, Governor. I'll have to see about that."

"No! Let them fight it out. Stay with me," he commanded, trying to catch her arm but Lona flung away from him and ran across the patio.

Madam Barcelona was angry. She threw open the door and sprang forward. She saw gamblers back toward the walls; some pushed out the front door allowing fresh air to tear at the thick smoke which hung lazily over the players. Two men pointed guns at each other. Doña Lona dashed between them.

"Go! Go! You know I do not allow any shooting here. Go!" ordered Madam Barcelona, her eyes ablaze.

The men stalked out of the room. The woman watched them go. Then with a sweep of her hands, she said, "Gentlemen. On with the games."

"Whew! What a fury!" whispered a stranger in a corner.

"Yes. We men call it her 'panther mood.' Watch her hands some time. But I'll say this: I have never known her to get so angry unless she was in the right."

Madam Barcelona did not return to the patio but passed through the series of rooms until she was in her own sala. She could see the Governor pace back and forth, obviously annoyed. She could not hear him hiss the word, "Hussy!" nor see him after he entered the hallway to stride on to the front door, but she guessed that he wondered whether anyone had been watching and knew of his embarrassment.

Manuel Armijo walked directly to his office. He dismissed his guard and sat alone. He was examining his favorite pistol, enjoying the click of the trigger, when he was startled by a knock

252

at the door. Hurriedly he put the gun in a drawer which he left open, and called, "Pass!"

A dusty tired messenger walked in, saluted and spoke rapidly, "I have just arrived, Your Excellency. It has been a long journey."

"Did I not tell you to be here by early July? What do you mean by such disobedience, you lout?" growled Armijo, showing his teeth.

"I could not avoid being late, Señor. I had to travel many extra hundred miles to catch up with General Santa Anna. I had great difficulties. Below in the Jornada, I rode ahead of the caravan and was attacked by Indians. I barely escaped with my life."

"Nonsense! Except for the messages, 'tis a pity that they did not scalp you. Let's have them. Now, go."

Governor Armijo tore the packet open, drew the candle nearer and read the short letter first and then looked over the long official paper signed by Santa Anna. "Aha! Good! I can fill in the date at my discretion. I know more of local conditions. I should say I do!"

Taking a new quill, Armijo filled in the date—August 7, 1843. He drew a curtain aside. A few people passed, homeward bound. He would wait. He walked the floor and rubbed his hands in gleeful satisfaction. "Now I'll crack them where it will hurt most. She will lose. So will he and be unable to return." Again he drew the curtain. No one was near. He picked up a hammer and a few tacks. When he saw no one on the palace portal, he tacked the paper to the door.

XXIV

"*POR DIOS!* SEE HERE! WHAT WILL HAPPEN
now?" exclaimed the first man who passed the palace the following morning. "Can you believe your own eyes? Signed by
Santa Anna too! It means ruin to many of us if that's allowed
to stand."

A crowd of men soon gathered and peered over each other's
shoulders to read the paper on the door, obviously official with
seal and elaborate rubrics scrawled under signatures.

"What on earth can that mean? All ports closed to wagons
from the East *and the South!*" cried a merchant looking over
his glasses at his neighbor. "Why man! No caravans to enter!
Not even from Chihuahua! What in heaven's name can be the
reason for such action? It spells disaster."

"I know. Disaster!" was the laconic reply for the man was
almost speechless.

Instead of going about their business, men left for their
homes. In half an hour everybody in Santa Fé had heard the
astounding news. Small groups of excited merchants gathered
on the plaza; others hastened to private patios where they dared
speak more freely. Condemnation of Governor Armijo and
President Santa Anna ran to white heat.

"Something's wrong!" . . . "Looks so to me." . . . "Someone asked Governor Armijo the reason. He lifted his shoulders and said gruffly, 'Too much trouble on the trails.' " . . . "What did he say then?" . . . "He shrugged his shoulders again and went on." . . . "But this is too drastic!" . . . "I'll say it is. I stand to lose money." . . . "So do I. It's outrageous!" . . . "But Armijo will lose also!" . . . "I know but he has plenty. I'll wager that Armijo cooked this up." . . . "Somehow I think so too." . . . "He'll have to set this aside." . . . "Go against Santa Anna? Not he!" . . . "Santa Anna acts hastily at times." . . . "Armijo could have this withdrawn." . . . "Somebody asked him to do this." . . . "What did he say?" . . . "He shook his head, threw his hands wide and just looked dumb." . . . "Something's wrong, I tell you."

Madam Barcelona heard much of this talk of the city. She guessed the real reason for the closing of the ports. Armijo might prate of danger on the trails to the East as much as he liked. Such an excuse hardly held good in regard to the Southern route. Once he leered viciously at her as he passed on the plaza. This tended to confirm her belief that he had learned somehow that José Lucero might be coming North before long. But to her patrons she said nothing.

Week after week rolled on insufferably dull. The ports remained closed. Merchants were powerless; Armijo arrogant. Business was at a standstill.

In her salas, Madam Barcelona chilled under the depression which pervaded the city. True, men came to gamble but their spirits were sluggish. The exhilarating verve always attendant upon the arrival of caravans was lacking. Balls were superficially gay. A subtle pall enveloped everyone. Discontent throbbed in the very air. Hatred of Manuel Armijo mounted.

Less cautious now, politicians felt the power of numbers and spoke out in Madam Barcelona's rooms. "We have word of another turnover down in Mexico," said one man who did not seek the privacy of the conference room. "You know, Madam, that there have been three such since Armijo grabbed the reins in '37. Now there's a fourth. We are again to have a constitutional government. The first departmental assembly meets soon. That will not set well with Armijo. No wonder he claims to be ill."

"Ill? Yes, ill at heart," exclaimed Madam Barcelona. "He knows how people scorn him. He's shown the white feather too often."

Some time later, no one, least of all Lona Barcelona, was surprised when Armijo appointed another to take his place and retired to his Alburquerque home in January of '44. Nor was she surprised, after the failure of two men in the high office, that General Santa Anna took the upper hand and definitely appointed Don Mariáno Martínez as constitutional governor. She agreed with her patrons that he might not be the wisest choice but she gloried in his courage when he revoked the edict against the entrance of wagon trains and proclaimed all ports once more open.

The first spring caravan to Chihuahua was announced as about to depart.

On Lona's desk was a pile of letters, for she had written often since José had left. Now she scribbled a last letter to him to send with the caravan.

"Surely now you can return with safety," she wrote and paused to glance out the window. Safety? Would there be any safety for him as long as Armijo was in the country? But Armijo was shorn of power. True. Nevertheless, he had an uncanny ability to return to office when he willed. But he was ill or said he was. Possibly he would remain in Alburquerque and, if so, he might forget his jealousy of her, his envy of her success and let her alone. Yes, Lucero could return. The odds were against Armijo's ever being in the old palace again.

256

Finally she wrote, "Governor Martínez is having trees planted on the plaza and along the streets. He plans an alameda near the chapel of the Virgin of the Rosary. You'll hardly recognize Santa Fé when you return, my dear. He is to establish a public school. I am delighted. The teacher is to be an Englishman by the name of Tatty. I shall send Anita and Luísa. I want them to have the best education the city can afford.

"Remember me to Lieutenant Miera. He must be a captain by now? Tell him that the girls and I miss him very much. I certainly do, for now I have no one with whom I care to ride the hills and deserts hereabouts as I did when you were away from Santa Fé the last time. I had a letter from Lucia, after you departed, telling me of their marriage. Pray convey my best wishes to them both."

With assurances of her love and her longing for his speedy return, Lona closed and sealed her letter. "His return?" she said to herself. "I wonder when that will be?"

Now it was the middle of August, 1846.

Three interminably long years had passed since José's departure, three years of danger to her lover. Lona sat on a bench on her patio portal. Her head was tilted back against the adobe wall. She was only vaguely aware of the birds chattering over full-bloom summer flowers. Somewhere someone was singing "La Paloma." A letter lay on her lap. So José had sold his mines! He was no longer well enough to carry on and had been rejected as a recruit for the Mexican army. He would come North in the fall. There might be trouble or delay on the way but come he would. She could count on him, this time, he wrote, for somehow he would be with her before long.

Little of importance to her personally had happened. Had she dreamed that so much time would elapse before she should see José, she would have ridden away with him that dark night so

257

long ago. So she thought now. The next year? Yes, it was in '44, that José had been so successful with his mines that he had decided to delay his return for a while. It was that year when Governor Martínez in the old palace had killed a Ute chief by crashing a chair down on his head, or the soldiers had. Stories varied. What fear had swept the city! People thought that the Utes might attempt a horrible revenge. But they did not. During the winter, the American, Ben Prewitt, let slip the word of a conference between Armijo and Martínez. It happened in the back of his own store, Prewitt had declared when rumors mounted that Manuel Armijo was scheming to return as governor once more.

Then in '45? Well, it was her fault that José had not come. In every letter, she had begged him to stay in Mexico where he was free and safe rather than come to her. She had been so sure that she was right. He had wanted to come. Yes. But it was lucky that he had not, for that autumn, Armijo actually did become governor again. She had had a tilt or two with him, then he had let her alone.

Now this was a year of war. War? It hardly seemed possible in sleepy old Santa Fé, that there could be war, bloody war anywhere. Yet traders had told her of trouble on the Río Grande near Matamoros, and of defeat for the Mexicans at Palo Alto and Resaca de la Palma. War! Cannon boomed somewhere. Men were dead or badly wounded. Women wept somewhere, and they helped when they could. But war, actual war was man's folly. The United States, the big bully, was pitted against Mexico.

Lona fell to thinking of Santa Anna. She knew that he was now in exile. Two years past, he had lost his wife and remarried about six weeks later. The wedding in the National Cathedral had been all but royal, she had heard, but Santa Anna himself had not been there! Another had acted as bridegroom. The

258

little bride had been escorted to Santa Anna's hacienda, *El Encero.* Of the General's downfall, she had heard also. He had been denounced as a rebel and had been forced into hiding. How she had laughed at the tale of Santa Anna with a few loyal friends waylaid by Indians! In spite of the General's disguise as a muleteer, the savages soon learned that they had captured the hated owner of the whole countryside. They knew the authorities were hunting him.

A priest interceded when the Indians were resolved to boil their victim, wrap him in banana leaves and present him to the officials, as a huge *tamale!* Lona smiled faintly now at the tale. But her smile faded when she remembered once more that Santa Anna was, at present, an exile in Cuba. He was needed in Mexico. Why didn't the Mexicans recall the one man who might lead them to victory?

The problem was not hers. Lona shook her head and walked out among the bushes for more light. She read José's letter again. Well, war or no war, José was coming. She was glad—glad in spite of her fears. There might be trouble at El Paso or on the Jornada. She prayed that he would come through safely. Perhaps after they were married, Manuel Armijo would not dare to molest them. Perhaps?

Lona dressed for the evening in a gown of brilliant red. She said to herself while she rearranged her hair, "Yes, my darling is coming and—so is the Army of the West!" American soldiers were on the way, she had been told, on their way to Santa Fé. "What will happen next? All I can do is to keep my business."

She sighed and added, "Yes, 'Patience, and shuffle the cards.'"

XXV

WHILE LONA DREAMED OVER THE PAST THREE years, a man walked into the palace to see Manuel Armijo. He was an Irishman, a successful trader who had often been in Santa Fé.

"Greetings to you, Governor and Commander-in-Chief," began the Irishman. He stepped forward where stronger candle-light fell on his slender black figure, his stiff white shirt front and high collar flaring above a black bow tie. His fine blue eyes were restless. Save for the quick batting of the eyelids, there was nothing to hint that the man was on an unusual errand.

"Ah, Señor Jim! Jim Magoffin. I'm delighted to see you. Many things have happened since you were here. More are at hand if the reports I have are true. Does a great army move toward Santa Fé?" Governor Armijo made a visible effort to smile genially while he looked down on the Irishman.

"Yes. The Americans are coming. They are not far behind me."

"I suppose that I should have you thrown in jail, Señor, but if you leave soon for the South all will be well. We are prepared to meet this army, Señor Magoffin. We shall have to fight, of course."

"Doubtless," answered Magoffin, smiling with lips that quivered, for the idea of Armijo's fighting bordered on the sublimely ridiculous. "I have an important message for you. I do not wish to talk here, for I must limit myself to the proper time for a short formal call. What I have to say concerns you very much. There is gold in it for you. Will you join me at the conference room over at Madam Barcelona's?" Señor Magoffin turned to depart.

"Gold, you say? I'll be there at nine. That is the best place to meet. Its semi-publicity disarms suspicion."

Promptly at nine, a guard thundered the usual announcement that His Excellency, the Governor, was arriving. He bowed and chatted for a moment with Madam Barcelona. "Aha! That is Señor James Magoffin," said Armijo, looking down the hall. "I must speak with him." With a quick bow, he left Doña Lona and strode away to greet the Irishman as if he had not seen him before. With a sweep of his hand, he invited Señor Magoffin into the conference room.

Gamblers who smoked near the front door followed the lead of Madam Barcelona's glance. All eyes were alive with suspicion.

When the door of the conference room closed, one man leaned over and said under his breath, "'A puerta cerrada el diablo se vuelve'—At the closed door the devil turns away—but not tonight! He stalked within. Didn't you see him, tail and all?" Another added, "Um! One American, far ahead of the Army of the West, alone in an ear-proof room with Armijo, hints of mischief. I wonder what they're up to?"

"I do not know, Señor, but if the Devil's in there, he'll cut the string and the cat will be out of the bag. You can be sure of that," replied Madam Barcelona with a wave of her hand toward the entrance to the large gaming sala.

Something more than mere curiosity held the woman in

261

the hallway. She walked its length again and again and glanced at the door. It remained closed. Not a sound could she hear. She chided herself as an eavesdropper but still something kept her pacing quietly up and down. At last, the door opened slowly.

"Twenty thousand, you say?" said Armijo, neglectful of caution.

"Aye, Ortíz—at Galisteo," whispered Señor Magoffin and the sibilant quality of his voice carried farther than he knew.

Madam Barcelona passed on.

Several days later, Doña Lona rode out to the Northeast, following the old trail to Taos. She went alone but found the road anything but lonely. Men on foot or horse, armed with rifles or bows, hailed her as they passed. Lona knew they were answering Armijo's call for troops. A group of Tesuque Indians halted and asked if the men of the East had come? No! "We no want fight Americans. They friends," the chief mumbled but led his men on.

Lona was about to wheel her horse to return when she saw some distance ahead a solitary rider, crouched far forward on his animal. The buckskin fringe of his coat flapped in the wind. There was no denying her squinting eyes. That was Beel. She waved her hand and saw a black hat answer high in the air.

"Heigh-ho! Lona!" shouted Williams from a distance. "Wal, I'm a buffler calf ef it ain't yersel'! Ridin' all alone?"

"Yes, I ride alone a good deal, Beel," answered Lona as she held out her hand. "It's good to see you. There's much excitement in the city. The American army comes. We may need each other. You've been gone for—let's see? Almost five years?"

"Yeah, some spell. I tole yer ef I heerd of big doin's down hyar, I'd be ridin' in, ef yer remember. Got word of Kearny and

262

his men a-marchin' while I wus loafin' with some Injuns, up North a piece. I says ter mesel', 'Lona might be needin' me. I'll skirr on down.' So hyar I be. Heerd the Mex air comin' in from everywhar ter fit Kearny."

"Yes. I met them riding toward Santa Fé, this very afternoon. Armijo wants men."

"Reckon he'll need 'em. From what I larned 'bout him up ter Bent's Fort, he's a damnable coward. Wus worse'n that back in '41. When I heerd 'bout his shootin' Howland and his men, I shu-ah ached ter draw a bead on him."

"Shooting is too good for him. Somehow he always seems to get off easy for his sins. What about you? Been trapping all this time?"

"Mostly. But I'm gittin' 'long in yeahs now. It's hard on any husky young un, livin' in snow an' ice fer months, gittin' frize up and then comin' down jes long nuf ter git thawed out. That's 'bout what it 'mounts ter. Lately I've been takin' it easy-like with the Utes. Now tell me more 'bout affairs 'round hyar?"

"It's safe to talk here," said Lona, glancing all about. "Armijo has spies everywhere. Few dare talk in the city. Lately, Beel," Lona unconsciously lowered her voice, "something happened. Armijo and that trader, Señor James Magoffin . . . Do you know him?" Bill nodded. "They were closeted in my conference room. I happened to pass when they opened the door. They did not see me at once. I heard Armijo say, 'Twenty thousand?' and Señor Magoffin whispered, 'Aye. Ortíz—Galisteo.' I have my own ideas about that. What are yours?"

"Um! Twenty thousand, eh?" drawled Bill. "Ef me ole thinker ain't wore too dull, I kin make a guess. The Americans air comin'. I'll bet Magoffin wus sent ahead ter dicker with Armijo. Ain't anybody heerd of his battin' an eyelash at a bribe, as fer's I knew. Armijo's sold out. That's what happened. Now

263

yer wait an' see. 'Galisteo?'—That ain't hard ter understand. That's whar the money'll be paid when Armijo clears out. Mark me word. I ain't ketched hints fer a thousand yeahs not ter be able ter draw conclusions and Ole Bill's usually been right, at that, Lona."

"That's what I think. Honestly, Beel, we've suffered under Armijo long enough. I do not mean myself. He didn't dare strike at me openly. He did secretly, a few years ago, when he closed the ports. I'm sure it was his doing. He thought that I expected goods that summer. It happened that I had not invested again. He planned matters so that José Lucero would not be able to return."

"José! You two haven't married yit?"

"No. He has been kept in Mexico twice. This last time, for three years. It was partly my fault. I warned him, begged him to stay away. I knew that Manuel Armijo would kill him somehow if he returned. Did you hear that José was ordered to go with Captain Lobato's company from Taos in '43?"

"Naw, I ain't heerd that. The ole skunk thought Lucero'd be kilt. Sort of a David-Uriah trick. Nothin' new. But life's made up mostly o' playin' ole tricks."

"Now about Armijo, Beel. He has declared that he will fight General Kearny at Las Vegas. Raw recruits have drilled for all they are worth. Of course, Armijo should engage any invading army. But . . . But, I'll admit that I'd like to see the Americans walk in and take over Santa Fé. Many people think as I do. We feel that it is the only way to dislodge Armijo. He has been a disgrace in the old palace for years."

"Armijo may try his guns at Vegas. I doubt it, though. Ef he ain't thar, we'll know fer sartain 'bout the twenty thousand deal, I'm tellin' yer."

More riders were now on the trail. The two talked of other matters and went silent. Suddenly Lona broke into a song.

264

"Eh thar, sing 'nother, Lona. Don't recollek evah heerin' ye sing afore. I cain't carry a tune. Not even ef I had a basket ter haul it in."

"I'm no singer, Beel, but I thought I'd give these men along the trail no hint that we have been talking about anything serious."

As they neared the top of the last hill, Williams said that he'd fall behind and take another trail in. She might expect him later, and he'd bring news.

Lona rode on slowly and halted at the highest curve of the hill. A cloud had hidden the sun. It was cooler.

Lona loosened the collar of her dark blue habit, and snatched off a multicolored rebozo from her head. Then her mind jerked her back to the present. And now trouble! She should hurry on. Tightening her hold on the reins, she dipped quickly through the Mascara Arroyo and galloped home.

Pedro was waiting. Lona tossed him the reins and walked on.

At the corner she stopped to watch the crowd and the men march and counter-march. They wore all manner of clothes, trim to ragged. Only sombreros suggested uniformity. Under the portals were the older men. Some women caught at their arms and begged for news. When must the men leave? Were all to go? Other women cried or stood dulled to numbness. A few children screamed in terror at the unusual confusion. Officers with clanking swords strutted by and gave sharp orders.

In the center of the plaza General Armijo, a fat clumsy man now, was astride a nervous mare gay in bright trappings. His long cape flapped in the wind. The purple plume on his high blue helmet whipped back and forth. His thin straight mouth under the heavy nose was hard-set. His blue eyes darted over the crowd. He knows there is possible danger for him in spite of the guards on either side. If he sent men to Vegas, he himself did not go, Lona thought. Finally drums rattled in march rhythm. As General Armijo led his men to their quarters, he passed near Lona. Did others see? She did. Armijo's hands were trembling!

"Coward!" whispered Lona. Would he actually lead his men into battle? A traitor, if he did not. It was his business to defend the country. Like a boomerang, her thoughts struck her own self. Was she a traitor at heart for hoping, as she certainly did, that the Americans would win? Well, if she were, she had plenty of company. Nobody would shed a tear if—if Armijo was shot down. No, nobody who amounted to anything. Even the men who fawned on him would not care.

It was late this evening, the fifteenth of August, when Williams came through the North monte room, deserted as were all the others. In the present excitement, there was no time for games. He found Lona waiting on the portal.

"Wal, I've larned heap much, Lona. But jes what's true is 'nother question." Bill sprawled out his long legs and fished for tobacco in his pockets. "Men air startin' the damndest rumors."

"What have you heard?" broke in Lona impetuously.

"Sich wild talk on the plaza! One thing's sartain. Armijo ain't sent any men ter Vegas er anywhar else. I heerd Colonel Kearny jes walked into Vegas. Didn't fire a shot! Then he got up on a roof an' made a speech. He tole the folks that he's takin' ovah the kintry. He made the alcalde swear allegiance ter the United States, Lona. Now, come mornin', a lootenant tole me 'bout two thousand men will march ter Apache Pass. The guns air on the way. Another soldier said thar wus a lot o' growlin' goin' on and he'd bet thar'd be a squabble ovah placin' the guns er somethin'."

"Apache Pass? Why, Beel, that's narrow! Armijo can wipe out all the Americans there. Somebody should warn Colonel Kearny," broke in Lona.

"Reckon that's already been done, the way messengers air ridin'. They ain't all ridin' fer Armijo, I'll bet me pipe. Saw two Taos Injuns jes a few minutes ago makin' off fer a trail everybody don't know 'bout. Injuns ain't fer the Mex any more. Nevah wus much but since '43, it's been different."

"What do you think will happen, Beel?"

"Why don't ye ask me somethin' easy, woman? Wal," continued Williams, thumping his right forefinger on the fingers of his other hand, "fust, Armijo's been threatened ef he don't fight. Second, he's a damn coward and now as skeer'd of his own men as of the Americans. Third, he's already sold out and got part of the cash, er I'm plumb loco. He's got ter skedaddle from som'ers." Bill looked up so seriously at Lona that she laughed outright. Then he grinned broadly under his graying red beard and rolled his eyes at her with impish glee.

"Here we two fools try to read the future and only tomorrow can tell," said Lona. She caught her head with her two hands and looked up at the heavy beams above her. "I have a 'hunch,' as you Americans say, that the coward will never stay at Apache Pass through one night. If that happens to be the case, he'll reach the Galisteo ranch by tomorrow night. I'm going to be there. I've a plan. Never mind what it is, Beel. But I want you there."

"Guess yer right. He might cook up a squabble jes ter have an excuse fer clearin' out. And . . ."

"I've got it, Beel. I'll leave with Pedro for the ranch in the morning. You scout around. Take the spyglass that Ewing gave me long ago. If you see Armijo leave, and you might at that, beat him to the ranch. It stands to reason that there's where the rest of the money will be paid over to Armijo."

"Ain't givin' a hint of yer plan? 'Pears like ef yer hellbent on bein' thar, ye'd bettah go. I reckon I kin guess what yer up ter, 'cept thar ain't no tellin' what a woman'll do."

"Go along, Beel. You men are more of a puzzle. Go now,

267

you old rascal. That's the plan. Now I must find Pedro."

Bill guffawed heartily and with, "Oh, you womin!" left the portal.

Not long after sun-up, while Lona and Pedro, both well-armed, rode for the Galisteo ranch, old Bill jogged toward Apache Pass by a side trail closed to sight from the main road. On a hill not far from the trail leading South, he tethered his horse, drew his black brim to his eyes and brought the spyglass into play. It was easy to locate the tall, ungainly figure of General Armijo and follow his movements. Arguments seemed hot, below there. Finally, Bill saw a barricade of felled trees being thrown up among the rocks this side of the gorge.

"Does the damn fool mean to let his enemy get through the pass, and then fire inter 'em?" Williams muttered to himself.

Bill turned his glass on down the pass but it could not penetrate the hills and follow the two Indians on the short-cut trail taken the night before. They had urged their mules to full speed, with thumping arms and legs in lieu of whips. At last they pulled into the camp of the Americans.

"How! How! Who we tell?" the Indians asked of Lieutenant Bill Emory.

"Colonel Kearny. I mean General Kearny," said the lieutenant correcting himself for he knew Kearny now carried a commission as general. It had arrived since the column had left Fort Leavenworth. "Come with me."

With radiant faces, the two Taos Indians walked to the mess where General Kearny was finishing a late noon meal. They bowed ceremoniously. The smaller one exclaimed, "Big Chief! We come. We come to white men from out of the East. Many moons gone, our wise men tell us you come. Then we free. The enemy in canyon, my brave. Make good medicine in your heart. Push them out."

268

No. Old Bill could not spy on that scene nor hear the words but there was no doubt in his mind that news of Armijo had reached General Kearny.

Williams had concluded that General Armijo would venture to hold the Americans back. But through his glass, in late afternoon, he saw Armijo point to the South, apparently with a command. Almost at once, guns were lifted on wagons. Horses were hitched up. Armijo awkwardly climbed into his saddle; gold flashed from his red and blue uniform. Now, about a hundred dragoons mounted. That was enough for Bill. He ran down the hillside to his horse and was away as fast as four legs and hardy lungs could serve him. He rode through the twilight and pulled up at the Galisteo ranch as a full moon loomed magnificently large over piñon-covered hills.

Lona heard Bill thud in and rushed to greet him.

"Beel! What news?"

"I tole ye Ole Bill didn't have ter be hit on the head to git an idee inside. Armijo's comin'." The story of the day-long vigil on the hillside followed. "Armijo can't come very fast. Not with the guns."

"Señor Ortíz and his wife have been most kind. I told them frankly why I had come. They say that they have had no word about any meeting here, but then, many ride by and stop. Pedro is on guard at the corral gate and has told the *peóns* what to expect. We ourselves must stay in this side room. Hide your horse where we have ours in that clump of trees yonder."

An hour later, two men rode up to the front portal and alighted. Bill and Lona could see them through the curtained window.

Only a few moments afterward, Madam Ortíz tiptoed in to whisper, "Madam Barcelona! It is true. Señor James Magoffin has just ridden in with a guard. He asked for an opportunity to speak privately with General Armijo, who'll be here shortly."

Half an hour later, Madam Ortíz again reported, "General Armijo has come! He told his men to gallop on down the road and wait. He asked to speak with Señor Ortíz for a few moments. My husband escorted him into the room where Señor Magoffin waited. They are in there now alone."

Williams slipped outside. He ordered Pedro to mass the *peóns* on the South side of the house and step out with them the moment he heard Doña Lona's voice. Then Williams hurried to the front of the casa and found Lona already there, holding the bridle of Armijo's horse. He took the reins into his own hands.

General Armijo soon walked out with moonlight full in his face. He saw a shawled woman standing near his horse and someone he did not recognize holding the bridle. He paid no heed, mounted in haste and reached for the reins but Bill held them securely.

The mantilla dropped. Armijo stared with eyes widening. Bill laughed.

Armijo screamed, "Lona! *Por Dios!* You! How . . . ?"

"Yes, Manuel Armijo. You coward! You traitor, fleeing your country! You, with your twenty thousand! I know! All Santa Fé shall know. Go! May the devil chase you!"

Armijo stiffened in his saddle.

Bill loosed the reins. Armijo wheeled his horse. Lona drew her gun and fired.

Armijo fell forward with his hand on his side, as his horse reared and plunged into a wild gallop.

"Good God! Did you shoot him?" gasped Bill. "I didn't expect that!"

"Shoot him? No. Didn't you see me fire into the air? A coward always knows he's a proper target for a bullet. He just imagined he was shot. He'll get agony out of that."

The crowd of *peóns* yelled their choicest epithets of abuse. Again and again came the rabid cry, "Trai-tor!"

"Gone!" hissed Lona, still gripping her gun. "Gone forever!"

"Yeah. Gone and unless I'm a numbskull prophet, he's the last Mex . . . No, he'll always be the last of the Spanish governors to us."

Lona stood looking Southward, watching the last of the Spanish governors fleeing in disgrace.

"THE AMERICANS COME!" EXCLAIMED LITTLE
Madam Alarid, bustling forward to grasp Lona's hand. Her
brown eyes glistened. "No one can prevent them now. Somehow it must be for the best. Anyway, there have been no fire-
balls bounding down the mountains. But then . . ." She caught
her breath sharply, put her hand to her cheek and pondered
for a moment. More slowly she continued, "Our chickens got
out of their shed, this morning. The cock crowed right in front
of the open patio door! Yes, he did, Lona. That's bad, you
know, but . . . but, maybe, it's too small a sign?" She looked
up questioningly. Deep concern was in her eyes.

Lona's lips quivered. As solemnly as she could, she answered,
"Yes, too insignificant, Señora. Men say it is the will of God.
You know we'll fare better with Manuel Armijo out of that
palace."

Madam Alarid did not reply but nodded her head and swayed
her chubby hand in time with the church clock while it struck
three. "But I wish that we'd had a sign, Lona."

Shouts on the plaza brought both women to the window.

"Look! There they are. How travel-worn their dark blue
coats are. Their trousers have yellow straps. See! They have

272

small visored caps. Let's go outside. I wish Madam Pino had lived to see this day."

Lona leaned against a portal post. Madam Alarid put an arm about Lona's waist and peered around her shoulder.

"How tired the horses are! Some of the men are shouting but not like traders, Lona?"

"They are exhausted, I guess. Even the flag in front seems listless."

"Why don't the folk under the portals cry vivas? Most of them are glad."

"I know, my dear," said Lona patting her friend's hand. "But they are afraid. Some families have fled into the mountains."

"Afraid of what? My husband said that messengers have reported that not a shot has been fired. Not one act of violence has been done since the Americans started way back at Fort Leavenworth. There was nothing to all those lies about how badly we would be treated."

"Nothing. But men are fearful lest Armijo return with an army."

"Oh!" said Madam Alarid and turned to greet her husband who came puffing through the crowd toward her.

"Ah, Lita. You are here. I did not want you to miss this." He bowed to Doña Lona and went on, "Strange, isn't it? A conquering army without any victory thuds in amid a few cheers."

The standard bearer wheeled his horse directly at the corner.

"Now it comes!" said Señor Alarid and took off his sombrero.

The American flag passed by. Its folds fluttered over the blue cap of the earnest young soldier who grasped the pole tightly in one hand and guided his mount with the other.

Flanked by officers looking stolidly ahead, rode a small man who smiled genially and occasionally lifted his blue cap.

"Hooray for General Kearny!" came from an American be-hind Lona's party. "Hooray!"

"That little man with the thin face? Is he the great General Kearny, Señor Alarid?"

"He must be. How plainly dressed. No epaulets."

"But so small!" she said. "Blond. Nice eyes. Beetling eye-brows. Good smile. But so small," she repeated.

"Many great generals have been small, Lona. Napoleon and . . ."

"I know," broke in Lona. "Simple. Dignified. I wish we could all shout huzzas, Señor."

"I wish so too but rumors are afloat, you know, that Armijo will return with a large army and drive the Americans out. How full the *garitas* will be then!"

"Aye, and walls blood-stained! Many will have to pay dearly for too much joy now," exclaimed Madam Alarid. She sighed deeply and clutched Lona's hand.

Her husband touched his wife's arm and pointed toward the main entrance of the palace. "You see the Americans are well received yonder. I suppose Lieutenant Governor Vigil will wine and dine the officers over there until the rest of the army come up. This was only the head of the column."

"Let's go in and have chocolate," suggested Madam Alarid. "You must stay with us and see the others come in, Lona, my dear."

Señor Alarid told of maneuvers at Apache Pass.

"Armijo surely showed a big white feather down there. Peo-ple talk about his having accepted bribes to leave the country." He paused and looked straight at Doña Lona. She was said to know more about this matter than anyone else. He wondered, but when she held her peace, he continued, "A man from the Ortíz ranch came in this morning and told a wild tale about your having been there. He said that you had given Armijo

274

a solid piece of your mind and then fired at him as he dashed away?"

"All kinds of rumors fly on such a day as this, Señor," answered Lona. The time for talking had not come. It was sufficient if word of the bribe was abroad.

Again huzzas came from the plaza.

"What a wild-looking lot!" commented Lona when she stood once more by the portal post.

"Yes, but they're jolly. More men answer. The tension has eased. Listen."

"To Hell with Armijo! . . . I'm for the Americans! . . . So am I! . . . Let's back 'em! . . . Hooray! . . . Huzza!"

The three stood by the Alarid door and watched the people surging forward toward the front of the old palace. Down the portal, they saw a black hat high over the crowd and recognized Bill Williams.

"Whoa, thar! This hoss has been gallopin' all 'round lookin' fer ye," said Williams who joined Lona near the adobe wall of the house. With a wrinkled flag across the front of his buckskin coat, Bill grinned like a schoolboy and fumbled with the hat in his hands.

"*Americano!* Where did you find that?"

"Ovah in Prewitt's store. He'd had it wrapped up on a shelf since Noah boarded the ark. Purty, eh? What did I hear? I'll be damned ef it ain't Prewitt's youngster twangin' 'Yankee Doodle' on his guitar. Com' on Lona. Let's git behind him and march ovah ter the palace. Gee, it's great!" Williams gripped Lona's arm and stepped high to the lively tune. "Pity, the cavalry don't have a drum and fife corps er a full-fledged band fer a day like this. Pity, I say. Horns and trumpets air not 'nuf."

"I think so too, Beel. It's been so quiet. Only a few huzzas. But the people fear."

275

"Yeah, I know, but you and I are sure that Armijo won't come back. Not that skunk!"

When Williams and Lona stood under the trees, she said, "Look at the crowd, Beel." He glanced about quickly and then his eyes fastened on a tall pole being lifted in front of the palace.

Milling about were Indians in bright blankets or buffalo robes, stolid but eager-eyed; Mexicans, in red, green or yellow shirts and tight leather breeches which flared at the knee; dark-skinned women, black shawled or in gay rebozos; American traders, with rumpled flags, others with ribbons, red, white and blue.

"Wonder what they're thinkin'," said Bill, his eyes on the flagpole.

Suddenly Williams caught Lona's arm with a stronger grip than he realized.

"Look! The pole is steady. Now . . . now! The flag! Up she goes!"

Williams had forgotten where he was. He jumped in the air and waved his own small flag. He yelled with all his lung power, one hooray after another. Finally a Mexican pulled at his coat and cried, "Hey, *Americano*. Think you're a sort of living flagpole?".

Williams caught himself again. He turned to Lona and tucked the stick of his own flag into his coat. "Guess I went plumb *loco,* Lona. But that thar flag looks mighty good ter me. Good Lord, but it's been a great day."

"Yes, Beel. News of today and history of tomorrow. It's seemed to me like a play on a stage."

Williams grinned. He rolled his gray eyes to the Southeast and said, "Listen, gal."

From the distance came the boom on boom of cannon firing a salute to the first American flag to float over Santa Fé.

276

When mid-morning came, Lona was again in the plaza, and, this time, alone.

In the glare of broad daylight, the jostling men were just people, people under a sea of sombreros.

She turned away from the crowd to watch the American officers on the palace roof. Now General Kearny spoke. She could not hear his words. Before he had finished, she slipped away. She must be ready for gamblers when the crowd broke. She wondered what José would think of all this.

While Madam Barcelona was more than usually busy in her salas, Williams mingled with the Missourians, delighted to be with his own sort. He drank, treated, gambled and "talked sense fer a spell." So engrossed was he that he did not come to see Lona for several days. Then, one morning, he marched in with a confident stride as if he himself had accomplished something great.

"That's the way the Americans do things, me gal. No bowin' ter old man 'mañana.'" Bill threw his head back. He seemed suddenly to have grown a foot. "Know what's happenin'?" Lona shook her head. "Wal, the Americans ain't been hyar five full days yit, but a bunch of 'em air up on the hill, ovah Northeast thar. Doin' what? Buildin' a fort, by God. Yeah, a fort. Not jes any old thing but with plans and all."

"Fine. No wonder you are proud, Beel. I hope the men get some extra money and can buy some new clothes. So many are ragged."

"Yeah, I know. They need money. Ragged or no, they do things. Bettah times air comin', Lona. Heerd ye air purty strick with 'em?"

"I have to be. They want to run the salas. They seem to expect me to be like their frontier gambling women. Bow and scrape to them? I won't. I get angry sometimes but I've kept

277

my tongue so far. If they do not learn their place, I'll order some of them out. I don't want to do that. They're fun-loving, full of laughter. Good losers, most of them."

"But not when they set out ter do somethin' big. Then they ain't fer losin'. They jes plug ahead and win."

Williams came now and then for a moment but it was a full week or more before he rushed in with astounding information. A priest from the lower country had come in, he said, and had told about town, that a Colonel with five hundred regulars had been marching North at the very time Armijo had fled. Now they were coming. Armijo had roused the whole Southland and gathered in volunteers. The priest declared that he'd been told a big army was on the way to wipe out the Americans. Williams laughed at the idea and reckoned that General Kearny might have to take a few men and go out to meet the enemy.

On the first of September, Williams came to Lona, bubbling over with joy because General Kearny was to start the very next day and he'd attend to the little matter of "givin' Armijo sich a lickin' that he'd scamper on South in a hustle." Williams wished he were younger. He would like to go too. He tangled up his long hair in his hand and continued, "Unless that thar Mexican Colonel has more guts than most of 'em and kin force Armijo ter fight, I have a sneakin' notion that, when Kearny gits down below thar, he won't find any Armijo. Don't run in his thick blood ter fight, Lona."

Lona nodded but said nothing so Bill rambled on.

"By the way, ye might be interested ter know that Jim's brother come in with a caravan, last night, Sam's his name. Sam Magoffin. Brought a bride, by cracky. I ketched a glimpse of her. Purty, dark-eyed young gal. A Kintuck beauty, er I'm a yappin' coyote. They're livin' ovah by the church, I've been told."

278

"Samuel Magoffin? I know. He comes every year, usually with his brother, Jim. So he has a bride? Good for him. Hope I'll see her but I'm kept closely here, these days."

"Wal, Lona, think I'll leave, come mornin', but not until I've seed Kearny and his men off. Ye see, the Gen'ral kin git 'long without me now." Bill grinned and rolled his merry eyes to meet Lona's. She laughed. "So I'll be traispin' up ter Taos, stay a spell and then go ter see the Utes agin. Now me plan is ter 'range fer an express ter be sent up ter me onct in a while and let me know what's doin' down hyar. Come winter, 'stead of trappin', think I'll amble back and size matters up for mesel'. Kinda ovahsee the Gen'ral, ye know. So it's good-by fer now." Bill stretched out his hand.

"Until winter?" Lona called after him.

XXVII

"SEE HERE, YOU MEN." COLONEL DAVID MITCH-
ell bustled into the palace office. "Kearny expects me to have a
cold thousand when he returns. You know we must have sup-
plies and open up communications with General Wool down
South. Everybody's turned me down. Got any ideas to offer?"
The Colonel sat down on a table, picked up a deck of cards the
Americans had used during siesta time and idly shuffled them.
"I tell you, I'm stumped."

"Tried 'em all? That storekeeper, Leitensdorfer, has the
lucre," suggested one man reaching for a bowl of fruit.

"Leitensdorfer? He wouldn't lend a cent. Not he! Prewitt's
got nothing. He'd lend in a minute if he had it."

"Might try the miners down at Tuerto. They tell me that
place is almost as large as Santa Fé," ventured another.

"No. The money's here somewhere if I can only find it."

"One thing's dead certain. General Kearny's not likely to
be in a good humor when he comes in. Chasing shadows isn't
his specialty. That priest needs a month or two in a nice little
cell for his yarn," said a burly fellow tilting back his chair
against the wall while he yanked off a huge hunk of tobacco.

"Sure'n it was me that was sorprised when I found oot,
Kearny'd be bitin'. Stood oop te raison Armijo'd be savin' his

old hide in Mexico as soon as he jolly well could," said a husky Irishman who turned toward the door when the catch rattled.

Lieutenant Emory tramped in, his face red from the sun, his eyes blinking. He did not wait to catch the drift of the conversation but asked abruptly, "Where's Doniphan?"

" 'Cross the way. That door. But Alex is working like the Devil. No siesta for him until he gets that code of laws finished. Kearny's got to have it before he leaves for California. Willard Hall's in there, helping, and he swears he'll scalp any man who disturbs them," said Colonel Mitchell.

"Well, he's not the only one who works around these parts. The men on the hill are sweating blood. The fort's coming along fine. But those men must have clothes. That puny eighteen cents a day extra won't buy many shirts and pants. We've got to have money."

"We were talking money when you came in, Emory. You're damn right. But I've scoured this town for a loan. You'd think that nobody ever heard of putting a peso by," growled Mitchell. "We can't sit around Santa Fé 'til Doomsday munching grapes." He rose and slapped down the cards that he had nervously shuffled again and again. His glance followed them as they fell. Suddenly with hand in the air, he yelled, "I've got it! Madam Barcelona. I'll try her. She's already won a nice little pile from me. Wonder I didn't think of her before."

"Right. She's your best bet, Mitchell. She's been mighty good to all the officers, ye know," came from the man with the long cigar.

"Be brushin' ye black curly hair and cute little moustache, laddie. Sparkle ye blue eyes. Smile ye damndest, an' ye'll make a killin'," said a grizzly-bearded Scotchman.

"Ze moustache. He impor-tant," ventured a Frenchman, waving his hands. "Ze moustache, he makes ze smash, Monsieur."

The men roared and Mitchell flushed. Such twitting bothered him even at forty.

"Eh, laddie. Never ye mind. We've all had te take it and never one of us did they call 'Colonel' so early. Never one of us builded the likes of your Fort McKenzie. Never one."

"Quit your blarney, you fellows. Now listen. If I have to walk into the ball tonight with her on my arm, you stop looking at Susan Magoffin long enough to bow your prettiest and dance with the lady or I'll have you shot at sunrise, by Hector," said Colonel Mitchell and whirled out of the room.

Colonel Mitchell knew that late afternoon was the time when gamblers deserted their games and strolled in the plaza, so he chose five as the hour for his call. He made himself as presentable as possible in his worn blue uniform with its long-skirted coat, by polishing every brass button and the hilt of his sword. It clicked in its scabbard when he walked briskly through the front door of the gaming salas.

Pablita was sweeping the Brussels carpet in the hallway and looked up in surprise. "Cards, Señor?" The man shook his head. "You want to see my mistress, Señor? She is resting but I am sure she will see you. If you wish, be seated in the conference room." She put her broom against the wall and left at once.

Madam Barcelona rose from her couch wondering why any officer of the American army should seek her at this time of day. She smoothed her hair, thinner now than in days gone by, and hastily slipped into a gown of black lace over turquoise blue which Pablita had laid out for the evening. Soon she was curtsying to Colonel Mitchell, who said apologetically, "It is good of you to allow me to see you at this time. I did not intend to disturb your rest, but, you see, I am one of those terrible ogres . . ."

Madam Lona laughed as she sat near the American. "Those ridiculous tales Governor Armijo spread! My friends knew

282

better, of course. I, myself, have known Americans well for many years. I like them, Colonel."

"I am grateful for such words, Madam," replied the officer. Unconsciously his face betrayed perplexity. He wondered just how to proceed.

"You are troubled about something, Señor. Can I be of service?"

"You certainly can, if you will. I'll come to the point immediately. No doubt, you have noted how badly our men need new equipment, new clothes and the like. We are too far from our base to obtain funds without great delay. Could you find it in your generous heart to lend our army some money? We need a thousand dollars." Colonel Mitchell paused and leaned forward. He had shot his arrow.

"A thousand dollars is quite a sum, Colonel."

"It is that, but the United States government will repay you," replied David Mitchell who enlarged on the situation in Santa Fé but tactfully avoided any reference to the fact that money was needed to outfit soldiers for the proposed march into Mexico.

"I'll have to think this over. The traders here should accommodate you. I am from Mexico. You may not know?"

"But do you not wish to be an American with us? Surely you will not join those who may elect to return to Mexico rather than live under our flag?"

"I shall not go South. I like the ideals of your country, Señor. But the war is far from over, I believe. It would go hard with me, should it become known that I had aided the invading army."

"But we have come to stay. The governmental set-up will be finished before General Kearny moves on West, the latter part of the month. The people seem to approve. We have had no word of any uprising of any kind."

283

"Probably not. Let me have time to think this over, before I give you my final answer. Right now, I must say no."

"Very well," said Colonel Mitchell. "You are coming to our ball tonight? Good. May I have the pleasure of being your escort, Madam? I hope that I am not too late with my request?"

"Thank you. I had other plans but I can cancel them. I'll be ready at half past nine."

Colonel Mitchell made a deep bow over Madam Barcelona's hand and left at once.

Lona sank down on a bench, tilted back her head and gazed at the blank wall across the patio. She must think this matter out. Mexico? It was years since the word had stirred her. How neglectful the men of the South had been of this north country! She had lost all respect. Yet suppose the Mexicans should be victorious in this war? She would suffer, perhaps be shot, if it were ever known that she had lent money to the American army. Apparently the newcomers *had* come to stay. If so, she would be safe. If she did lend, several men would know about the matter. Among a group of men, she reflected, there is always, at least, one who never in his life has considered sacred any promise to a woman. Never, unless it was linked deeply into his own precious life. He would idly let the word slip. There might be trouble somehow. Most of the people in Santa Fé would not call her traitor even though they, like herself, were glad that the Americans had come. What should she do? Perhaps a solution would come clear before the night should pass.

With Colonel Mitchell, Madam Barcelona entered the ballroom trimmed with American flags and already hazy with smoke. She smiled and bowed courteously to her friends and took a place at the far end of the room near the musicians.

While she swung through the first dance with Colonel Mitchell, she was not unconscious of the fact that she was not only one of the most handsome women in the room, but she was also one of the most conspicuous. Against the bright colors of the dancers, her black dress gleamed. It was of satin with many ruffles, unlike the dull black worn by the duennas against the wall. Her red fan, red rosette at her neck under her black mantilla and red heeled slippers proclaimed her a dancer, not a wall flower. At forty, she was not an old woman to sit in a corner with her feet resting in the lap of a servant crouched on the floor. Let the women who liked that sort of thing do so, not she.

Madam Barcelona did not lack for partners and, as she danced gaily, she gave no hint that, here and there, she saw the disapproving glances of Americans, directed especially against Colonel Mitchell. Such, she thought, were born of false ideas about her and her business. She would outlive that if the Americans stayed. She would force them to change their minds.

"Who is the one little American woman yonder? She is charming. Who is she?" Madam Barcelona inquired of Colonel Mitchell.

"She is Susan Magoffin. I mean Mrs. Samuel Magoffin. She came from Missouri recently. Quite an accomplished young lady. Strait-laced as you'll find them. I'm told that she keeps a journal of her trip. She'll have plenty to say of Santa Fé and much more about Mexico, no doubt. In a few weeks she and her husband will go on South, war or no war."

"I caught her eying me suspiciously with her big brown eyes, as if she thought I were some sort of assistant to the Devil himself. She probably disapproves of playing cards and thinks me quite wicked."

"Pray pay no attention. You have as much right to your life

285

as she has to hers. Customs vary in different parts of the world, you know. What's wrong here is right there. Why bother?" He dropped the subject with "Let's have a glass of wine?"

When Colonel Mitchell claimed her for the last dance, Madam Barcelona had almost forgotten Susan Magoffin. She was flushed with pleasure since the American officers had treated her royally.

"You have been such a delightful partner, tonight, Colonel. I do like you Americans," she said as she walked leisurely to her salas. She invited the officer to sit with her for a few moments in the conference room still well-lighted with candles.

"I've been having a battle with myself about this loan, Colonel," she said when she sat opposite him. "It's Mexico versus the United States. I must admit that I care nothing for Mexico. Almost everybody thinks as I do. We should be either independent or belong to the States."

"You do belong to us now, Madam."

"Perhaps. But the war is not over?"

"True. But we have taken New Mexico and we will not relinquish it. You may count on that," said the officer.

Madam Barcelona sat quite silent with her hand to her cheek while Colonel Mitchell said nothing but watched her face.

"I'll risk it," she replied suddenly and left the room.

When Pedro brought in a heavy bag of silver, she said with a smile, "There, Colonel Mitchell. Please count the pesos."

While the click of coins filled the air, neither spoke.

"I am more than grateful, Madam Barcelona," said Colonel Mitchell and hastily wrote a receipt. "You shall not regret this. I assure you that I will take great pains to close the lips of the few men who know of my quest for funds."

"I hope you can do this for me. No one should know of the transaction." She looked down at the note in her hand. "No one should know."

286

On the way to the old palace, David Mitchell was glad that the night was densely dark. He slipped by one candle-lighted lantern at the corner and hurried diagonally across the plaza. He found a few men again loafing in the same office where the spreading cards had suggested a visit to Madam Barcelona.

Candles pushed together in the center of the table made a well of light that illuminated faces clean-shaven or smartly-trimmed for the ball. It was reflected from starched white shirts, caught the yellow stripes down the seams of blue trousers and touched the patent-leather belts of their long coats hanging up on pegs. The soldiers took their feet off the table and rose as the Colonel entered.

"Well, men, here's the thousand," said Mitchell, heaving the heavy bag on the table with a thud. The coins gave one sharp tinkle. "McGinnis and Allen are to guard this tonight. Now every man jack of you, put up your right hand. Swear, if you guess where I received this money, that you will forever hold your peace, come what may. That's only fair."

"I'll say so," said a lieutenant. "She's no bouncing Betsy of Missouri. A lady, if ever I saw one."

"Yeah, and if our men don't check their impudence in her salas, there'll be a bone or two broken, by God," snapped a second lieutenant in a far corner of the room.

"Sure'n yer roight," broke in the Irish sergeant. "Sure'n, lookit, Sor?" McGinnis held his big fist toward Colonel Mitchell. "Let ony man of us squawk . . ." McGinnis shook his fist. "This is roight good medicine fer loose hinges on any man's trap, I'm tellin' ye."

When morning came on that eleventh of September, 1846, the two women most prominent at the officers' ball of the night before, sat at their desks. Susan Magoffin and Lona Barcelona. Lona had been reading a letter which a messenger had brought early that morning. It lay in her lap. She thought of its news but, when Pablita passed the window, her mind turned on the work for the day and then slipped easily to memories of the evening before. She was glad that she had loaned the money. The Americans did need it. What a splendid ball! What a good time she had had! Only that one clash of eyes with little Mrs. Magoffin had marred the night. She knows nothing of me and little of my business, yet she sat like a judge. I know. What a look of intense disapproval swept her young face! Perhaps some day, Mistress Susan may grow up. Are all Anglo-Saxon women like her? How many people in my life have come and gone with only a flash of eyes!

Lifting the crackling paper, Lona shrugged her shoulders and reread her letter. It was from José Lucero. Again he was detained . . . had reached Chihuahua . . . was ordered to serve in an army office . . . affairs had taken on an edge since Santa Anna had been recalled from exile . . . might be on duty for three months or more . . . would ride North as soon as possible . . . hoped she would allow the banns to be read on his arrival . . . no leaving Chihuahua for the present . . . faithfully . . . love. So she must wait again, and again her business must go on.

Lona sighed.

Susan patted the round white collar and cuffs of her plain brown dress and smoothed her dark hair, parted in the middle and drawn down over her ears too severely for her eighteen summers. She had bought vegetables for the day from a little girl, "and a cunning piece she was too." She had given orders to a servant and been interrupted by a caller, an Indian, with whom she had talked both English and Spanish and noted that he was "well dressed in new boots, pants, hat and white blanket-coat." Now she sat in a straight, high-backed chair and

288

wrote of the ball: "Among the officers of the army I found some very agreeable, and all were attentive to me." Her pen ran on, forgetful of tildes or correct spelling. *"El Señor Vicario was there to grace the gay halls with his priestly robes. . . . There was 'Dona Lona' the principal montebank keeper* in Santa Fé, a stately dame of certain age, the possessor of a portion of that shrewd sense and fascinating manner necessary to allure the wayward, inexperienced youth to the hall of final ruin."

And Susan sighed.

XXVIII

DURING THAT AUTUMN, THE AMERICANS CONtinued to "do things," much to Madam Barcelona's delight. The fort on the hill was finished and called "Fort Marcy." The regulars of the army made nights unwontedly harsh with Indian whoops, wild yells and prolonged tooting of trumpets which they had found somewhere in the city. What a clatter and clamor they did make! But that was like Americans, thought the mistress of the gambling place when she ordered Pedro to keep doors closed to shut out the noise.

All Santa Fé was surprised when, down from Taos, came Charles Bent to be installed, without fanfare, as governor. But not Madam Barcelona. She had known Señor Bent, years before, as a capable captain of trade caravans, a man of marked ability, friendly to all classes of people. She rarely saw him on the plaza but noted, when she did, that Governor Bent did not swagger. He was no Armijo.

Neither did General Kearny make much ado when he left for California. Nor did Colonel Sterling Price and his Missourians when they marched in some ten days later. She liked this new military commander. He was jolly, adored by his men, and always so courteous when he came to test his luck. He was less severe than Colonel Doniphan who now marched in the

West against the Navajos. It was high time that soldiers went after the rascals. The Navajos had carried away some people on the outskirts of Santa Fé when everyone was busy watching for the coming of General Kearny.

Later, when one of Doniphan's officers told her triumphantly of a treaty with the Navajos, Madam Barcelona quirked her lips. She did not remind the young man that treaty on treaty had been made before, with those treacherous Indians, and broken. She asked how matters stood down in Mexico. Had any word come?

"Not much," answered the Captain. "Now and then, a messenger does make Santa Fé. We heard recently that Santa Anna was allowed to run the blockade at Vera Cruz and has gone to the capital. Undoubtedly men by the thousands will rally about him. It seems Santa Anna is stumping about boasting, 'I am the nation!'"

Madam Barcelona laughed heartily.

"Aping Louis XIV now, is he?" commented Madam Lona. "The last I heard was that he strutted like Napoleon. He has yet to prove that *he* is the state. You are probably right about his army. He has but to whistle. Men come. Then he must march against the Americans under . . . ? Who is the general?"

"General Zachary Taylor, Madam, and a good fighter. He had little trouble taking Monterrey in September."

"Yes, but Santa Anna is or has been victorious on a battlefield."

Changing the trend of thought, Madam Barcelona asked, "What is this that I hear about Colonel Price? I'm told he is not strict enough here in Santa Fé. Some discontent creeps throughout the city."

"Possibly, but in the end all will be well, I assure you."

"What of Taos?"

"Well, I understand that the people there are a bit restive but perhaps that is to be expected from a community so far away."

"Somehow I do not like such news, Captain. Bring me better before long."

Several weeks later, something happened.

A gentle snow drifted down over the patio. It was well past midnight. Lona was sitting at her window, looking at the light on the snow, for the moon had tricked the storm and broken through a rift in the clouds.

Lona heard a knock. She leaned forward, turned her head to catch the direction. Someone was at the West door.

No light flashed in Pablita's room so Lona knew that both her servants were asleep. She would not waken them.

Another knock!

Hastily catching up a candle and some matches, Lona tiptoed through the snow on the flagstones to the saddle-room. She lighted the candle again. The knocking continued. There must be a very urgent reason for such a call. Fumbling with the latch, she opened the door narrowly.

"*Gracias á Dios!* Doña Lona. I come. I mus' tell," cried a small figure huddled in a black shawl flecked with snow.

"*Santa María! Pase!* What brings you?" exclaimed Lona when the trembling girl stepped within. The one candle flickered feebly. "Why, Sarah! What is it?"

The mulatto did not speak. She rolled her big black eyes in fear, the whites glistening. She pressed a finger to her lips.

Lona quickly led the way to her own room. It must be very important news to force her hard-working servant out on a night like this. Lona felt the girl clutch at her skirt.

"Someone there?" whispered Sarah. "In the dark?"

"No, Sarah, no one is here," answered Lona, patting the girl's shoulder when they went within.

292

"What's wrong? Has that husband of yours been beating you again?"

"Yes, but not tonight. He kill me if he know I come . . . come to you. But I mus' come. I mus' tell."

"What is it?" urged Lona kindly, putting her hand over one of Sarah's. The girl clutched her shawl with the other. While snow flakes on her shoulders melted in the warmth of the fire, Sarah tried to speak.

"Doña Lona. The men . . . drunk . . . They say once 'Nineteen' . . . Now, they say Christmas eve . . . Shoot Americans . . . Shoot all . . . Shoot Governor. . . . You do something?" Her eyes bulged and again the whites glistened as she rolled her glance to the closed door and the curtained windows.

"Are the men at your house?"

The mulatto nodded and went on, "Drunk . . . All . . . Five . . . They say 'Kill!' Once my husband, he . . ." Sarah raised her arm and drew her hand swiftly across her throat. "The knife! He say he kill me . . . if I tell. Tonight he too drunk. No see me. I run. I no like men kill. You no like. You tell?"

"Yes, I'll do something," Lona promised. "No one must know that you have come tonight. You're a brave girl—a good girl. Now you run home."

"Think spooks come after me? I 'fraid." Sarah's teeth chattered. She drew her arms closely about herself and shivered in fear.

"No, no, Sarah. There are no ghosts. You will be safe. Keep near the walls and run. The men must not miss you."

Without a word more, Lona led the way to the door and Sarah slipped outside. The latch clicked far too loudly, and her own heels struck the flagstones like hammers, Lona thought, as she crossed to her room.

She stood taut before the dying fire. Then she walked back and forth, her eyes intent on the floor. Something must be done . . . and quickly. Probably there were many men involved in this plan to kill the Americans. Yes, many more. American soldiers could quell any uprising if they were forewarned. The Colonel must know. . . . She must not trust any messenger. . . . She must go herself, and at once.

Hardly realizing what she did, Lona changed her dress for one of black and threw a heavy black shawl over her head. She hurried to the West room, picked up her saddle and was on the way, thankful that, for the moment, the moon was hidden and a rising wind whipped the snow.

The saddle was heavy but Lona did not feel its weight. She reached the corral and spoke quietly to her horse. She pushed and tugged until the saddle was in place. Then, pulling with all her might, she tightened the cinch. She opened the gate, and sprang into the saddle.

As Lona rode at a moderate pace by the barracks, she shook her head. She did not believe the Colonel was asleep in his own quarters. He had been in her salas, that night, and had left very early. Lona knew that he often spent the night at the Chaves ranch. She had heard him say that, but not tonight. Yet intuitively, she felt that he had ridden out there. She would take the chance. She must find Colonel Price.

Heading Northward she rode through the Mascara Arroyo and up on the more level ground. She spurred her horse into a gallop along the trail to the Chaves ranch.

The storm was over. The moonlight was clear and cold. The wind whirled the fluffy snow from the roadway and scattered it across the flat. The heavy silence of the desert was broken only by the soft thud of the horse's hoofs on the damp ground. Snow fell from *chamisa* bushes without sound. A jack rabbit stopped on the trail, stretched his high ears, looked and jumped out of sight.

The horse seemed to understand the need of haste. Dipping into a shallow arroyo, he tried to rush the opposite bank. He stumbled and almost threw Lona. Snorting, as if in disgust at his clumsiness, he pulled himself up and gained the flat beyond. Here the wind had spent itself. He ran more easily, took a depression again and suddenly shied.

Ahead was a waning campfire shielded with a few rocks. A horse was tethered near. Wrapped in a blanket lay a man apparently sound asleep. Not wishing to disturb the lone camper, Lona started to make a detour. But, in a second, the man was on his feet, a tall, gaunt figure. He pushed his cap back. It had two ears!

"*Por Dios!* Is it you, Beel?" she shouted and rode toward him. "It is Lona. How on earth do you happen to be way out here?"

"Wal, by the jumpin' hind legs of the great craw-faced cricket! Lona! What in thundah air ye doin' ridin' with the moon out on a desert?"

"But you?"

"Wal," drawled Bill. "Got into town late tonight and somehow I didn't like the looks I got thar, 'specially from some of the fellers down side lanes. I thought I'd jes cut out hyar and get me shut-eye. Nevah sleep inside if I kin help it. A bed's the work of the Devil himsel'. Come mornin', I'll do some snoopin' 'round and find out what it's all 'bout. But you . . . out hyar?"

"Beel, I had to ride tonight. I must reach the Chaves ranch and return before dawn. I have news for Colonel Price. It is bad," said Lona, not wishing to reveal her secret, at once, anyway.

"Bad? That's the feelin' I got in the city. I shu-ah breathed it right in the air. Mind tellin' me?"

"I . . . I should tell Colonel Price first. But, after all, Beel, you are the one to go North and give the warning. Some men, in Santa Fé and perhaps in Taos are planning a revolution."

"Revolution, eh?" growled Bill. "What's the date fer the uprisin'? Did ye git that?"

"Yes, Christmas eve. They mean to kill the Americans. The Governor is in danger and every officer. There's no sense in it. The Americans have been good to us. They must be saved. I'm riding to see Colonel Price."

"Wal, now I'll hitch up me old nag and be goin' 'long. Ye're the darndest gal I've evah knowed."

"No, Beel. Please! I am not afraid. I must go on alone. I'll return this way. Wait for me here. I'll be going," she said and spurred her horse into a gallop. There was still a half mile to go.

Not a light was visible when she approached the long, spacious house, darkened by the broken shadows of cottonwoods and stripped bushes. There was no snow. The storm had skirted the place.

Apparently no one was about. Caution urged her to study the trail. She halted for a moment. Not a sound. She pulled the reins and started again.

Suddenly a bullet whizzed over her head. The Western warning to turn back! She understood, wheeled her horse and soon found a slope which hid both herself and her horse. She slipped from her saddle and listened breathlessly. She had seen no one. Who could have given such a warning? She must not spend precious moments pondering about that. She must reach the ranch house.

After tying her horse, Lona circled through high *chamisa* and bent over while she walked. A few feet below the corner of the

296

great wall of the ranch she could see the full length of the roadway for the first time. Yonder was a sentinel! Yes. Then she was right. He was on duty because the Colonel was a guest. Otherwise there was never a guard.

Lona crouched down to watch the man, walking so straight, with long cape swaying and stout boots tapping on the hard ground. How far was his beat? Surely not beyond this corner? Possibly. That side wall was being repaired. Adobe bricks were stacked high beside a pile of loose dirt screened for plaster and ready for the morning's work. The sentinel was coming. How far? Good! Just for a look down the broken wall. He turned sharply. After he was beyond the gate, Lona dashed across the road and hid behind the adobes. But she had crunched a dry twig! How it cracked in the night silence!

Quick taps. The sentinel was running. Now he stopped. She could feel him near. She heard him scratch a match to light a cigarette. A moment later his steps were steady and growing fainter.

Cautiously Lona groped her way to the wall. Here was a lower stretch of adobes but recently laid. She climbed over carefully. A hurried step, dry flower stalks cracked. She listened. To her great relief she heard no quick tapping of boots. Then more deliberately she made her way to a door and knocked. She knocked again. Someone stirred within. A lock creaked and a thin line of candlelight flashed from the edge of the door. A sleepy old man's voice quavered, "Who's wanted?"

"Colonel Price," whispered Lona and immediately the door swung wide. She went quickly inside with her shawl drawn well over her face. "I must see Colonel Price. Is he here?"

Hardly had the question left her lips when the Colonel walked from his room wrapped in a dressing robe, his dark curly hair and side whiskers tousled, his heavy eyebrows bent to a frown over stern brown eyes.

"Did you say that you wished to see me?" he inquired and relaxed his frown.

"Yes, and alone for a moment, if I may."

The old man handed the candle to the Colonel and withdrew at once.

Lona dropped her shawl from her face.

"Why, Madam Barcelona! What brought you here?"

"Sir, scarcely two hours since, I learned of a conspiracy against you Americans."

"Conspiracy? Are you certain, Madam?"

"Most certain. The time for the uprising is Christmas eve. Men plan to kill all Americans."

"Do you know the names of these men?"

"Only one, Sir, but his name must appear among others. If you will call in the morning at ten, I'll have a list."

"I'll be there promptly, Madam. I think we need not worry. Pray tell me how you reached the door unannounced? Is my guard asleep?"

"No. The sentinel is on duty. He fired. I turned back but came through the bushes and over the wall. I was determined to do what I could to save the Americans."

"And you did not fail, Madam," said the Colonel smiling warmly. "We are most grateful."

"The thanks are due another, Colonel. I will pass them on. My part has been small indeed. Now, I do wish to leave without the guard seeing me, if possible. No one should know that it was I who came. No one."

"I understand. I will escort you home if you can wait a moment?"

"No. No, I thank you. My horse is tethered not far away. I must go alone."

"Then leave by the kitchen door. This way. I'll whistle for

298

my man. When he comes you can escape unseen." He unlatched the main door without a sound and set it partly ajar. Then he walked outside.

Three shrill whistles cut the air.

The sentinel came on the run.

"What of the watch, tonight?" asked Colonel Price loud enough for Lona's ears.

"All seems quiet, sir, although I have had a strange feeling that someone prowls about. I saw one rider. I thought he might be a member of that band of thieves who have been so bold lately. Three in the morning is no time to be abroad. So I fired the warning. The man wheeled and was gone in a moment. That is all, except some crackling sounds."

"A coyote, perhaps," suggested the Colonel. "Come in. I have not slept well. I wish to send a message."

As soon as Lona heard the door close, she tiptoed through the gate. A few moments more and she had mounted and trotted her horse away. Not until she saw Old Bill's fire did she relax in her saddle.

"I saw him, Beel," was all she said of her venture. "Now, man, you must carry the word to Taos. There's no one else whom I can trust. Ride like a merciless wind."

"Of course, I'll go. But, you can count on me scamperin' back as fast as I kin. Want ter be on hand hyar. Old Fetcham's achin' ter spit fire. She'd like nothin' bettah than ter land a bullet in any damn rascal that's jes a-searchin' fer trouble. Yeah, I must be hyar ef thar's ter be a show. Bless ye, Lona gal. I ain't seed the likes of ye, in all the twenty yeahs I've knowed ye."

"Keep my name between your teeth. Ride to beat the wolves. Now I must hurry. Dawn will be here soon." Lona scanned the East but it was dark as yet. Then she turned to Williams. She leaned from her saddle, caught his hand and held it close in both of hers. "How wonderful it has been to have you for a friend, Beel, through all these years. Adiós!"

Bill Williams looked away across the snowy desert. Lona had never said anything like that before. Awkwardly he put his other hand over hers. His eyes met Lona's, straight and fair. "Folks say I'm hard, hard as granite, say I'm 'most a savage but ye've allus brought out the white man. Allus, Lona gal."

Slowly Williams withdrew his hands. He mounted his own horse, and lifted his fur cap with its flapping ear shields. "I'm lettin' ye go on alone. I know ye ain't 'feard. I kin make time cutting North from right hyar. I'll be makin' me own trail again. Adiós."

Not far out among the bushes, Williams muttered to himself, "Reckon I 'most forgot how soft and fine a woman's heart kin be. What a cussed fool I wus, back thar in Missouri, pushin' mother and Arabella 'way from me and playin' I didn't have no feelin's. And I nevah onct looked up Mary. Mary!" He halted his horse and looked back to the other trail. For a second, the silhouette of the woman on the galloping horse cut black against the sky and then was gone.

Promptly at ten, the next morning, Colonel Price, trim in his well-kept uniform, called at the salas and was ushered into the conference room. He paced the floor, noting idly the rich carpet, the hand-carved table with its bowl of bright dried asters. He knew how women buried them in sand until they were dry and then brought them out to cheer a winter room. They could not wilt in the heat coming from the small corner fireplace ablaze with snapping cedar and lazy-burning piñon.

In a few moments, Madam Barcelona was at the door curtsying low in a wide-skirted wine-colored silk. An old locket

300

edged with pearls fell below her white lace collar. Colonel Price caught the picture the handsome woman made while he bowed in return.

"You officers are always on time, Colonel. Pray be seated."

"We should be, Madam, especially when a woman has done what you have. You have courage, Madam. And now, have you names?"

"Yes. I have seven. That was all I could get this morning. As for danger, last night? Somehow I never thought of it. I was so intent on finding you. Now you can do something to prevent the uprising, I am sure. I know that there are many more men involved in the plans."

"No doubt. But I shall soon learn of the others."

"From what I have gathered, Colonel, the first date was for Saturday, the nineteenth. Men were to meet in the church and, at the midnight bell, sally forth and seize the guns; others were to seek you and Governor Bent and do you to the death. Then a general massacre was to take place. As usually happens the world over, Colonel, among a group of conspirators, some of the men could not hold their plans secret. A woman heard. No woman wants bloodshed. She came to me. She had been threatened with death if she told but her man had unburdened *his* soul. He could not keep the secret. To my mind, Sir, she is a heroine."

"It could be no other than a man who first told the secret," said the Colonel rather reluctantly.

"I shall never divulge the name of the woman who sought me. Unless someone jumps at conclusions and states as fact, something not really known, no one will ever guess that I came last night."

"You may be sure that my lips are sealed, Madam," promised the Colonel rising. "It will be my duty, to see that there is no

301

bloodshed. And now, Madam Barcelona . . ." Unconsciously Colonel Price slowly spaced his words. "Believe me when I say that no words can express my appreciation and gratitude. I thank you . . . thank you in the name of the United States of America."

XXIX

WHEN COLONEL PRICE HAD GONE, LONA SUD-
denly wilted. She called Pablita. "Let me sleep as long as I will,"
she ordered. "Do not waken me unless there is some important
reason."

Late in the afternoon, Pablita became uneasy. This long
sleeping in the daytime was unusual. Could Doña Lona be
ill? Carefully she opened the door and felt of Lona's forehead.
No. There was no fever. Lona only stirred; she did not
waken.

An hour later, Pablita came again. Doña Lona was still
asleep but she roused and opened her eyes when Pablita gently
touched her shoulder.

"Doña Lona *mía,* you have slept long but you would wish
to know. Señor Lucero is here."

"José?" exclaimed Lona now fully awake. "José! Help me
dress, Pablita. While I arrange my hair, find that light green
dress. He likes green. Oh! My fingers are clumsy."

As soon as she was ready and the couch to rights, she bade
Pablita run and tell Don José to come at once.

"Ah, my darling." José's brown face beamed. When at last
he freed her, he asked, "You are not ill? Pablita said you have
slept the day away."

"No, *querido mío,* I am not ill but I was tired. Oh, I am so happy. Now you will never leave again. Never."

"Never. Shall we have the banns read at once? It has been an eternity since we first pledged."

"A little more than an eternity, I think." Lona smiled and drew back, keeping her hands in his. "How well you look! And the journey must have been hard?"

It was a long story José had to tell. At the office in Chihuahua, the commandant saw that he could not expect much more work from Lucero and gave him an honorable discharge. Luckily a chance came to join a caravan for El Paso. Everybody there, as at Chihuahua, was in a dither with fear of Americans.

"Rumors of spies made talk of closing the port, so a group of us took horse and got out of there in a hurry," said José. "The Jornada was no joke, but it was not scorching hot. It's enough to give one the 'hippo,' as the Americans say. I'll bet our faces were a *vara* long before we got through. All the upper country was a-buzz with Colonel Doniphan's plans. Then too, the air literally vibrated with tales of a great Mexican army marching North. Men corralled wagons and looked after their animals. I was positive those rumors were lies but I could not allay their fear. Some people enjoy the shivers."

"Did you come via Socorro?" asked Lona, remembering the wide plaza, the rambling low old inn and the great trees along the irrigation ditch. "Has it changed much?"

"No. Mexican towns cling to the earth like barnacles to rock, and grow about as fast. Socorro just lies asleep in the sun. What a place it is for the guitar! I declare I believe every home has at least one. But music or no, the place was gloomy. So many of Doniphan's men have been ill and sent back to recuperate from typhoid or rheumatism. Many are sick of blumy. Never was a town so woe-begetting. Alburquerque was not much better either."

José lifted Lona's hand and kissed it. "I thought much of you, sweetheart, on the deserts when the dust devils played."

But Lona had not heard enough news, so she asked, "Did you tarry with caravans when fear ran so high?"

"No, Lona, darling, I was bound for Santa Fé and a girl I know."

Lona's eyes glistened. "Did you hear of the Magoffin caravan?"

"Yes, but I did not see it. Those people were in San Gabriel. Oh, I forgot to say that James Magoffin is in jail in Chihuahua. They thought him a spy."

"Perhaps he was. I wish you had seen little Susan Magoffin."

Lona laughed and told José about the ball and affairs in general during the past few months in the capital. José listened intently. "Is there any possibility that the Mexicans will win the war?" she asked eagerly.

"All on edge for news, aren't you, my girl?"

"Yes, and as usual, bizarre news travels fast."

"As for winning the war, Lona. One of the last things I heard came from a fellow of the far South. I rather suspect he bore messages for officials in Santa Fé. Anyway, he said that General Santa Anna . . ."

"So they recalled him, did they?" exclaimed Lona. "Sometimes I'm all for Mexico, at others, equally hopeful that the Americans will win."

"Oh, yes. I thought you knew that. Well, the General reached San Luís Potosí finally, with several thousand men and found several thousand more there. He was desperate for cash and off-keel on discipline or drill, so the army was wobbly on its feet. Any number of little devils and ghosts tag at his coat tails. He's not quite the hero-god as in days gone by."

"All this talk and we haven't either one of us mentioned the girls. Luísa married, last summer, as I wrote you. She is happy in that small home of hers. Anita lives with her and will probably marry within the year. Poor dears. They never did know very much of their 'Mother' as they call me. There was never a time when I thought it wise for them to live here. I tried to visit with them as often as I could, but lately I have been a very poor mother indeed. They certainly did grow to be very correct little ladies under Madam Suazo's care."

Christmas eve came starry-clear. Because of deep snow on the mountains the air was crisp and cold but not biting enough to numb the fingers of musicians who strolled about plucking at strings.

Over Santa Fé floated lazy smoke. Small bonfires flared, here and there, before plaza portals, along streets and even on mud roofs of homes throughout the city. Men dipped tall pitch-soaked torches in the bonfires. With these flaming *achones,* they lighted the street procession of priests and acolytes in vestments of red, white and gold, followed by a double line of sober men who carried their sombreros and were in turn followed by women in black shawls. All carried candles save those who bore the cradle with the Christ-child image, the banners, the crosses, or swung brass burners which filled the air with sweet incense.

Among the women walked Madam Barcelona but, when the procession was over, she hurried to her rooms bright with candles. She picked up a deck of monte cards and dealt with lightning speed. Her laughter was high and nervous. She knew many people from far districts had assembled in the city for church festivities; some were at her tables. She wondered if the Americans, even though forewarned, would be able to suppress an uprising if one broke out, in spite of the arrests which

306

they had made. Action might have been more generally planned than the Americans suspected. Unconsciously she halted her game when the midnight bell rolled. Everybody listened. No shots sounded. At once, the tense spirit that had pervaded her salas throughout the evening gave way. Men and women played on with gaiety. Her own feeling of relief was so keen that she soon handed her deck to an assistant and sought José.

"Well, at least, the suspense of this night is over," she said when she walked into her own room. "My dear, this has been a nervous evening." She sank on the couch and looked at José who had been writing at her desk. The tip of her tongue warmed with the desire to tell him the story of her ride to see Colonel Price but she bit her lip. It was better to say nothing.

When morning came, José wandered about the plaza but, although he saw scowls a-plenty, there was no hint of trouble. Stopping near a portal post, he watched the sand-laded wind lift papers and debris from the celebration of the night before. He saw a few merchants doing their share of cleaning up, but the plaza still looked unusually unkept.

Near by stood a stranger, an Englishman in buckskin with a serape over his shoulder and a sombrero drawn down far over his weather-bitten young face. He eyed the handsome, well-dressed Mexican. "Are you also a stranger in Santa Fé, Señor?"

"Hardly a stranger. My home was in Zacatecas, not long since. Have you just arrived?" asked Lucero. He noted that the Englishman carried his shoulders in square military fashion. He had quick contemptuous eyes.

"Came in on the twenty-second. I thought that I'd find something better than this. Santa Fé is the most miserable prairie-dog town that I've ever seen. Outrageously dirty, don't you know. The mud houses look like dilapidated brick kilns. My word! The only clean things around are the stubble corn fields everywhere about. I fancy you think so too, if you are from the South."

"Well, after a celebration, Santa Fé plaza is not a pretty sight, I admit. As for the houses, Sir, many have fine interiors. And there are some splendid people here," said Lucero. Then he introduced himself.

"My name's George Ruxton," said the Englishman. "I've just come up from the South. The Comanches have been bad. I was warned all along the way but, with a servant or two, I saw it through."

"Traveling alone in this country is dangerous. I'm glad that you arrived safely," said Lucero courteously. "Perhaps you will find Santa Fé more to your liking if you will tarry a while."

"Tarry," growled the stranger. "It's more than I can abide. Those rowdy, filthy Missourians all over the place don't help matters any. They call themselves soldiers. Ye gods! Soldiers! My word! They should see an English company."

"The Americans are a tough-looking lot, I know, but they are not as bad as they look, Lieutenant," ventured Lucero, realizing that no explanation of the plight of the Americans and no excuse for their laxness would weigh with an English soldier.

"Did Armijo have any discipline over his men?"

"Armijo?" laughed Lucero. "I should say not. If they did anything for that brute, it was only through fear. It's lucky he's gone. I hope he'll never come back."

"No danger of that. He started going and he's still going. I met him down below Chihuahua. He was with a caravan under a German, named Spiers, bound for the fair at San Juan. His wagons rode like ships at sea on that plain. Spiers had forty or thereabouts. Armijo had seven loaded with cotton goods."

"So you actually saw him? Did you speak to him, Sir?"

308

"I rather fancy I did! Armijo rolled his mountain of fat out of his American dearborn and asked the price of cotton in Durango. Then he asked what people in Mexico were saying about the capture of Santa Fé. I told him bluntly that everybody thought that General Armijo and the New Mexicans were a pack of arrant cowards."

"What did he say to that?" broke in Lucero, leaning over to catch every word the Englishman might say.

"He waddled at once to his dearborn and said as he went, 'Adiós! They don't know that I had but seventy-five men to fight three thousand. What could I do?'"

"The damned liar!" exclaimed Lucero and launched into an account of the affair at Apache Pass as he had learned of it.

"What a general!" laughed Lieutenant Ruxton. "Fit for this motley crowd of lazy loafers—Indians, Mexicans and good-for-nothing Americans. I say! My word! This place disgusts me." With a curt good-by Ruxton left Lucero and strolled on.

At lunch, Lucero regaled Lona with an account of his meeting with the Englishman. "I guess we need fear Armijo no more, Lona." They both laughed.

"Tomorrow," exclaimed José joyfully.

"Yes, tomorrow, we'll wed. Oh, by the way, my darling, there's something we should do. The girls brought it over this morning. What? Wait and see. Please ask Pedro to bring a step-ladder into the large sala."

In a few minutes Lona followed Pedro.

"Let's take down the Mexican flag, José. Leave the Spanish one on that side. Put this opposite." She held up the tricolor of France. "That means mother to me." Lona stepped back. "Yes, the angle is right. Now put this in the middle. Let the folds fall so." It was a new flag. The stars and stripes.

"Right," continued Lona while she took José's hand. "French

309

and Spanish in blood we are, but, from now on, my dear, we'll be American."

For a moment they stood thinking so intently of the future that neither heard a moccasined foot on the threshold. Finally Lona turned. "Ho, there, Beel!"

"I thought ye'd come to it, Lona. It looks mighty fine up thar. Mighty fine. Howdy, Lucero," he said and shook hands pump-handle fashion. "I'm rippin' glad ye've come." He turned to Lona. "Wal, the big show didn't come off. Somehow I jes knowed it wouldn't, so I dawdled 'round Taos, a-feelin' fer news. Couldn't larn much but, one night, I wus nosin' 'round up on the loma, near whar ye ust ter live, Lona. I seed a feller go into Pablo Montoya's house. I watched fer a spell, not thinking much 'bout Montoya, 'cept that I knowed he wusn't a good boy back in '37. Then 'nother feller went in and one or two others. Couldn't see no light in the house. Might be he wus havin' a run of poker back inside.

"Lucero, do ye know . . . ?" Bill checked himself for he saw Lona quickly run her hand over her chin and leave one finger pressed against her lips. He caught the hint and ended, "Ye've won as fine a gal as I've evah knowed."

Before Williams left, he consented, after some coaxing, to take supper with Lucero and Lona. He returned promptly at six and ate heartily, handling his knife and fork as awkwardly as a child. They talked of times gone by, laughed at old jokes and discussed present news. When Williams finally rose to go, Lona said, "You must come tomorrow before the seven . . ."

"No, Lona gal," interrupted Bill. "But I'm wishin' ye both will be as happy as ye desarv' ter be. That's meanin' much." He choked a little and glanced quickly at her, hoping that she had not noticed. Somehow he could not brook the idea of Lona's marrying anybody, yet he . . .

"I'll be leavin' afore ye're up. I cain't help in the marryin' business, ye know. No. I'll not be thar. It's me fer hittin' the trails agin. Now, adiós."

Williams shook hands with both and, while he crossed the darkening patio, he turned, raised his hat in the air and said slowly, "Happiness ter ye, Lona." Wandering down the alley lane, he muttered to himself, "She's still jes a leetle bit like Mary."

Lona had raised her hand in answer. A lump rose in her throat. That hat high in salute! There was something, something that reminded her suddenly of that day, long ago, when Young, astride his horse, had raised his hand in farewell. Ewing had never come back. But then, Bill would come again. He always had.

The winter day was just breaking when Lona put on her wedding dress. It was of the customary black, but of handsome satin with full skirt and close-fitting bodice. Her only jewelry was a heavy gold chain with a cross, and long gold earrings which had belonged to her mother. She knew that José planned to wear the conventional black American clothes, top hat and all. Somehow she wished that she could wear color. She smiled as Pablita helped her dress and adjusted a black mantilla over her high comb. Then she stepped forward to look in the mirror but Pablita cried, "No! No! Doña Lona," and quickly turned it to the wall. "It will bring bad luck if you look in a mirror, now that you are ready. No!"

"Very well, Pablita, I'll not look," said Lona and told the maid to wait in the large sala. From her jewel chest Lona drew the old pearl-studded case which had belonged to her mother. From it she lifted her locket. She opened it, thinking less of Rudolfo than of the beautiful young mother who had worn it, so serene and lovely, but had she been happy? Then carefully, Lona put the locket back and slipped the case out of sight. She would wear the locket no more. After all it had been no talisman. From the drawer in her desk she took a thin pile of letters and laid them on the fire. Now she belonged wholeheartedly to José.

Already the musicians were tuning their instruments in the large sala. They were to precede her carriage to the church. Soon Pedro came to tell her that all was ready.

Lifting the curtain of her dearborn, in the gray of that early day, Lona saw the church, La Parróquia. Her eyes lifted to the square face of the clock in the middle tower. In a small inset above the clock was its bell where a small wooden figure of a negro struck the hour. When it struck again, the wedding would be over and the bell in the North tower would ring in her nuptial mass.

At the steps in the wall, Lona found Señor Pino waiting to offer his arm. Dear kindly Señor Pino, a friend these twenty years. He was old and thin now. He was to take her father's place. Lona looked toward the hills. Something fluttered. It was only the American flag floating over the flat-topped, revetted walls of Fort Marcy. A new day! thought Lona as she walked slowly into the church.

Within, Lona scarcely heard the musicians. Her eyes were intent on the blaze of many tapers on the white altar in the apse where priests waited. She did not consciously see the two life-sized wax figures of friars, one dressed in blue, the other in white on either side of the altar nor the high window covered with a rich red curtain through which the morning light was stealing sluggishly. At the altar stood a group of friends, holding lighted candles. Suddenly she held one and so did José.

After the mass, at the entrance to the church, the bride and groom received congratulations and good wishes. Señor Pino stood by. There were the Alarids. Pablita and Pedro. Madam

312

Suazo with Anita and Luísa. Others. A group of American soldiers and officers waited their turn. On the outskirts of the crowd were many Mexicans. Lona knew that they planned the usual noisy charivari with laughter and music. As she walked away to her carriage with José, Lona leaned over Madam Alarid's shoulder and whispered, "Be sure the ladder is ready."

When twilight of the wedding day deepened, Lona enveloped in a black shawl and José in a serape crossed the adjoining roofs and climbed down the ladder to Madam Alarid's roof, safe now from well-wishing fun-makers.

Madam Alarid came swiftly forward, her fringed shawl flying out like wings from her outstretched arms. She kissed Lona. Then the three walked through the patio to a sala in which Señor Alarid welcomed them to the blazing fire.

"Lona, my dear," began Madam Alarid anxiously, when the two were alone in an adjoining room for a few moments. The little lady tilted her head upward. "You did not forget and look in the mirror after you were dressed for the wedding?"

"No. Pablita saw to it that I did not. I would have forgotten."

"It would have been bad, very bad if you had," chirped Madam Alarid obviously relieved. "I had a friend once who did forget. Everything was ready at the church. The guests were there. The priest. But she refused to go and be married."

"Refused? I would never have done that," replied Lona.

"Probably not. You are so modern in your ideas. But, after all, things do happen after signs. My friend did not marry for years and then not happily. The man never married. By the way, the sun has not shown all day, Lona. The sun should shine on a bride. I am sorry for that. Do not scorn such a sign, my dear. Be on your guard. Unhappiness may not come to you in your marriage but, mark my word, something sad lies ahead."

LONA RADIATED HAPPINESS. SHE JOKED WITH
Madam Alarid about her prediction of trouble ahead. "Here it
is the twentieth of January and everything is still going well,"
Lona argued. But her friend answered that, although her husband did not talk much about signs, he had agreed with her
that something bad would happen.

"Ah, no," Lona said aloud, but to herself she added, "it's
just sheer nonsense." She kissed the timid old lady. "I'm going
home now and plan for a grand ball."

Late that afternoon, Lona sat at her desk making a guest
list. The ball must be finer than any that she had ever given.
Singers with guitars were passing through Burro Alley. She
had not thought of it before, but it was true there had been
little singing during the past few weeks. She knew that business had been light for a while but . . . Now for the dance.
It would be the first with José as host. Her head was bent over
the list when Pedro ran into the patio, calling in a strange
frightened voice.

"Doña Lona! Doña Lona! A revolution broke out in Taos
yesterday."

"Revolution?" exclaimed Lona as she opened her door. "No!
No, are you sure?"

314

"Yes. Governor Bent was killed early in the morning," Pedro's voice broke when he added, "and scalped, too!"

"Scalped!" gasped Lona. *"Santa María!* Others killed?"

"Luís Lee. Others. I did not hear their names," Pedro was saying when José rushed in.

"He's right. It's true, Lona. A massacre in Taos. A messenger rode in a while ago, his horse all a-lather. He said Padre Martínez had sent him. When he left for Santa Fé, the mob was galloping toward Turley's mill, over in the Arroyo Hondo."

Speechless, Lona sank on a bench. So her ride had failed!

"It was early in the morning when the riders came from Ranchos de Taos and the pueblo to swell the crowd," José continued. "They went insanely wild. 'Taos lightning' did its worst. The men rushed to the Governor's house. They knew he was there on a visit. The messenger left too soon after the attack to bring accurate details."

"He was a good friend to everybody, José," Lona said slowly. "What will Colonel Price do? Have you heard?"

"No, not yet. Something drastic must be done."

"Madam Alarid's gray day prophecy!" gasped Lona.

A few days later, Lona and José learned that soldiers had been called from Alburquerque to protect the capital while Colonel Price and a fairly large number of men were absent in the North. They knew that fear pulsed throughout the city but that it did not compare with the anguish of the year of '37 except in the families who were linked with the revolution.

To Lona, that year of '47 always remained a horrible nightmare. The interest in her business dulled. The terrible news of strife took heavy toll of her strength and lines deepened in her face, but even so, she forced herself to smile.

She listened to an account of the battle at the Mission church in the Taos pueblo where the Americans won and many Indians fell. She knew of the hanging of Pablo Montoya, who had styled himself, "The Santa Anna of the North" and of the trials which were held in the old palace during that depressing spring and summer. She heard the cracks of rifles at the old *garita* below Fort Marcy where those found guilty of murder fell beside the old wall. Caravans from the South brought tales of defeat suffered by the Mexicans and of General Santa Anna, crushed, but allowed to go into exile in distant Jamaica. In fact, Lona's whole world seethed in a maelstrom of trouble.

Finally, that long year passed. One day in January of '48, Lona returned from *La Fonda,* laughing.

"José, I've had the best laugh in over a year. Funny things do happen even in the midst of trouble. Never 'til now have I known the facts about the escape of Don Tomás Ortíz. I've been listening to Doña Ana Ortíz at the inn. She dares to talk now. Did you ever hear the real story?"

"No. Only a jumble of rumors. What happened?"

"Well, Don Tomás knew the soldiers were after him. It had leaked out that he was one of the leaders in the conspiracy of over a year ago. One day, they decided to search the house of his brother, Padre Juan Ortíz. When the soldiers came, every woman in the place fled but Doña Ana. She said that she was making toast and she wasn't going to let it burn. Not for a million men. She met the searchers with her fork high. They wouldn't attack a woman with a fork. No! Doña Ana stood there in her red apron, her face flushed with anger, her hair awry, holding that fork. She told the men to go ahead and search if they wished.

"They wanted to see the storeroom. So she led them on, pointing with that fork. She said that she had hard work to keep from laughing outright when they examined the pile of supplies which were all ready to be sent, as they actually were, that night, for the use of Don Tomás on his flight. Somehow it did not occur to the soldiers to go out on the balcony where Don Tomás was hiding."

"Strange that the Americans didn't do a good job of it. I guess that fork was too much for them," interrupted José laughing.

"Yes. Doña Ana said she did not know that she had the fork in her hand until she started to help Don Tomás dress as a servant girl, not even when she was bidding a messenger run for Pedro Trujillo. When Don Tomás was ready, the two lowered him down to the garden."

José broke into a laugh. "I'll bet Doña Ana made him put on women's shoes and a sun-bonnet."

"She did that. Señor Trujillo insisted on carrying Don Tomás on his back and go by way of the trail over there beyond the church. They started for the home of Tomás's left-hand sweetheart, Doña Peregrína. On the way, Don Pedro met some soldiers who asked him who it was that he was carrying. He told them that it was his daughter who was very ill and he must take her home at once. Señor Trujillo must have had a grand laugh when he landed Don Tomás safe in Doña Peregrína's arms."

"I'll bet my last peso he did," interrupted José.

"And then," continued Lona, "Don Pedro hid some horses down by the river. He gave a signal and Don Tomás started for the river with a water jar on his head. Then, by all the gods, José, if he wasn't met by soldiers! They just asked 'the woman' where Peregrína lived and, if Tomás Ortíz was there? 'Oh, yes,' he assured them. 'He was in the kitchen there' and pointed to the house."

"Good Lord! Tomás had his troubles. Anything more?" asked José.

"Yes. Don Tomás was so eager to get to the river that he

317

threw the skirts over his shoulder and ran. Then, some of the shiftless *vagamundas* who live in those hovels near the arroyo, yelled to the *gringos* that the man was Don Tomás, himself. But he and Señor Trujillo mounted and rode furiously down to Galisteo. There Don Tomás got fresh horses, money and provisions and kept on going. I'll bet my salas that he didn't get a good breath until he pulled into Chihuahua." Lona bent over with laughter.

"So that's how the man escaped, the man who wanted to kill all Americans and be governor, eh?" José remarked and joined Lona again in laughter.

During the following summer, Madam and Señor Lucero visited the new inn on the plaza, new in name only. It bore the pompous title, "The United States Hotel." Its proprietor, long-legged, spare Ebenezer Spindle, slowly dragged his tangled anatomy out of a big rocking chair, drew a thin hand over the gray stubble of a beard on his thinner face and stepped forward to greet the couple cordially. For him, every visitor afforded him a chance to show his "hotel." Lona looked at the ill-kept bar, the dining room untidy with its dirty pine table and old sideboard too heavily loaded with poor earthenware dishes and worn silver-plated knives and forks. It is far from Madam Pino's *La Fonda,* she thought.

"Long Eben" insisted on mixing a new drink for his guests, which he called a "gin cocktail." "Yonder," he continued, "is a fine new up-to-date American gambling house." He directed them to it with a snake-like twist of his left hand while his right released his pipe for a cloud of smoke.

When the pure air of the outdoors had dissipated the smells of "The United States Hotel," Lona suggested that they make a visit to the gambling place, that night. She would like to see how the Americans ran their business. "Long Eben" had said, "They keep the tallest kind of an elephant there." She knew of other new gambling dens. Her own North room patronage had fallen off but she said gaily to José, "What difference does it make? We are rid of some bad rubbish."

"A good-will visit, Lona?"

"Yes. I'm going to take along enough money to play if the right opportunity comes. Just to cater to their love of show, I'll wear extra necklaces and rings," Lona laughed. "Americans surely do like to parade and see others on parade as well. I'll match their taste tonight."

Pedro drove the dearborn to the long low building recently plastered with *tierra baillita,* so light in color that it glowed in the night. At the door, Lona ordered him to loosen the bits of the horses and wait.

Passing through the barroom which already smelled of cheap, vile brandy, Madam and Señor Lucero were greeted with a hearty "Howdy, folks!" and a clownish bow. As soon as the proprietor had regained his five feet ten, he sensed the advertising value of such a visit and urged "Madam Barcelona," as he called her, to accept a "bank" table for the evening, stipulating that the earnings of the table would, of course, go to the house but that, since she was such a well-known dealer, he would allow her a percentage greater than that which he usually gave his dealers.

Madam Barcelona accepted the invitation and began to deal her monte cards so expertly that a crowd gathered about her table. There was no sound of guitars but laughs of winners, growls of losers, a drunken ditty or two, created plenty of noise, through which came the regular call of the man at the roulette wheel. "Hyar ye air, gents. A good game. The ball's ready to hum. Fun fer yer money. Step up, gentlemen."

319

Late in the evening, Lona noticed a rather short young American stranger enter the room with a Missouri teamster as guide. They stood by her table watching. During a break in the game when a great pile of coins changed hands, she gave them critical attention. That driver's not much more than a boy, she was thinking when his eyes met hers squarely with an expression of pity and contempt.

"Cussed monte woman," the Missourian muttered and walked away.

When José and Lona were again at home, talking over the evening, Lona told him about the young American who had called her a "cussed monte woman." José flushed. "I wish I had heard him. I would have pinked him."

"That would have done no good, José." Lona laughed but not gaily. "The Americans believe they are always right whether they know what they are talking about or not. They bring their idea of a gambling woman from their frontier dives. José, I fear that some of our people are being influenced against me. But what does it matter?" Again Lona raised her head and laughed but José knew that the words had stung.

Late next spring the Taos scout, Antoine Leroux, sauntered into Madam Barcelona's North rooms. No one was about so he stepped into the patio and sat with his head leaning against the wall under the portal, his long hair and beard black against the adobe. He was pulling hard on his pipe when Madam Lona came from her own sala. She did not recognize the man as she walked toward him.

"I'm Antoine Leroux, Madam," the man said in Spanish after he had risen.

"Ah, yes. I remember you now, Señor Leroux. It was you who brought me a message from Señor Young so long ago. I remember."

320

"Yes, I'm the man. Now strangely enough, I've come to bring you a message from your old friend Bill Williams. I promised and here I am, Madam."

"Williams?" asked Lona anxiously. "I heard recently that he had gone into the mountains and had not come back. Is that true? Old Beel always returns sooner or later."

"But this time, Madam Lona, he will not return," Leroux said slowly.

Lona sat down beside him. "Tell me all you know," she ordered.

"Perhaps he's better off now," said Leroux. "Bill was old, bent and gray. He was growing queerer and queerer. He told me that he wanted to die in the mountains. Not long before he left this time for the Río del Norte, he declared to a group of us that he had dreamed again that a bear put his paw on his shoulder. He believed that meant an Indian would kill him. When he died, he said that he'd come back as a buck elk. He warned us never to shoot an elk with certain markings. The Mexicans who were with him say that the Utes killed him."

"But I thought he and the Utes were friends."

"Yes, they were. It all goes back to that ill-fated Frémont expedition. Colonel Frémont would have his own way. It was his fourth expedition through the Rockies and he thought he knew everything. Bill Williams was in the party and gave him good advice. It was a bad winter to be traveling anyway. Williams told the Colonel that he should take a southerly trail but Frémont would not. The result was that eleven out of the thirty-two men died on the way. It's a wonder they didn't all die. When Frémont got to Taos, he blamed Williams for his disasters. That was nonsense to the mountain men."

Leroux paused and fingered his cap. "I don't know whether Williams got wind of Frémont's talk or not. He went into the mountains anyway, along with Doctor Ben Kern and some

Mexicans to get the fixin's that they'd cached. They came up with some Apaches. Bill wasn't feeling kindly toward that tribe. Anyway, over in the mountains he found that a band of Utes had joined the Apaches. Perhaps he thought that he had to fight or be called a coward. I don't know. I believe he did not expect to have to fight Utes when he went out. Williams was not the kind to turn on his red friends."

"It's hard to believe," answered Lona. "Old Beel gone! Never to come again. Never! Thanks for coming to tell me, Señor Leroux. Thanks. Beel was a wonderful friend to me."

It seemed to José that Lona was never quite her old self after the death of Bill Williams. He wondered if she had ever loved Bill. One day he asked her frankly.

"No, José, dearest. I never loved Beel but he had a rare capacity for friendship. I miss him very much. Sometimes years passed when we did not meet but I always knew that somewhere in this great West was Beel, and that the day would come when he would return. Real friendship and love are twins."

"I guess you are right, *querida mía,*" replied José. "But you must shake off the weight of sorrow. If there is a happy hunting ground, as the whites have taught the Indians to believe, Old Bill is still hunting and still your friend."

Lona tried to be gay, for she loved José. She thought that she succeeded but he knew better. She tried to look after her business but it had lost its interest.

Although she was far from old, Lona sensed decline. She struggled against the idea but she did not fear. She smiled at the forward look and buoyant health of Pedro and Pablita, who were to leave for a visit to old Mexico. Sarah and her husband would take their places for the while.

Lona made gifts to friends in need and to her church. She visited the sick as she had always done, trying to bring them

322

cheer, but her own heart was leaden and for a reason that she could not fathom.

Less than two years later, Doña Lona fell seriously ill. Pain in her right side wracked her body. Her two adopted daughters came to care for her. José sat constantly by her side. She always tried to smile for him.

One morning, Lona asked that her bed be turned to the window. She was gently raised on pillows. Outside all was blurred. A great wind swept clouds of dust through the patio. Sarah with a red rebozo around her head and shoulders was pushing against the gale.

Lona sank in her pillows. "Red! Dust!" she whispered. "Pablita, bring me my lock—" Then she was silent.

José leaned over her. What was it that she wished? A locket? He had never seen a locket. He watched Lona's face grow paler. "Lona! Lona!" Maybe her own name would bring her back. Again he called, "Lona . . . Lona de Estrada!" But Lona did not hear.

www.ingramcontent.com/pod-product-compliance
Lightning Source LLC
Chambersburg PA
CBHW020641030726
47498CB00002B/311